PRAISE FOR
JULIE ANNE LONG'S PREVIOUS NOVEL,
THE RUNAWAY DUKE

"Wonderful and charming . . . at the top of my list for best romance of the year . . . It is a delight in every way."

—LikesBooks.com

"Thoroughly enjoyable . . . A charming love story brimming with intrigue, witty dialogue, and warmth."

—Rendezvous

"Hilarious, heartrending, and tender . . . ample suspense . . . A guaranteed winner."

—CurledUp.com

"A must-read . . . Combining the ideal amount of romance, suspense, and mystery, Long gives us a marvelous and dazzling debut that overflows with intelligence, wit, and warmth."

—Romantic Times BOOKClub

"Two fantastic lead protagonists . . . Fans will want to run away with this delightful pair."

—Midwest Book Review

Also by Julie Anne Long

The Runaway Duke

JULIE ANNE LONG

NEW YORK BOSTON

Cover design by Diane Luger
Illustration by Alan Ayers
Typography by David Gatti
Book design by Giorgetta Bell McRee

Warner Books

Time Warner Book Group
1271 Avenue of the Americas
New York, NY 10020
Visit our Web site at www.twbookmark.com

Printed in the United States of America

First Paperback Printing: April 2005

10 9 8 7 6 5 4 3 2 1

For Ken—for uncommon patience
in the face of second-book angst. And maybe I owe
you a dinner or something, too.

Acknowledgments

My gratitude to Melanie Murray, because—well, because she rocks; to Bill Reiter and David Blackburn, for serendipitously owning and graciously loaning to me the *exact* books I needed, just when I was beginning to believe they didn't exist; to the friends and loved ones who believed me when I swore I wasn't *shunning* them, honest—I was just really, really, *really* busy (honest); to Elizabeth Pomada, for her unflagging belief in me; to all the lovely people who wrote to me about *The Runaway Duke*—your warmth and enthusiasm fueled *To Love a Thief,* and I hope you enjoy it just as much as *Duke;* to Elizabeth Fulton for her kindness and wisdom; and to Cecil, who used to oversee every word I wrote from his perch on my desk . . . I miss you, my dear buddy.

To Love A Thief

Chapter One

Come at once, Gideon, the missive said. *Uncle Edward is dying.*

Uncle Edward was *always* dying.

"If the man doesn't actually die soon, Laurie," Gideon Cole gloomily told his friend, "I may just strangle him." He crushed the note in his fist.

No one knew the precise nature of Uncle Edward's illness, only that it seemed to require him to be bedridden and waited on hand and foot and had created handsome dowries for each of the parish doctor's five daughters. For five years Lord Lindsey had in fact been the most jovial sick person Gideon had ever seen. And because Gideon stood to inherit the baronetcy and his uncle's extraordinary estate, Aster Park, Edward sent for him every time he felt a twinge.

Uncle Edward was forever feeling twinges.

Tremendously *ill-timed* twinges.

Gideon yanked off his hat and pushed his fingers agitatedly through his hair. The warmth of the day was oppressive; the crowds that eddied around them on Bond Street felt oppressive, the circumstances of his life felt oppressive. He wasn't looking forward to returning to the chambers at Westminster, to donning his wig and robes and eloquently pleading a case while beads of perspiration raced each other down the back of his neck. At least it was a case he would win easily.

Kilmartin—Lawrence Mowbry, Lord Kilmartin—sighed a long-suffering sigh. "By all means, go to your uncle instead of to Lady Gilchrist's ball, Gideon. I'm sure Jarvis will be happy to dance all the waltzes with Constance in your stead—yet again."

"You're not helping, Laurie."

"And you're not listening, Gideon. You cannot afford to leave the *ton* now that Jarvis seems to be making a run for Constance. Jarvis *already* has a title and a fortune. And he's not exactly a gargoyle."

Usually Gideon found Kilmartin's particular brand of insight—honesty undiluted by tact—bracing. Today, however, his pride was tender. "Constance is fond of me," he insisted stubbornly.

"Of you, and grand houses and new carriages and fine clothes and *attention* and—"

"Hullo, Cole! *Wonderful* to see you! How are—oh, hello there, Kilmartin."

Gideon and Kilmartin swiveled to find the genteelly graying Lord Wolford hovering on the periphery of their conversation, merrily swinging a walking stick. Gideon tensed briefly, and then he remembered: he'd repaid Wolford. Gideon's father had owed a fortune to nearly everyone in the House of Lords at one time, but Gideon had repaid all of them methodically—alphabetically, in fact, because given the sheer number of debts, it had seemed the only fair way to go about it—after his father's death. Being a "W," Wolford had been one of the last, but he'd been more or less gracious about it: "Seems the apple fell a good distance from the tree in your case, m'boy" had been his precise words. Meaning that Gideon was nothing like his father, Alistair Cole, who had left behind mountains of debt and a trail of disillusioned friends when he'd shaken off this mortal coil. Gideon had taken Wolford's words as a compliment, and he'd done his best to ensure the truth of them ever since.

"Congratulations on the Griffith case, Cole." Wolford gave Gideon's back a manly thump with his free hand. "Very impressive work, indeed."

"Thank you, sir. It was a pleasure to win it for him."

The marquis fanned out his gloved fingers and began counting off. "First Shrewsbury's property dispute, then Lord Culpepper's sticky little problem with his estate manager, and now Griffith. You're making quite a name for yourself, m'boy. Shawcross is looking to fill that position in the Treasury, and your name came up, among others. Have you given any thought to a political career?"

Gideon noticed Kilmartin struggling to keep his face straight and resisted the urge to give him a little kick. Gideon fully intended to be Chancellor of the Exchequer, at the very least, someday; he'd mentioned it to Kilmartin two or three—or four thousand—times. And Shawcross—*Marquis* Shawcross—was Constance's father.

"It has crossed my mind, sir," he said mildly.

"Do let me know if I can help in any way, will you?"

You can ask Shrewsbury, Culpepper, and Griffith if they ever intend to pay me. He didn't say it. There were a number of reasons the *ton* held Gideon Cole in high regard, and discretion was one of them. "I shall, sir, and I thank you."

"Well, I must be off, but we really must share a drink and a chat at White's soon. Oh, and you come, too, Kilmartin."

Wolford administered a paternal pat to Gideon and ambled away.

Kilmartin shook his head as they watched the crowd absorb the marquis. "'*Oh, and you come, too, Kilmartin,*'" he repeated, bemused, and shook his head. "All that admiration. Almost makes me want to work for my living, too."

By way of response, Gideon merely lifted a brow and regarded his friend in amused, unblinking silence.

Kilmartin struggled to maintain an earnest expression, but Gideon's see-through-your-soul barrister stare made it impossible. "Oh, *very* well, then. Of course it doesn't. But people have been congratulating you on the Griffith affair all morning. What must it be like, I wonder, to be so popular?"

Gideon snorted. "If it's any comfort to you, Laurie, I would *much* rather be rich than popular. And furthermore," he added, before Kilmartin could get the urge to remind him that it was probably his own bloody fault he wasn't yet rich, "if I were rich, I wouldn't be in my current . . . *absurd* predicament."

"Gideon," Kilmartin continued more gently, "I know you're fond of your uncle, but you know very well he isn't *actually* dying. Have you considered that Constance's patience may not be endless? Perhaps she'd like a titled husband before she's in her dotage. Perhaps she's uncertain of your intentions."

"Uncertain of my *intentions*? Nonsense. I have it all planned, Laurie: I'll buy the town house—the one on the corner of Grosvenor Square that Constance wants so badly—"

"Because it's the biggest, most *expensive* town house on Grosvenor Square—"

"Of course," Gideon defended. "Constance wants only the very best of everything."

"And this includes you, presumably."

This made Gideon smile. And Gideon's smile, the slow sultry curve of it, could crack the heart of any woman between the ages of eight and eighty. "Naturally," he continued smoothly, eliciting a snort from Kilmartin. "As I was saying, I'll buy the town house, and then I'll present it to her—with a little speech, perhaps: 'Constance, I would be deeply honored if you would consent to spend all the Seasons of your life with me in this town house. Will you be my wife?' "

"Very romantic, Gideon," Kilmartin said dryly. "There's just one thing: Jarvis wants that town house, too."

This brought Gideon up short. "How do you know that?" he asked sharply.

"I'm afraid *everyone* knows that, Gideon. And there are now entries in White's betting books wagering not insignificant sums on the possibility that Lord Jarvis will be engaged to Lady Constance Clary before the end of the season. Seems he'd like to spend all *his* seasons with Constance, too. You've a serious rival now."

Gideon silently took this in, as around them hoards of men going about their business created the music of Bond Street: the jingle of tack and clatter of hooves, voices raised to outdoor volumes. He inhaled deeply and resisted the impulse to yank his hat off again; he half suspected he always allowed his dark hair to grow just a little too long just so he could work his fingers through it in frustration.

"Bloody hell," Gideon muttered grimly, at last. "All the wagers used to be about me."

Kilmartin nodded sympathetically. "Used to be."

"But didn't you hear Wolford, Laurie?" Gideon could

hear desperation creeping into his tone, and it irritated him beyond measure. "Constance's *father* has mentioned my name in connection with the position in the Treasury. Surely it's because Constance believes we are close to an . . . understanding."

"Wolford said your name was *among* those mentioned. Who knows? Perhaps Jarvis was mentioned, too."

"I doubt Jarvis has done a day's work in his life." Gideon didn't entirely succeed in keeping the bitterness from his tone.

"I'm not sure the Treasury cares very much whether he has, Gideon."

This response irritated Gideon all the more because no one knew the truth of it better than he did. As with everything, it was about money and titles. And Jarvis had them: a grand family, and money, and a title. Gideon did not. What he *did* have was rather a knack for making the best of the only truly useful assets bequeathed to him by his father: a charm that was just shy of roguish, and looks that pleased on first glance and riveted on the second. His imposing height usually caused that first glance; his face—dark, dark eyes set into an arresting merger of slopes and angles and hollows that hinted at strength and sensitivity and something slightly more dangerous—did the rest.

But while Gideon's looks and charm may have opened doors, years of hard work and careful choices, of banishing risk and stifling impulse and using rules as ladder rungs to scale the ranks of the military, the law, in society, had earned him the regard he now enjoyed in the *ton*. And it was a measure of this regard that the idea of an engagement between Lady Constance Clary, the daughter of a wealthy marquis and the uncontested jewel of the season, and Gideon

Cole, former soldier and near-penniless barrister, had so far been greeted not with mirth . . . but with indulgence.

Though the "near penniless" part was a bit of a secret.

And again, was probably his own bloody fault.

Jarvis, on the other hand, need only be *Jarvis*—wealthy and titled—to be considered worthy of Constance and a position in the Treasury. It was simply how things were.

He did it: he yanked off his hat, swept his fingers through his hair again. "All I need is thirty pounds, Laurie, as a first payment on the town house—the solicitor promised. And then I'll make payments, and—"

"That town house must cost at least a thousand pounds, Gideon. Tell me, exactly how much money do you now have?"

Damnation. Kilmartin knew him too well.

And when Gideon remained stubbornly silent, it was Kilmartin's turn to arch a knowing brow. Unfortunately, Kilmartin's brows were so fair they were nearly invisible, which robbed the gesture of a little of its eloquence.

"I have Aster Park," Gideon, ever the barrister, countered. "Constance covets Aster Park."

Everyone coveted Aster Park. It was one of the grandest estates in England, a veritable ocean of land that gobbled money and managed to create just enough income in the form of beef and wool to justify its own existence. It had been a shock to everyone when Gideon's uncle had inherited it a few years after Gideon's parents had died, from a relative so distant he'd hardly been more than a rumor in their family.

"You don't quite have Aster Park *yet*," Kilmartin reminded him relentlessly. "Gideon, if you want my advice, you'd best stay in London and go to Lady Gilchrist's ball, if only to remind Constance why she is so very . . . *fond* of you."

Gideon fell silent again, tracing and retracing the contours of the problem in his mind. His bloody, *bloody* uncle. He *was* fond of the man. And what if he *was* actually dying this time? Dying while Gideon circled a ballroom with a beautiful heiress in his arms . . .

"You could just hit him," Kilmartin half jested. "Jarvis. Take him out of the running."

Gideon gave a short laugh. "I don't *do* that sort of thing anymore, Laurie."

He *had* done that sort of thing at one time; that sort of thing was how he'd met Kilmartin: about a decade ago at Oxford, he'd lunged at two large boys who were tormenting a small plump boy. An hour later he'd had two black eyes and a friend for life in Kilmartin (the small plump boy), and all four of them had received demerits for fighting, of which Kilmartin was still rather proud.

But he didn't do that sort of thing anymore. Largely because it was precisely the sort of thing his father would have done.

Kilmartin was no longer either small or plump, but he still had to tilt his head back to look Gideon in the eye. Which he did now, his pale eyes squinting in the sun despite the shelter of his hat. "Well, look at it this way, old man. Even if Constance is taken off the marriage mart, you would probably still have your pick of young ladies."

"Yes," Gideon said, because he hadn't the strength for false modesty today. "But I want Constance."

Kilmartin made an exasperated noise. "Why *do* this to yourself, Gideon? Why choose the most difficult female of them all?"

"Oh, come now, Laurie. You should know by now, no

matter what, I *always* choose the most difficult of all." He grinned, an attempt to make Kilmartin grin.

But Kilmartin was having none of it. He studied Gideon shrewdly instead. And then his shoulders slumped as realization set in. "Bloody hell, Gideon. This is about your Master Plan, isn't it?"

Gideon paused again. Sometimes it was deucedly inconvenient to be known as well as Kilmartin knew him.

"I want Constance, Laurie," he said softly. "I *need* Constance." He'd *earned* Constance, he wanted to add, but didn't, because he wasn't certain Kilmartin would understand. Laurie was heir to a viscount; his family was ancient, his fortune seemingly permanent. Unlike Gideon, he'd never watched his father bring his humble family to untold social altitudes with a roll of the dice, only to bring them crashing down again in precisely the same way; he'd never watched his mother and his sister hold their heads high amidst the losses and whispers; he'd never received word that the ship carrying his parents to India—Gideon's father, the eternal gambler, the eternal optimist, had dragged his mother off in search of new fortune to replace the lost one—had been dashed to pieces in a storm.

Gideon had been just eighteen and still at Oxford when his parents died, his sister seventeen, and they'd been left nearly penniless. They'd sold the family home; Helen married a wealthy Yorkshire farmer who'd offered for her. It had seemed a sound decision at the time. Gideon knew better now.

Gideon had told Kilmartin about his Master Plan one night at Oxford after too much wine—and regretted it ever since, really. He wasn't sure Laurie fully understood the need to ensure his future was nothing—*nothing*—like the life his father had provided for his family, with its constant vertigo of fluctuating fortune, the pride and the shame.

But Laurie was a good friend. And after a moment, he shrugged in resignation. "Well, perhaps you can persuade your uncle to die when Constance goes off to visit her cousins in the country—isn't their house party in a day or so? And when she returns for the Braxton ball, she will find you a baron and master of Aster Park and Jarvis will lose all appeal."

In spite of himself, Gideon laughed. "Oh, Uncle Edward would never be so obliging. He would—"

Gideon could not have told anyone what made him spin around at just that moment. Perhaps it was the same instinct that had enabled him to dodge musket balls at Waterloo and come home with senses and limbs intact. But spin he did.

And that's how he saw the girl just as she was dipping a slim hand into his coat pocket.

Gideon seized her wrist. Frozen in shock, breathing hard, they glared at each other.

The impressions came at him swiftly. Her wrist, thin as a child's, her skin almost shockingly silky, her pulse speeding with terror beneath his thumb. A high pale forehead, luminous in the afternoon sun, a pink mouth nearly the shape of a heart, a pair of extraordinary aquamarine eyes ablaze with panic and outrage. And freckles, a collection of tiny asymmetrical splashes of gold, across her nose. Almost unconsciously, he began to count them. One, two, three, four—

"*Oof!*"

Gideon dropped to his knees, gagging for breath. While he had been counting her freckles, her knee had come up between his legs with brutal accuracy.

And she was gone, absorbed into the crowd as though she had never been anything more than a shadow.

* * *

Lily ran. Her skirt clutched in both hands, her bare feet slapping down hard on the dirt street, she expertly weaved and dodged through the crowds of men and women and horses and the piles the horses left behind. She ran until her lungs were as hot as a blacksmith's forge, until her heart was a hammer in her chest, until, at last, she was in St. Giles again.

The difference between St. Giles and Bond Street was like noon and twilight. Prone bodies reeking of gin, prostitutes leaning against walls and out of windows, street urchins skulking, buildings sagging under the weight of their years. Raucous laughter and arguments, competing vendors calling their wares. *Home. Thank God.* On the heels of her alarming near-capture, it was all strangely comforting.

It was his hair that had caught her eye—longer than most fashionable gentlemen wore it, and dark, but with red hiding in it: when he'd yanked off his hat, it had briefly glowed like a coal burned almost all the way down to ashes. She'd seen the gleam of gold in his pocket when he'd thrust his hands into his very fine coat; *a watch,* she'd thought. He was very tall, taller than most of the crowd, but he'd seemed so restless, so absorbed in his conversation with his friend, a man with the pale, open face of someone who'd known little of worry or care . . . so oblivious . . .

She'd been *so* wrong.

And his *eyes* . . .

Later. She'd think of his eyes later.

As she rounded a corner into the alley where McBride kept his shop, a hand fumbled out to grip her shoulder. "Oi, Lily, give us a kiss, luv—"

Lily threw her elbow back sharply; she heard a grunt and a torrent of good-natured curses as the hand dropped away.

"*Always* wi' the elbow, Lily Masters! Just one kiss, is that too much t' ask, I ask ye—"

"Ah, but yer too slow, Tom," she tossed over her shoulder, grinning. Lily had deadly sharp little elbows. They made splendid weapons. Nearly as good as knees.

They tried, the boys did, but none of them could catch her—unless she wanted to be caught. And she *had* wanted to be caught—once. It was partially McBride's fault: he'd given her a copy of *Pride and Prejudice* and—unwittingly, as McBride could not read—a collection of erotic stories written entirely in French, and though Lily was fairly certain this wasn't exactly how Mama would have wanted her to apply the little bit of French she'd insisted Lily acquire, she'd found the book riveting. Both books made the goings-on between men and women sound so much more complicated and elegant than the sort of thing that went on in alleys all over St. Giles, or what Fanny did upstairs for money at the lodging house, and Lily had wanted to discover the truth of it for herself.

Nick, the boy's name was. Blue eyes and a clever wit, lips more clever still; he'd known what he was about. The kiss, brief though it was, had been like a match touched to a rush light: the sweet warmth wicking through her, the beginnings of weakness, of *want*, had taken her quite by surprise. She'd put a stop to it immediately, pushing Nick away; she'd seen the lodging rooms filled with starving women and children and screaming sickly babies. She wasn't about to allow curiosity, or an occasional yearning to touch and be touched, to trap her forever into a life of squalor. *Never willingly put yourself at the mercy of a man, Lily*, Mama had once said.

Besides, Nick was no Mr. Darcy.

But she was glad to have done it; it was good to know

that something as seemingly simple as a kiss could draw the will straight out of you. And she thought she now understood how Mama, who had been a lady longer ago than anyone could remember, could have come to marry a man like Papa and stay with him even through the loss of everything.

When Lily reached McBride's shop, she stopped and waited a moment to allow her indignant heart to slow its pumping before she pushed open the door.

McBride was vigorously scrubbing at something on the counter with a cloth; the movement made what was left of his gray hair spin out from his head like streamers on a maypole. He looked up when he heard the door open, and when he saw Lily his face split into a delighted open-mouthed smile, revealing teeth and gaps where teeth used to be in equal measure.

"Oi, Lily me love, and when oh when will ye be me bride?"

"Oi, McBride, I'm assemblin' me trousseau even now."

"Yer *troo-sew*!" He cackled appreciatively. "Ah, Lily, ye've a wit about ye, ye do. Say more things to me in that voice of yers. Like smoke from a fine cigar, it is. A man could forget 'is troubles jus' listenin' to ye speak."

"And 'ow would ye know anythin' of fine cigars, McBride?" Lily teased. "Or troubles?" He always made a great fuss about her low, distinctive voice, insisting it belonged in the body of an expensive courtesan and not a mere slip of a girl.

"Ah, Lily, the things I once knew . . ." His eyes went dreamy for a moment from memories, or perhaps from the bottle of gin he'd had with his midday meal. "Well, and what have ye brung me today? Nay, dinna touch the wood here," he said hurriedly, when Lily moved to rest her elbows upon the counter. "I've spilt summat what will take yer skin right off."

Among other things, McBride was an apothecary. He specialized in treating ailments brought about by indiscriminate lovemaking, but he also offered a range of elixirs for those unable to make love at all. "I've summat fer the ups, and summat fer the downs," he maintained cheerfully. His clientele spanned all social classes and he charged them ridiculous sums for his cures. They were usually desperate enough to pay it and too mortified to ever complain if the cures didn't precisely work as advertised.

Lily looked askance at the noxious vapor rising up from the little pool on the counter. From the looks of things, the potion would cure the problem by eliminating the anatomical source of it forever.

"A cure for piles?" she guessed.

"A cure fer the pox. Needs a little work yet. Have ye any goods fer me today, me love?" McBride also made a tidy living as a trafficker in stolen things.

Lily dipped her hand into her apron pocket and spilled her day's slim haul onto the counter a safe distance from the wisping puddle of pox cure: a watch fob and two silver buttons.

"Is it gold?" she asked McBride eagerly when he poked a long finger at the watch fob.

"Hmm . . . I dinna ken, luv. I'll give ye four shillings fer it."

"Four shillings!" Lily was indignant. "And do ye take me fer a fool, now, McBride?" They both took great pleasure in the haggling.

"Four shillings ha'pence, then."

"Five shillings," Lily insisted. McBride glared at her, outraged. She glared back.

"Five shillings, then." He sighed. "Lily, me love, 'tis cruel ye be."

Lily snorted and held out her palm. She suspected she was benefiting from McBride's soft heart. He'd tried before to give her more money than her haul warranted, but she was not foolhardy enough to protest today—not when she and her sister, Alice, needed to eat. Besides, at the rates McBride charged for his potions, he could probably afford to buy a town house in St. James Square.

"And a shilling for the buttons," she added.

McBride sighed and begrudgingly counted the coins out into her palm, mumbling something about how she was robbing him blind, she was. She handed him back the shilling, grinning impishly. "Spend it on yerself, McBride."

He took the shilling, smiling in return. "I've a book fer ye, today, as well, Lily." He was awed by the fact that Lily could read, and he saved every book that came his way for her. He'd inadvertently helped her amass a truly eclectic library, including an encyclopedia of animals, a volume of Greek myths, the works of Shakespeare, and of course, *Pride and Prejudice* and the book of bawdy stories.

"*Robinson Crusoe*," she read aloud from the cover of the book. "Thank you, McBride. I will cherish it."

"See that ye do," he said sternly, embarrassed suddenly by his own generosity.

Lily smiled, stood on her toes to lean across the counter, kissed his stubbly cheek, and dashed from the shop.

Gideon had returned to the Westminster chambers with a slight limp. *Bloody little pickpocket and her deadly aim.* But then again, he'd been even more impassioned than usual during his summary today; one juror had even been moved to tears. Perhaps he should *thank* the pickpocket.

"Well done, Mr. Cole."

"Impressive as usual, Mr. Cole."

"Excellent summary, Mr. Cole."

Gideon nodded and murmured his thanks to his colleagues as he wended his way through the small crowd to join the other barristers in the chambers at Westminster Hall. He always allowed himself but a moment to savor a courtroom victory before he once again threw himself upon the mercy of the solicitors who milled about, looking for barristers upon whom to bestow their cases. Fortunately, Gideon, with his habit of winning, was in demand with solicitors. He was particularly in demand with one solicitor, unfortunately.

And oh, dear God, *there he was.*

Mr. Dodge was small and top-heavy; his round torso overhung two twiggy little legs, a fringe of graying hair encircled his otherwise shiny pate, and the alert beak of his nose supported a pair of spectacles through which peered a pair of sharp blue eyes. Those sharp blue eyes were scanning the courtroom for his prey: Gideon Cole.

Gideon had faced Napoleon's hordes. He'd been in any number of bare-fisted fights. He'd once even fought a duel, though he could scarcely now remember over what.

But only Mr. Dodge could strike terror into his very bowels.

Mr. Dodge knew his weakness.

As surreptitiously as his height would allow, Gideon inched toward the courtroom's exit.

"Oh, Mr. Cole—"

Gideon lengthened his stride, forcing the solicitor to scuttle after him in an undignified manner.

"Mr. Cole! I'd like just a moment of your time, if you would, Mr. Cole," Dodge panted, unperturbed by this frosty reception.

"I've given you all the moments I intend to give you, Mr. Dodge."

Mr. Dodge managed to scurry around Gideon's long-legged frame and plant himself in his path. "I do think I have a case that will interest you, Mr. Cole," he said firmly, his beaky little nose pointed up at Gideon.

Gideon groaned and covered his face with his hands. An interesting case was precisely what he feared. "Mr. Dodge, I don't *want* to hear about any orphans cheated of their inheritances or any such tragedies."

"But it's not an orphan this time, Mr. Cole."

Gideon parted two fingers and peeped cautiously out.

"It's a widow," Dodge informed him brightly.

Gideon jerked back. "Go away, Mr. Dodge."

"But Mr. Cole—"

"I mean it, Mr. Dodge. Find some other foolish, soft-hearted barrister to torment."

"I fear you're the only one, Mr. Cole," Dodge told him sympathetically. "And you're so very good at it. You always, always win."

"And I'm never, ever paid."

"Oh, now, gentlemen such as yourself don't need money, do they? You've a tree that sprouts pound notes on an estate somewhere." Dodge thrust a sheaf of papers at Gideon. The case's brief.

"Very funny, Mr. Dodge." Gideon snatched the papers from him. "Who is this widow?"

"A dressmaker by profession. She's worked very hard all her life, built a tidy little business for herself. And now her dead husband's brother is trying to steal her house out from under her. Claims it's legally his."

"Has she any money?" Gideon asked despairingly. "Any chance I might earn more than a shilling from this?"

Mr. Dodge beamed at him. "None whatsoever."

"I hate you, Mr. Dodge."

"I know, Mr. Cole," Dodge said cheerfully. "You will take the case?"

"I will look into it," Gideon grumbled. But they both knew it was virtually a certainty that Gideon would take the case. Which would prevent him from taking other more *lucrative* cases.

Which was why it was Gideon's own bloody fault he wasn't yet rich.

"You're a good man, Mr. Cole," Dodge said softly.

Gideon snorted and made a shooing motion, a half-smile playing at his lips, and Dodge tottered cheerfully off, whistling a little tune.

Widows, orphans, the elderly . . . Gideon didn't know why Dodge took on these kinds of clients. But Dodge, as a solicitor, was under no obligation to support the lifestyle of a gentleman of the *ton*, with the lodgings and fine clothing and entertainments it entailed. Dodge was already married; he didn't need to woo the daughter of a marquis with the promise of a town house on Grosvenor Square. And Dodge, Gideon was willing to wager, didn't have a Master Plan.

Gideon stared grimly down at the brief. He thought of Helen in Yorkshire and the last letter he'd had from her, the words cheerful and careful on the surface and wrenching beneath. He thought of Constance, and how she would greet the news that Gideon Cole all but gave away his services when she'd assumed he'd been busily amassing the sort of fortune befitting the daughter of a marquis. Astonishment, confusion, contempt . . . he imagined them flickering in succession across her gray eyes. She would likely feel betrayed.

She'd be right to feel that way.

Gideon lifted his head from the brief and rubbed a weary

hand over his eyes. A decade after Oxford, he was still leaping to the defense of the defenseless. But he suspected the visceral pleasure he took in it had become an indulgence. The dressmaker . . . well, perhaps this particular dressmaker would have to fend for herself.

"Mr. Cole, there is one thing I neglected to mention."

Dodge *again*? Gideon leveled a knee-bucklingly hostile glare at the solicitor, but Mr. Dodge seemed unaffected; perhaps intimidating glares merely glanced off his spectacles like sunbeams.

"It's about your former client, Mr. Wesley."

Gideon brightened a little, albeit warily. Wesley was a farmer; Gideon had shared a number of very satisfying conversations with him about the Leicester Long Wool, a breed of sheep Gideon thought might thrive at Aster Park. "How fares Mr. Wesley?"

"I've unhappy news, I'm afraid. Mr. Wesley has passed away."

Gideon felt the sadness sink through him like a stone. *Well,* he thought mordantly. *This day improves by the minute.*

"But he remembered you in his will, Mr. Cole." Mr. Dodge continued gently. "With utmost gratitude for helping him to save his farm. Here you are: thirty pounds."

And then Dodge pushed the sheaf of bills at Gideon and tottered away again, just as though he were an ordinary solicitor and not a veritable messenger from the gods.

"Lily!" All exuberance, Alice ran to Lily for a hug. Alice had been instructed to be wary of everyone but Mrs. Smythe and Fanny while Lily was out, but Lily knew fresh gratitude each day she arrived home to find Alice safe, because reticence didn't come naturally to Alice.

"We've bread and cheese for dinner tonight, dearest. Are you hungry?" The moment Lily set foot over the threshold of their room she flung the dialect of St. Giles from her like a tattered cloak. For her mother had raised Lily and Alice to be ladies. Though it had been several years since either of them had spoken to any *actual* ladies. And Lily, meanwhile, had learned the patois of St. Giles as diligently as she'd learned French; it was part of her costume, a key to her survival.

"Oh, yes! Today I helped Mrs. Smythe with the cooking and washing up," Alice told her proudly. "And look, she gave me a penny." She pushed a penny into Lily's hand. It was warm and moist; clearly Alice had been gripping it all day.

"I'm proud of you, Alice. 'Tis no mean feat to extract a penny from Mrs. Smythe. Did you perhaps cast a spell on her?"

Alice giggled. "No! She just said I was a good worker. I *wish* I knew how to cast a spell."

A good worker. At ten years old, Alice was "a good worker." A ten-year-old girl should be *playing* at working, not earning a penny to give to her sister to buy food. Lily thrust a sharp metaphorical elbow into the thought; she could not afford to let it catch hold of her, for there was little she could do about it. "You are a miracle worker, then. Mrs. Smythe is as tightfisted as they come."

Mrs. Smythe had a figure like two barrels stacked one atop the other and a face as hard as a brick. Neither Alice nor Lily had ever seen her smile, but the bricklike effect was softened somewhat by the four or five long gray hairs fringing her chin, which fascinated Alice. Lily always had to remind her not to stare.

The very best thing about Mrs. Smythe was her implacability: no matter how long you had lived under her regime, no matter your circumstances, you were out on the street if your rent was late by even a moment. Mrs. Smythe's rules intimidated the worst rogues from attempting to take rooms, which kept the lodging house reasonably safe and her rents higher than most. Lily had honed her pickpocketing skills specifically to satisfy Mrs. Smythe's requirements.

Alice giggled again. "Maybe I *did* say some magic words without knowing it. Perhaps they were, 'Mrs. Smythe, shall I sweep the floor now?' "

Lily tweaked her sister's long blonde braid. "Well, from now on every time we need something good to happen, we'll say to ourselves, 'Mrs. Smythe, shall I sweep the floor now?' And then we shall wait for the result."

Alice laughed, delighted by the idea. "*Mrs. Smythe, shall I sweep the floor now? Oh, Mrs. Smythe, shall I sweep the floor now*?" she sang, skipping about the room.

Her mother, the daughter of a curate, would have been aghast at the thought of her daughters casting spells, but Lily joined in the song anyway as she sliced cheese and bread. She'd gone straight from McBride to the bread shop, and then to the cheese shop, and then bought a small nosegay of violets for Fanny, because Fanny was always kind and informative—particularly regarding the use of knees and elbows—and would never think to do such a thing for herself.

But her purchases had exhausted Lily's take; she'd be out again tomorrow hunting for coins and watch fobs.

"If our song really is magical, tomorrow it should be raining pennies," she said through bites of bread.

"We'll buy shoes," Alice said dreamily. "And a great house like the house in your story. Tell a story, Lily."

Lily had always catalogued the world sensually, through her eyes and ears and fingertips, and her impressions spilled out in the form of stories. The old nag that pulled the flower cart became a unicorn; Mrs. Smythe became a child-eating giantess, McBride a wizard with potions that went sadly awry. She spun stories at night until the room seemed to throb with magic, giving each character its own voice, its own mannerisms; the stories warmed the two of them better than gin. And Lily knew this because she'd *tried* gin—once. Vile stuff, like swallowing sour fire. She hadn't tasted it again.

Rather unlike Papa.

"Which story shall I tell? The one about the great house? Or a new one?"

"The one about the great house."

"Well, once upon a time, two beautiful princesses—"

"Named Lily and Alice."

"—named Lily and Alice," Lily confirmed, "lived in a grand, grand house, a palace, made all of brick and marble, with rooms enough for everyone in St. Giles."

Alice frowned. "But we don't want *everyone* to stay with us. Not Mrs. Smythe."

"Oh, of course not. We shall be very discriminating."

"Perhaps McBride," Alice suggested magnanimously.

"Certainly McBride," Lily agreed. "And the house was surrounded by green lawns as far as the eye can see, and trees and fountains were everywhere, and swans and peacocks, too."

"Tell me again about the peacocks."

"They are great shiny birds, with long proud feathers like this." Lily fanned her hand out behind her bottom and wiggled it, to make Alice giggle. "Like the birds in our book."

"Can we eat them?" Alice asked bloodthirstily.

"No, our cupboards will be so full of beef and cheese that we would never dream of eating a peacock."

"Oh my," Alice breathed.

"And there's a prince," Lily added suddenly.

"A prince?" Alice was fascinated. "There's never been a prince before."

Because I've never seen a man quite like this before. "Yes, a very tall prince, with broad shoulders, and . . . thick straight dark brows like this." Lily placed her fingers across her own fine brows. "And cheeks like . . . like this." She sucked in her own cheeks to illustrate high slopes and elegant hollows. "And a bold nose. Rather saves him from being too pretty. And hair like fire."

"His hair is on fire?" Alice was alarmed.

"No, goose. His hair is very dark, but it shines in the sun like . . . lit coal. His eyes are dark, and he has very fine clothes. And a firm grip," she added, a touch resentfully.

"A firm grip?" Alice was puzzled. "Is he handsome?"

Lily hesitated, remembering those dark eyes fringed by lashes so thick she'd been tempted to reach up and brush her finger across them. Staring down at her in cold, confident fury, clearly a man unafraid of much of anything, particularly her. But then, in the space of a breath, his gaze had become . . . something else. Interest? Wonder? She'd felt the change as physically as his fingers closed around her wrist; she'd felt in the very center of her, a shock of heat, like lamplight blooming.

Right before she'd kneed him in the cods.

She smiled a little; it had been a terrible thing to do to a man. But it wasn't as though he'd given her much of a choice.

"Well, yes. Very handsome," she admitted.

"All right," Alice conceded begrudgingly. "He can live with us, too. And do Mama and Papa live in a house like that in Heaven, Lily?" Alice's blue eyes were beginning to mist over with sleepiness.

Lily thought about this. No doubt there was a place for handsome wastrels who married the orphan daughters of curates, drank up their money, and then died, leaving their wives and daughters penniless in St. Giles. She just wasn't sure heaven was it.

When Papa died, Mama had given up caring about much of anything, so it fell to Lily to put food on the table and keep the roof over their head. She had tried applying to shops, to great houses: none would have her. So she'd stolen her first watch fob. Desperation had blunted her fear, and success had given her courage, and courage had made her bolder. When she discovered she was *good* at relieving gentlemen of small shiny things, a certain amount of pride began to shine through the shame of it, and she began to revel in her own resourcefulness. There was great satisfaction in knowing she was keeping her family together.

If Mama had guessed how Lily had gone about it, she'd never said a word.

But Lily had other memories, too, memories her sister was too young to share: of safer and more comfortable homes, of soft laughter between her parents, of playing simple tunes on a pianoforte that had later vanished along with the house and everything in it. Of seashore trips. Of shoes.

Lily looked down into Alice's wide blue eyes, so like Mama's. *What will become of us?* was a thought she rarely entertained; *there is only today* was the refrain that comforted her.

"Yes, Mama and Papa live in a house like that in Heaven," she told her sister softly.

"That little pickpocket got you right in the . . . in the . . . *baubles.*"

Gideon pulled his gaze away from Lady Gilchrist's ballroom to look askance at Kilmartin. "I was *there*, Laurie. I see no need to reminisce."

"What was she after? Your watch?"

"My great-grandfather's *gold* watch." The jarring clarity of the girl's eyes haunted him—such a remarkable color. And he'd read outrage in them, too, as well as panic, as though his attempt to prevent her from helping herself to his one cherished family heirloom had been sheer effrontery on his part. He'd walked gingerly for hours after. He shook his head wryly. *Women.* A cruel, confusing species to be sure.

He returned his eyes to the ballroom, where a chandelier poured soft light down upon rows of dancers in the throes of a reel. Reels embarrassed Gideon; all that clapping and twirling ill-suited the dignity of someone several inches over six feet tall. When he could do so without causing great offense, he waited them out. Constance, however, appeared to be enjoying this reel inordinately.

Perhaps because she was partnered with Lord Jarvis.

Lord Jarvis, who *already* had a title and a fortune and wasn't exactly a gargoyle.

Jarvis was a decent enough fellow, Gideon conceded reluctantly. Blond. Affable. On the whole, completely inoffensive. Apart, that is, from his interest in Constance.

Kilmartin followed Gideon's morose gaze. "'Constance,'" he mused. "An ironic name, when you think about it. She doesn't seem terribly 'constant' now, does she?"

"Are you *trying* to cheer me up, Laurie? If so, I wish you would stop."

Kilmartin shook his head sympathetically, and they returned to watching the dancers in silence.

"What does Constance see in him?" Gideon asked finally.

"*Besides* the money and title and all that property?"

Gideon slowly turned an amazed expression toward his friend.

"Oh, sorry, old man," Kilmartin added hurriedly. "I suppose that wasn't terribly helpful, either."

Gideon lifted one eyebrow in confirmation and resumed his Constance vigil. "At least I am dancing all but two waltzes with her this evening."

Kilmartin sighed. "Gideon, as your friend, I feel obliged to tell you your conversation lacks something these days. Or rather, it lacks *everything* but two things: work and Constance. You used to be *fun.*"

"Fun?" The notion surprised Gideon. "I was never *fun.*"

"You *were,*" Kilmartin disagreed firmly. "The time you put the lizard in Cunnington's bed—remember that? The morning you hid everyone's boots? The mule races? Or—my favorite—the night of the opera dancers?"

Ah, the night of the opera dancers. Gideon recalled a good deal of champagne and giggling, followed by a frisky chase around a settee and a very satisfying conclusion *atop* the settee. He smiled to himself, a slow, sweetly sinful smile that sent fans and eyelashes fluttering all over the ballroom.

Kilmartin was right: *Work and Constance.* His Master Plan *had* begun to feel a bit like an endless, steep marble staircase.

But at the very top Constance glowed like a compass star.

What the bloody hell was Jarvis saying to make her laugh so merrily just now? How amusing could a reel possibly *be*?

"I do take your point, Laurie. But . . . *look* at her."

Kilmartin dutifully looked at Constance. As usual, her dress was in the first stare of fashion: pale and floaty and slightly daring, held up at the shoulders by two mere wisps of fabric. Tall, bright of hair and fair of skin, she dominated the room the way the sun dominated the sky.

Gideon often felt like Icarus when he looked at Constance.

"I don't care what you say, Gideon, she rather frightens *me*" was Kilmartin's subdued-sounding verdict. "She's so . . . so . . . very . . ." He stalled like a cart mired in mud.

"My point *precisely*," Gideon completed with relish.

Finally, Constance's bright head dipped in an elegant curtsy, and Lord Jarvis led her from the floor, his face flushed with pride and exertion; heads turned to watch them. And as Jarvis made his bow and drifted away, three young women appeared and attached themselves to Constance. The handmaidens, Gideon and Kilmartin secretly called them. They orbited Constance like moons, as though they couldn't help it, as though their natures required it.

Kilmartin took two steps away from Gideon to find Lady Anne Clapham, but then he paused and turned, his expression thoughtful. "Do you know what Constance needs, Gideon? A rival. Someone exotic, someone just different enough from her to throw her off her game. That ought to tip the balance in your favor."

Gideon gave a short humorless laugh. "Pity such a creature does not exist."

When it was time for the waltz, Gideon steered Constance (or was steered *by* Constance—it was often difficult to discern the difference) about the ballroom floor like a great golden galleon, conscious of and pleased by all the eyes watching them. They were well matched; he knew it pleased Constance as much as it pleased him.

"Would it bore you if I told you how lovely you looked tonight, Constance?" He said her name proprietarily; he wondered if she had yet allowed Jarvis to call her by her first name.

"Oh, a compliment could never bore me, Gideon."

"But doubtless you've been complimented in the very same way all evening."

"But not by *you.*" She tilted her head back and peered at him through flirtatiously lowered lashes.

Gideon knew a challenge when he heard one. "Well, perhaps, then, I can arrive at a more *original* compliment," he teased. "Perhaps something along the lines of . . . your eyes are the color of the sky above the moors on a wintry evening . . ."

Too late he recalled that Constance had no patience for metaphor; she vastly preferred the tangible. Her angelic face hid a breathtakingly literal mind.

"Really, Gideon—'*moors.*' How very florid. Perhaps you could compliment my gown instead. I'm the only young lady in the *ton* to have anything like it, and it was very dear."

"The only young lady? That *is* impressive. How did you manage it?"

Constance lowered her voice confidingly. "I bribed most of the dressmakers in the *ton*!" She gave a wicked little giggle. "And that *would* have worked a treat, but then I learned that Miss Fortescue had already ordered the dress. So I said to her, 'Miss Fortescue, you've such lovely *plump* arms, that new type of sleeve would *never* suit—perhaps a puff would be more appropriate?' I aver, Miss Fortescue will wear puffed sleeves for the rest of her life. And she canceled her order, of course."

Gideon gazed down at her, bemused, as he so often was in her presence. Constance took her clothing very seriously. "It must be an awesome responsibility to wield such influence over the young ladies of the *ton*, Constance." He was half jesting.

"Oh, but it *is*," she said in all gravity. "But it's also very important to *win*."

Gideon could hardly disagree, as he'd devoted almost his entire life to winning. He hadn't yet resorted to bribing dressmakers, but who knew what measures he would take if circumstances called for it? "Well, no other young lady would carry that gown off quite so well as you. It is exquisite."

She looked pleased enough, though Gideon had the sense that he was confirming something she already knew. He immediately fished about in his mind for more compliments, as they were, after all, the grease that kept conversation with Constance flowing smoothly, and could very well lead to other topics if he kept at it.

"How does your uncle fare, Gideon?" she asked suddenly.

The question disarmed him; he was touched. "Poorly, as usual, I'm afraid."

She was quiet for a moment. "He's been ill for *such* a long time. One might even begin to believe he'll be ill . . . forever."

And suddenly a cold little finger of suspicion jabbed below his heart. *Perhaps she'd like a titled husband before she's in her dotage*. Kilmartin's words.

"Uncle Edward may expire any moment." Surprise made his words emerge more clipped than he had intended.

Constance seemed to brighten a little. "That *is* a shame. Pity, isn't it, that he cannot enjoy his properties as they should be enjoyed? Papa has always *greatly* admired Aster Park."

"Has he?" Gideon knew full well the marquis admired Aster Park. *Everyone* admired Aster Park, particularly Constance. He recalled strolling alongside her during her first and only visit to the estate, during a house party Kilmartin had persuaded Gideon to hold. Her conversation had been light, but she'd scrutinized the rose and statue and kitchen gardens, the lakes and fountains and labyrinths and trees, with the coolly critical eye of Wellington inspecting his regiments. And Gideon had seen the gathering covetousness in her gaze.

"But *I* always thought all those big American trees should be planted in a more orderly fashion, not in those great messy clumps. You know, I think I may yet discover a talent for horticulture, Gideon."

Great messy clumps? "I should not be surprised if horticulture turned out to be your great calling, Constance."

She laughed at that. "Now you are teasing me. Tell me, did you win in court today?"

"Of course." He smiled reassuringly.

"And did they give you a good deal of money for it?" Constance had no real understanding of the legal system, a fact that tended to work beautifully in Gideon's favor.

"Oh, a *good* deal," he said airily. It wasn't precisely a lie. "In fact . . . I thought I'd buy the town house on Grosvenor Square. The one on the corner."

"Oh!" Constance's gray eyes widened. "But I thought— That is, Malco— That is, Lord Jarvis is interested in that . . . in that property as . . . as . . . well . . ."

And then Gideon watched a slow flush paint Constance's face up to her eyebrows as she realized precisely what she'd revealed.

Bloody hell. So it's "Malcolm," is it?

And so it seemed the betting books had the right of it.

Violins and cellos measured off a subtly charged moment. "I can see why he might be," Gideon managed smoothly at last. "It *is* a handsome property."

"Yes," Constance agreed just as evenly. "I always

thought it would make a wonderful wedding present for some fortunate young woman."

And then she laughed, a breathy girlish laugh. But the words were not lightly intended; a gauntlet of sorts had been thrown down. Gideon noted the message with no halt in rhythm or change of expression. A cold little knot formed in the pit of his stomach; his mind whirred.

"Will you miss me when I'm in the country?" Constance's head inclined coyly.

Gideon knew mere compliments would no longer do; strategy was now required. Gideon's barrister's mind swiftly rifled through the facts. Constance wanted only the best of everything, and clearly Constance had begun to believe Jarvis had as much, possibly more, to offer her than Gideon Cole.

But *why* did Constance want the best of everything? Because Lady Constance Clary not only *loved* to win—she *needed* to win. Because she always won. And Kilmartin was right: in the absence of a title and fortune, what Gideon needed—what he needed *for* her—was a worthy rival. Quickly. One capable of convincing Constance that what she *needed* to win . . . was Gideon Cole.

And if a rival would not obligingly, magically appear . . .

He would invent one.

Gideon gazed out over the ballroom and saw Kilmartin sail by in the clutches of Lady Anne Clapham, his face, as usual, dreamy with contentment. They puzzled Gideon a little, Kilmartin and Lady Anne Clapham. Gideon typically felt something more . . . *active* in Constance's presence. Admiration, uncertainty . . . things that kept him alert, tensed the muscles of his stomach.

"Forgive my distraction, Constance. It's just that when I saw Kilmartin, I recalled he has a cousin he would like me to meet."

"A cousin?" Constance sounded almost incredulous. She was usually the first to know and assess any newcomer; no doubt she found it nearly impossible that Kilmartin could have a cousin she knew nothing about.

"Yes. I cannot quite recall her name . . ." Gideon's voice drifted—strategically—along with his gaze. Constance's fingers tensed in his hand; she was nearly vibrating with curiosity now.

Gideon returned his gaze to Constance. "But I shall of course miss you while you're away, Constance."

And he would of course buy a town house while she was away, as well.

The waltz came to an end, and Gideon looked lingeringly into Constance's eyes, which now held a faint light of uncertainty; he bowed lingeringly over her hand and reluctantly took his leave of her. *Take that, Constance. I was a soldier, and now I am a barrister. I know how to win.*

Chapter Two

Lily was of two minds about portly men: they often made good quarry, because they tended to move more slowly. However, sometimes they strained their clothing, and tight clothing allowed pickpockets scant room to maneuver.

But the particular portly man Lily had her eye on looked prosperous; the walking stick he clutched in his huge fist sported what appeared to be a genuine gold top, and his clothing, at least his coat and trousers, was beautifully made and generously cut. Most importantly, a chain dangled tantalizingly from his coat pocket. *A watch.* Splendid! Successfully retrieving this particular watch would make up for yesterday's failure.

Her dress had long ago faded to somewhere between gray and brown, and this was a great help when it came to blending into masses of people and disappearing into shadows. She sidled through the crowd, her head lowered, until she was flush with the man and within reaching distance of his pocket. Heart racing, she stretched out her hand. It vanished into his pocket and closed over the delicious smooth metal of the watch; her touch was expert, almost indiscernible; if it was detected at all, it was usually mistaken for a breeze.

And then . . .

Well, it happened so quickly.

Someone in the crowd stumbled and swore, jostling her quarry, who stumbled and swore in turn, and took an awkward step to right himself, his head turning to watch his feet—

Just as Lily was extracting her hand from his pocket.

His hand clamped around Lily's arm. "*What the bloody hell do you think you're doing?*" He squeezed until she cried out in pain; her fingers splayed open and the lovely watch fell and skittered, winking in the sunlight, across the ground. The man bent forward to sweep it up, dragging her down with him; his grip didn't slacken. She twisted and kicked out, but it was becoming horribly clear he did not intend to release her.

Terror sucked the air from her lungs.

God help me, she prayed. And then, absurdly, *Mrs. Smythe, shall I sweep the floor today?*

In a mere hour, thanks to Mr. Wesley's thirty pounds, Gideon would be the owner of a London town house: the one on the corner of Grosvenor Square. He consulted his watch and superstitiously quickened his pace toward the square, as though Jarvis was racing across town to buy it out from beneath him. He'd been assured by the seller's solicitor that this was not the case, and yet—

A sudden barrage of *basso* bellows and curses stopped him cold. Good *God*, what an unholy racket. Gideon scanned the crowd for its source: something—or rather, someone—was thrashing in the grip of an enormous man, and this enormous man was doing the shouting.

Curiosity and a strange sense of urgency propelled Gideon closer; the fluttering of a tattered skirt told him the captive was a woman. A *small* woman.

"Here now, what is this?" he demanded in his barrister voice.

"*This wench tried to steal my watch!*" the enormous man roared indignantly. The girl continued to twist so violently in the man's grasp that her face was a blur, but the man obviously had manacles for hands; she couldn't free herself. Finally she stopped thrashing, panting desperately, and her eyes flicked toward Gideon.

Good God! Those *eyes.* It was the girl who had tried to steal *his* watch the day before. "You really ought to give this up," he told her dryly. "Clearly you aren't any good at it."

She merely scowled at him and kicked out at her captor, whose nether regions, unfortunately for her, were protected by great rolls of flesh. The enormous man effortlessly held her at a safe distance from his person and gave her a hard shake, like a terrier with a rat in its jaws.

Fury warped the air in front of Gideon's eyes. She might be a thief, but the man dwarfed her, and he was deliberately hurting her now. "Let her go," he heard himself say. "She won't do it again."

"Let her *go*?" The man was aghast. "I will not! My grandfather's watch! The little pestilence belongs in Newgate! I've a mind to take her straight there."

"I sympathize, but surely—"

"She needs to be taught a lesson!" the man bellowed, freshly enraged. He shook the girl again. Her head snapped forward and back, like the head on a doll.

The metallic tang of rage burned the back of Gideon's throat, crawled over his skin on cold spiky legs, tightened his lungs until his breath came shallow. Oh, a clean fist to the jaw would take this beast down easily.

But he didn't do that sort of thing anymore.

"Five pounds if you release her," he said quietly instead, his voice a deadly thing.

The man suddenly went still, surprised by the offer; his fist remained securely wrapped around the girl's arm. She gave a token twist, but winced the moment she did.

Gideon couldn't bear it.

"No, sir," the large man reiterated. "I don't know what you want with her, but she's going to prison, if I have any say in it."

"Ten pounds."

"Not for any price, sir."

"Not for thirty pounds?"

A loaded silence fell over the strange little trio. The enormous man studied Gideon curiously for a moment. *Say no,* Gideon thought. *Ignore my insanity, and I'll be on my way.*

"Show it to me," the man demanded instead.

Gideon looked at the girl. Her entire body heaved with her breathing; her eyes fluttered closed. The flesh of her thin arm, covered in the worn cloth of her dress, bulged between the man's huge fingers.

Slowly, as if in a dream, Gideon pulled the precious thirty pounds from his pocket.

The enormous man snatched it and pushed the girl at Gideon.

"Enjoy your prize, sir." He stalked off.

When Kilmartin opened the door to his lodgings, he found a thunderous-looking Gideon Cole clutching a filthy scrap of a girl by the arm.

"Congratulate me, Kilmartin. I seem to have purchased a pickpocket."

"What on—what have you—" Kilmartin spluttered as Gideon pushed past him into the house, dragging the girl along with him.

Gideon pushed the pickpocket firmly into one of his friend's sitting room chairs. "Don't move a hair," he commanded her. She glared back at him sullenly, but remained perfectly still, apart from the rapid rise and fall of her breathing. Her chin went up; her spine stiffened. *Proud for a thief.*

"Yes, for thirty pounds." Gideon turned to Kilmartin and gave a short, near-hysterical laugh. "She tried to steal a watch from a huge fellow, who planned to turn her over to the authorities, and so I gave him thirty pounds to turn her over to me instead. *And*—you'll enjoy this part, Kilmartin—she's the very wench who tried to steal my watch yesterday."

"But Gideon . . ." Kilmartin spoke gently, rather the way one would address an escapee from Bedlam. "*Why?*"

Gideon yanked off his hat and pushed an agitated hand through his hair. "God, I wish I knew. It was . . . a reflex. It just . . . it just infuriated me to watch that enormous man shake a girl who could never possibly defend herself against him."

"But she's a *thief,*" Kilmartin explained, straining for patience. "And you're a *barrister.*"

"I know," Gideon groaned.

"Why didn't you just *hit* him?"

"I don't *do* that anymore, Laurie."

"And why did you bring her to my lodgings? She'll get fleas or some other vermin on the furniture, no doubt."

"Oh, please, Kilmartin. Your furniture would be improved by the addition of a few fleas."

Out of the corner of his eye, Gideon thought he saw the girl's mouth twitch a little. He turned swiftly to look at her, but found her face a sullen blank. Perhaps he'd imagined it.

They turned to look at the pickpocket, who was now scanning the room with her huge eyes. "Calculating how much you can get for the candlesticks?" Gideon snapped. She glanced at him—guiltily, he thought—and returned to gazing straight ahead, her hands folded in her lap. And then Gideon pictured the man's hand clamped around her thin arm; the girl would likely have a bracelet of bruises. More gently he asked, "Did that man hurt you? Are you injured?"

The pickpocket's eyes widened in surprise; she gave her head a little shake: no.

"You could just turn her loose, like a rat," Kilmartin suggested hopefully.

"*Thirty pounds*, Kilmartin. Every penny I had. I was on my way to buy the town house in Grosvenor Square. I rather hoped to make a wedding gift of it." Gideon threw himself onto Kilmartin's settee and slouched in frustration.

"Perhaps you can give the pickpocket to Constance as a wedding gift instead."

"Oh, *very* amusing, Laurie. Do you know what I now have to offer Constance? Precisely nothing."

"And here I thought Constance loved you for your own dear self."

Gideon hurled his hat at Kilmartin, who dodged it.

"You know I would loan the money to you if I could, Gideon. But my father still controls my funds."

"I know you would loan it, Laurie, and I thank you. But I would never ask it of you. I must do this myself."

"Doing things yourself is vastly overrated, Gideon."

"If you say so, Laurie." There was a pause; Gideon jounced his knee in thought. "Perhaps we can find the girl some sort of employment."

"Does she talk?"

"She hasn't yet. I've considered that she may be mute. Though she seems to understand English well enough."

"Ah. So you've purchased a mute female pickpocket. I must say, Gideon, it doesn't rank among your wiser investments."

A little gingerly, Kilmartin moved closer to the girl and peered into her face. She turned to glare at him. He reared back in surprise.

"Good God, Gideon. She's a bit of a looker, isn't she? Those *eyes*. Freakishly lovely, really. You didn't have something less . . . *savory* in mind for her, did you, when you bought her?" Kilmartin turned back to Gideon looking half worried, half intrigued.

"Oh, for God's sake, Kilmartin." Gideon was disgusted. "And take care not to get too close. She kicks."

"I also *bite* . . . if sufficiently provoked."

The two men swiveled in unison.

She *spoke.*

Not only could she speak, but that . . . that *voice.* A low drawl with an edge of ragged velvet, it was unlike anything Gideon had ever heard. It shivered through him, like a tongue applied to the back of his neck, or fingernails dragged gently up his back. In that voice, "I also bite" sounded less like a threat and more like . . . an erotic *promise.*

His own voice seemed to have retreated in deference to the splendor of hers. "So you *can* talk," he finally managed. "Why have you not spoken until now?"

"Perhaps the *mood* did not take me." She crossed her arms over her chest defiantly.

Impudent wench. And again, that voice. There was nothing of the street urchin in either her timbre or phrasing. She sounded like a grown woman, like a *lady*. More like a lady, in fact, than most of the young things that romped about in reels at balls and parties all over the *ton*.

"Who are you?" Gideon demanded. "What is your name?"

Her arms remained crossed; her mouth remained closed; her gaze remained sullen.

"If you do not tell me your name *now*, I will call you other names that, I assure you, will not please you in the least."

"Why should I tell you anything?" the girl hissed.

"Because, Miss Whoever-You-Are, I will make sure you spend the rest of your wretched life in Newgate if you do not. You've cost me thirty pounds."

The girl studied him, the pulse in her throat beating visibly. After a moment, her expression shifted a little; she'd decided, it seemed, to take his threat seriously. "Lily." The word was etched in resentment.

Gideon and Kilmartin were quiet. Gideon wondered if Laurie was thinking the same thing: Oddly, "Lily" suited her, ragged and begrimed though she was.

"And do you have a surname, Lily? Or do you even know who your father was?"

She scowled at him. "Do you know who *your* father was, Mr.—?"

"Cole. And of course I know who my father was."

"I asked," Lily drawled, leaning forward earnestly, "because I've never known a *whoreson* to know the name of his father."

Gideon heard Kilmartin's sharp intake of breath even as he felt his own face growing warm. Lily leaned back again, seemingly pleased with the impact of her insult.

"Miss—?" Gideon's voice was gentle.

"Masters," she revealed sullenly.

"Miss Masters, you underestimate the gravity of your predicament. You do understand what I just said, am I correct? You understand words like 'underestimate' and 'gravity' and 'predicament'?" He didn't trouble to disguise his sarcasm.

Lily glowered at him.

"Because the typical pickpocket would not, you see."

"*I*," Lily emphasized, "am not typical."

"Hear, hear," Kilmartin murmured. Gideon turned to glare at his friend before returning his attention to Lily.

"You are a terrible thief, Miss Masters."

"I am an *excellent* thief, Mr. Cole."

"You were caught at least *twice* in two days. Not an impressive record."

"Mr. Cole, were you ever a soldier?" She sounded impatient.

Gideon was surprised by the question, and, quite frankly, curious enough about it to answer it simply. "Yes."

"If you missed your target twice out of a hundred or so times you fired your musket, would you consider yourself a 'terrible' shot?"

Kilmartin gave a quick appreciative laugh. Gideon threw him a repressive look.

"So . . ." Gideon's tone was silky. "You admit you've stolen at least a hundred times, Miss Masters?"

This quieted Lily.

"I am a barrister, Miss Masters. Do you know what that means?"

"You torment the poor?"

"I send lawbreakers to prison."

Another silence from the pickpocket.

"Where do you live Miss Masters? Why do you pick pockets?"

"I live in St. Giles, Mr. Cole, and that should be answer enough for you."

"But you could find other work, Miss Masters. As a scullery maid, perhaps."

There was a pause; her eyes flicked away from his. "I've my reasons, Mr. Cole."

Gideon studied her. "You're well-spoken . . . for a *thief*, that is," he allowed. "How did that come to be?"

Her head snapped back toward him. "How is any of this your business, Mr. Cole?"

"Thirty pounds makes everything about you my business, Miss Masters. Was your mother someone's mistress, perhaps?"

"My mother," Lily said through a jaw that all but clenched, "was a *lady*."

"A *lady*, was she?" Gideon's voice was saturated with skepticism. "No doubt, then, she would find you a disappointment at the moment."

Her expression shifted subtly, darkening. "No doubt," she repeated softly.

The room fell silent. Gideon stared at Lily thoughtfully, his fingers drumming his thighs. And then a rogue inspiration swam into his mind. He indulged it.

"*Parlez-vous français?*" he barked. Kilmartin jumped.

"*Je parle français un petit peu.*" Lily looked startled by her own response.

French delivered in Lily's rough velvet voice was simply

devastating. Gideon and Kilmartin fixed her with dumb-struck stares.

She was well-spoken, she knew a little French . . . what other ladylike accomplishments lurked beneath her feral façade? Gideon was reluctantly, increasingly fascinated. He studied her for a moment longer. And then . . .

"Kilmartin . . ." Gideon could hear the portent in his own voice. "I've an idea."

Kilmartin looked worried. "Gideon, I don't think it's a good idea for you to have ideas."

"No, just wait. Hear me out. Miss Masters, can you read?"

"Of course." The girl's chin was up again. The *pride* in her. As if there had never been any question of a pickpocket being able to read.

"Do you dance?"

A snort from the pickpocket.

"I'll take that as a no. How old are you? Do you know?"

She looked away from him.

"You may as well tell me, Miss Masters."

"I am twenty years old," she divulged begrudgingly.

Gideon eyed Lily Masters speculatively. Those singularly lovely eyes, that vulnerable pink heart of a mouth . . . As unlikely as it seemed, Lily Masters could very well be quite presentable beneath the rags and grime. Her hair was pinned up indifferently, but she seemed to have a good deal of it, and it was difficult to see what kind of figure she had beneath that ragged dress, but she was definitely slim. And then there was that voice. *Dear God.* The contrast between her ethereal appearance and her courtesan's voice was mesmerizing. The *ton*, he was sure, had never seen anything quite like her. She had been taught to speak like a lady; she even spoke a little French. She had wit and pride—

No. It was madness. It would never work. She was a thief who preyed upon unwary men—by her own admission. It would be like setting the fox among the hens.

And yet it *could* work. It *might* work. Gideon had very little to lose at this point, and much to gain. And it might, in a way, help him recoup his thirty pounds. He felt something welling up in him, something that had been dormant for a very long time.

A taste for risk.

He supposed it lived in him like one of those fevers soldiers often acquired in the South Seas, the kind that went dormant only to reemerge in desperate times.

Apparently he was still his father's son after all.

"Kilmartin," he began innocently, "do you recall saying that Constance needed a rival? Someone exotic enough to throw her off her game and tip the balance in my favor?"

Kilmartin frowned, puzzled. And then understanding broke like a sunrise on his face.

And rapidly turned into alarm.

"No, Gideon. No, no, no. You've gone quite mad. It would never work."

"But *look* at her, Kilmartin," Gideon said excitedly. "*Listen* to her. It *might* work. With a little polish, we can pass her off as your country cousin—by the way, I already told Constance you had a country cousin you wished me to meet, just to make her painfully curious—and we'll teach her to dance, to walk properly, and all that. We'll take her to Uncle Edward's house while Constance is away—"

Kilmartin was aghast. "She'll steal the silver plate and copulate with the footmen."

Gideon watched with interest as a deep color flared in Lily's cheeks; she turned her head swiftly and her throat moved in a hard swallow. *So she understands "copulate," does she?*

"My uncle's footmen are long past being interested in copulation," Gideon told Kilmartin. "And we shall keep her so occupied she won't have time or strength to steal or think of anything else. It *could* be great fun, Laurie. And you *have* been complaining about how dull I've been. She need only know enough of the *ton* to pass through it socially for a month or so. We'll watch her very carefully. And then, once Constance has capitulated and I am safely engaged, we can release her back into the wild."

"You must truly be desperate, Gideon." Kilmartin sounded woeful.

"I *am* desperate, Laurie. You know how important this is to me. I was so close, Laurie. It's my—"

"I know: your Master Plan. So just to be very clear: you're proposing to keep the pickpocket at your uncle's house while Constance is away, reform her, unleash her upon the *ton* as my 'cousin,' make Constance so jealous she'll beg you to marry her, and then release Miss Lily Masters with a pat on the bum? Is that the new leg of your Master Plan?"

"In a nutshell."

"*No.*" This came from Lily, who was breathing swiftly again.

"It's this or Newgate," Gideon said cheerfully. "Or there's also transportation to Australia. So many lovely options."

"No . . . I cannot . . . you cannot . . . you see, I've a sister . . ." The pride and impudence were gone, and Lily was all trembling panic. The transformation was remarkable.

Gideon went still. *I've a sister.* He knew about sisters. Twin pangs of guilt and regret always arrived with any thought of Helen.

Kilmartin sighed. "There are *two* of them?"

"How old is your sister, Lily?" Gideon softened his voice.

There was a pause. "Ten years, Mr. Cole." She met his eyes, but the words were delivered reluctantly; she was clearly loath to divulge anything about her sister. *Protective.*

"We'll fetch your sister. And then we'll leave for my uncle's house this afternoon."

Lily's eyes began to dart about the room, as though she was searching for some way, any way, out of Kilmartin's lodgings.

"I wouldn't try it, Miss Masters. You owe me thirty pounds."

"'Tis not as though I begged you to rescue me, Mr. Cole. I believe you have only yourself to blame for your loss."

Gideon smiled. "And yet I *did* rescue you. And so you are in my debt. Or do thieves have any honor at all? I've always wondered."

That did it; he'd sensed it would. Her chin went up and her slim back went rigid again. "I suspect *you* know little of honor, Mr. Cole."

"I'm certainly willing to give you an opportunity to find out how much I *do* know of honor, Miss Masters."

Kilmartin was shaking his head. "You are mad, Gideon. Mad."

"But you *will* help, Laurie?"

"Of course," Kilmartin said cheerfully. "It might very well be grand fun."

Chapter Three

"Oi, Lily, fine choice for yer first one, lovey," Fanny called down from her open window. "*Cooey*, jus' *look* at that cove. Where *did* you find 'im?"

A quick hackney coach ride under the unrelenting watch of the towering Gideon Cole, who had a loose but determined grip on her arm, and Lily was once again in front of Mrs. Smythe's boarding house. Fanny was leaning out of her upstairs window, and her bosom was leaning out of her bodice.

"'E's a special case, Fanny," Lily shouted up. "'E's 'avin' trouble gettin' 'is *staff* to rise. It jus' sort of lays there, like. Very sad. 'Is name is Gideon Cole, by the way." Lily raised her voice to make sure as many people as possible heard her. "*Gideon Cole*."

Heads everywhere up and down the street turned to get a look at Gideon. Even the prostrate drunks managed to lift their heads.

Gideon shot Lily an unreadable look. She was very pleased with herself.

"Oooo, ye poor lad," Fanny cooed down at Gideon

sympathetically. "Come up to me, luv, I *know* I can get yer pole to rise. I'll ride ye proper. Unless ye prefer the boys?" she suggested helpfully. "We've a lovely selection of boys in St. Giles."

Lily didn't trouble to disguise her smile.

"'Staff'?" Gideon murmured with equanimity to Lily. "'Pole'?"

Bloody gentry cove and his bloody poise, amused by everything, thinks he owns the world, Lily quietly seethed. And then she could practically hear her mother's voice in her head: *Don't say "bloody," Lily.*

"Lovely accent, by the way, Miss Masters. You're certainly versatile," Gideon added.

Lily ignored him.

When she pushed open the boarding house door, the dank smell of the hallway rushed out to meet them like a huge eager beast. Lily was uncomfortably conscious of the contrast between her home and Kilmartin's plush lodgings. For a brief moment, she fervently wished that she really did have fleas, just so that a few could have made themselves at home in Kilmartin's furniture. "Freakishly lovely," was she? It made her want to growl.

Suddenly a low rumbling started up beneath their feet, and then the tired slats of the boarding house floor began rhythmically jumping. *Thud, thud, thud, thud.*

It heralded the approach of the formidable Mrs. Smythe.

Her voice reached them before she came into view. "I'll 'ave no shoutin' in me halls, Lily Mas—"

Mrs. Smythe saw Gideon Cole.

She froze as though she'd run smack into the flat of a shovel. And then the lower half of her face twitched, and convulsed, and then suddenly, improbably . . .

Mrs. Smythe was smiling.

It was horrible.

"And 'oo 'is *this*, Lily?"

Dear God, Mrs. Smythe was not only smiling, she was *flirting.*

Gideon bowed to the matron, who uttered a strange helpless little syllable that sounded almost like a coo.

"Alice!" Lily called desperately. "Alice, where are you?" She attempted to free her arm; Gideon refused to relinquish it. At last her sister came running up the hall, her braid flying out behind her. She halted abruptly behind Mrs. Smythe and peered around her at Lily. Alice's eyes, confused and frightened, traveled the long length of Gideon, and then skipped to Lily's face.

"Lily?" her voice quavered.

"We're going on a journey, love," Lily said gently, wishing Gideon would let her speak to Alice privately. "This is Mr. Cole. We'll be traveling with him. I will be . . . in his employ for a while."

Gideon bowed politely to the little girl. "Pleased to meet you, Miss Alice."

Alice said nothing; she merely stared, bug-eyed and stone-faced and silent, up at Gideon.

And then Gideon smiled at Alice. Lily watched the smile happen, the slow lift of his fine mouth, the soft warmth flooding his eyes. And she couldn't help it, really; her own heart skipped a beat.

Before Lily's very eyes, Alice melted. She grinned up at Gideon with the gap-toothed grin normally reserved for Lily. *Little traitor,* Lily thought.

"I'll need some of my things, Mr. Cole." Lily wasn't anxious for Gideon Cole to get a look at their meager little room. "I can fetch them myself now, if you'll just . . . let . . . *go. . . .*" Lily tugged fruitlessly away from the warm fingers curled loosely around her arm. Surely his fingers would have cramped by now. Surely no one could maintain a *clutching* position this long.

"Oh, I am sure you *can* fetch them yourself, Miss Masters." Gideon sounded amused. "But I will accompany you to your room. *Thirty pounds*," he added softly, a reminder of her debt to him.

Lily glowered and inhaled sharply, but that turned out to be a bit of a mistake; the scent of Gideon Cole rushed into her. Sometimes a stiff wind blew in from the sea, strong and cold enough to be scoured clean of the London odors that usually rode it, and his scent was a little like that: fresh, sharp, a hint of portent. It worked on her senses like gin; her glower wavered, along with her courage.

She was out of her depth with this man.

Lily lifted her chin and met Gideon's dark eyes with a stare that she hoped belied her own quivering uncertainty. His eyes might be amused now, but she'd seen them coolly murderous when he'd first caught her hand in his pocket. As civilized as he appeared at the moment, Gideon Cole was very likely not a man to be trifled with. And he *had* threatened her with Newgate.

And though it was his own bloody fault he was out thirty pounds, it was *her* own bloody fault she'd needed rescuing at all. She wasn't without a sense of honor.

Or gratitude.

Or, for that matter . . . curiosity.

And then Mr. Cole surprised her: he slowly uncurled his fingers from her arm and smiled down at her faintly. His eyes were amused; one eyebrow was lifted. A dare. *Show me how honorable you really are, Miss Masters.*

Lily almost smiled; she appreciated a good dare. She decided to opt for dignity: instead of kneeing him in the cods and fleeing, she lifted her chin haughtily. "Very well, Mr. Cole. Follow me."

Gideon turned to the lodging house proprietress with a gentle smile. "If you will excuse us, Mrs. Smythe?"

Wordlessly, Mrs. Smythe stepped aside, as though she too were ceding her authority to Mr. Cole.

Lily and Alice Masters were curled up against each other on the coach seat across from Gideon, asleep, their ragged brown-gray skirts falling about them like the wings of molting doves. They were both much too thin, their wrists and the ankles above their dirty bare feet seemed much too fragile.

And now that the initial rush of giddiness that typically accompanied a risk had ebbed, Gideon suspected Kilmartin's initial assessment was correct: He *was* mad.

He laughed softly, ruefully, to himself, and shook his head. *Am I truly this desperate?* Had everything in his life, including the ragged girl sitting across from him, become a means to an end?

And yet, a wicked little voice in his head said: *Imagine what it would be like to pull one over on the* ton.

His behavior had been faultless for years; he'd learned that if one hadn't a title or money, one's behavior had *better* be faultless. He'd stifled impulses, channeled his temper, an attempt to build a life more stable than the one his dazzling, reckless father had provided for his family.

And yet . . . was he truly any better off? Was Helen?

His Master Plan. He'd formulated it from the wreckage of his family's fortunes: wealth and property and position, security and permanence—all of the things his father had managed to smash to kindling—he'd have them all before the age of thirty. How ironic if a page from his father's book—the book of reckless gambles—turned out to be the thing that won Constance at last, and opened the door to the future he'd envisioned for a decade.

If this works, I'll never take a risk again, he told himself.

Ha! was what the wicked little voice in his head had to say to that.

Gideon turned to the source of folly, the pickpocket he intended to turn into a diamond of the first water. Lily's long dark lashes quivered against her cheek; asleep, she looked as innocent as her sister. And yet he had difficulty believing she was at *all* innocent.

There was the little matter of the books, for instance. Lily Masters had brought six books with her, as matter-of-factly as if they were necessities. An encyclopedia filled with drawings of animals. A volume of Greek myths. *Pride and Prejudice*. A collection of Shakespeare's works. *Robinson Crusoe.*

And a book filled with erotic stories written entirely in French.

While Lily and Alice slept across from him, Gideon surreptitiously read a few pages of the book. And then another few pages. And then, because he couldn't help himself, he read half the book. The author certainly had a way with description: sensual demands, soft moans, expert stroking, complicated positions—everyone in that book, men and women alike, seemed to be enjoying themselves immensely, in chairs in front of mirrors . . .

Over and over and over.

Gideon clapped the little French book shut and slid it a safe distance away from him on the coach seat. The stories were too stirring for a man who hadn't done any flesh-wallowing for far too long now.

Je parle français un petit peu, Lily Masters had said. *I speak a little French.* To what use did she put that French? Was this little book a *manual* of sorts? And yet . . . *a good choice for yer first*, the prostitute had shouted down to her. He remembered her blush in Kilmartin's lodgings. If she had been initiated into the flesh trade, it had likely been only recently.

Gideon shook his head ruefully again. He *was* mad. So be it. He now knew the extent of his own need to win. His own equivalent of bribing the dressmaker.

He felt in his pocket for his grandfather's watch, and was relieved to find it.

Lily stirred and opened her eyes, then sat up abruptly and leaned forward to peer out of the coach's tiny window.

They were hurtling up a drive lined with trees, tall straight ones, prim as sentries. Through them she could see a flash of something red—brick? And then more and more and still more red brick unfurled before her disbelieving eyes, and the afternoon light struck sheets of light from the correspondingly endless rows of windows. She dropped her gaze to the vast pillared portico, tinted amber in the lowering sun. A fountain leaped skyward in the courtyard.

She raised her hand to shield her eyes from the brilliance of the place; her heart swelled with its beauty.

"My uncle's home," Gideon said simply. "Aster Park."

Lily merely nodded once, an admirable attempt at feigning indifference. Somehow she suspected Newgate didn't hold a candle to Aster Park.

Lily and Alice stood in the grand tiled entryway of the house, gripping each other's hands. Lily's eyes had gone huge, expanding to accommodate the grandeur of the room in which they stood. Gideon watched her shoulders go back and her chin go up, as though the house itself was an adversary she intended to best.

He was reminded of Constance's first visit to Aster Park. Her beauty, her confident tranquillity, her bloodline—Constance had seemed as touchable as a star then. She'd stood in nearly the same place as Lily stood now, her cool gray eyes assessing fixtures and furniture, and her verdict, delivered lightly—"I wouldn't mind living here myself, Mr. Cole"—had landed on Gideon's ears like a benediction.

From that moment, an understanding had slowly grown between them; that understanding, it seemed, had been too long on the vine. He fought back another surge of restlessness.

"Is this our palace?" Gideon heard Alice whisper to Lily.

"Very like is," Lily whispered back.

"Then is Mr. Cole the prince?"

"*Prince*?" Lily scoffed. "He hasn't even a title."

Once again, despite himself, Gideon found himself fighting a smile. The *cheek* of the girl.

He stepped forward to speak to Gregson, the footman. "How do you fare, Gregson? Someday you really must tell me your secret. You never age a day."

The elderly footman, who was almost as bent as an inverted *J* but still taller than Gideon by inches, looked pleased. "Thank you, sir. 'Tis the air at Aster Park, to be sure. I am happy to see you, sir, and your uncle will be delighted as well."

"And is Uncle Edward still dying, Gregson?"

"Yes, sir."

"Is he dying any worse than before?"

"No, sir. The same as always, sir."

"Very good. I'll be up to see him as soon I get the dust off. And by the way, Gregson, may I introduce to you Miss

Lily Masters and her sister, Miss Alice Masters? They are cousins of my dear friend Lord Kilmartin, who should arrive tomorrow, and will be my guests here for some time. Will you kindly see that rooms are prepared?"

Gregson goggled at the bedraggled, barefoot girls.

"And we'll need two baths drawn at once, if you would, Gregson."

Gregson's lips parted; he looked tempted to reply, *Good God, we most certainly* do. Instead he said, "Very good, sir. I'll speak to Mrs. Plunkett."

"We'll need some clothing, too, Gregson. Something for Miss Lily and something for Miss Alice, as well. There was an . . . er . . . coaching accident. And unfortunately, all of their trunks were destroyed along with their clothing."

Gregson didn't even blink. "That *is* unfortunate, sir. I am glad, however, that the two young ladies are sound. Mrs. Plunkett will be able to obtain some women's clothing."

"You're a wonder, Gregson. Thank you. One more thing: Mrs. Plunkett does count the silver each evening, does she not? And locks it up tightly?"

Gideon could practically feel the heat from Miss Masters's glower.

The faintest of frowns wrinkled Gregson's brow. "Yes, sir. But of course, sir."

"Very good, Gregson. You may go."

Gregson turned on his heels and began to walk away.

"But Lily, I've never had a bath," Alice whispered.

Gregson slowed his stride almost imperceptibly just then, as though Alice's words had struck him between the shoulder blades. Gideon stifled a laugh. A lesser man than Gregson might have stumbled in shock.

Gideon returned his attention to Lily. "Should anyone

ask, you and Alice are Lord Kilmartin's cousins from Sussex."

"And it seems we've had an unfortunate coaching accident."

"My, you're a quick study, Miss Masters. Tell me, how much do you think you could get for that gold clock?"

"Not a farthing, Mr. Cole. My fence has *some* taste."

Gideon laughed; she'd surprised it from him. "Listen to me, please, Miss Masters: you will have your baths, and then a dinner will be served to you in your room."

"What will there be for dinner?" Alice piped up as Lily tried to shush her with a pat.

Gideon smiled down at her. "What would you *like* for dinner, Miss Alice?"

"Peacock!" she declared.

Gideon blinked. "Ah. Well, we've peacocks here at Aster Park, but they mostly stroll about the grounds looking pretty. We don't usually serve them for dinner. Perhaps you'd like to see them tomorrow?"

"Oh, yes!" Alice breathed. Gideon glanced at Lily. She was wearing a strange expression, a sort of tender turbulence, as though an internal struggle was taking place.

"Very well. I'll have one of the footmen take you to see the peacocks in the morning, Miss Alice. For dinner, there will be cold roast of beef, no doubt."

"Lily *said* there would be beef." Alice sounded smug.

When had Lily mentioned beef? Gideon looked questioningly at her; she merely gazed back at him blandly. "I must away to London once more, but I will return to Aster Park by tomorrow midday."

"Don't hurry on my account," Lily murmured.

Gideon acknowledged her with a sardonically lifted brow. "Lord Kilmartin will join us tomorrow, as well, and we shall meet with him to discuss our . . . arrangement. You shall breakfast in your room. Meanwhile, I know you will not consider . . . curtailing your stay, Miss Masters, or veering from your story, or leaving your room. Unless, of course, you place little value on honor. And have an interest, shall we say, in decidedly less comfortable accommodations."

Lily's eyes snapped comprehension at him, as he'd known they would. He had alluded to Newgate chiefly for the pleasure of watching her eyes flash; it was like watching lightning crack in a dawn sky, quite wonderful, really. "And besides, where would you go? There's nothing about for miles and miles."

Lily's mouth opened; she no doubt intended to issue a scathing rejoinder, but Mrs. Plunkett's strong, solid form ambled into the room just in time.

"Mrs. Plunkett, allow me to introduce Miss Lily Masters and Miss Alice Masters. Until tomorrow, then, ladies." Gideon bowed and surrendered them to the competent care of the housekeeper.

Mrs. Plunkett handed Lily a long brush, a cake of white soap that smelled as if it had been carved from the floor of heaven, and two thick white cloths. A huge copper tub of steaming water sat on the floor between them. A great wet miracle.

For years Lily had retrieved water from the public wells, and what little she'd been able to bring back to their rooms in Mrs. Smythe's boarding house was usually boiled for tea. It had been impossible to ever draw enough for a bath; and even if she could have, she wouldn't have known where to find a bathtub. She and Alice had swabbed themselves with cloths dampened in basins, cleaning themselves as best they could without benefit of a mirror. It was likely she'd had baths when she was younger, but they were not among her memories.

A *whole tub* full of hot water was an unspeakable luxury.

Mrs. Plunkett, the housekeeper, was a woman of few words. "A coaching accident?" she asked. "Lord Kilmartin's cousin?"

"I suppose so," Lily murmured, staring at the tub longingly. "Oh, that is, yes. A coaching accident."

If Mrs. Plunkett wondered how a coaching accident could have coated the two Miss Masterses in what looked like an irrevocable layer of grime as well as shredded the clothing they wore, she refrained from comment.

"Alice will go first," Lily said quickly.

Mrs. Plunkett eyed Alice dubiously. "Ye'll need a whole other tub fer yerself, Miss Lily. We'll set the water to boil now."

"Thank you, Mrs. Plunkett." Lily's voice had gone faint.

Lily shifted in the bath; the scented, soapy water lapped gently at her shoulders and breasts. And then, to her astonishment, tears pricked at her eyes.

She couldn't remember the last time she'd wept; there had never seemed to be a point to it, really. And now she was about to weep over a *bath*. It made her furious. *Bloody Gideon Cole.*

It was just all so much . . . *bigger* than she was. The house. The overwhelming array of rich textures, the wood and gilt and marble, everything clean and gleaming. The servants. The *silence*. It was never, ever silent in St. Giles. The bath cradled her tenderly; she could not recall the last time she'd been cradled tenderly. The soles of her feet stung a little where the soapy water found raw places and fine cracks, the result of racing shoeless through London's streets.

Thank you, Mama, she said silently and fervently, a sort of prayer. Because at least she more or less knew how a lady should speak, a few "bloody"s and "whoreson"s notwithstanding. She'd been able to pull that ladylike demeanor around her today and wear it like battered armor in front of Gideon Cole.

The scented water lapped at her soothingly. *There, there, now,* it seemed to say. *No need to take on so.*

Lily had managed to coax a tremendously skeptical Alice into the copper tub. But when the water began to grow dark, Alice became convinced it was because her body was dissolving into it, turning her into so much Alice soup. Lily was able to stifle her sister's shriek of horror with her hand just in time.

A short time later, Alice was splashing as happily as a duck. Lily taught her how to scrub herself clean, working the soap into Alice's hair, taking rags gently to her face. Scrubbed of the layers acquired from living in St. Giles, Alice was beautiful. This made Lily want to cry, too.

Lily abruptly sat up and raised herself out of the tub. The water suddenly felt like hands holding her down; she needed to be moving. Sometimes it caught up to her when she was quiet and still; it rose and crested and crashed down over her: fear. Not the sort of fear she could simply run from, the way she'd run from Gideon Cole a mere few days ago, a knee in the baubles and then off you go. It was far, far larger and less tangible.

Fortunately, quiet moments were few and far between in St. Giles. And if sometimes she jerked awake at night bathed in sweat, her heart battering her ribs, Alice was next to her and could be prodded awake for conversation.

Get a hold of yourself, Masters, she told herself sternly.

If she was equal to London, to *St. Giles*, for that matter, then she was equal to this house.

And perhaps even equal to Gideon Cole.

The room was like a plush cave, all velvet hangings and dark furniture and candlelight pulsing in globes. The heavy draperies had not been parted in years, but the windows may have been opened once or twice—Gideon seemed to recall Mrs. Plunkett insisting upon it.

In the middle of the soft dim room was Lord Lindsey's bed, and Lord Lindsey occupied it like a castaway surrounded by the vast sea of his house and land.

There was a tacit agreement among all those who knew and cared for Uncle Edward: no one was to question why he was ill; no one was to question whether or not he *was* ill. The servants, of course, would never dare, and Gideon, who was heir to the title only because his two cousins had been killed in the war, felt he had no right. So for years, Edward had been indulged in the way that extremely wealthy men are often indulged. If Edward said he was ill, he was ill.

And yet, while Lord Lindsey spent his days in bed, he never seemed any less formidable for it.

"Uncle Edward?"

No response.

It had been more than a decade since his uncle had soundly thrashed him and his cousins for stealing his cigars and then turned around and taught them how to smoke one properly, but Gideon couldn't help fidgeting. His Uncle Edward, a steely, wry counterpoint to the breezy charm of Gideon's father, had never let him get away with anything.

He cleared his throat and tried again. "Uncle Edward?"

"So," came a decidedly petulant voice from the bed at last. "I see you were in a tearing hurry to see your dying uncle."

"I'm always eager to see you, Uncle Edward; you know that. I apologize for the delay. I was detained by business in town."

"I was *dying*, Gideon."

"You're *always* dying, Uncle Edward." The words were out of his mouth before he could stop them. Gideon was horrified.

The shocked silence radiating from the bed was almost comical.

And then, much to Gideon's astonishment, Lord Lindsey chuckled. "Impatient for the title, are you?"

"Of course not, Uncle Edward."

"Perhaps just a *bit*?"

Gideon paused, and then he sighed and pulled a chair up next to his uncle's bed. He was struck anew by how vigorous Edward looked. There were obvious effects of age—his thick hair was nearly white, his skin loose and lined—but Lord Lindsey's eyes crackled with alertness and his posture as he sat up in bed was erect. "There's a certain daughter of a marquis whom I believe is impatient for the title, Uncle Edward. I, truthfully, would prefer you to live forever."

Lord Lindsey chuckled again. "Ah, and here we have a fine example of how a barrister is able to court the daughter of a marquis: your silver tongue. You remind me of your father, you know. Lord, I miss the man, glorious wreck though he was. Who's the girl? The big blonde daughter of Marquis Shawcross? It's been some years since I've seen her, but I imagine she's grown into a strapping lass. She'd be a good match."

Gideon smiled a little to hear Constance described as big and blonde. "She's lovely and tall, and yes, she's quite the finest young woman in London." He wasn't about to tell his uncle about Jarvis and the betting books and Constance's lust for property.

"You are seven- and twenty now, Gideon. You can set up your nursery without a title, you know. And you *should.* And then bring all your children round to stay. Marry that girl. *One* of you Coles should make a good match." There was a slight edge to these last words.

Gideon tensed, but thankfully Lord Lindsey said no more. His uncle had made his feelings about Helen's marriage plain—scathingly plain—long ago. The subject remained a tender one; they talked of it rarely.

"Soon, Uncle," Gideon said softly. "I plan to."

"Ah, yes. You and *plans.*" Uncle Edward was amused. "Shawcross owns more of England than even Kilmartin's family. And he wouldn't hurt your career one bit. How are you fixed for blunt, by the way? You're prospering?"

"Of course, Uncle Edward," Gideon lied. "How are you feeling?"

"Oh, never worse, m'boy, never worse," was the cheerful reply. "The doctor should be by a little later with my simple and some gossip, however."

"Has he managed to marry off the last of his daughters, sir?"

"I think she was hoping to have a crack at you, Gideon. But the curate nurtures hopes regarding her which are not entirely unwelcome, or so I hear."

Gideon laughed. Life, and the game of marriage, was simpler here in the country than in the *ton*; he felt a brief pang of *what if . . . ?* But if one intended to be Chancellor of the Exchequer, one didn't marry the doctor's daughter.

"So, m'boy, will you be staying for a time or is it right back to London for you?"

"I thought I'd stay for a few days, sir. Kilmartin will be

joining me tomorrow—we thought we'd get in some shooting and what-have-you before the season begins in earnest." If he were careful, his uncle would never know Lily or her sister was even under his roof.

"What a shame," Uncle Edward teased. "I know I'm a demanding old sod, Gideon. I am happy to have your company."

Demanding, Gideon thought with affectionate exasperation, did not begin to describe it. "I am always glad to see you, Uncle Edward. I'm at your service."

Their chamber, like the bath, like the rest of the house, made Lily feel almost angry: what gave *anything* the right to be so grand?

A thick carpet, patterned in twining green vines and faded pink roses, sprawled on the floor; Lily slipped her feet out of her borrowed slippers and curled her toes into it, reveling in its undreamed-of softness. A pink velvet tufted chair sat before a little writing desk; she'd arranged her books upon the desk, and she decided they looked well enough there. A great oaken wardrobe stood against one wall—empty, as far as she knew, for they'd taken her clothes away along with Alice's—and a dainty dressing table sat opposite it. And a fire, clean and smokeless, crackled cheerily in a fireplace. This was a marvel: she'd always had to do battle with the fireplace in their room at Mrs. Smythe's. Old Smokey, she and Alice called it.

In the round mirror over the dressing table Lily saw a girl, big-eyed with the strangeness of her surroundings, swimming in Mrs. Plunkett's borrowed nightdress. Her shining, newly clean hair seemed much . . . well, *larger* than usual. As though ecstatic to be free of grime, it waved with wild abandon about her face and down her back.

Alice flung herself on the bed; Lily sank down next to her. Not surprisingly, the bed turned out to be deliriously comfortable, too, so they spent a moment oohing and ahhing together over it.

Alice was wearing what appeared to be a little boy's shirt as a night rail. Lily took the hem of it between her fingers and rubbed it wonderingly; the shirt was so fine she knew she could have gotten more than a penny for it from Mrs. Bandycross, a fence in St. Giles who specialized in such things. She snuggled down under the blankets next to Alice, and the blankets, unsurprisingly, were heavy and smooth, of good wool.

"'Tis very quiet here," Alice mused, wrinkling her nose. "But I might like to stay forever, anyhow. Do you think Mrs. Smythe will give our room away?"

"I paid her for it through the month, so she'd best not if she knows what is good for her," Lily said with more bravado than confidence.

"If she does give it away, perhaps Mr. Cole will make her give it back to us. Perhaps he will give her a good whacking."

"A good *whacking*?" Lily turned to her sister. "More likely he will simply *smile* and Mrs. Smythe will swoon like a great . . . great . . ."

"Cow."

"Cows don't swoon, Alice."

"They would if they saw Mr. Cole."

Lily was not inclined to disagree with her.

"He looks like your prince, Lily. He has dark hair and dark eyes."

"As does half of London. *McBride* has dark hair and eyes." Her sister was a little too astute.

"McBride has only a little hair. Mr. Cole has a great deal."

Yes. A great deal of silky-looking hair that glows like a lit coal in the sunlight.

"I like him," Alice concluded sleepily. "Tomorrow I am to see the peacocks."

And Lily's heart squeezed. Didn't Gideon Cole see or care how cruel his careless kindness to a little girl was? It wasn't fair to give Alice these things only to take them from her in a few weeks' time.

And yet . . . though she'd managed to keep Alice fed and clothed and off the streets for years, *she* had never yet been able to show Alice peacocks, or feed her cold roast of beef for dinner. Or give her a quiet place to sleep cocooned in fine wool blankets.

She could only tell stories of them.

"We are only staying here for a very short time, Alice," Lily warned. "Remember? I am only in Mr. Cole's employ for a short time."

"But I *might* like to stay forever," Alice repeated, on a yawn.

"Yes, but we're—" Lily stopped herself and sighed. It was a fruitless argument; she would return to it another time. "Shall I tell a story?"

"Yes, please." Alice snuggled down next to her.

And because telling stories was her singular talent, Lily felt a little mollified, of use to her sister once again. She sorted through the day's images. Trees like ranks of soldiers, stoic Gregson's tall, bent frame, and this house, a house that could comfortably accommodate gods and goddesses . . .

"Once there was a kindly old wizard named"—Lily thought a bit—"George, whose job it was to carry the weight of the world on his back. Soon he was so bent from his burden that he asked the gods if he might rest a while. But the gods said to him"—Lily lowered her voice to give it godlike gravity—"'George, we have need of you now more than ever. A great army of immortal soldiers is even now marching toward our homes. . . .'"

And so a fantastic tale unfurled, and Lily's low soothing voice was Alice's lullaby. Her sister's eyelids grew heavier as the fire burned lower, until Alice was snoring softly.

What will become of us? The treacherous thought crept in, beckoned by the silence and stillness.

Don't think about it. There is only now. This thought had always been Lily's own lullaby. She repeated it until, despite the deafening silence and the newness, she fell fast asleep.

Chapter Four

Gideon pounced upon the solicitor the moment his beaky little nose poked into the Westminster Court chambers.

"I've been looking for you, Mr. Dodge."

"You were looking for *me*, Mr. Cole? Are they building snowmen in hell, then, sir?"

"Very amusing, as usual, Mr. Dodge. About your case—the dressmaker—"

"You'll take her case, Mr. Cole?"

"Yes—"

"Very good, sir." Dodge beamed, and began to walk away.

"—upon one condition, Mr. Dodge."

Dodge halted midstride. There had never before been a *condition*. "A condition?" he repeated, cautiously.

"Yes. This dressmaker—Madame Marceau—is she truly French?"

"About as French as you or I, Mr. Cole."

Gideon's mouth twitched into a smile. "Please tell

Madame Marceau that I will take her case. But that I will need to be paid in dresses."

Dodge's bright little eyes went wide. "Pardon me, but did you say dresses, sir?"

"Yes, Mr. Dodge."

"*Ladies*' dresses?"

"Do you know of any other kind, Mr. Dodge?"

"I suppose not, sir."

"Day dresses, evening dresses, pelisses, and all the various fripperies that go with them. And some dresses in a smaller size, too. I'll need them very soon. I would like Madame Marceau to pay a call at this address the day after tomorrow, during the afternoon. Here is the direction." Gideon handed Mr. Dodge a slip of paper. "If she can do this for me, I will take the case."

"I am assured she is an excellent seamstress, Mr. Cole."

"Good. But I primarily have need of a swift one. And if you would tell her . . ." Gideon hesitated. "Tell her . . . greens and blues and golds would suit." He cleared his throat self-consciously.

"Greens and blues and golds," Dodge repeated slowly, like a spy attempting to decode enemy intelligence.

"And one more thing, Mr. Dodge."

A decidedly bemused Mr. Dodge was staring down at the slip of paper in his hand. "Yes, Mr. Cole?"

"I will be on holiday for a few weeks, both in the country and in London. I shall keep you apprised as to when I intend to return to work."

Dodge's brows flew upward so swiftly his spectacles rose along with them. "*You*, sir? A . . . a . . . *holiday*? But you don't—you never—"

"It's rather a working holiday, Mr. Dodge."

"Oh." A relieved sigh.

Gideon could almost hear the man's thoughts: the natural order of things hadn't come to a complete end after all: Mr. Cole would be *working*. He was taken aback. Though it was tremendously satisfying to get the better of Mr. Dodge, apparently Kilmartin had the right of it: *work and Constance*. It was a sobering thought.

"Thank you, Mr. Dodge. Try not to miss me while I'm away."

The Gentleman & Lady's Companion, the book was called. It had arrived with a tray of eggs and fried bread this morning.

"You're to come with me, Miss Alice." Alice eyed Mrs. Plunkett's outstretched hand somewhat warily, and then looked up into Lily's face, seeking permission. Lily nodded.

A grin split Alice's face and she slowly slipped her hand into Mrs. Plunkett's. "I'm to see the peacocks!" she crowed. And off the little traitor went.

A note was tucked inside the book, the handwriting on it tall and angular and impatient, much like the person who had written it.

> *LM—Read as much of this book as you are able by midday today. Do not leave your room. Take particular notice of page 20. —GC*
>
> *P.S. Thirty pounds, Miss Masters.*

Lily turned to page twenty, certain whatever she found there would be nothing short of infuriating. The words across the top did nothing to dispel her suspicion:

Instances of Ill Manners to be carefully avoided by youth of both sexes.

A helpful list of examples followed:

- *Lolling on a chair when speaking or when spoken to, and looking persons earnestly in the face without any apparent cause.*
- *Surliness of all kinds, especially on receiving a compliment.*
- *Distortion of countenance, and mimicry.*
- *Ridicule of every kind, vice or folly.*
- *A constant smile or settled frown on the countenance.*
- *All actions that have the most remote tendency to indelicacy . . .*

She couldn't resist a smile. *All actions that have the most remote tendency to indelicacy?* She supposed that meant breaking wind was out of the question.

But the list droned on, if printed words could drone. *So,* Lily thought. *I am not to pull faces, or smile or frown, or jest or think or breathe or move or—*

She clapped the book shut. It wasn't as though her mother hadn't already instilled these things in her, more or less. And granted, perhaps her demeanor had suffered a little tarnish through exposure to St. Giles. But why on earth would anyone *want* to be a lady of the *ton*? Newgate was beginning to seem like an appealing option. She was tempted to fling the book on the bed, but she placed it gently there instead. It was a book, after all, and it was difficult not to think of it as precious.

She pulled her vast borrowed nightdress off over her head, pulled on her borrowed pinned-together sack of a gown, and pushed her feet into a pair of big borrowed slippers. Mrs. Plunkett had produced a brown ribbon for her as well. Lily had never had a ribbon of her own, not one to keep, anyhow—in St. Giles, ribbons were currency. Some pickpockets specialized in ribbons and silk handkerchiefs, as they were always popular with fences; her own goals were loftier, of necessity—she needed to meet Mrs. Smythe's rent. She held the ribbon wonderingly; it slithered through her fingers, a satiny snake. Heaving a practical sigh, she used it to tie her large clean hair back from her face.

Her toilette thus completed, she took a tentative step outside of her room. Honestly, what could one step possibly hurt? She *would* read Gideon Cole's stuffy little book. In a moment.

The quiet of the house was unnerving; the smallest sounds, creaks of doors opening, distant voices—servants?—made her start. The very absence of noise was almost like the loss of hearing itself. And so she took another step, for the comfort of hearing her own feet strike the marble.

Her one step led to another. And then another and another, until she was halfway down the marble-tiled hall. The walls went up and up; ornate molding marked the place where they ended and the ceilings began. Sconces were spaced evenly, the candles in them freshly trimmed and unlit. Wax candles, from the looks of things, not tallow. An unspeakable luxury.

I've gone and fallen into one of my own stories.

Delight and trepidation quickened her heartbeat. *Just a few more steps forward . . .* she thought. *Then I'll return. . . .*

Quite a few more than a few more steps later, she found herself in a gallery of sorts: a series of portraits lining a curving flight of stairs. Ancestors, perhaps? Men in wigs, women in outlandish enormous ruffs. Dark-eyed boys posing with frolicking dogs, men with muskets. She inspected each of them as she scaled the stairs. Here and there a suggestion of height recalled Gideon, and those dark eyes seemed to run through the family throughout the centuries. But not a single bloody ancestor was anywhere near as handsome as he was.

Then again, she didn't know how anyone could paint light into hair, or fathoms into eyes.

McBride, Lily thought, as she rounded a curve in the stairs, would have *fits* in this house. A single silver candlestick—and there seemed to be candlesticks everywhere, even in places that surely one didn't need to light—would set her and Alice up for months, years even. She could just tuck one of those candlesticks into her overlarge sleeve and—

Be hauled off by her ear to Newgate by Gideon Cole.

She felt a twinge of guilt at the thought of him; perhaps she *should* return to her room and read the odious little book . . . She did, in a sense, owe him thirty pounds. . . .

When I've run out of stairs.

She paused to impishly trace the plump little buttocks of a carved cherub; *hundreds* of those little blokes cavorted up the banister, entangled in carved grapes and vines. Up and up she went, past nooks sheltering blank-eyed marble busts; they gave her the shivers, those sightless eyes and bodiless heads; she moved past them quickly.

If the bloody *stairwell* seemed enchanted, she could only imagine what the rest of the house was like: no doubt as vast and complex as all of London. And as soon as she began to think of the house as another sort of London, it began to seem less intimidating, for she'd managed London well enough. It wasn't the *house's* fault it was so grand.

And there wasn't a bloody speck of dust *anywhere*. For a moment Lily thought she wouldn't mind that job; polishing those whimsical cherubs, giving them names: *Oi, Denis, can I dust yer bum for ye?* She covered a giggle with her palm.

When Lily finally ran out of stairs she found herself in front of a door leading into an intriguingly darkened room. Naturally, she stopped to peer in.

"*Who goes there*?"

Lily jumped back.

"I know you're not a servant, m'dear, and you're most definitely not my nephew or any of his friends."

Lily froze, panicked. "But how did you know?" she finally blurted.

There was a pause, during which Lily could practically *hear* a smile.

"By your gait. And I know you are a young lady by the lightness of your step. Gregson, you see, walks as though he's part of a funeral procession, and Mrs. Plunkett walks as though she's staggering under a great weight, and—well, let's face it, she more or less is—"

Lily laughed, charmed.

"—but you, m'dear, walk as though you're in a tearing hurry to get away from something or get *to* something. Gideon walks rather like you; he's a restless soul. But his footfall is a good deal heavier and his stride longer. So the question remains: Who are you? You're already part of the way in; you may as well come closer and let me get a look at you."

It was an oddly cheerful and hale-sounding voice to be emanating from such a dim room, and Lily was too painfully curious now not to follow orders. She took a tentative step through the doorway.

A white-haired gentleman was sitting up in bed. By the

light of the candles pulsing in globes arranged about him, she could see that his face was soft with age, the skin beneath his jaw drooping, his eyebrows sticking out in gray tufts. He was watching her with delighted interest.

"Ah, I see I was right! I would not have troubled to flirt with you if I hadn't been certain you were very pretty. And oh! See how she blushes to be told she is pretty."

"Oh, were you flirting, sir?" Lily teased, getting into the spirit of things.

He laughed, pleased. "Oh-*ho*, so she's a bit of minx, too! I'm Lord Lindsey, m'dear, and you still haven't told me your name. Who are you? Come closer. You're not my nephew's bit o' muslin, are you? Gideon could certainly use one."

The words were so friendly Lily didn't even consider taking offense. She remained where she stood, however; she'd heard plenty about elderly lords of the manor and their propensity for friskiness. And regardless of his supine position, this one didn't look incapacitated.

"I'm Lily Masters, Lord Lindsey, and I am Lord Kilmartin's cousin from Sussex."

Lord Lindsey laughed. "And you're not at all taken aback by my suggestion that you might be a bit o' muslin. You *are* an unusual young lady, Lily Masters. Why are you wearing a pinned-together sack of a dress? It looks as though it may belong to Mrs. Plunkett."

"It *does* belong to Mrs. Plunkett. I was in an unfortunate coaching accident, sir. All of my clothing was ruined."

"Your slippers as well, Lily?"

Lily looked down at the slippers loaned to her by Mrs. Plunkett. "How can you see my feet?" she marveled.

"The reflection from the bureau mirror, m'dear. Come closer and chat with me. I'm a bored and sick old man, and I promise I will not bite, regardless of how tempted I might be."

"I would simply bite you back," Lily retorted playfully, and then clapped a hand over her mouth. This wasn't McBride. This was Lord Lindsey, a *baron*. One could not tease a baron about *biting*.

But Lord Lindsey merely laughed again, altogether pleased. "And listen to that voice of yours, Miss Masters. Like a great velvet settee, it is; one could sink right into it. You *are* an original. Tell me you are not married so that I may feel free to fall in love with you. Do I know your parents?"

Lily eyed him cautiously. So far, she knew only three things about who she was supposed to be: she was Kilmartin's cousin; she'd been in an unfortunate coaching accident; she was from Sussex.

Oh, and one more thing: she wasn't to ramble all over the house.

"I am unmarried, sir. And I doubt that you knew my parents. They died long ago."

"Ah. I see." Sadness swept down over Lord Lindsey's face. "I lost my sons, both of them, in the war. And their mother after that."

His grief was a sudden and almost palpable presence in the room; Lily was awed by the weight of it. "I am sorry for your loss, Lord Lindsey," she told him softly.

"And I for yours, Lily." They shared a commiserating silence for a moment. And then he patted the bed; she moved forward and pulled a chair up next to it.

"Why are you ill, Lord Lindsey?"

He turned to her, his eyes wide with surprise, and was silent for so long that Lily grew a little anxious. Perhaps young "ladies" were not supposed to ask direct questions of barons, no matter how friendly they might be.

"Nobody knows, Lily, nobody knows," Lord Lindsey finally answered wistfully. "And nobody even asks me those sorts of questions anymore. The doctor arrives, he takes my pulse, he gives me a simple of some sort to drink, and yet I am always the same."

"When did you fall ill, sir?"

"It must have been . . . oh, let me see. After the war. I took to my bed and I've scarcely moved from it since."

Ah. He'd been ill since he'd lost his sons. It was grief, no doubt. Lily understood the impulse to let the darkness of it wash over you like a dreamless sleep; she had known the temptation to surrender to it, especially after Mama had died. But she'd always had Alice to care for; Alice had given her a purpose. She wondered if Lord Lindsey felt any sort of purpose. Perhaps after taking to his bed out of grief many years ago, he was now unable to get out of it from sheer habit.

"Do you ache? In your belly or head? Can you walk?"

"Good God, child. You *do* ask rather a lot of blunt questions."

Oh no. Now Gideon would haul her off to Newgate for offending his uncle. And she'd only been trying to help. "It's just . . ." Lily stammered. "It's just that I know an apothecary in St. Giles who can cure most anything at all. Particularly the pox."

Lord Lindsey barked a startled laugh. "The po— My *God*, Miss Masters, but you're a caution. Unfortunately, my problem is not quite that simple. And I've a fine physician of my own."

"But he hasn't yet cured you, has he, Lord Lindsey?"

At this bold statement, Lord Lindsey inhaled sharply and drew himself up to his full sitting height. He studied Lily, his blue eyes glittering and inscrutable, as if she were an interesting specimen he intended to shoot and stuff and mount.

In the silence that followed, Lily could hear a clock somberly ticking away seconds.

"No, he hasn't yet cured me, Miss Masters," Lord Lindsey said at last. "Though I suspect *you* may be able to." He smiled rakishly then, and Lily's heart gave a strange kick; even at his advanced age, Lord Lindsey's smile was remarkably similar to Gideon's. And Gideon's smile was . . . a *weapon.*

"Would you join me in a game of cards, Lily? Entertain a bored old man?"

"Well, certainly, Lord Lindsey. But we cannot *see* our cards properly in such dim light. I'll just open the curt—"

"No, Lily! It would—"

But Lily had already briskly pushed aside the heavy draperies. Light flooded violently into the room, sending the dust in the air into a swirling frenzy. Lord Lindsey threw his arm over his eyes.

A moment later, he cautiously lowered it again. And then he smiled, blinking sheepishly, as though someone had caught him in the midst of playing a prank.

"Lord, but I've forgotten what tyrants women can be. Very well, Lily. We'll have cards *and* sunlight. I *may* call you Lily?"

"Certainly, Lord Lindsey. But I should warn you—I am a very good card player."

"As am I, Lily. As am I. I hope you are in a betting frame of mind."

"And *I* hope you do not mind losing."

Lord Lindsey laughed.

* * *

Gideon was halfway down the hall to his uncle's bedroom when a sound stopped him in his tracks: the unmistakable "pop" of a card being dealt from a faro box.

It was followed, to his burgeoning horror, by a throaty giggle.

What in the name of Lucifer—

He was in his uncle's room in two long swift strides.

"*Aarrgh*!" The brightness of the room attacked him. Gideon covered his eyes in defense. Since when had the sun been permitted into his uncle's domain?

He was not the least bit pleased to hear more giggles mingling with a rusty chuckle.

Gideon lowered his arm again, blinking to accustom himself to the sunlight. And then he blinked again, attempting to make sense of the tableau that had come into focus before him.

Uncle Edward was sitting up. In a *chair*. At a *table*.

And across from him sat a wicked, barefoot angel.

Her hair, the color and gleam of old gold, was held loosely away from her face with a ribbon; it spilled in a sort of haphazard splendor down her back and framed her face in loose spirals. Her newly scrubbed skin was pearl and rose, flushed from laughter, and when she turned to look at him in the full sunlight her eyes were nearly translucent, as though the sky itself shone through them. There was a large pair of slippers on the floor near her feet; Lily had obviously kicked them off in order to be more comfortable, and ten pink bare toes were curled into the carpet, as though luxuriating in the feel of it. Cards were splayed out on the table, and a small heap of coins sat in front of her. All she lacked was a cigar and a snifter of brandy and a halo.

Transfixed, his breath lost, he stared at the revelation that was Lily Masters. And as he stared, Gideon felt something inside him, something he could not quite identify, break loose from its moorings, shifting his equilibrium perilously.

"Back from London, are you, son? Are you going to stand there and gape like a looby, Gideon, or will you make your bow to us and say good afternoon? Miss Lily Masters of Sussex has been beating me at faro. She has an apothecary friend who will make me well, she says. We've written to him for an elixir." Lord Lindsey winked at Lily.

"Have you, now?" Gideon drawled. Lily looked a little worried at his tone. *And well she should.* "I am glad to see you . . . up, Uncle Edward." Gideon struggled to keep his voice even. His uncle. At a *table*. Playing *cards*.

"She's a caution," his uncle continued, as though his being "up" was something that occurred every day. "She has graciously allowed me to call her Lily. You didn't mention she'd be joining Lord Kilmartin."

"Oh, Miss Masters is quite . . . *gracious*." Gideon delivered the last word with all the irony he could muster and watched with some satisfaction as storm clouds began to move over Lily's clear eyes. "And her visit was something of a . . . surprise. Miss Masters, we've an appointment this afternoon, do we not?" Gideon kept his voice even and polite. His eyes, however, told a different story, of that he was certain.

"Yes," Lily answered faintly. "I suppose we do."

"Must you take her away, my boy?" Lord Lindsey sounded disappointed. "Very well, then. Lily, promise you'll visit again."

"I promise," she said, in the same faint voice. She quickly stood up from the table.

"You'll want your shoes, Miss Masters," Gideon said mildly.

"Oh." She thrust her little feet back into the big slippers.

"Help me back into bed, will you, Gideon? And pull the curtains closed. Silly girl insisted on sunlight." Lord Lindsey smiled. "Shake hands with me, Lily, there's a good girl, and come see me tomorrow."

Lily gave Lord Lindsey her hand and smiled, an open smile, warm and joyous and teasing. It struck Gideon in his solar plexus like a tiny comet.

And left in its wake a sizzling, irrational jealousy that it had not been directed at him.

"Don't forget your winnings, m'dear."

Gideon watched Lily sweep a handful of pennies and shillings into her palm. "Thank you, Lord Lindsey. I *will* see you again." She cast a sidelong look at Gideon.

Gideon helped Lord Lindsey back into his bed and closed the curtains against the invading light. *Like putting a toy soldier back in his box.* His uncle was not a toy for Lily Masters to play with at whim.

"Shall we, Miss Masters?" Gideon's voice was grim.

He steered her into a nearby sitting room. The blue room, his aunt had called it when she was alive; carpeted and draped and upholstered in a full dozen shades of blue, not all of them complementary, and furnished with ridiculous spindly French furniture.

"You were told to stay in your room, Miss Masters."

To his astonishment, her eyes widened in surprised amusement. "And you assumed that I *would*? Besides, I took but a few steps—"

"Which led directly to my uncle's room. Did you *really* think you could seduce a sick old man, Lily?"

Lily's jaw dropped. "*Seduce?*" she squeaked, outraged. "But I've never . . . he probably could not . . ."

Her cheeks colored; it was like watching wine slowly being stirred into cream.

"You've never *what*, Miss Masters?" His tone was silkily amused. "My uncle probably could not . . . *what*?"

Lily remained quiet for a moment. "Why are you asking me these things?" Her voice had gone thin.

Gideon paused. "I'm deeply concerned about my uncle's welfare, Lily. And you're in possession of a rather interesting book, which leads me to believe that you may also be in possession of some rather interesting . . . *skills*. Which you may attempt to practice upon him. He's sick and elderly, and despite the grandeur of this house, he is *not* a wealthy man."

"Book?" Lily looked puzzled. And then: "Oh." A wave of mortification swept across her face as understanding took hold.

"Yes. 'Oh.' "

"It was a gift," she said swiftly.

"From an admirer?" Why on earth should he want to know that?

There was a beat of silence. "Of a sort."

"I read the book, Miss Masters. It was very enlightening."

"Oh? I understand only a very little of it."

"Then why are you blushing the color of a peony?"

Lily was silent; she glared her embarrassment at him.

"Do you value that book?"

"Yes. As I said, it was a gift."

"Perhaps," Gideon mused, "I will take it from you and sell it."

Lily inhaled sharply. "Oh, very clever, Mr. Cole. Believe it or not, I *do* understand that stealing is wrong. But it is necessary."

"*Necessary?* There *are* other options, Miss Masters. You could sell flowers, or—"

"My body, Mr. Cole? Is that what you're implying I do? Would you find that preferable to my taking your watch?" Her cheeks flamed with fury.

Gideon looked down at her small proud chin, her soft, full mouth. "No," he said softly, at last. "I would *not* find that preferable, Miss Masters."

Lily blinked hard, like someone who had been charging full speed at a bolted door only to have it swing open at the last minute. Gideon smiled a little.

"But my watch is precious to me, Miss Masters. It belonged to my grandfather. And you would have taken it from me without a care, is that not so?"

"I cannot afford to give much thought to such things, Mr. Cole."

"Because a conscience is a burden to a thief?"

Lily paused, and then sighed deeply. "Mr. Cole, have you a sister? A brother?"

And it was as though she had suddenly stabbed one of her slim fingers into a wound. "Yes," he said, when he was certain his voice would be steady. "I've a sister. Helen."

"Do you care for her?" Lily's tone had gone somewhat gentler.

He said nothing, but he suspected his expression answered her question, for Lily nodded once to herself, as if she'd confirmed some suspicion of her own.

"What *wouldn't* you do for your sister, Mr. Cole?"

In a moment, it was his turn to nod once, conceding the point to her as though they were indeed in a formal debate.

"I do know of other options," she said. "None of them, apart from one, would have provided enough blunt to keep a roof over my head and food on the table and Alice at my side and off the streets."

He just watched her; he knew how people lived dozens to

a room in St. Giles. He knew they used gin to stay warm; he knew of the violence and illness and misery that often ensued. He suspected she was telling the truth.

"I did . . . I did try," she faltered, in the face of his unblinking gaze.

"What did you try, Miss Masters?"

"I applied for work at great houses. And shops. No one would have me. I've no experience of that sort of work, you see, and not enough education for any other sort. And would you hire someone who looked the way I did only a day ago?" She hurried on as if she couldn't bear to hear his answer to that question. "And families who have need of serving girls are usually unwilling to also take on small sisters. And so I . . . well . . ."

For some reason he wanted very much to salvage her pride. "You would make a terrible servant, Miss Masters. Perhaps a better colonel."

"Thank you, Mr. Cole." She looked genuinely pleased.

He couldn't help it; he smiled again.

"I have provided for my sister for years now, you know," Lily continued. "We are doing well enough." Her voice thrummed with pride.

"If not for me, Miss Masters, you would very likely be sentenced to transportation to Australia at this very moment."

"I hear 'tis quite fine this time of year."

He refused to smile at that. "The life you lead is dangerous, Miss Masters."

"I know. It's not as though I enjoy it."

There was a pause. "Oh, I think you enjoy it a little," he murmured.

And God above, she smiled at him then: an unrepentant smile, broad and mischievous and dazzling and young. The beauty of it *hurt*; it stopped his breath. Gideon took an involuntary step back, a peculiar act of self-defense.

"*Thirty pounds*, Miss Masters. I suggest you return to your room and read your book as instructed, lest you wish to discover just how *fine* it is in Australia at this time of year. And my uncle is not a plaything. If you attempt to seduce him, or to steal anything from him . . . I *will* know it."

To Gideon's profound relief and boundless regret, the smile disappeared as quickly as it had flashed into being, and Lily spun on her heels, the skirts of her big borrowed gown whipping about her ankles. She bustled toward the door—by God, he'd never seen someone move so quickly.

But when she reached the door, she paused. And spun around to face him again.

"I have a question, Mr. Cole. It concerns honor."

Gideon gave a short laugh. "You wish to engage me in a philosophical discussion, Miss Masters?"

"No, I wish to ask you whether I am a *prisoner*, or whether I will be free to go if I repay my debt."

"You're hardly in a position to return my thirty pounds, Miss Masters. There isn't a fence for miles around. I looked into the matter for you."

She ignored the goad. "But if I *am* able to repay your thirty pounds while I am here . . . will I be free to go?"

"If you're thinking of asking my uncle for thirty pounds, Miss Mas—" A motion caught his eye; Lily's fingers had idly fallen atop the back of a plush velvet chair; he watched her eyes fly briefly wide in startled pleasure. "—Miss Masters, I hardly think that qualifies as an honorable way to repay my debt. Taking advantage of . . ."

Her finger was now moving over the velvet in a furtive, almost imperceptible stroke. Gideon's breath hitched; the gesture was both heartbreaking and faintly erotic. It made him want to put everything at Aster Park beneath her fingers, just so he could watch her expression change.

"... that is, er ... taking advantage of an ill and elderly man ..." He was aware his words lacked a certain coherence at this point. Her finger was tremendously distracting.

Lily's hand stilled. "*I* never ask anyone for anything, Mr. Cole."

He raised a brow. "Of course not. You just *take*."

Her head snapped back indignantly; her mouth parted on a planned retort. But then she seemed to think better of it; she closed her mouth and studied him instead, her forehead slightly furrowed. He returned her appraisal with an unblinking, challenging one of his own.

And then it happened.

Slowly, simultaneously, wryly ...

They smiled at each other.

An acknowledgment that they were each, despite themselves, taking an unexpected pleasure in their exchange.

By God, the girl was a thief by her own admission, but she reasoned like a barrister and had more pride and sheer *spine* than the majority of the men he knew. Gideon found himself absurdly gratified by the respect he now read in Lily's eyes.

"Very well, Miss Masters," he said softly, suddenly. "If you can come by thirty pounds *honestly* while you are here ... you are free to go."

Her smile broadened.

"Will you promise to cooperate with our plans"—and here her smile took on a mischievous edge—"to the best of your *ability*, Miss Masters?"

"All right, Mr. Cole."

"And there is, of course, no guarantee that this undertaking is anything more than folly."

"Oh, I couldn't agree more, Mr. Cole. But as a start, you may have *this*." Lily thrust her handful of winnings at him; startled, Gideon opened his hands for it. "Two pounds. I believe that brings my debt to *twenty-eight* pounds, Mr. Cole. You should know I told Lord Lindsey only that I am Kilmartin's cousin from Sussex. And he is *not* a sick old man, Mr. Cole; he's a bored and *lonely* and coddled old man looking for an excuse to get out of that bed."

Speechless, Gideon watched her spin, the skirts of Mrs. Plunkett's big borrowed dress whipping about her ankles, and bustle purposefully toward the sitting room doorway.

She paused again when she reached it.

What a pity he would have to spoil her dramatic exit.

"The stairs, Miss Masters, are to the left, and your room on the second floor."

She squared her narrow shoulders, and then turned left and disappeared down the hall, her too-large slippers clacking on the marble.

And Gideon, his hand full of two pounds' worth of coins, stared bemused at the doorway for quite a few minutes more after the sound of her footsteps had faded away.

Chapter Five

"Mr. Cole was *right*, there are peacocks, Lily, and oh, how pretty they are, and they make a sound just like ladies in distress, like this: *help help help*. And Boone—Boone is the gardener—he says peacocks make good guards, as good as dogs, even—"

"Mmm. You don't say? *Honestly*," Lily managed to utter beneath the flow of Alice's words, just in case Alice required a response from her. But as it turned out, it was really more of a monologue than a conversation. Lily ignored the words after a moment and studied her sister, whose thin cheeks were glowing a healthy pink from her day in the sun and fresh air.

"What did *you* do today, Lily?" Alice finally asked, magnanimously.

"Oh, I read a book today." The hated *Instances of Ill Manners to be carefully avoided by youth of both sexes* sat on the writing desk, looking just as strict and humorless on the outside as it was on the inside. After her confrontation with Gideon Cole, she'd dutifully absorbed the book's contents, and felt as though she'd spent an entire day being admonished.

She'd discovered something interesting, however: the words *Property of Gideon Cole* had been scrawled in a youthful hand on the inside of the cover. Perhaps this book was responsible for turning Mr. Cole into . . . whatever he happened to be. A thorn in her side. Her gaoler.

An object of increasingly unnerving fascination.

A tap sounded at their chamber door. Lily opened it to find a maid bearing yet another note.

> *LM—Kindly join myself and Lord Kilmartin for dinner in the first floor dining room at 8:00. Bring Alice. Be clean. Given your talent for exploration, I imagine you can find the dining room without my assistance—GC*

"My, you've a funny look on your face, Lily." Alice had kicked off her slippers to walk the winding vine pattern in their chamber carpet.

Was Gideon Cole goading her or teasing her? Lily suspected both. She felt her skin heating again. Confusion, irritation, amusement . . . an odd breathless pleasure . . .

I am out of my depth with this man.

Then again, she was no stranger to exploring new depths.

"We've been invited to dine downstairs this evening, Alice."

"Dinner?" Alice marveled. "Imagine having dinner two nights in a row!"

Kilmartin and Gideon cradled their glasses of port lovingly. Port was really meant to be an after-dinner libation, but since no one but Gideon was about to monitor their manners, the two of them had decided to indulge before dinner, and were feeling as smug as two schoolboys about it.

"So how fares our . . . protégée?" Kilmartin wanted to know.

Gideon lifted his glass up and peered into its depths, as if he could read the answer there. *How fares our protégée?* Perhaps it was the port, but the question called to mind ten pink toes curling into the carpet . . . a finger sliding over velvet . . . and a smile as unexpected and enchanting as a shooting star.

And his uncle. Upright and playing cards in a room ablaze with sunlight. And again, perhaps it was the port, but all of these things seemed somehow part of the same miracle.

"Improved by a bath," Gideon finally answered. For some reason, he found it difficult to meet Kilmartin's eyes.

Kilmartin gave a quick laugh. "Gideon, are you quite certain you wouldn't prefer to abandon this fol—" He faltered to a stop. Gideon looked up. Lily Masters was standing in the dining room doorway, her chin aimed skyward and shoulders back as usual. Alice fidgeted at her side. Both girls looked scrubbed and rosy. And hungry, if he was not mistaken.

Gideon and a goggling Kilmartin scrambled politely to their feet.

"*Improved?*" Kilmartin whispered to Gideon. "You're a rascal, Cole."

Gideon ignored him. "Good evening, Miss Masters. Miss Alice."

She hesitated. "Good evening, Mr. Cole." A hint of irony in her voice acknowledged her role as reluctant guest.

"And you remember Lord Kilmartin?"

"Good evening, Lord Kilmartin," Lily turned her fresh-scrubbed visage up to Kilmartin.

"Good . . . good . . ." Kilmartin stammered.

Gideon shot Kilmartin a *get a hold of yourself* look. "And may I present Miss Alice Masters?"

Alice stared at Kilmartin, her small hand, the one Lily wasn't holding, fidgeting in her skirt. "He's very fine, but not so fine as Mr. Cole," she whispered at last to Lily, who squeezed her hand a little too late to censor her.

Kilmartin bent toward Alice. "That's what everyone else thinks, too," he whispered conspiratorially. Alice giggled.

Ah, Gideon thought. *If only grown-up women were as easy to charm as the little ones.* "Shall we?" He motioned to the table.

Footmen emerged from the shadows to pull chairs out for each of them. "Sit," Gideon commanded the girls, who did as told. They looked bemused when the footmen pushed their chairs toward the table. Alice giggled and Lily shushed her, but her lips were pressed together, as if she were stifling giggles of her own.

The footmen reappeared bearing dishes domed in silver. With subtle flourishes, they lifted lids to reveal venison, fish, roast fowl, and peas; they deftly served portions to each diner and retreated again, their footsteps silenced by the thick carpet.

Gideon cleared his throat. "Now, Miss Masters, when you are a guest at a dinner party—"

He was interrupted by the clink of metal against porcelain.

Lily and Alice had . . . attacked their dinners.

Meat and fish and fowl vanished into their mouths, peas were shoveled, juices scraped up with the sides of forks, their hands nearly a blur. Gideon and Kilmartin watched, spellbound, as Alice chased the last of her peas around with the avid focus of a big game hunter, trying and failing to stab it. She finally smashed it with the flat of her fork and licked it off, beaming.

In unison, Gideon and Kilmartin turned to Lily; she was dreamily sucking the tines of her own fork; her plate glistened bone white.

The men had yet to touch their own dinners.

Gideon's chest tightened; he could only imagine how scarce food must be to them.

"Would you like more?" he asked gently, finally.

Both girls nodded eagerly.

"I suppose we should add 'how to dine' to our curriculum," Kilmartin murmured.

Gideon sighed.

Chapter Six

Lily had just doffed her enormous borrowed nightdress and donned her enormous borrowed day dress when a tap sounded at the door. She yanked it open to find the stoic Mrs. Plunkett bearing a tray of eggs and fried bread and another missive from Gideon Cole.

She relieved Mrs. Plunkett of her breakfast tray, mumbling her thanks.

"You're to come with me, Miss Alice," Mrs. Plunkett said.

"Hurrah! Good-bye, Lily!" Alice stood on her toes to give Lily a quick hard hug and then went off hand in hand with the housekeeper, all signs of reticence gone. Alice had been bouncing about the room excitedly from the moment she'd opened her eyes. Apparently today she was to help Boone the gardener plant flowers and help Cook make bread and cookies in the kitchen.

Lily gazed after them longingly and then sighed and settled onto the bed. She sank her teeth into her bread and shook open the folded note.

LM—Kindly report to the blue sitting room on the second floor for a discussion of our mission. Be on time. There are fine clocks simply everywhere, but no doubt you've done an inventory of your own. You will play cards with Lord Lindsey, and meet with the dressmaker thereafter—GC

Cards with Lord Lindsey? Lily smiled at that; apparently the baron had insisted.

But then she read the note again, and could feel her temperature rising. She might be a strange patchwork creature, part urchin, part lady. She might be thirty pounds—correction, *twenty-eight* pounds—in the man's debt. He might be unreasonably beautiful and a little too clever . . . but she *did* know the word "please" was part of a gentleman's vocabulary. And she was growing a little tired of its exclusion from his missives. It had been *years* since *anyone* had told Lily Masters what to do.

All right then. She *would* cooperate with Mr. Cole . . . to the best of her ability.

She smiled a wicked little smile to herself.

"Thank you for your punctuality, Miss Masters." Surrounded by the overwhelming variety of blues of the blue sitting room, Lily's eyes were two vivid wonders.

Lily nodded to him curtly.

"Miss Masters, perhaps you are unaware of this, but it is considered impolite not to respond when you are spoken to: in short, when someone, for instance, *myself*, says, 'Thank you,' you will reply, 'You're welcome.'"

Lily rolled her eyes.

"Did you read your book, Miss Masters?"

"Yes, Mr. Cole, I read your little book."

"Did it perhaps say anything about, oh, eye rolling?" he asked mildly.

Lily furrowed her brow thoughtfully. "I read something about 'distortion of countenance,' I believe. But there was no specific mention of eye rolling." For Gideon's benefit, Lily distorted her countenance by crossing her eyes. And then, her face as clear and sweet as a rosebud, she turned to Kilmartin.

"Good morning, Lord Kilmartin."

"Um . . ." Kilmartin stammered.

Gideon sighed. Despite his pedigree, Kilmartin had never developed any sort of immunity to beautiful women. "You'll have to do more speaking than that, Kilmartin, if you're to be of any use here. Collect yourself."

"Quite right, quite right, Gideon," Kilmartin said hurriedly. "Good morning, Miss Masters. Please do take a seat." He had claimed an entire blue settee for himself.

Lily gave him a little curve of a smile and selected one of the delicate blue chairs to settle upon.

Gideon eyed those chairs and decided it was safer to lean against the mantel. "Help me, Miss Masters, for I'm confused. I seem to recall a discussion about cooperation yesterday. Did I imagine it?"

Lily cast her eyes up to the ceiling, which was painted all over in blue-robed cherubs. "Hmmm . . . well, yes. I recall that discussion as well. But you see, at the time, I *thought* I understood what 'cooperation' meant. This morning I learned I was mistaken."

Gideon crossed his arms and studied her in growing irritation and amused curiosity.

Her return gaze was a shade too wide to be truly innocent.

"All right, Miss Masters. Your point, please."

She looked a little disappointed; she had hoped, perhaps,

to toy with him a bit. He saw reluctant respect in her eyes again. He cherished that particular expression.

"Well, it's this, Mr. Cole. I thought the word 'cooperation' implied . . . a certain unity of purpose. Perhaps even a partnership. But this morning I received an *order*."

Gideon frowned. "An order?"

" 'Be on time,' " Lily quoted from his missive. Her pique was showing. "Not '*please* be on time.' An *order*. Nary a 'please' to be seen on the bloody thing. I *said* I would cooperate, Mr. Cole. You needn't order me about."

"Oh, you're right, Miss Masters, he *does* do that." Kilmartin sat up very straight suddenly, as though he'd just had an epiphany. "Orders *me* about now and again, too. A holdover from his military days, I expect."

"Bloody irritating," Lily groused.

"*Isn't* it?" Kilmartin agreed, getting into the spirit of things. "It's usually when he's in a hurry, I've noticed. And sometimes when—"

"*Thank* you both very much for the education." Gideon's barrister voice, low but resonant, cut them off. "Miss Masters: I apologize. Will that do? I will acquaint myself with the word 'please.' "

She smiled a little, pleased with herself.

"As I said yesterday, Miss Masters, I'm not entirely convinced this undertaking isn't pure folly. Our mission, after all, is to turn you into the sort of young lady of the *ton* who will outshine Lady Constance Clary, a true diamond of the first water and the daughter of a marquis."

Lily snorted.

"Thank, you, Miss Masters, that *was* a lovely sound. And as I can't recall ever hearing Lady Constance Clary snort, we'll have to discourage you from doing so."

Lily frowned and opened her mouth; Gideon continued

quickly. "And while we shall not, for now, dispute that you were raised a *lady*"—he watched Lily's face go mutinous—"we need to ascertain whether we've only a little polishing to do—whether we need only scrape St. Giles from you like barnacles from the hull of a ship, as it were—or whether it's . . . well, as I said, folly."

"*Barnacles?*" Kilmartin was delighted with the image.

Lily was not; lightning crackled in her clear eyes again. "My mother was the daughter of a curate, Mr. Cole, and she raised me to be a *lady*. To speak as a lady, to—"

"Well you see, *that's* odd, Miss Masters, because I can't recall the last time a *lady* called me a whoreson. I'm fairly certain Lady Constance Clary doesn't even know the word."

"Barnacles," Kilmartin repeated happily. "Words like—well, words like that, Miss Masters, are barnacles."

Lily ignored him. "Then it's a wonder Lady Constance Clary is able to refer to you at all, Mr. Cole."

Gideon couldn't help it: he smiled again. Lord, but she was quick with a retort; it was as invigorating as a lawn tennis volley. *I probably shouldn't be enjoying this quite so much.*

"Miss Masters, what are your pursuits?" he asked suddenly.

"My . . . my pursuits?"

"Yes. How do you spend your days?"

"Well . . . I pick a few pockets, visit my fence, buy a little dinner for Alice and myself if I've enough blunt. I read. I tell stories to Alice. Sometimes I pass the time talking and playing cards with Fanny, the prostitute upstairs."

Kilmartin made a choked sound, which unfortunately triggered a full-blown fit of coughing. Gideon sighed and strolled over to the settee to thump him between the shoulder blades.

Lily looked distinctly pleased with herself once more.

"You may be surprised to learn that those are not the typical pursuits or accomplishments of a young lady of the *ton*, Miss Masters." Gideon stopped thumping Kilmartin. "What sort of stories do you tell Alice?"

Lily's eyes widened warily. "Just . . . stories, Mr. Cole."

"About . . . Mr. Darcy, perhaps? Or maybe a . . . prince?" Gideon asked the question solely to see her cheeks go pink again, and they did. Like watching the sun tint a dawn sky, it was. She stared at him, her expression battling between stormy and embarrassed and amused appreciation.

"What about needlework, Miss Masters?" Kilmartin interjected brightly. "Do you count it among your accomplishments? Or drawing? Or archery? Constance wins all the archery tournaments; she would hate to be bested. Perhaps Miss Masters excels at archery."

This sobered Gideon. "I am *not* outfitting Miss Masters with a bow and arrow."

Lily looked disappointed. "I am quite deft, Mr. Cole."

"Precisely my fear, Miss Masters."

"I don't suppose you play the pianoforte, Miss Masters?" Kilmartin had begun to sound a little discouraged.

"I—" Lily paused. Gideon watched an intriguing shadow of longing pass over her face. "No, I don't play the pianoforte."

"Do you ride, Miss Masters?" Kilmartin tried again, a little desperately. "Lady Clary is an exceptional horsewoman. Perhaps you can best her there."

"Never been on a horse in my life." Lily sounded grimly triumphant.

"Constance is an exceptional *everything*, Laurie," Gideon replied smoothly. "I suppose Miss Masters can be seen riding with me in your high flyer, rather than on horseback."

"You'll like my high flyer, Miss Masters," Kilmartin said cheerfully to Lily. But he sent Gideon a worried look.

A slightly disheartened silence followed.

Gideon raked his fingers through his hair. "Well, it's not as though she'll be expected to demonstrate needlework or drawing, necessarily. We can perhaps work around the pianoforte, though young ladies are often asked to perform. We'll just begin by telling everyone that . . . Miss Lily Masters is Lord Kilmartin's cousin, from Sussex, near the town of Wilmington, and that her father is a very wealthy gentleman who owns land, and ships, and—"

"Do I have a horse?" Lily had begun to look intrigued.

Gideon blinked. "I beg your pardon?"

"A horse. Perhaps this Miss Lily Masters of Sussex is an equestrienne. Perhaps she has a horse of her own back in Sussex."

"But we've established you don't ride, Miss Masters."

"But Miss Lily Masters of *Sussex* might ride. Just not in London."

"Very well. Miss Lily Masters of Sussex has a horse."

"What is his name?"

"His *name*?"

"The horse's name."

Gideon drew in a long breath through his nose, and let it out again. "Anything you like, Miss Masters, with perhaps the exception of 'Baubles.'"

Lily looked pleased. "McBride. Miss Lily Masters of Sussex has a horse named McBride."

McBride? Gideon let that pass for now. "As I was saying, Miss Masters, we can say that your father is an extremely wealthy gentleman—he owns stables full of horses, land, houses, ships, canal shares, and just about everything near Wilmington. And by *gentleman*, I mean he hasn't a profession."

"I *know* what a gentleman is, Mr. Cole. I often wonder whether you do."

Kilmartin laughed at that. Gideon sent him a quelling look. "And perhaps your pursuits can include long walks and . . . and reading."

And when Lily's eyes went wide and she swiftly looked down into her lap, he knew at once they were both thinking of the same thing: that insidiously compelling little French book.

He briefly lost his powers of speech.

Kilmartin swiveled his head from Gideon to Lily and back again, confused by the sudden awkward silence.

"Sounds bloody dull, if you ask me," Lily said to her lap, finally. "Walking, reading."

"Barnacles," Kilmartin said sadly. "Words like 'bloody,' Miss Masters, are barnacles."

Gideon felt drained suddenly. How to explain the intricacies of the *ton* to this girl, who knew London's darkest district but had never navigated the velvet battleground of a ballroom? Who spoke like a lady but who used "bloody" like an ordinary adjective? She probably easily knew as much about lovemaking as the average St. Giles whore, if the book was any indication. But she couldn't very well share that information in the drawing rooms of London.

Folly. I should send her home. He looked at Kilmartin again, gave a slight shake of his head.

And then suddenly Lily Masters took a deep breath; her chin elevated to a defiant angle.

"Ten pounds."

"I beg your pardon, Miss Masters?"

"Ten pounds against my debt says I can prove that I can do it."

"*What* can you do, Miss Masters?"

"Rival Lady Constance Clary."

Gideon gazed at her a moment, bemused. "Miss Masters . . ." he began gently. "Lady Constance is the daughter of a marquis. She is beautiful and wealthy, she wears the finest clothes, rides in the finest carriages, wins archery contests, sets fashions and ends them—I could go on and on. She's the most admired young woman in the *ton*. She makes very certain of it."

This recitation merely seemed to make the set of Lily's jaw go more stubborn. "Ten pounds, Mr. Cole."

He smiled faintly. "Miss Masters . . ."

"You don't think I can." It was a statement, not a question. It was also a dare. Two pink spots of indignant pride sat high on her cheeks.

Gideon looked at the pickpocket in her big borrowed dress, her hands clasped in her lap, spine rigid and chin high. The girl was like an épée: forever parrying. Where did it come from, that confidence, that fight, that *pride*?

And then it occurred to him: the same place he'd gotten his own confidence, and fight, and pride. It had been built and tested through use, like a muscle. Whereas Constance's effortless grace, her correct conversation, her tranquil confidence, had been virtually issued to her as part of her birthright. Constance would not *expect* to be challenged, for she never had been.

And one of the most effective battle strategies, he knew, was the element of surprise.

Lily's debt to him stood at twenty-eight pounds. And he was his father's son, after all: one taste of risk left him open to another. He could risk ten pounds to see what she proposed to do.

"*How* do you propose to rival her, Miss Masters?"

"Ten pounds if you deem me successful, Mr. Cole?" She was all tension.

"Very well, Miss Masters."

"Your word of honor?"

"You have my word of honor," he said softly.

The tension visibly left her; she turned to Laurie. "Lord Kilmartin, if you would pretend to be Lady Clary?"

Laurie sat bolt upright. "If I would *what*?"

"Pretend that you are Lady Clary, and that we have just met."

Kilmartin shot a pleading look at Gideon; Gideon turned his palms up with a grin. "You'll make a splendid Lady Clary, Laurie. Go right ahead."

Kilmartin sighed gustily and turned to Lily. "How do you do, Miss Masters?" he chirped.

"Very well, thank you. And how do you do, Lady Clary?"

"Exceptionally well. Your gown is *lovely*, Miss Masters." Kilmartin was finding his feet in his role.

"Thank you, Lady Clary," Lily said smoothly. "And may I return the compliment?"

Two pairs of eyebrows, Gideon's and Kilmartin's, rose, admiring her graceful response.

"Why, *thank* you, Miss Masters. And is this your first visit to London? From what part of Sussex do you hale?"

"I live near Wilbeyton, Lady Clary."

"*Wilmington*," Gideon stage-whispered.

"Wilmington," Lily corrected without batting an eye. "I was in London once before, as a child."

"And how do you find London now?" Kilmartin–Lady Clary asked.

Lily's eyes went dreamy. "Oh, London is heavenly. The crowds, the noise, the excitement, so much to do and see. And everyone has been so exceptionally kind. But I do long for Sussex now and again, and McBride, my horse. Sweetest nature, he has, and a star right"—She pointed to her forehead—"here, you know. A coat as black as night. I named him for my father's old groom, who had a long somber face."

Gideon stared. The words spun out of her like fairy dust. He could detect no trace of the feral girl who'd thrashed in the grip of the huge man only yesterday—apart from the faint aura of defiant confidence that surrounded her and her determinedly erect posture. Her expression was benign as a blossom. Poor Kilmartin seemed downright mesmerized.

"And what other pursuits do you enjoy in Wilmington, Miss Masters?"

"I enjoy long walks very much! Oh, and reading. I often read to my neighbor Fanny, as she has just the one eye."

Kilmartin blinked, a little startled.

"What became of her other eye?" Kilmartin–Lady Clary asked.

Lily leaned forward conspiratorially. "It was an archery accident, you know. Fanny was the best archer in all of Sussex, but one day during a tournament a misfired arrow took out her eye and sailed away with it—right to the center of the target! And the person who aimed the arrow would have won the tournament, apart from the . . . well, you know. Fanny's eye."

Kilmartin was agog.

"It was blue," Lily added. "The eye."

"How very dreadful!" Kilmartin managed faintly after a moment.

"And it's why, you see, I wouldn't dream of dabbling in archery anymore. One can have a terrible accident, like poor

Fanny. And I do so enjoy looking out at the world through *two* eyes."

Gideon was agog, too. It was both brilliant and unnervingly convincing: Gideon was fairly certain the image of an airborne eye wouldn't leave him anytime soon. Nor would Miss Lily Masters of Sussex be in any danger of being invited to participate in archery tournaments. Even Lady Constance Clary would think twice about archery tournaments upon hearing that story.

"Well, she is fortunate to have you as a friend," the Kilmartin version of Lady Clary said, recovering himself. "What sort of things do you read to her?"

"I read Shakespeare to her, and novels, too. Fanny is particularly fond of novels. We just finished *Pride and Prejudice*. I adore a happy ending, even if one must suffer a bit to get to it." She gazed at Kilmartin limpidly, her head tilted.

Kilmartin gaped at Lily, captivated.

Gideon cleared his throat.

Kilmartin jumped. "Ah . . . right," he stuttered. "Have you . . . have you been to Brighton, Miss Masters?"

Lily paused. "Oh. Well . . . yes. Have *you*, Lady Clary?"

"Naturally," Kilmartin said, a testing glint in his eye. "But I wondered what *you* would think of it, Miss Masters, as it is in your part of the country."

"The sea . . ." she began hesitantly, glancing at Gideon for confirmation that Brighton did indeed include a sea. He nodded. "The sea air is quite invigorating. Papa takes us every year."

"What is your father's profession, Miss Masters?" Ah. Kilmartin was clever; it was another tricky question, one that could even be construed as an insult.

"Profession, Lady Clary?" Lily seemed gently puzzled. "My father hasn't a . . . *profession*. He merely owns a great many things. Land and houses and horses and ships and canal shares. *Those* kinds of things."

She concluded by lifting one brow, indicating the question was untoward—*gentlemen* did not typically have "professions"—but that she would generously forgive the asker. *This* time.

Kilmartin turned to Gideon then, a grin slowly spreading over his face as though they had all just bested a common foe.

"How—?" Gideon said to Lily, amazed.

"Stories. Not needlework, not riding, not archery. Stories." The pink spots of indignant pride had faded and she looked—not smug, but definitely satisfied with herself.

And Gideon had to admit to a certain awe. It wasn't difficult to imagine Lily in the doctor's parlor, chatting amongst the doctor's daughters like an ordinary well-bred young lady. Well, an ordinary young lady with astonishing eyes, and a soft bud of a mouth, and . . .

He wasn't quite ready to cede victory to her. He pushed himself away from the mantel and paced a little, thoughtfully rubbing his knuckles over his chin. "All right, Miss Masters. It seems you *can* convincingly portray a refined young lady." She frowned a little, objecting to the word "portray." "But our goal is more complex. . . ."

"What he means, Miss Masters," Kilmartin interjected, "is that we need to convince Lady Constance Clary that she wants to marry Gideon, despite the fact that Gideon has no title, no property, and no money. And only passable looks."

Gideon shot Kilmartin a wry look.

"You must be very much in love with her," Lily said softly.

Gideon froze mid-pace. The word might well have been "treason" for how strangely provocative it sounded in that little room. And she'd said it so *easily*. Kilmartin, damn him, was looking at him expectantly, as if he too would have liked the answer to that question.

"You've been reading too many novels, Miss Masters," Gideon finally said stiffly.

Lily still looked puzzled. "And you've no money? Haven't you—I mean, you *must*—that is to say, this house is very grand—"

"Gideon spent his last thirty pounds on *you*, Miss Masters," Kilmartin said.

Lily went very still, as though she'd stopped breathing.

Gideon felt his face warming.

"But your uncle . . . couldn't you ask your uncle . . . ?" she stammered.

"My uncle hasn't a spare sou. And besides, *I* never ask anyone for anything, Miss Masters." He tossed her words to her, the ones she'd used on him only yesterday.

"That's right," she shot back. "You just get *pickpockets* to do the work for you instead."

Gideon's head went back a little with the force of the volley. He heard Kilmartin stir uneasily on the settee.

He regarded Lily in measuring silence again. She gazed back at him.

And then, seconds later, again: two slow, simultaneous smiles, pleased and wry, curved their lips, as though they had each passed some sort of mutual test.

And yet . . . Gideon still wasn't quite ready to cede her victory. He had another test in mind.

"And if Lady Clary were to say to you, 'Miss Masters, you've such lovely plump arms, that sleeve would *never* suit! Perhaps you should try a puffed sleeve instead?' "

"Does she *really* care so much about sleeves?" Lily was clearly bemused.

Gideon privately agreed that sleeves hardly ranked in the hierarchy of important things, but loyalty to Constance kept him from saying so. "Trust me, Miss Masters, fashion is an important battlefront in the *ton*, and Constance is Wellington."

Lily pondered this. "Then I would say"—and she leaned forward, her tone sweetly confiding—" 'You're absolutely correct, Lady Clary. Which is why my dressmaker is developing a *new* sleeve especially for me.' "

Again: *brilliant*. A sleeve especially for someone else would drive Constance *mad*.

"Miss Masters . . ." he said slowly, shaking his head in wonder, "I believe . . . well, you do have the idea: parry everything. In other words, be yourself. Only with stories."

Lily's chin angled proudly again, and she allowed herself a small triumphant smile.

"But don't forget, Miss Masters," Kilmartin added mischievously, "you also need to pretend you're utterly enthralled with Gideon in order for this to work."

And then Gideon watched, with great satisfaction, as those fair smooth cheeks colored and her confident smile wavered a little. "I hope you've a book for *that* one, for I can't imagine how I'll do it." She addressed this to her lap again; she'd lowered her eyes.

Kilmartin laughed.

"Oh, if you blush in just that way, Miss Masters, I do believe people will get the general idea." Gideon's voice was soft, amused. She jerked her head up and met his eyes; her expression was again battling between wanting to laugh and wanting very much to throttle him.

"Well, I suppose we just need to scrape off the barnacles now," Kilmartin mused. "And polish the hull."

"And how much remains of my debt, Mr. Cole?" Lily demanded.

Because he was feeling devilish, and because her breath appeared to be held, he made her wait for it.

"Congratulations, Miss Masters. You've only eighteen pounds to go."

And again, despite themselves, they smiled at each other.

Unfortunately, Gideon wanted to begin scraping barnacles right away. He called it a "deportment lesson," and he'd decided it should take place in a room featuring sturdier furniture and fewer porcelain things, since Lily would have to practice "walking" and he had no wish to completely destroy the blue room. Or so he said. He also wanted to see her curtsy.

Practice walking, indeed, Lily fumed to herself. She likely did more walking in a single week than all of the young ladies of the *ton* combined.

But you walk like a thief, Miss Masters, Gideon had said. What could that possibly *mean*?

She supposed she had her own accursed pride to thank for all of this. It was the *look* the two of them, Gideon and Kilmartin, had exchanged that had done it, made her open her mouth and wager the ten pounds. It was as if they had been on the brink of giving up on her, as if she, Lily Masters, had nothing to offer them. And it had slashed her pride to watch Gideon Cole's beautiful dark eyes regard her almost *pityingly* . . . As if she could never possibly measure up to that paragon, Lady Constance Clary.

She'd like to see Lady Constance Clary survive in St. Giles.

So now they were in the ballroom, a vast room filled with echoes and overhung with two enormous chandeliers. The floor was honey-colored and slick as a mirror, and Lily was seized with an overwhelming urge to slide across it in her bare feet.

Gideon wasted not a moment. "Miss Masters, will you do us the honor of showing us your curtsy?"

Lily sighed. She clutched fistfuls of her borrowed gown and ducked into a quick little squat.

Lord Kilmartin burst out laughing; Gideon shook his head sadly. "Miss Masters," he said with exaggerated patience, "you are not lowering yourself over a chamber pot. The point of a curtsy is to greet a friend or new acquaintance. We must address your, shall we say, *form*."

"Er . . . Gideon . . ." Kilmartin sounded hesitant.

Gideon turned to him, a question on his face.

"Who will show Lily how to curtsy properly?"

Gideon's take-charge demeanor faltered and he momentarily looked nonplussed. Lily was delighted; she didn't trouble to disguise a smile.

"Well, I rather thought *you* would, Kilmartin. You've more female relatives than I."

"But God knows, Gideon, you've been the recipient of far more curtsies than I."

"But you're . . . you're closer in . . . *height* . . . to Miss Masters, Laurie."

"Ah, Gideon, but you've considerably more grace than—"

Gideon sighed gustily. "Oh, for God's sake, Kilmartin. We'll *both* curtsy. Now pretend you're a young lady. You can be . . . Lady Constance Clary again. I shall be Lady Anne Clapham."

"How on earth do I get myself into these things, I ask you . . ." Kilmartin grumbled. But he dutifully rose to his feet. Clutching the hem of his coat in his hands, he slowly lowered his sturdy frame into an exquisite curtsy. "Good afternoon, Lady Clapham."

"Good afternoon to *you*, Lady Clary." Gideon, aka Lady Clapham, clutched the hem of his own coat and executed a curtsy so flawless that Kilmartin's eyebrows shot up in appreciation. "And may I present to you my friend Miss Lily Masters?"

Lily decided watching these two men curtsy was almost worth being captured and dragged to Aster Park. The two of them were a study in contrasts: Kilmartin's face a sort of pale square topped in fair cropped hair, his eyes a light blue, his lashes and brows barely a color at all; Gideon all elegant defined angles and dramatic darkness—the thick slash of his brows, his richly colored hair and eyes—against fair skin.

Gideon turned to her in all seriousness; apparently curtsies were an earnest business. "Miss Masters, when you make your curtsy to Lord Kil—er, Lady Clary, don't *rush* through it. Pretend . . . you are . . ." He paused, his eyes rose to the ceiling in thought. ". . . Oh, pretend you are a . . . willow bending in the breeze."

When Kilmartin snorted, Gideon looked a little discomfited, as though a belch rather than a pretty description had slipped from him. But truth be told, the image captivated Lily. *A willow bending in the breeze* . . . how *would* a willow greet its friends? Lily could not recall having seen a willow, but she'd read of them; her mind's eye filled with lissome green branches caught and tossed by a breeze.

All right, then.

She gathered loose folds of her dress in her hands and dipped slowly, lowering her head to show Gideon and Kilmartin the part that divided her dark gold hair. She rose up again.

"Oh, *well* done, Miss Masters!" Kilmartin clapped his hands. "Fit for presentation at court."

Lily smiled at him but then turned, reflexively, to Gideon; she could not seem to help it. Gideon was studying her quietly; she looked to him for approval—and *why* should she want his bloody approval?—but his eyes were unreadable.

"Yes," he said softly. "That's the curtsy you should perform each time, Miss Masters."

"One barnacle scraped away," Kilmartin said with satisfaction.

Lily's lesson in "walking" was far less successful than curtsying, unfortunately. She'd discovered the extent of Gideon Cole's patience.

It had a *very* short reach, his patience.

"What *is* the bloody rush, Miss Masters?" Gideon and Kilmartin had abandoned their coats to the ballroom chairs, and Kilmartin was sprawled across several of them, sweating. Gideon pushed a hand through his hair in frustration. The afternoon sun had found its way into the ballroom, and it picked out the deep reds hidden in his hair. In her mind, Lily began to list the colors: rust and bronze and copper and—

"Miss Masters, if you would *please* pay attention."

Lily returned her eyes to Gideon's face. *Bloody handsome tyrant.*

"You are not running from the watch or from an angry barrister whose pocket you have just attempted to pick," he continued ironically. "You are entering a ballroom, or a drawing room. There is no need to *bolt*. And lower your chin, for God's sake. You are not a pugilist."

"Walking," Lily said through gritted teeth, "is merely a

way to get from one place to the other. I can't imagine why anyone would want to prolong it."

"Yes, Miss Masters, but walking is also a way to announce *who you are*." Gideon waved one arm impassionedly. "How you *view* yourself in the world. The way you hold yourself, the way you move, how you occupy a space, tells other people a good deal about you, tells them *how* they should think of you. Listen to me: it's *very* important, Miss Masters."

Lily studied Gideon, reluctantly fascinated. Actually, she knew this to be true: this was how she chose whose pockets to pick.

Kilmartin's stomach made a noise, something between a growl and a whine. "If you're going to orate, Gideon," he drawled, "I think I'll go see about luncheon." He levered himself up and began pushing his arms into his jacket sleeves.

Gideon slowly lowered his gesturing arm and sighed, his shoulders slumping a little.

"Very well. I will join you, Laurie. Miss Masters has an appointment with Lord Lindsey, anyhow. And Miss Masters . . . after you meet with the dressmaker, if you would *please*"—he drawled the word facetiously—"return to this room for a dancing lesson?"

Lily struggled not to distort her countenance into a frown. *Maddening, bloody*—"It would be my *pleasure*, Mr. Cole."

He paused then, and considered her a little wryly, as if deciding whether to say something else to her. He did. "And Miss Masters, some people *do* walk merely for the pleasure of it."

"Do *you*, Mr. Cole?"

Gideon opened his mouth, and then closed it again, and

swiftly turned away from her and collected his coat from the chair.

"You know where to find my uncle, Miss Masters," he said.

The two gentlemen bowed to her and Lily, surprising herself, dipped into a beautiful curtsy in response. When she rose up again, Gideon's eyes were on her, and she could have sworn she saw something flash across them, a hot flare there and gone, but then again, it could have been a trick of the light.

"Where did you learn to play cards so well, Miss Masters?"

Lily had arrived in Lord Lindsey's rooms to find him wrapped in a handsome dressing gown, sitting up at the table. Cards had been dealt, little sandwiches were stacked on a plate next to a pot of tea . . . and all the softly glowing candles had been snuffed. The curtains were pulled open a civilized degree, letting in a pleasant beam of light, rather than the torrent Lily had unleashed yesterday. She smiled at the compromise.

"Are you sure it is my skillful play, Lord Lindsey, or are you allowing me to win . . . *again*?" She was two pounds closer to freedom.

Lord Lindsey laughed. "Minx! Anyhow, I promise you, today I am *trying* to win, but you are besting me. And I am no amateur at cards, I will have you know. With whom do you play at home?"

"Well, I play a good deal with my neighbor Fanny, for she's time enough between custom—" She caught herself just in time and looked up at Lord Lindsey swiftly. He was watching her alertly, but not *too* alertly; he merely seemed interested in what she had to say. "For she has plenty of time, as . . . as her children are grown."

The lie came easily, and it sounded natural even to Lily's ears. *Lying, stealing—Mama would be so proud.*

Thankfully, Lord Lindsey merely nodded and selected another card. "And what else are you doing to pass the time here at Aster Park, Miss Masters?"

Lily thought of the odious little brown book. "Reading."

"*Reading*?" Lord Lindsey sounded appalled. "A young girl like you, on days as bright as this one? Surely you should be about visiting the neighbors, or going on long walks to see some ruin?"

"I've . . . I've not the clothing for visiting quite yet, Lord Lindsey. Though I am to see the dressmaker this afternoon."

"Oh, quite right. Forgive me, child. 'Unfortunate carriage accident,' and all. You look quite presentable to me even in that great sack of a gown, but then what does an old man know? So what is it you are reading?"

The title of the book was burned on Lily's brain. "The book is called *Instances of Ill Manners to be Carefully Avoided by Youth of Both Sexes*. I discovered it in my rooms, and found it quite . . . interesting. I could not put it down." *Forbidden* to put it down, more accurately, she thought resentfully.

Lord Lindsey lowered his chin and lifted his brows at her in deep, skeptical silence.

Lily selected a card of her own. "The book is inscribed, '*Property of Gideon Cole.*'" Her nonchalance was masterfully feigned.

"Oh. *That* book." Lord Lindsey sat back for a moment, looking grim and reflective. "Before Gideon lost his parents—my brother Alistair was Gideon's father—he was an impulsive boy, more than a little headstrong, always in motion, always up to some mischief. But then his parents died . . . and, well, he somehow got hold of that little book, and I aver, he attended it with more devotion than our own curate attends the Bible. And, well, I don't suppose you can argue with the results. He's done very well for himself."

But oddly, Lord Lindsey looked more wistful than proud as he said it.

Lily recalled Gideon's dark eyes snapping with passion, his hand flailing the air for emphasis this afternoon. *It's* very *important, Miss Masters,* he had said, exasperated with her.

But a little green shoot of sympathy poked its head up through her resentment. Sympathy for a high-spirited boy who had lost his parents and had turned to a book of rules to make sense of a world gone suddenly and painfully senseless. Lily could have told the young Gideon that planning was futile, that no set of rules could keep the whims of fate at bay. She had learned to live by one rule only: *There is only today.*

It had served her reasonably well . . . up until the moment she had arrived at Aster Park.

"But why *you'd* want to read that book is beyond me, Miss Masters," the baron continued. "I would think it would quite ruin *you.*"

"Quite," she agreed darkly.

"And, oh, now see, you've won again. I *am* losing my touch."

"You were telling a story, Lord Lindsey. You were merely distracted."

"Ah, so that is your strategy, is it, Miss Masters? To distract me?"

"You are clever to catch me out, Lord Lindsey." She demurely lifted her teacup to her lips.

He laughed again. "So tell me, Lily, are you going to marry your cousin?"

Lily choked on her sip of tea, and settled the cup back down on its saucer a little roughly; porcelain rang against porcelain. "I . . . I beg your pardon?"

Lord Lindsey chuckled, pleased with himself. "Ah, you see, you are not the only one with the power to startle. Perhaps you *should* marry Kilmartin. He's a good sort. Not terribly interesting, but then he's rich, so he doesn't have to be. He would be kind to you. Perhaps you'd do him some good."

Lily wasn't certain whether she should be amused or appalled. "No, sir, Lord Kilmartin and I have no plans to marry."

"No? Have you any sweethearts, Lily? Oh, look, you've gone pink, a minx like yourself, I'm surprised at it. No matter: you will find a sweetheart in London. Or rather, they will find you, I am most certain of it. You'd likely do Gideon some good as well, but his sights are fixed on that big blonde daughter of a marquis, and perhaps it's just as well. It would be an excellent match for him."

You've no idea just how fixed, Lily wanted to say. The reminder of the specific reason for her presence at Aster Park darkened her mood. She raked her winnings toward her. *Three pounds closer to freedom.*

Mrs. Plunkett appeared in the doorway of the room. "Miss Masters, the dressmaker is here to see you."

"Well, if you must have new gowns, Lily, I suppose you must. Until tomorrow?" The baron looked hopeful.

Lily's cheeks warmed with pleasure. "Of course, Lord Lindsey."

The baron pushed his chair back and levered himself upright, and then, slowly and rustily, he bent into a handsome bow.

Lily was suddenly grateful she could offer him a perfect curtsy in return.

Chapter Seven

Madame Sabine Marceau's face was pure Plantagenet: long and oval, prominent-nosed, as time-honored and English as the Tower of London. Her figure, on the other hand, was all modern elegance. Her walking dress, a tawny jaconet, was puffed at the shoulders and snug in the arm and flounced at the hem; a tiny tasteful bustle bulged behind. Her brown hair was parted in the middle and meticulously curled, and a perfect little straw bonnet, heavy with silk flowers, cupped her head.

The dressmaker whipped the bonnet off and tossed it onto a little chair.

"Oh, thank *goodness* you are pretty!" were her first words to Lily. "'Tis so unutterably dull to dress the plain ones."

Well, that was two "pretty"s in as many days, Lily thought. Perhaps it was true. "*Am* I pretty?"

Madame Marceau patted Lily's cheek with a gloved hand. "*Aren't* you a funny little thing! 'Am I *pretty*?'" she mimicked, and laughed merrily.

Lily tried with some difficulty not to distort her countenance into an irritated frown. Laughter did *not* answer her question. She suspected she was *St. Giles* pretty—but then again, after enough gin, *everyone* in St. Giles was pretty—and perhaps she was pretty enough for Lord Lindsey, whose eyesight seemed sharp enough for a man his age.

But was she *London* pretty? Was she . . . *Gideon Cole* pretty?

Gideon had used that grand word—"beautiful"—to describe Lady Constance Clary. Lily would have preferred to be beautiful. But she had too much pride to press Madame Marceau for clarification.

She shivered in her overlarge borrowed shift while the dressmaker circled her like a bird of prey, clucking and mumbling things under her breath like "yes, yes, of course" and "probably not" and "hmmm."

"You've a lovely trim figure and even a bosom, Miss Masters, so we needn't use padding. And you've coloring to treasure—that hair, those eyes. I can *do* something with you, yes I can," Madame Marceau crowed triumphantly. Briskly—Madame Marceau was nothing if not brisk—she stretched a tape measure over and around various parts of Lily's body, so matter-of-factly that Lily didn't have time to consider whether she might be embarrassed to stand in her shift before a complete stranger.

Madame Marceau stood back and assessed her. "We should probably go light on the flounces, since you're so slight, but we'll use tucks and embroidery to splendid effect, a little tidy vandyking, too, I think. Ruffs are all the thing for day dresses, you know, and all the rage in Paris, but they might swallow your little neck up—perhaps we can get away with just a frilled shirt-habit."

Madame Marceau might as well have been speaking

Chinese. "Of course. Tidy vandyking and frilled shirt-habits," Lily agreed ironically.

The modiste arched a brow. "I'll explain all about vandyking, Miss Masters, and the rest, when your clothing arrives, for you'll most certainly need to know those sorts of things. Oh, yes. I can see it now: patent net over a pale blue slip—I have the perfect satin for it, too—caught up in puffs at the hem, a simple sleeve. And a low neck, to show off that lovely bosom. Has he given you pearls yet?"

Lily was astounded. "*Pearls?*"

"You are fortunate, indeed, Miss Masters, to have a protector as kind as Mr. Cole. And he has *taste* as well."

"*Protector*?" Lily repeated incredulously. "*Kind?*"

"Are you just learning the English language, Miss Masters? You're sounding a bit like a parrot. You needn't be shy about it with me. He's just the most beautiful-looking man, isn't he? If anyone deserves to take his ease with a woman, I would say Mr. Cole does. And you're an interesting choice."

Take his ease with a woman. Lily almost smiled. What a pretty phrase for it. But then, because her bloody fertile imagination sprouted anything planted in it, an explicit image blossomed: Gideon Cole, his long body leaning over her, his hot eyes holding her motionless. His arm slowly curling around her waist, his lips lowering, lowering, and then . . .

Touching her lips. Opening against them . . .

Lily threw an imaginary elbow into the image; it dissolved. But traces of it lingered in her warm cheeks and weakened limbs, like an illness.

"But . . . but . . . I am Miss Lily Masters of Sussex. I am Lord Kilmartin's cousin," she recited weakly.

"Of course you are, dear." Madame Marceau gave her another little pat and rolled her eyes. "That's what he told me as well. Never you mind. You should be proud, as he's a very fine, hardworking barrister. He has helped many a penniless sort and gets nothing out of it, as far as I can see."

"He gets to win," Lily muttered. "He gets *that* out of it. He very much enjoys *winning*."

"Oh, and win he does. You should see him at it, Miss Masters," Madame Marceau continued with relish. "So tall and well-spoken, standing up there in front of the court, eating his opponents alive. He won a case for my cousin, and I fair swooned watching him."

Lily didn't want to imagine it, but it was far too easy: Gideon's speaking eyes fixed on the court, a strategic devastating smile or two, his resonant voice raised in demand or dropped in silky persuasion—the opposition would never have a prayer.

Madame Marceau was still talking. "He would be a wealthier man today if he didn't take on cases like mine," she declared. "And I am happy to be of assistance to him, for he very likely cannot afford to dress you himself. Let alone your sister. You'll have your new things in a week or so; I'll set my girls upon the job."

Alice, too? And more slow reluctant warmth rayed through her. He'd thought of Alice, too. How long had it been since *anyone* had given special thought to the two of them?

"I cannot wait to see you in satin and velvet," Madame Marceau continued. "Can you picture it? Or a white muslin walking dress, a row of gathered crepe across the bodice—" She dropped her hands on Lily's shoulders and turned her toward the mirror.

Lily only saw the same girl she'd seen in the mirror over her dressing table; her tiny gold freckles conspicuous against her pale skin. *She looks more frightened than I feel,* Lily thought, bemused. *But perhaps I am more frightened than I know.* Of what? Not of clothes, certainly.

Perhaps of Gideon Cole and this . . . this treacherous *weakening*.

"He suggested sea greens and blues and golds," Madame Marceau murmured, "and I do believe he is right, but perhaps some white as well. Yes. You'll be quite striking in white."

An odd pang took Lily, and her breath caught. Had Gideon Cole really thought about her in terms of color—thought of her eyes, her skin, her hair?

Madame Marceau whisked her businesslike gaze up and down Lily's length. "You'll need bonnets and slippers and gloves and half-boots, too, of course. I'll see to it. Mr. Cole took my case when I'd nothing to offer him, and then he requested my assistance with outfitting you, Miss Masters. He knows full well what that will mean to me—very likely an increase in business, once the *ton* gets a look at you. He's a rare man, Miss Masters. Now lift your arms straight out, please."

Greens and blues and golds. Absently, Lily lifted her arms; Madame Marceau snaked the tape about her limbs.

"Please do not move, Miss Masters, or I may inadvertently stick you with a pin."

Lily would have welcomed a pin stick. Anything to shake her from the peculiar torpor brought on by all this thinking about Gideon Cole.

"Turn toward me, my dear. And do hold still."

And Lily, who two days ago had taken orders from no one, turned and allowed Madame Marceau to take her measurements. Because, God help her, she *wanted* to be dressed in greens and blues and golds.

* * *

Bloody hell, where again was the ballroom? Lily began to run, but then remembered a lady wasn't *supposed* to run, and slowed her pace. Her slippers clacked a guilty tattoo across the marble: *I'm late, I'm late, I'm late, I'm late.*

Triumph! She finally found the ballroom, and it was only five minutes past the hour. Gideon and Lord Kilmartin were standing in the center of it, their heads, one dark and one fair, close together, quietly conversing. The addition of Gregson the footman, Mrs. Plunkett, and Molly the kitchen maid, clustered warily together, expressions studiedly bland, was a bit of a surprise, however.

Gideon looked up. "Miss Masters, so glad you could join us." He glanced pointedly down at the very watch she had attempted to relieve him of a few days earlier, and gave a low sardonic bow.

I'm only late by five bloody minutes, you tyrant. "The pleasure is mine, Mr. Cole." She looked back at him evenly. There was a silence. "Oh," she mumbled, remembering to curtsy.

The corner of his mouth twitched; he was suppressing a smile.

"I've something for you, Mr. Cole." She jingled the three pounds freshly won from Lord Lindsey in her palm. Gideon took it and pocketed it without question, just as though they were merchant and customer.

"I see my uncle allowed you to win yet again."

"*Allowed?*"

Gideon smiled crookedly, pleased at her indignation.

"Fifteen pounds to go, Mr. Cole," she said, almost but not quite under her breath.

He ignored her. "We thought we'd begin with reels and quadrilles, Miss Masters, since they are more complex. In a few days, we will address the waltz. Mr. Gregson, Mrs.

Plunkett, and Molly have graciously consented to participate in your lessons."

Gregson, Lily thought, didn't *quite* look gracious. He was *struggling* to look gracious. But he'd probably had as much choice as she did in the matter.

"Kilmartin will accompany us on the pianoforte. He's quite talented in that regard, though you wouldn't guess it to look at him."

"Damned with faint praise," Kilmartin acknowledged cheerfully, taking his seat at the instrument.

Lily glanced over at the pianoforte, and a bittersweet memory flared: she was a little girl, seated at a pianoforte, feet dangling, picking out a simple tune. Mama stood over her smiling proudly.

Stop it, she told herself sternly. There was even less point in reviewing the past than there was in living in the future. *There is only today.*

She looked away from the pianoforte and with a start found Gideon's eyes on her, simply watching. Again. As though he somehow knew she'd been paying a visit to her past, and was patiently waiting for her to return.

"Now, reels, Miss Masters," he began, strolling toward the center of the floor and beckoning for her to follow, "are comprised of a series of figures, or movements, performed by the dancers. For example, the figures might be comprised of a spin, or a few steps forward and back again, or a slide. The variations are, in fact, almost infinite. We will also learn the Sir Roger de Coverley."

Lord, but the man's trousers fit him beautifully. They were a soft fawn color, snug all the way down until they disappeared into the tops of his tall gleaming boots. It was a pleasure to watch his long legs stride across the room, even if his intent was to lecture.

"Miss Masters, are you paying attention?" Did the bloody man sound *amused,* or was she imagining it?

"The Sir . . . who?"

"The Sir Roger de Coverley. It's a dance that typically ends dances and balls, and you will most definitely need to know it."

"And what," Lily asked politely, "is the point of the dances?"

Gideon frowned a little. "The 'point,' Miss Masters?"

"Yes." Lily was puzzled by his puzzlement. "Why do you do them? Why are they important?"

Gideon looked bemused. "There isn't a 'why' to them, really. It is simply what one does."

"When one is a member of the *ton*, as you say."

"Yes."

Lily brightened in comprehension. "Perhaps it is like peacocks."

"Peacocks, Miss Masters?"

"Peacocks do a sort of dance for each other before they mate. Fan their feathers, that sort of thing."

The hush that fell over the ballroom was almost tangible. Confused, Lily swiveled her head toward the servants, who were gazing at her in mute, appalled fascination.

Kilmartin ended the silence with a burst of laughter. "Oh, I think you have the right of it, Lily! Peacocks, all of us. And most particularly Lady Constance Clary."

She turned to Gideon, bloody Gideon, who was studying her again. His expression was peculiar; a struggle between laughter and lecture and . . . something softer she couldn't quite identify.

"Miss Masters, you needn't concern yourself with the *why* of it," he finally said gently. "You merely need concern yourself with the *how* of it. Reels and quadrilles are considered great fun."

"Do *you* enjoy them, Mr. Cole?"

Gideon opened his mouth, and then closed it again and frowned.

"You *do* seem to spend rather a lot of time doing things you do not enjoy," Lily muttered.

Gideon paused as though he intended to respond, but then he turned to Kilmartin abruptly. "All right, then, Laurie."

It was an order for the music to start. Kilmartin bent to the task; a jaunty tune sprang into the room, and Mrs. Plunkett, Gregson, Gideon, and Molly the maid bowed, curtsied, and then marched across the smooth honey-colored floor toward each other. *Stomp, stomp, stomp.*

And then they marched back away from each other again.

Grim as soldiers, they marched forward, looped arms with the person across from them, and swung each other about. And then they backed away from each other, and stomped forward and—

They did it all again.

Good God, but it was silly. Gideon's face was a study in stoicism, a man enduring penance. And the contrast of Gregson's dour face and the jaunty music . . .

Well, suffice it to say, aspects of her education were proving to be extraordinarily entertaining.

But much to her surprise, the music had set her foot to tapping. And after a few bars Lily conceded that . . . well, perhaps she wouldn't mind learning a reel. It would probably be preferable, anyhow, to counting the colors in Gideon Cole's hair as the ballroom light played over it, or watching his broad shoulders move beneath his coat as he spun Molly around . . . lucky Molly . . .

The music ended and the man in question finally stepped out of the reel formation, looking relieved to have gotten it over with. Lily did not miss the look of longing Molly favored upon him as he strolled toward Kilmartin.

"Do you think you can follow the dance now, Miss Masters?"

And then he saw the expression on Lily's face. "You're not going to say five pounds, are you, Miss Masters?"

"I was going to wager three, but now that you've mentioned it . . ."

Gideon cocked his head speculatively. "You cannot wager over *everything*, Miss Masters. You *are* in my debt."

"But you, Mr. Cole, appear to be a wagering man."

He paused again, as though wondering about this. "I suppose I am," he agreed equably, sounding half amused. "Let's make it interesting, shall we? Five if you do it perfectly—I do mean *perfectly*—the first time."

"And if I do not?"

"We add three pounds *back* into your debt."

"Oooh . . ." Lily breathed in admiration. She gave it a second's thought. But she of course couldn't resist the terms. "Very well, Mr. Cole."

She moved to take Gideon's place in the little foursome, Gideon signaled to Kilmartin, and the jaunty tune started up again.

Lily promptly bowed when she should have curtsied and clonked her head against Gregson's smooth pate. *Bloody hell.* Just like that, she'd lost three pounds.

She rubbed her forehead and kept moving; over the music, she heard Kilmartin and Gideon laughing, the beasts. Thankfully, apart from looking slightly put-upon, Gregson seemed entirely unaffected. His skull was probably a good deal thicker than her own.

She gamely went on to execute the rest of the reel *perfectly.*

Well, perfectly, with one or two exceptions, where she inadvertently invented her own dance steps, surprising Gregson yet again. Still, it had all come right in the end.

When the tune ended, Gideon signaled for the dancers to do it again from the beginning. Kilmartin gamely bent his blond head over the keys, and the tune, which Lily was now sure would haunt her in her sleep, started up again.

Lily noticed Gideon watching her, his eyes almost never leaving her, his lips curved in a slight smile, as she curtsied and stepped, her big dress lashing her ankles as she spun. *Glad* he's *enjoying this.* But his watching eyes made her aware, yet again, of wanting to impress him, of wanting to show him how little challenge a silly reel presented to someone from St. Giles. So she put a little extra flourish into her next spin.

Unfortunately, the extra flourish sent her heavy dress whipping a little too violently about her ankles, which knocked her sideways into Mrs. Plunkett, who then collided with Molly, who collided with Gregson, until all of the dancers were ricocheting off one another like billiard balls. Thankfully, Mrs. Plunkett provided a rather soft place to collide; Gregson's bony frame offered considerably less give.

More hearty laughter floated Lily's way from over near the pianoforte. *Beastly men.*

But the dancers got it all sorted out again. And by God, by the third time they performed the reel—it took a little while for Kilmartin to recover his composure enough to play the song again—Lily had forgotten Gideon Cole was watching her at all and was thoroughly enjoying herself. She was almost sorry when the music crashed to its third, strident, cheerful finish.

It was then that Gideon held up a hand.

"Thank you, Gregson, Mrs. Plunkett, Molly. We will likely call upon your services yet again, but for now, you may return to your duties."

Poor Gregson looked as though he considered Gideon's words a threat, but Mrs. Plunkett and Molly looked ruddy and almost pleased about their impromptu exercise. The servants bowed and curtsied and exited the room in a hasty yet orderly fashion.

Gideon turned to Lily. "Not a bad showing for your first dancing lesson, Miss Masters. You only trod upon poor Gregson twice. And was that a new dance you were inventing? Very bold of you."

He was teasing her; the light in his eyes told her that. "Perhaps I *shall* invent a new dance," she said airily. "Does Lady Constance Clary invent her own dances?"

Gideon paused. "When Lady Constance Clary dances, no one can take their eyes from her."

It wasn't an answer. It was more like an *ode*. Kilmartin, bless him, snorted from the pianoforte bench.

"Thankfully, Miss Masters, you will have more opportunities to practice," Gideon continued, ignoring Kilmartin.

"Oh, *thankfully*." The words came out a trifle more acerbic than she had intended.

Gideon studied her, and she wondered for a moment if she'd made him angry; he looked as though he was struggling with something, or several somethings.

"Gratitude," he said softly, finally, "*is* an appealing quality in a young lady."

"You should be careful, Mr. Cole," she retorted. "You may surprise everyone and actually be amusing one day."

Kilmartin laughed again. It *was* truly lovely to be appreciated by Lord Kilmartin.

But Gideon didn't laugh. Instead, a fleeting expression—could it actually be *admiration*?—illuminated his face.

"Eighteen pounds, Miss Masters," was all he said. "We shall see you at dinner."

"Lily, Lily, Lily!" Alice burst into their chambers and lunged in for a hard hug.

Lily laughed and closed her arms over her sister. She had done this hundreds of times before, but today the sensation was oddly disorienting: Alice didn't feel or smell like Alice anymore. Her fine little borrowed dress was still warm from the sun, and she smelled of soap and the outdoors, grass and earth and sweaty little girl. Whereas in St. Giles, Alice often spent most of her days indoors and smelled of . . . well, truthfully, as did Lily, Alice usually smelled of St. Giles.

Lily felt something hard digging into her hip. She put her hands on Alice's shoulders and moved her back a little, and discovered it was the tiny porcelain fist of a doll Alice was clutching by the arm. The doll was missing most of its hair, and what was left seemed to have a tenuous grip on its scalp.

"Alice, where on earth did you get a doll?"

"Oh! This is Zebra." Alice stood back from Lily and cradled the doll in her arms.

"It's a doll, Alice. Not a zebra."

"No, that's her *name*. Like in our big book of animals. I thought it was pretty."

"Oh. You're right, of course. It *is* a pretty name. So how did you come to own Zebra?"

"Mr. Cole sent for her."

Lily went rigid. "He sent for her? What do you mean?"

"Mrs. Plunkett told me he sent word to a neighbor about

a little girl who needed a doll, and they sent over Zebra. Isn't she *beautiful*? I took her gardening this morning. With Boone. We only got a little dirty."

Boone, Mrs. Plunkett, Mr. Cole, the garden, the peacocks . . . Alice's world was expanding; her natural exuberance, reined in of necessity by the dangers of St. Giles, had room to stretch here, to bloom.

"She's . . . yes, she's lovely. Zebra is lovely."

And Lily suddenly found it difficult to breathe. A memory came to her: she was a little girl, standing on the seashore hand in hand with her mother, watching waves lick closer, and closer, and closer to her toes. And her mother had explained how the waves had shaped the cliffs in just this way, with these little relentless licks.

And as long as she stayed here, Lily suspected she would have about as much choice in the matter as the cliffs had: Gideon Cole would reshape her defenses, erode them away. She resented this softening; it felt a little too much like hope. And hope—the Mr. Darcy, little-French-book kind of hope—threatened her pride, for she knew it was simply ridiculous where she was concerned. The man was kind; the man was beautiful; the man intended to marry the daughter of a marquis.

Never put yourself at the mercy of a man, Lily.

Lily had never dreamt her imagination could be as much enemy as friend.

A tap sounded at the door; it could only be Mrs. Plunkett.

"Miss Masters, you are invited to join Mr. Cole and Lord Kilmartin for dinner," the housekeeper told her. "Miss Alice will eat with the staff in the kitchen. I shall take her."

Alice now took Mrs. Plunkett's hand as naturally as if it were Lily's, and Lily fought a little surge of jealousy toward the housekeeper. *Unworthy of me,* she thought. Alice *knew* their stay here was only temporary, yet Lily feared she was becoming too accustomed to the wonder that was Aster Park, and would grieve for it when they left. And witnessing Alice's grief would be painful.

Eighteen more pounds, and she could be herself again. Her days, her life, would be her own once more, full of risk and danger, but her own, and blissfully simple and straightforward.

Though she might just regret not getting a look at herself in greens and blues and golds.

"Thank you, Mrs. Plunkett." Lily wasn't sure whether she should curtsy to the housekeeper or not, but she did it anyway. Surely Mrs. Plunkett deserved a curtsy for enduring Mr. Cole all these years.

"Perhaps the first thing you must understand, Miss Masters," Gideon told Lily gently when her chair was pushed up to the table, "is that food in the *ton* is obscenely plentiful. You can heap your plate and clean it, and heap your plate and clean it . . . and still there will be more. A hostess is judged upon the quality of her table, and will do her best to make sure her guests stagger away from it twice as big as they were before they sat down."

Lily's expression flickered from disbelief to wonder to defensiveness as he spoke, and her cheeks went a little pink and her chin rose to its usual defiant angle as full understanding dawned: he was telling her she should not dive into her plate like a gull upon a fish.

Gideon couldn't bear to watch her discomfort; no one should feel ashamed for having been hungry much of the time. He hurriedly continued.

"And though in many circumstances it makes sense to eat

as quickly as possible, in the *ton* eating is considered a leisure activity; an opportunity to make pleasant conversation with your neighbor at the table. In fact, as absurd as this sounds, it is considered good form to leave a little on your plate."

Lily silently took this in, fidgeting a little with the snowy napkin folded at her setting; he watched the hectic color fade from her cheeks as her pride settled back into place. No doubt she was silently ascribing this behavior to the general peculiarities of the *ton*.

Kilmartin was regarding Gideon with faint interest, too. "Never quite thought of it that way, Gideon."

"I have," Gideon remarked shortly. "Now, Miss Masters, the fashion in the *ton* is to serve yourself from the platters on the table. On occasion, the servants will do the honors, as they do here at Aster Park. There is no way of knowing how many dinner parties we will actually attend, but no doubt there will be at least one attended or hosted by Lady Constance Clary. And odds are you will be exposed to a good many kinds of rich food."

Lily glanced up suddenly and smiled impishly. "That doesn't sound like much of a hardship."

His mind turned to pottage. Those sudden smiles of hers were as dangerous as flying cannonballs.

"Perhaps Miss Masters should practice serving herself, then?" Kilmartin suggested into the dumb silence that followed.

Gideon cleared his throat. "Very well, then. We shall begin with the meat. Allow yourself a slice or two at a time, Miss Masters," he guided, "and employ leisurely movements."

The table was set with numerous gleaming dishes, and Lily reached—or more accurately, lunged—for the silver serving fork resting on the platter of sliced roast of beef.

Gideon stifled a sigh. *Fast* seemed Lily's sole speed; she wasn't without grace, but her grace was like that of a hummingbird; all economy and purpose of movement. Honed through picking pockets and fleeing, no doubt.

"Slowly, Miss Masters, as you reach . . . and don't dangle your sleeve through the candle, as it is considered bad form to go up in flames at a dinner party."

She giggled. An enchanting, genuine, entirely unexpected sound. And suddenly Gideon wanted to make her do it again, and then again, the way one wanted to hear a lovely piece of music over and over. "You remind me a little of Dodge, Miss Masters," he teased.

"Dodge?"

"The solicitor who dogs me. Little man, quick as a sparrow. Foists these cases upon me that I cannot refuse to—"

Gideon stopped. What was he *doing*? Certainly he'd never discussed Mr. Dodge with Constance; he could easily imagine her confusion if he were to bring the subject up: *Why does Gideon want to bore me?*

But Lily was waiting, her head tilted in curiosity. "What does he look like, Mr. Dodge?"

Gideon hesitated. It was seductive, the interest he saw in her eyes. He was certain Lily Masters saw a world populated with characters, and Mr. Dodge was most certainly a character. He surrendered to the urge to talk about him. "Little chap, bald, the brightest blue eyes you've ever seen. He looks like a pigeon, too, round on top and twiggy on the bottom."

Lily laughed, pleased with the vivid description; her eyes had gone a little abstracted, as though she were forming a picture of Mr. Dodge in her mind. And suddenly this mundane part of Gideon's world took on color and light.

"And why do I remind you of him?" she asked.

"Oh, I suppose because he's a quick devil. Moves like you do. I never can dodge him, you see; he always manages to catch up to me."

"So his name is perfect for him!" Lily looked pleased by this.

"I suppose so."

They smiled at each other, easy smiles, momentarily engrossed in the simple story.

"Like my parents," Kilmartin remarked idly.

"What's that, Laurie?" Gideon turned his smile toward his friend.

"The two of you rather reminded me of my parents just then. Father would talk about business, Mother would ask questions, they'd laugh . . . quite nice, really." He sounded wistful.

Gideon's smile froze in place, and he stared at Kilmartin mutely, uncertain as to why he should feel . . .

Caught.

"Roast beef, Gideon?" Laurie asked mildly. He pushed the platter toward him.

Alice was snoring softly next to her, her grubby little doll clutched in her arms. But Lily could not sleep. She was a little too full of roast beef, a little too tired of being required to move sedately, and the silence of the house enclosed her like a great bell jar.

Perhaps she could light a candle and read?

What she really wanted to do was run, expend her bottled energy. She was unaccustomed to confinement; it chafed at her, banked her restlessness. She smiled a little, picturing how the servants would react if they were to discover Miss Lily Masters, Lord Kilmartin's cousin from Sussex, racing through the hallways in her big dressing gown. Would an actual emotion register on Mrs. Plunkett's face?

She slipped out of bed, wrapped herself in her borrowed night robe, and lit a candle. Cupping the flame with one hand, she turned the chamber doorknob, slipped out, and padded silently and swiftly up the stairs to the library, the marble sending little rivers of chill up her legs through her bare feet.

She peered in; a fire was burning low there, throwing soft light and odd, uneven shadows about the room. Surely this was wrong; surely a servant should have doused the fire by now? She hesitated in the doorway, listening. She heard nothing, so she took a step in.

She saw him then. His long body filled a chair, his legs casually spread, his hands cupping a small red book; he seemed absorbed in it. In a nod to comfort, his shirt was open a button or two at the neck; dark hair curled intriguingly up out of it. The firelight burnished his skin, deepened the hollows of his cheeks, revealed red glints in his lashes, much like the ones hiding in his hair.

Even in repose, there was something taut and expectant, perpetually vigilant, about Gideon Cole. It made Lily want to murmur to him, the way you might to a restive animal. A rain of awareness washed her senses almost raw. *How could anyone or anything be so beautiful?*

And then Gideon glanced up and saw her. He went utterly still.

Their eyes held for an almost absurd length of time, but strangely, it was not the least bit awkward; his face, in fact, reflected the same gentle mystification she felt.

And then, as if shaking himself from a dream, Gideon began to rise to his feet.

"Miss Masters—"

"Oh, please do not stand, Mr. Cole," she stammered. "I am sorry to disturb you. I'll just go back to my—"

"No," Gideon said quickly. "That is to say, don't go, Miss Masters. That is to say, you *needn't* go."

Lily paused. If she didn't know better, she would have said that Gideon Cole was *flustered.*

He sat down again and closed the book he was reading, turning it over in his lap. "There's very little of any value in this library, Miss Masters. You might perhaps try my uncle's study. There's some gold plate lying about, I believe."

"You don't consider books of value, Mr. Cole?"

"Some of them, yes." He paused, regarding her thoughtfully. "You enjoy stories very much, don't you, Miss Masters? Reading them, telling them?"

"Yes."

"Why do you suppose that is?"

"Well, very likely because they are amusing, Mr. Cole."

Gideon regarded her silently for a moment. "Do you know why *I* read stories?" His words were gently ironic. As though her answer had disappointed him. "*I* read them to escape the sordid, everyday difficulties of my life. To make it more . . . bearable."

Lily gave a shocked little intake of breath, and her face went swiftly hot. Was he *mocking* her?

When she spoke again, her voice was cold and formal, signaling her intent to take command of their conversation. It shook a little, however, and she cursed herself and him for it. "Mr. Cole, now that I am here, I would like to speak to you about Alice."

"Alice is delightful."

"Yes, she is. You arranged for her to have a doll."

"Are you jealous, Miss Masters? Would you like one, too?"

"Very amusing, Mr. Cole. I grant that it was kind of you to think of Alice. But she may become accustomed to such luxuries, and as you know, her life in St. Giles does not allow for them."

Again he studied her quietly with those unfathomable eyes; she grew apprehensive. And his next words, gentle though they sounded, stripped yet another layer from her.

"Does the issue lie, Miss Masters, in the fact that *you* cannot give her those things?"

Lily's breathing quickened with something akin to panic. *He's probably a bloody good barrister.*

"We were happy, Mr. Cole," she hissed. "Alice and I were doing quite well before you and your bloody thirty pounds."

"Oh, yes. *Quite* well," he repeated cynically. "What if something befell you in your 'daily rounds,' Miss Masters? What if I hadn't happened along when I did? What of Alice? Do you *care*?"

It was as though he had landed his fist in her gut. But before she could give vent to her fury, he surprised her.

"I apologize, Miss Masters." His voice carried a soft self-rebuke, and his hand went up to rub his brow absently, as though he wished he could erase the thoughts that had led to his words. "Truly. That was unworthy of me. I know how deeply you care for your sister. In fact, you should be congratulated on how well she has turned out. I just . . . I just want you to see that you should give some thought to your future. Not everyone who catches you will pay thirty pounds to free you."

It was not condescension, precisely, but Lily found it infuriating nevertheless.

"The future, Mr. Cole? You can plan all you like, but *no one* can truly prepare for the future. Not even you. *Despite* your desperate measures and your Master Plan and your bloody thirty pounds."

His expression changed then, his features tightened; her words had struck home. His lovely long fingers restlessly plucked at the arm of the chair.

"And why," she added, near tears, which infuriated her further, "do *you* care?"

A log, nearly devoured by flame, tipped into the lowering fire. Lily's bare feet once again felt the chill of the floor; she absently chafed one against the other.

And the silence stretched.

Gideon shifted restless in his chair, took in a deep steadying breath, released it. "I'm not sure why I care, Miss Masters," he admitted softly. He sounded genuinely puzzled. "But I do."

And then he smiled. It really wasn't much more than a rueful, self-mocking lift of the corner of his mouth, but there was a hint of vulnerability in it. And God help her, that smile spiraled right around Lily's heart and tugged it nearly clean out of her chest.

Her anger evaporated. Lily studied him, and he met her gaze evenly; her heart tripped. Something was taking shape between them; it was like hovering on the threshold of a dark room, in that moment before your eyes adjust and the outlines of things become clear. She was afraid to say anything more, to step any farther into that room, for fear of crashing clumsily into something.

I could walk into his eyes, she thought. *Happily disappear right into them.*

Gideon cleared his throat, as though he wanted to speak before she could say anything. "What sort of book were you after, Miss Masters? Perhaps I can direct you to it."

"Oh!" His solicitousness on the heels of her thoughts made her blush. "Would that be . . . would that be all right?"

"'Tis a library, after all." He sounded faintly amused. "Are you fond of novels? Or perhaps of . . ." He faltered almost imperceptibly. "Of . . . of poetry?".

Odd. It was as though he feared he was making some sort of prurient suggestion.

"I don't know much of poetry. Though I've a book of Shakespeare's works."

Gideon smiled faintly, and then he tilted his head back, his eyes on the shadowy ceiling; the firelight gilding his throat. " '*The sun's a thief, and with his great attraction, robs the vast sea* . . .' " he murmured.

Lily's heart gave an astonished kick. Hearing those familiar words in this place, in his voice . . . She waited. But he didn't seem inclined to continue.

" '. . . *The moon's an arrant thief, and her pale fire she snatches from the sun* . . .' " she encouraged softly. She could have recited the rest to him, but she wanted to hear it in his voice.

Instead Gideon slowly lowered his head and regarded her wonderingly. "You know it."

Lily nodded.

"It's beautiful," Gideon admitted after a brief silence. He sounded almost . . . shy.

Lily hated to ruin the moment for him, but she couldn't resist an opportunity to make a point. "And it's all about how everything is a *thief*."

Startled, Gideon laughed, and she laughed, too, because she couldn't help it: he had a wonderful laugh. It was full of the boy he must have been, and she wished he didn't ration it the way he seemed to. Their eyes met again; faint smiles curved both of their mouths, and Lily could think of nothing to say.

And then, as if freed by the laughter and darkness and firelight, Gideon's gaze began, gradually, to lower. It followed the length of Lily's bare throat, went to the loosed hair spilling over her chest, dropped to her waist, where a cord wrapped twice around her closed her robe. Slowly, slowly, his eyes traveled the curve of her hips, down her thighs, down her calves, to where her bare feet touched the floor. A most deliberate and thorough and unsubtle perusal.

And as surely as if his open hand were skimming over her bare skin, gooseflesh rose beneath Lily's robe; her skin felt stung with heat, her breath came short. Again, that sense of lamplight blooming below her belly, fanning out in her veins.

And he was only *looking* at her.

I'm out of my depth with this man.

He'd pulled at her like a swift current from the moment he'd locked his hand around her wrist on Bond Street. And Gideon Cole was not a Nick, who could be kissed out of curiosity and pushed away and forgotten. If Gideon Cole were to deign to reach for her now, she knew there would be no knees or elbows. She would come to him. And promptly be swept under. It was terrifying, really, how quickly pride and reason had deferred to the urges of her body.

Gideon returned his eyes to her face, his expression again decidedly unreadable. And now Lily understood: Gideon Cole's thoughts were most active when his expression was least readable.

There was a story in her French book: a man and a woman made love as they watched one another in a mirror, mindless with pleasure. And Lily thought . . . *I would love to see Gideon Cole's face when he makes love . . . to be the person who makes his eyes change . . . who makes him lose himself in pleasure. . . .*

Gideon drew in a long breath. "Miss Masters. I think you should return to your chambers now."

His tone acknowledged a danger to them both.

And wordlessly, in silent agreement, Lily spun about and padded quickly out of the library.

Chapter Eight

When Lily finally slept, strange dreams beset her: Gideon Cole was preparing potions behind McBride's counter while Lily attempted to sell him his own watch: "Five shillings," she demanded of him. He smiled at her; one of his teeth was missing. "Give us a kiss, luv," the dream Gideon purred. She was just leaning forward to oblige him when—

"Lily, wake up!" Alice was tugging at her arm, and Mrs. Plunkett was tapping at the door. Groggily, Lily pushed her limbs into her robe and staggered to the door.

Mrs. Plunkett was on the other side of it, and, wordlessly, the housekeeper handed over a tray of breakfast, a note . . . and an intriguing paper-wrapped bundle. Lily looked up into her face quizzically, but if she thought she'd find any clues there, she was sadly mistaken.

The housekeeper led a skipping Miss Alice away, and Lily tucked her hair behind her ear and sat down on the bed to read her note.

LM—Here is your schedule for the day:

10:00	*Deportment*
11:30	*Conversation*
1:00	*Picnic*

A picnic?

3:00	*Cards with Lord Lindsey*
4:30	*Dancing*
6:00	*Dining*

Yes, Miss Masters, you will accompany me on a picnic. You will learn today that some people do walk simply for the pleasure of it.—GC

P.S. Do be careful, or Willoughby may replace Mr. Darcy in your dreams.

Her heart tripping oddly, Lily tore open the paper to discover a book and . . . a pair of thick, soft, wool . . . stockings?

Sense and Sensibility, the book was called. By the same author who had brought Mr. Darcy into her life. And Lily smiled slowly, a lovely warmth heating her cheeks.

But . . . stockings?

And then she recalled: last night, in the library—she had attempted to warm her feet by rubbing one against the other.

He sees everything.

And all at once, elation and a delicious, tingling sort of terror made a wishbone of her, and the book and stockings might well have been rubies for how she felt about them. Two gifts. Two unmistakable, no doubt deliberate, reminders of a few minutes of intimacy shared in a firelit library. Could it be, for the first time in her life, she was being . . . wooed?

To what purpose?

Lily was not entirely naïve: she *did* know that gentlemen did not take proper young ladies on picnics unchaperoned. But perhaps gentlemen took *pickpockets* on picnics.

And what, then, did gentlemen do?

In truth, though her mother would hardly approve, she couldn't wait to find out.

Kilmartin had risen late, so Gideon decided to breakfast alone, attended by nothing but the clear morning sunlight flooding into the dining room, the near-silent to-ing and fro-ing of servants, and the pleasant hum of his thoughts. A small stack of correspondence lay next to his plate; the handwriting on one letter made him tear it open immediately.

I must confess I'm now a little afraid, Gideon, it said. *But please don't say anything to Uncle Edward. I'm sure everything will be all right.*

A cold hand closed over Gideon's heart.

Of course, in the way of all the Cole women—of all Coles, with their accursed pride and mordant humor—she'd concluded, *Then again, if I can endure you, I suppose I can endure anyone.*

It was signed, *Yours affectionately, Helen.*

Her letters had contained hints over the past few months, hints only a brother could interpret. He'd had suspicions ever since his last visit to her; he'd never voiced them to a soul, not even to Kilmartin.

But not once, not even when she was a child, had Helen admitted to being frightened. Of *anything*.

It was an affliction, the Cole family pride. It had enabled

Helen and his mother to keep their heads up when their fortunes came crashing ignominiously down; it prevented Helen and Gideon from ever asking for help.

But now . . . an urgency pressed down on Gideon's chest. *Perhaps I'll come when you have your own home, Gideon,* Helen had told him last time he saw her. *But I don't think I can face Uncle Edward.*

He placed his fork neatly next to his plate; his appetite had fled. *I'm trying, Helen.* The letter drooped in his hand; he stared unseeingly over the dining room table.

What kind of man was he if he couldn't protect the people he loved?

10:00 Deportment

"No, no, *no*." Gideon Cole seemed infected with urgency this morning; he paced the plush little blue room like a tiger incredulous at being caged. "Take smaller steps, Miss Masters. Stand upright, but not *bolt* upright. And please, *please* do something about that chin. You look as though you intend to throw your fists, or spit."

Lily paused amidst the sea of blue and stared at him with astonishment, resentment burgeoning. What on *earth* had happened to the soft-eyed man who'd spouted poetry and undressed her thoroughly with his eyes and sent her stockings and a book? Perhaps she *had* dreamed him. Nothing about Gideon's demeanor this morning suggested he'd be receptive to thanks for his gifts, or to any kind of acknowledgment of . . . whatever it was that had begun in the library. He was remote and impatient and infuriatingly focused on the matter at hand.

"Perhaps we should put a book on her head?" Kilmartin suggested. "It worked for my sister."

"I know where *I'd* like to put a bloody book," Lily said meaningfully.

Gideon's sense of whimsy was conspicuously absent today. "And it's *that*, Miss Masters. That's precisely the sort of thing you must *never* say. Need I remind you of our mission and your *eighteen-pound* debt? Lady Constance Clary is a lady personified; your demeanor absolutely must not excite comment, unless it is of the complimentary sort."

Kilmartin eyed Gideon critically from his perch on the settee. "Gideon, you seem to be in a . . . mood."

Gideon stopped pacing for a moment and took a deep breath; he dropped his head briefly and exhaled. When he lifted his face again, some of the tension had left it. "Please forgive me." The words were stiff but sincere. "There's much on my mind." He included Lily in the apology with a sweep of his dark eyes.

"Work and Constance," Kilmartin guessed.

Gideon paused. "Of course. Work and Constance."

No, it's something else, Lily thought suddenly, with a pang of intrigue. That little pause, the almost imperceptible tightening of his features, told her that. *Something else is troubling him.*

"Miss Masters," Gideon continued in a more reasonable tone, turning to her, "we are no longer disputing that you were . . . shall we say . . . gently reared. But you seem to have acquired a habit of using . . . certain words and . . . well, *expressions* . . . and these will quite expose you as a fraud if you use them in the *ton*. A well-bred young lady would not use these words—certainly, Lady Constance Clary doesn't use these words—and they would not slip out of her even if a cannonball were dropped upon her toe."

"Barnacle scraping time," Kilmartin said cheerily.

"Certain words, Mr. Cole?" Lily's expression went

somber and she cast her gaze heavenward, as though considering the concept. "Do you mean, I should not say, for example, 'Mr. Cole, you are a bloody whoreson'?" She turned wide eager eyes on him, as though seeking approbation.

From somewhere behind Gideon, the settee creaked as Kilmartin shifted uneasily.

"Or . . ." Lily continued musingly, when Gideon remained ominously silent, "perhaps I should not say, 'Mr. Cole, you're a tyrannical bast—' "

"Miss Masters?" Gideon's voice was mild.

"Yes, Mr. Cole?"

"Are you quite through?"

She sighed. "I suppose so."

But he was smiling a little now. And Lily realized that she had been trying to make him smile, to soften that taut expression on his face.

"Close your mouth, Kilmartin," Gideon added. Behind him, Kilmartin clapped his dropped jaw shut.

"See what you've done to poor Kilmartin, Miss Masters? You've quite shocked him speechless."

"Those words come in useful in St. Giles," she muttered.

"And you must never, never, *never* men—"

"—tion St. Giles. All right, all right, *all right*. What *does* one do if a cannonball drops upon one's toe?"

"Scream?" Kilmartin suggested from the depths of the settee. "Yes, perhaps a scream, just a scream."

And suddenly, Lily was a little tempted to test the appropriateness of a "scream, just a scream." And damned if Gideon's eyes weren't now glinting with amusement, as though her thoughts were written all over her face.

"If you feel a temptation to use the word 'bloody,' Miss Masters, might I suggest you replace it with the word 'goodness'?"

"Hasn't quite the same punch as 'bloody,' I know," Kilmartin commiserated with her. "But it's what's required of young ladies."

Lily was beginning to feel a reluctant sympathy for all the young ladies of the *ton*. Perhaps she should start a fashion in *swearing*.

11:30 Conversation

Analysis of the word "bloody" quite naturally led to the conversation lesson. The three of them remained in the blue room, Mrs. Plunkett brought in some tea, and Kilmartin only put up a token struggle when he was requested once again to perform the part of Lady Constance Clary. Lily suspected he was perversely enjoying lampooning the woman. Gideon, it was understood, would once again play Lady Anne Clapham. It seemed only fair.

Lily doubted Lady Anne Clapham paced rooms as much as Gideon seemed to.

She took her seat next to Kilmartin on the settee. Her back straight but not too straight, her expression sweetly welcoming, she turned to him and prepared to be bemused yet again by the habits of the *ton*.

"Miss Masters, you must tell me something." Lord Kilmartin, aka Lady Clary, leaned toward Lily confidingly. "What do you think of Lady Clapham?"

Lily glanced at Gideon, aka Lady Clapham. "She is a perfect bast—"

"*Miss* Masters . . ." The two words from Gideon were a warning delivered on a sigh.

Lily bit back a smile and began again. "She's a decent sort."

Gideon held up a hand. "Miss Masters, when someone like Lady Clary asks you a question like that, the proper response is 'agreeable.' It is a safe word. A genteel word. A ladylike word. For if Lady Clary ever were to ask you such a question about Lady Clapham, she is fishing for gossip or hoping to lure you into saying something appalling she can repeat later, thus slurring both you *and* Lady Clapham."

"But that's perfectly awful." Lily was a little aghast.

"That's the *ton*," Gideon and Kilmartin said in unison.

"What if I can't abide Lady Clapham?"

"You will 'abide' everyone, Miss Masters. Which is how *you,* of course, will be quickly perceived as 'agreeable.'"

Lily was growing more and more convinced she could not "abide" Constance Clary.

"And furthermore," Kilmartin added a little haughtily, "*everyone* can abide Lady Anne Clapham."

"Yes, yes, Laurie," Gideon soothed. "She's lovely."

Lily was bewildered. "Does *no* one ever say precisely what they think?"

"It's *society*, Miss Masters," Kilmartin explained gently. "Imagine the chaos that would ensue if people actually said what they thought."

"But perhaps if you were to say what you thought in just the right way—"

"Miss Masters," Gideon interrupted. "You may say what you think, but never *all* of what you think. You may say, for example, 'I find *Pride and Prejudice* to be an excellent novel,' but you must *not* say, 'Mr. Darcy haunts my dreams at night and gives me fits of longing.'"

Kilmartin turned to Gideon, half incredulous, half amused.

Lily's cheeks had gone a little warm. "Mr. Darcy does *not* haunt my dreams." He *had*, in fact, on more than one occasion.

Gideon's crooked smile told her he suspected the truth. "Do you understand the difference, Miss Masters?"

She sighed, her shoulders slumping in acceptance. "I suppose so."

"And if ever you find yourself at a loss for something to say, simply look enigmatic. You will find your conversation partner so disconcerted that the topic will be changed in no time at all."

Kilmartin looked up at Gideon with another faintly amused expression. "Is that what *you* do, Gideon?"

"It works," Gideon said shortly. "Can you appear enigmatic, Miss Masters?"

As it turned out, Lily *could* appear enigmatic, though it didn't come naturally to her. It required, she discovered, that one look inward and think of something else. Lamb chops. Peacocks. *Dark eyes. A sensual mouth.* "Enigmatic," Lily thought, might just become a very useful strategy for enduring Gideon Cole. That unreadable look of his—he must have cultivated it to endure the *ton*. It seemed a suffocating way to live, burdened with layers of careful masks.

Kilmartin pushed himself upright and retrieved his watch from his pocket to review the time. "Well, Gideon, Miss Masters, as much as I am enjoying our lesson, I must go away to London for the rest of the day. I need to persuade Aunt Hester to be our hostess for our stay in the *ton* and to be Miss Masters's chaperone for the duration. And it will take some doing, I assure you."

"Your Aunt Hester? Wasn't she the Countess . . . something?"

"Yes, she is the dowager Countess Avery. She's about a hundred years old and irritable, just so you fully understand the sacrifices I make for you."

"It's much appreciated, Laurie." Gideon said it somberly. "Oh, admit it, your life would be dull otherwise."

Kilmartin bowed, and when he was upright again, he was smiling wryly. "I will see the two of you tomorrow midday, unless something untoward befalls me. Like Aunt Hester's cane."

1:00 Picnic

They convened for their picnic near the fountain, and Gideon took one look at Lily's wary expression and almost laughed. He could hardly blame her: He'd been decidedly charmless all morning.

"Miss Masters, you are going on a picnic, not to the gallows. Picnics are considered a pleasant way to pass the time."

Lily turned that expression up to him. "Very amusing, Mr. Cole. It seems to me that everything you do is 'considered' something. Nothing just . . . 'is.' "

Gideon was struck silent by the observation. She was right, he decided, with a mixture of irritation and amusement. Just about everything he did these days, from dancing to dinners to conversations, came wrapped in a carapace of duty and ambition.

And yet . . . *some people do walk for pleasure,* he'd told her with amused condescension, as if he were an expert on the subject. *Do* you, *Mr. Cole?* She'd wanted to know. Words thrown down like a gauntlet.

So he'd given it some thought. And if he was being honest, not even his first stroll through Aster Park's grounds with Constance could qualify as "pleasure": he'd awaited her judgment of the place the way he awaited a verdict in court, with the same heightened anticipation, the same sense of consequence.

To find a memory of walking for pure pleasure, he'd had to rifle through a decade of remembrances. But he did find one: the very first time he'd wandered over Aster Park's grounds.

It had been like . . . trespassing in Eden.

He hadn't yet become a *complete* prig. This picnic was evidence: Because he'd *known* Kilmartin would be away this afternoon. And like any healthy, normal young man who'd had the astonishing good fortune to find himself alone in a darkened library with a fetching, robe-clad young lady, Gideon had immediately conspired to get her alone again. After Lily spun on her heel and padded out of the library, he'd feverishly scrambled for a pen and foolscap so he could revise her agenda for the following day. And then he'd sent her gifts, for God's sake. He was grateful Mrs. Plunkett was the most impassive creature on earth; she hadn't even blinked when he'd requested stockings at dawn.

But this morning, at the very last minute, his sense of honor had reared up, and he felt faintly abashed by the feverish revision of the agenda and the gifts, the way one might after a night of drunken carousing. Not quite abashed enough to cancel the picnic *altogether*, however. So he'd asked Mrs. Plunkett to send Alice out to join them, too.

"Alice will be joining us," he told Lily.

"She will love a picnic," Lily said, though her face darkened subtly; was that the barest hint of disappointment? Gideon felt a very masculine surge of gratification.

Alice came bounding up a moment later, carrying a long knobby stick. Lily looped one affectionate arm around her sister. "Where did you get a stick, Alice?"

"It's a musket," Alice declared. "It will protect us from the wild boars in the park."

"Then I shall feel very safe," Gideon said somberly.

Alice gave him a pitying look. "It's not really a musket, Mr. Cole. It's a *stick*. I was *pretending*."

Gideon met Lily's eyes; they were dancing. "Oh, you're quite right, Miss Alice, I see that now. Perhaps I need spectacles."

"McBride wears spectacles," Alice volunteered.

"And who is McBride?" Alice would no doubt be a wonderful and unwitting source of information about Lily's life.

"We've a lovely lunch in the basket, Alice," Lily interrupted. "I think there may be some cakes."

Alice was immediately diverted by the topic of food. "I helped the cook with the cakes."

"You helped gobble them up, you mean," Gideon teased.

Alice giggled, and Gideon laughed, too. Sometimes there was nothing so purely rewarding as a ten-year-old girl's giggle.

He glanced at Lily again; he caught her eyes just as they were swiftly moving away from him, but he'd seen in them a hint of begrudging warmth.

"Shall we? We will walk to the edge of the park and have our picnic there. For *pleasure*, Miss Masters."

"As they do in the *ton*. As a lesson." It was a statement, but Lily's eyes held, as usual, a challenge.

"Why else?" He agreed airily.

He picked up the basket and took a step forward.

They walked across the green in silence for a minute or so, an oddly companionable silence, while Alice raced ahead and whacked things with her stick, or pretended to shoot at boar, or gleefully pursued the fluff of a blown dandelion as it sailed by, caught and tossed by the soft breeze. The sky was a rare brilliant blue, empty of clouds, and it was almost as though they were the only three people on earth.

Gideon would have thought Lily's gaze would be roaming the magnificent parklands, but she was staring steadfastly forward, instead, like an acrobat walking a tightrope.

Aster Park had been landscaped by Capability Brown himself, and the result was a masterful blend of serene order and the illusion of wildness. Neat stone pathways wound through calculated disarrays of flowers and thick, informal stands of old trees—beeches, oaks, maples, and chestnuts, many of them American varieties—and humble English flowers flourished everywhere, elevated to elegance by their thoughtful placement. Vast green expanses of lawn spilled like lakes between all of it.

Gideon had once known every inch of the park; he'd wandered over it discovering little universes within universes: a stone roughly the shape of a sleeping cat embedded in the walkway near the statuary; a grand old monster of an oak tree—reputedly a sapling when William the Conqueror set foot on English shores—that thrust up through the ground like a defiant fist; a secluded trickle of a stream that hosted dragonflies and hummingbirds and tall nodding lilies. And the practical things fascinated him, too: the flock of fat sheep—he could just see them now, if he squinted, looking like tiny blown dandelions in the distance —and the vast, fertile kitchen gardens, redolent of rich dirt and green leaves, which yielded enough vegetables and fruits to feed the denizens of the park and some of the neighboring town, as well. If he hadn't become a barrister who intended to become Chancellor of the Exchequer, he suspected he'd be perfectly happy being a farmer.

Great messy clumps, Constance had called those big American trees. Thanks to the impulsive purchase of a pickpocket's freedom, Aster Park—or rather, the *promise* of Aster Park—was about all he had to offer Constance now.

Aster Park, and his charming self.

He felt another rush of impatience. Bloody *impulse*. He wondered if Jarvis now owned that town house.

"And how is my walking, Mr. Cole?" Lily's ironic question cut through his thoughts.

He glanced at her. "Slightly better, Miss Masters. Although I imagine it would be difficult to bolt like a thief while trudging along grass in a long skirt."

"Oh, I could probably manage it." The words were idly disdainful. And then Lily slowed her pace thoughtfully. "In fact . . ."

She stopped walking altogether and turned resolutely to him. "Ten pounds, Mr. Cole."

"I beg your pardon?"

"Ten pounds says I can race you to that stand of trees . . ." She pointed to a cluster of beeches about fifty yards off . . . "and win." She turned back to him, all sangfroid and challenging upraised brows.

Gideon stared at her incredulously. "A *footrace*? Don't be absurd, Miss Masters. Ladies don't—"

"Afraid you will lose?" she sympathized sweetly. "Ah, well. I know how you would *hate* to lose." She shook her head regretfully and trudged forward again.

Gideon stayed rooted to the spot and stared toward the cluster of beeches, perched like a bouquet at the far edge of his vision. And the wildness he'd deliberately tamped into a stupor so long ago began to stir and kick at the walls of its pen.

There was no one about to see him.

Lily was still trudging forward, her hands clasped behind her, looking for all the world like a professor on his way to teach a class at Oxford. Gideon took three long steps to catch up to her.

"Which is precisely why I *won't* lose, Miss Masters."

She stopped again. They eyed each other in measuring, cocksure silence.

"So you'll wager ten pounds, Mr. Cole?"

"*Ten* pounds? Robbery! Five."

"Nine."

"Eight, and that's my final offer."

Another silence. A few yards away, Alice hurled her stick through the air like a javelin, and then trotted off to retrieve it.

And then, though he could hardly believe he was doing it, Gideon lowered the picnic basket to the ground. "On the count of three."

Lily's mouth went thin and determined. She kicked off her slippers and clutched her skirt in her hands, lifting it a little off her ankles, and Gideon shook himself out of his coat. He folded it carefully before placing it on the ground.

"One . . ." he drawled "Two . . . *three*!"

They bolted.

And it felt extraordinary.

Air ripped into his lungs; he pumped it out again, relishing the sensation. The wind raked his hair as he plunged through it, and in moments, the strictures, the concerns, of his life loosened and flew from him, until at last he was nothing more than a creature running for the pure joy of running.

Well, that and *winning*.

The beech trees were closer. He began to silently gloat, which he knew was unworthy of him, but he knew he was going to win this race. He risked a glance at Lily.

Aargh! *She was ahead of him!* Good God, but the girl ran like a wild thing, low to the ground and with utter abandon. Her ribbon came undone and twisted through the air, and the gold plume of her hair burst out behind her, like the tail on a comet.

No *girl* was going to best him in a footrace.

He stretched out his legs, eating up more ground, his boots thumping hard over the grass, but it was no use: he was out of practice, and she was born to it. He tried for one final burst of speed, but Lily reached the trees and touched one, and then bent to catch her breath, her delighted laughter ragged from her run.

And then she had the nerve to stand there and tap her foot until he loped up behind her and touched the same tree. To add insult to injury, Alice was already there, too, jumping up and down and clapping. God, that little girl must be able to leap like a flea.

"Hurrah for Lily!" he heard her exult over the low roar of his own panting.

"Lily is very quick," Alice added sympathetically, bending down to peer into his reddened face.

"And I've had a good deal more practice," Lily allowed. She wasn't even *breathing* hard anymore.

He glanced up from his doubled-over position. It was a shameful amount of time before he could speak. "Good . . . answer . . . Miss . . . Masters." Gideon wanted to drop to the ground and catch his breath; he would shoot himself before he would do that in front of her. "Very . . . gracious."

"And how much remains of my debt, Mr. Cole? Speak only when you can breathe again."

He tried to laugh, but he hadn't enough breath for it yet. Lily was red-cheeked and perspiring, her hair was a wild tangle, her smile brilliant. Enjoying her victory, but not to an intolerable degree, thankfully.

When Gideon's lungs felt slightly less like overworked bellows, he stood upright again. "I'd better fetch our basket," he told the girls, with some recovered dignity. He ambled, limping a little, back to where the picnic basket had been deserted. Along the way he spotted Lily's ribbon, a little sliver of gleam in the grass. He plucked it up and ran it thoughtfully between his fingers, enjoying the slide of satin; he was tempted to pocket it as a memento. He found her slippers, too, or rather, the overlarge pair loaned to her by Mrs. Plunkett, and collected his jacket, and limped back with all of them.

"It was because I was wearing boots," he explained when he returned.

"Oh, of course." Lily soothed. "That must be why you . . . *lost*." She grinned wickedly.

Her smile was more infectious than cholera. He grinned foolishly at her in return.

And then, as his breath and his senses returned fully, he began to *feel* foolish. It was impossible to imagine Constance red-faced and sweating from a headlong run; he imagined her expression if she could see the urbane Gideon Cole doubled-over from a *footrace* with a *girl*.

His face must have darkened, for he saw the light fade from Lily's eyes as well.

"I found your ribbon." He handed it to her. She took it from him and ran it through her own fingers thoughtfully, her face turned down so he could not see her expression. And then she wound it around her hair and tied it back. It didn't make her look any more like a lady.

Or any less appealing.

He handed her slippers to her, too; she dropped them to the ground and pushed her feet into them.

"Well, Mr. Cole. What do we do now?" Lily's tone was neutral again.

"Eat!" This came from Alice, and sounded more like a demand than a suggestion.

"Capital idea, Alice. Let's spread our blanket out now, shall we?" Gideon flipped open the picnic hamper and pulled out a folded square of blanket. He shook it open with a great flourish, and it landed on Alice's head, much to her delight. She made a great show of fighting her way out from underneath it, giggling, and Gideon laughed with her, because it was impossible not to, really.

Smiling again, Lily helped them straighten the blanket out on the ground, and thus cushioned by the blanket and canopied by the full greenness of beeches and oaks, Gideon unpacked the basket with great ceremony.

"And what have we here . . . ?" he mused, peering into the basket. "Oh! It's . . . good heavens, it's *cold chicken*!"

"Hurrah!" Alice approved, clapping.

"And next we have . . . could it be . . . it's *lemon seedcakes*!"

The girls were giggling now.

"And look at this . . . I can hardly believe our luck . . . it's *cheese*!"

Where had this come from, this . . . *silliness*? It fizzed up out of him, shaken loose by the run, perhaps. He'd never wanted so badly to make two females giggle, and Lily's giggle was pure music.

He doled the food out all around, and they all fell upon it; the girls ate like locusts. He really should be admonishing Lily, he thought. Launching into a lesson: "Never, Miss Masters, eat with both hands." Something along those lines.

Perhaps . . . perhaps later. He found himself rolling up his shirtsleeves; the warmth touched his bare arms and seeped into him until he felt something like languor. *This must be why I typically avoid outdoor amusements,* he thought. *They make you indolent.*

A few bees buzzed curiously about their meal and left again. And then a butterfly winged by for a visit, and was admired effusively by all of them.

"This is what Heaven looks like," Alice informed him, gnawing a piece of bread with cheese, waving her arm about to indicate Aster Park's grounds. "Lily said so. And Mama lives in a house just like that—" she gestured toward the big brick house in the distance— "with Papa."

He turned to Lily. "Ah. So this is what Heaven looks like, Miss Masters?"

Gideon watched her take a deep breath, as though gathering her courage, and gaze out over the swath of green they had just run across. She scanned the stands of trees, the delicate bobbing brilliance of early summer flowers, the white specks of fountains in the distance.

And as her face slowly became luminous with awe, Gideon could feel her wonder flowing into his own veins like a lovely liqueur, and it was as though he was experiencing Aster Park for the first time all over again.

"So many kinds . . ." Lily said softly, almost to herself.

"Kinds?" Gideon was puzzled.

"Of green. I never knew . . ." she trailed off, giving her head a wondering little shake.

"Which is your favorite?" he found himself asking.

She didn't even need to consider the question. "That one." She pointed up at a leaf on the tree sheltering them, still curled in upon itself, poised to unfurl. "It's so . . . delicate, you can almost see through it. You almost fear for it, this fragile new thing."

Her words kicked strangely inside him: *You almost fear for it, this fragile new thing.*

"Do *you* have a favorite green, Mr. Cole?"

"Well . . . yes," he confessed. And so help him, he'd never admitted this to anyone. "That one," he gestured to an oak leaf through which the afternoon sun shone. "It is a mature leaf, and yet when the sun shines through it . . ."

". . . it looks almost new again," Lily sounded pleased at the idea, a little smile curved her lips.

"Just before the sun begins to set is when I like it best," he continued almost gingerly, like someone stepping out over untested and possibly perilous ground.

"Oh! Yes, it's a kind light, that time of day," Lily agreed. "It gilds everything. It's as though everything on earth is allowed to be beautiful in that moment. Even St. Giles," she added, with a rueful little smile.

Gideon stared at her, and suddenly he felt strangely lightheaded, as though he'd taken his first full clean breath in years. He was seized with an impulse to show Lily the cat-shaped stone, and the ancient oak, and the secluded stream, and all those fluffy sheep, just to hear what she would say. Just to watch her eyes change.

"But this *is* what Heaven looks like, Lily, right?" Alice insisted.

"Oh, of course." Lily frowned a little, as though there had never been any question about it.

Bored with them, Alice decided to take her stick down closer to the lake to see what might be swimming there, leaving Gideon and Lily alone on the blanket amidst the carnage of their meal. Sunlight pierced their canopy of leaves and found tiny rainbows in the strands of Lily's hair, and Gideon found his thoughts drifting in a decidedly less innocent direction. *Firelight on fair skin, a spill of gleaming hair . . .*

Last night, as he watched her, he'd imagined reaching forward and gently, gently, loosening the cord that closed Lily's voluminous borrowed robe . . . deliberately postponing, heightening, the breathless shock of pleasure he knew would accompany the sight of her body, bare to him . . .

His reverie was interrupted by a tickling sensation; he glanced down. A tiny black insect was struggling through the hair on his forearm.

Lily leaned forward and gently touched her finger to him.

And it was just a whisper of a touch, but it burned through him like a cinder. Gideon's breathing suspended; his senses ignited. What was she—

She was rescuing the insect. The tiny creature clambered aboard Lily's nail; she deposited it on the grass with a slight smile of satisfaction. Lily looked up into his face. "It was trapped," she explained softly.

Their eyes met and held again. Gideon couldn't speak; a strange ache had started up in the pit of him, and he couldn't seem to free his gaze.

It was Lily who finally looked away, her expression unsettled. And Gideon, feeling faintly ridiculous, tried to command his anarchic thoughts and senses back into formation.

"Lily! Mr. Cole! Look!"

Alice had gouged something long and dark and muddy up from the lake with her stick. Some old roots, it looked like.

"Don't touch it, Alice." Gideon and Lily spoke at once. Their heads swiveled to look at each other quickly; just as quickly, they turned away from each other again, blinking self-consciously.

Alice obediently hurled whatever it was back into the lake and began swishing the stick about looking for other disgusting or intriguing objects worthy of inspection.

"How long have you cared for Alice on your own, Miss Masters? What became of your parents?"

Lily turned back toward him and looked intently into his face, searching perhaps for his motive for asking, or for a reason not to answer. "I could tell you anything I like about my parents, and you would never know whether or not it is true."

"But you will tell me the truth," he hazarded.

Lily hesitated a moment more, and then shrugged. "Mama was the daughter of a curate, a widower, who died and left her very little money. Papa was . . . well, Papa was many things. I think he at one time may have been a soldier. But mostly he was a gambler and a drinker," she concluded with a wry twist of her mouth.

"What became of them?"

"They . . . they passed on. Mama is gone three years now. Papa died a few years before her." The old grief flickered across her face, like a dying fire given a prod.

Three years of caring for her sister on her own . . . three years of risk on the street. He wondered how Constance would have fared if left to her own devices in St. Giles. Constance was so accustomed to winning, so innately an aristocrat; perhaps she would simply will men to hand over their watches to her.

"My parents died when I was young, too. When I was seventeen." His own words clanged oddly in his ears. He hadn't said them aloud to anyone in years; partly because the grief had defied words when it was new, and later he'd had no wish to revive it by talking of it, even with Helen. But for some reason . . . he wanted Miss Masters to know that he understood something of loss. "They were at sea and . . . there was a storm. Their ship was dashed to pieces. I was at Oxford. And after that, I looked after my sister.

And . . ." He smiled a little, ruefully. "Well, my father knew a little about gambling, too." And oddly, then, he missed his father. His father had considered life one delightful surprise after another.

Lily lifted her eyes to his, and he read understanding in them, but not the sort that made him want to shake away from it, not the cloying sort, and he was relieved and strangely comforted. They were silent together for a time, turning to watch Alice kneel and drag her fingers through the lake water.

A winged insect of unknown genus circled them determinedly; Gideon waved it away. "Have you any living relatives, Miss Masters?"

"None that I know about, and I know not where to look."

"But it must have been difficult to care for Alice on your own for so long. Wouldn't you like someone to take care of you, too?"

"By 'someone,' do you by any chance mean a *man*, Mr. Cole?" Lily's mouth twisted wryly.

He said nothing, for this was precisely what he'd meant.

"Men," she scoffed, wrapping her arms around her knees. Her big dress gapped a little at the bodice; Gideon forced his eyes up into the oak leaves. It would be interesting to see Miss Masters in her new wardrobe when it arrived. "Most men can hardly care for themselves, to hear Fanny speak of the men who go upstairs to see her. And Papa was certainly no help in that regard. I will *never* allow myself to be at the mercy of any man—I would rather care for myself and for Alice on my own. There's more freedom in it."

"But immense responsibility."

She frowned a little, puzzled. "I suppose I don't see it as responsibility. It's merely . . . life."

Merely life. The simple strength in those two words resonated in Gideon like a bell.

He turned his head back toward the handsome house sprawling at the edge of the green, the house that would one day belong to him—and to Constance, who would, if all went according to his Master Plan, be his wife. Constance would *never* run like a wild thing; her athleticism was channeled into archery or riding or dancing, things requiring grace and decorum. He wasn't even certain Constance ever *perspired*. Constance was always patently, thoroughly a lady. Which was why he regarded her so very highly.

Wasn't it?

"While we are asking questions, Mr. Cole . . ."

"Yes, Miss Masters?"

"Why do you insist upon following that little rule book when it has nothing to do with who you *really* are?"

His head snapped toward her. Lily's smile held a hint of mischievous triumph. But, oddly, a little sympathy, too.

He could ignore the question, he supposed, or scoff at it. But his sense of fair play demanded he attempt to answer it for her. "Those rules exist for a reason, Miss Masters. And if your mother was a lady, she knew those reasons, too. There's a . . . comfort in symmetry, in knowing that everyone in your social circle shares the same customs and mores. In times of joy and pain, there's a comfort in knowing how to behave, in knowing . . ."

"How to marry the daughter of a marquis?" Lily completed ironically.

Gideon said nothing; he looked away again, uncomfortable; a strange pressure was building in his chest. "My father lost everything my family owned, Miss Masters, and I've worked very hard for my position in life. An excellent marriage is something everyone should aspire to."

Lily nodded thoughtfully, as though ceding this point to him. "Yes . . . but to me, those rules feel like . . . wallpaper pasted up to cover over one's true self. Everyone is your friend, and yet everyone is a stranger. And they make no allowances for the whims of fate."

The whims of fate? Like paying thirty pounds for a thief? "Those rules are a civilized place to begin a friendship, Miss Masters. And they make one more *able* to tolerate the whims of fate."

Lily was studying him; he could feel her eyes upon him. "Do they?" she said, again ironically.

He could not recall ever having a conversation quite like this, let alone with a woman. He was unaccustomed to mining his soul; it had begun to burn and needle him, like a limb shaken from sleep.

"*Surrender!*" Alice bellowed from near the stream. She was aiming her big stick at an unfortunate tree, a stand-in for a French soldier, no doubt.

They both turned to watch her. The play of emotions on Lily's face when she looked at Alice—the concern, the affection, the irritation—were all the things one felt for sisters. But she was really more mother than sister, and had been, he suspected, even when their parents were alive.

"Where is your sister now, Mr. Cole?"

Gideon turned his face away from Lily. "In Yorkshire." Two curt words.

Alice was shouting something else now; it sounded like "*Charge!*" It was followed by a hearty thwack. Some poor beech had just been smote.

"It seems we are not so different, Mr. Cole," Lily ventured when Gideon said nothing more. "We both know something of loss. And responsibility." She smiled a little, watching Alice. "And sisters, I would guess."

His building inner agitation propelled Gideon abruptly to his feet. "You've an appointment with my uncle, Miss Masters. Please do try to walk like a lady, rather than a thief, as we return to the house. And if there is one thing you should learn from today, it is this: A *lady* would never issue an invitation to a footrace."

She looked up at him, held his gaze for a moment before speaking. When she did, her words fell on him like a fine snow. "Somehow, Mr. Cole, I doubt a *gentleman* would accept one."

She rose nimbly, ignoring his outstretched hand, and walked away from him to collect Alice. "Ten more pounds, Mr. Cole," she said over her shoulder. "And by the way, thank you for the stockings and the book."

3:00 Cards with Lord Lindsey

Lily arrived for cards to find the baron dressed—and not in a dressing gown, but in a coat and trousers and boots, all several years past fashionable, but all beautifully made. Lily knew this from the years she'd spent studying gentlemen on London streets; one did get a sense for the current fashions, and who was likely to be carting about gold watches based on the quality of their clothing.

"You seem a bit subdued, Miss Masters. Are you feeling well?"

"Hush, Lord Lindsey. I know you are trying to distract me. I do not intend to lose this hand. Have some tea."

Lord Lindsey chuckled and obeyed. As Lily studied her hand, she heard a long sip and the comforting chink of porcelain meeting porcelain as he returned his cup to his saucer. "You've lost the last hand because you're *already* distracted, Miss Masters. You seem a bit flushed. Have you been outdoors without a bonnet?"

Lily looked up at the old baron, a little bemused. It was rather nice to be fussed over. But being outdoors without a bonnet was *nothing* compared to being outdoors without shoes for the past several years of her life.

She wasn't about to share this little observation with Lord Lindsey.

"Yes. There was a picnic," she said shortly.

"And did you enjoy yourself?"

"Aster Park is beautiful," she replied after a moment. It wasn't exactly an answer to his question, but truthfully, Lily didn't know the answer. Had she enjoyed herself? Admittedly, there was a great deal of pleasure to be had in simply *looking* at Gideon Cole. Especially when his shirtsleeves were rolled up and he was leaning back on his strong forearms, his long body outstretched, his head tilted up to catch the sun.

He'd done that only briefly, however. And then he had been all restless vigilance again, all probing questions. And then cold and closed, making sure she knew her place.

But there had been a moment, when she'd rescued the little black insect: he'd held so very still, and watched her so breathlessly, so intently, that her heart had bumped against her ribs. As if trying to escape from her chest to go to him.

It hadn't been desire she'd read in Gideon Cole's face. It had been a sort of . . . bewildered longing.

That makes two of us, Mr. Cole.

Because her rescue of the insect hadn't been entirely selfless. The impulse to touch Gideon had been overwhelming; the copper hair curling up out of that taut, muscular arm—

Her confusion made her feel even more confined and restless; the danger of life in St. Giles seemed simpler, easier to navigate, somehow more *honest* than the peculiar danger she now felt; it was easier to know what to do about those grasping hands, those "Lily, give us a kiss, luvs!" than this relentless tug she felt toward Gideon Cole. *Ten more pounds and I can leave.*

Oh, but the park itself . . . no words could describe it. Well, perhaps a single word could: Eden. Surely one couldn't *own* Aster Park. Surely Aster Park itself did the owning.

"Won it in a card game—Aster Park," Lord Lindsey mentioned idly.

Lily nearly spit out her tea. "You *didn't*!"

"Of course not." He smiled roguishly. "But I thoroughly enjoyed saying so just now."

"You're a rascal, Lord Lindsey."

"That I am, that I am," he agreed absently, mulling his cards. "Truthfully, I inherited the property and the title from a distant relative. . . . Very unexpected thing, it was." He made his play, selecting and discarding a card.

"Good heavens. I can hardly imagine what that must have been like." Lily made her play and Lord Lindsey arched a brow, conceding defeat. She smugly raked her winnings toward her with one hand.

"Oh, it was quite an adjustment, I must say. I moved my family—Beatrice, the boys—from a little cottage in the country into this immense place. Pity no real money came along with it. Aster Park is rather an albatross of sorts, truthfully. But it manages to eke out a sort of income for us—beef and wool, you know. We've made do for some time."

"Your boys must have loved it here," Lily said, and then she could have bitten her tongue. She would hate to see grief sweep down over Lord Lindsey's face again.

But to her relief, he merely looked pensive. "Oh, they may have. But it was Gideon who took a real interest in the landscaping and such—he loved this place the moment he set eyes upon it, and I swear he prowled over every inch of it. He was at Oxford by the time the park came into my hands, and then his parents died and Helen up and wed that farmer in Yorkshire. I was dead against *that*. Waste of a perfectly smashing girl, if you ask me. A more pigheaded pair of children never— Well, anyhow, there were very few picnics here at Aster Park. I must say, it's odd to see Gideon at . . . *play* at all, as it were."

"Oh?" Lily tried to sound casual, but she was desperately curious.

"I didn't think the boy knew *how* to stop working, really. Ever since his parents died he worked at . . . well, *everything*. Got himself beaten quite a bit for his trouble, too," he added cheerfully.

Lily felt faint. "Beaten?"

"Well, the boy never would bend. Young boys are animals, Gideon was poor—and so all those rich lads at Oxford goaded him for it. He fought back, and they thrashed him. It's a time-honored school tradition, you see. But his pride probably got him beaten more than was strictly necessary. He'd come home for the holidays with blacked eyes."

Lily could hardly believe Lord Lindsey was being so cavalier about such a thing.

"But that's . . . that's *awful*."

"That's life, Miss Masters," Lord Lindsey said gruffly, rifling through his cards to determine the quality of his new hand. "Gideon knew the risks he was taking when he continued on at Oxford. But he had plans for himself. And Oxford is where you meet the people who will help you achieve those plans."

Like becoming a barrister. And marrying the daughter of a marquis.

"And then there was your cousin. They used to pick on

poor Kilmartin, too, as he was shy and plump. Terrible thing to be at Oxford, shy and plump. Gideon got himself beaten even more on Kilmartin's behalf: He'd leap to the defense of anyone, that boy. Once Gideon and Kilmartin were friends, however, the whole of the pack backed off. Damned if Gideon didn't earn their respect for standing up for himself. Still has it," the baron added proudly. "They're his clients now, and friends."

Oh, damn. Lily didn't want to care about Gideon Cole, or the things that drove him and the deeper reasons for them. She didn't want to care about, wonder about, the pain that flickered across his face whenever his sister was mentioned. She didn't want to feel again this treacherous weakening or want, she didn't want to feel . . . *tenderness* . . . she didn't want to—

She didn't want to *like* him.

"Your draw, Lord Lindsey."

Lord Lindsey drew, and cleared this throat. "Perhaps you can persuade Gideon to go on more picnics, Lily. The boy needs to play."

Oh, he's not a boy, Lord Lindsey. He's most definitely a man.

She wondered if Lord Lindsey would encourage more picnics if he'd known about firelight, and stockings, and poetry . . . and a look of bewildered longing.

6:00 Dining

Gideon sent a note up with Mrs. Plunkett informing Lily and Alice that the gentlemen would be dining alone. A little port, a cigar, some manly conversation about politics and horses . . . He would be himself again by the end of the evening.

He most certainly hadn't been himself all day.

He repaired to the drawing room with Kilmartin and the two sank into comfortable chairs, chosen, no doubt, by his uncle or some other sensible male ancestor with an aversion to the spider-legged furniture that overran the rest of the house.

A fire was leaping merrily in the grate, and Gideon leaned over it to light his cigar. He tugged the rich smoke into his lungs and watched for a moment the colors in the flames, the soothing lick of ambers and oranges and hot reds . . . *Firelight on fair skin, a spill of gleaming hair that begged his hands to plunge into it* . . .

"And so . . . are you determined to go forward with this thing, Gideon, or were you thinking of stopping?"

Gideon looked up, startled. "Stopping . . . ?"

"Our project. Miss Lily Masters versus Lady Constance Clary. Your Master Plan. Pay attention, Gideon. Or have you consumed too much port?"

"No," Gideon said quickly.

"No to the port, or to the stopping?"

"To both. I wouldn't dream of stopping now."

"Are you all right, Gideon?"

"Distracted, Laurie. Thinking about—"

"Don't tell me: work and Constance."

Gideon smiled. "Right again."

"I must admit Miss Masters is quite a find, Gideon. Almost makes one want to wade on into St. Giles and reform the whole of it."

"You," Gideon told him pointedly, "wouldn't last a moment in St. Giles."

Kilmartin looked briefly offended, and then sighed. "I suspect you are correct." He took a pride-assuaging draw on his own cigar, stretched his legs out, and crossed them at the ankle.

"Besides, I'm very nearly certain Miss Masters is one of a kind," Gideon added.

"Then it's lucky for you it was your pocket she attempted to pick."

Lucky? Gideon let that one lie. He shifted his body and tapped his fingers on the arm of the chair a few times. "You don't like Constance, do you, Laurie?" he asked suddenly.

Kilmartin looked up sharply. "Well," he began carefully. "It's not so much a matter of *liking* . . . I mean, one doesn't go about saying, 'I *like* Athena' . . ."

Gideon's mouth twitched. "What *is* it a matter of?"

"I'm not sure. . . . She's certainly very beautiful, in an entirely conspicuous way. She has fine manners and connections. . . . You would do very well with her as a wife. She rather intimidates me. But you know all of that. It's just . . . well, and please don't take offense, Gideon—"

"What is it?"

"I would prefer that she cared more for you." Kilmartin looked a little anxious about the revelation.

Gideon nodded once, thoughtfully. "You don't think she does?"

"Oh, after a fashion, of course. But mostly I think Lady Constance Clary cares for Lady Constance Clary."

"Don't you think it's a luxury, Laurie? Ensuring that one is, as you say, *cared for* in a marriage."

"Oh, see, now you've gone sarcastic. You should not have asked; I should not have answered. You may be right. No doubt you'll be very happy with her."

Gideon sighed. "Sorry, Laurie. Forget I asked at all." He pulled on his cigar until the tip glowed red.

"Perhaps if she sees that Miss Lily Masters harbors a *tendre* for you . . . she will discover how much she truly does care for you," Kilmartin offered.

Gideon's heart bucked. "A *tendre* for me? Miss Masters?"

"It's your plan, isn't it, Gideon? Miss Lily Masters of Sussex will outshine Constance and pretend to adore you, thus securing your engagement to Constance, and et cetera."

"Oh. Of course." Gideon moved restlessly in the chair again, and so help him, he could feel his face going warm, and it wasn't due to the fire. "So . . . have we a hostess in the *ton*? A 'chaperone,' if you will, for Miss Masters?"

"Yes, Aunt Hester has agreed to put us up in her town house there. I'm lucky to have so many cousins; she wasn't the least bit suspicious about the sudden appearance of a Miss Masters. The three of us can stay with her for the . . . well, duration. Which I assume means as long as it takes for you to get engaged or concede defeat. Or for Miss Masters to steal something important from a ball guest. I'm certain she won't," he added hurriedly. "She does rather clean up nicely. She's a game little thing, isn't she?"

The corner of Gideon's mouth quirked wryly. "Our thief." He returned his attention to the fire.

Kilmartin was silent for so long that Gideon finally looked up in surprise. His friend was studying him, his brow faintly furrowed.

"What?" Gideon said, irritated.

"Do you realize, Gideon . . ." Kilmartin said slowly, "that you just made the word 'thief' sound like an endearment?"

"I beg your pardon?"

"'My *dear*.' 'Our *thief*,'" Kilmartin demonstrated. "Rather like that."

Startled, Gideon turned quickly away. His entire body was tense, he realized; he unclenched his jaw and uncurled his hands from the fists they'd balled into, rolled his neck to loosen the stiffness.

"You're drunk, Laurie," he finally accused, and Kilmartin snorted a soft laugh.

Gideon reached for his port again; the thick sweetness of it made him feel as though he were replenishing his own blood. "And it will of course be our secret that you and I are staying with your aunt to keep an eye on Miss Masters, and not in our own lodgings?"

"Of course."

"Will Lady Anne Clapham mind you squiring about your 'cousin'?"

Kilmartin smiled dreamily. "Lady Anne knows how I feel about her. She shall not mind."

Kilmartin was very irritating, Gideon thought, when he was being dreamy. "Won't it bother you to deceive her?" he prodded, a bit testily.

"I shall simply tell her the story when we are old and gray, and we'll share a laugh." Kilmartin stood suddenly. "Well, I'm for bed. Drink the rest of your port, Gideon. I think you need it."

Gideon gave him a strained smile. "Good night, Laurie."

But Kilmartin was wrong; the port was in large part encouraging the urge he surrendered to now. He turned his eyes back to the fire and lost himself in a fantasy that had grown increasingly, uncomfortably, tantalizingly more explicit.

He wished he'd never read that bloody French book.

In his mind, he unwound the tie and nudged the robe from Lily's shoulders; it sighed to the ground. And there she stood bare, slim white limbs cast in firelight, lips parted with desire; the long shining spill of her hair falling modestly across her breasts, across the crook of her legs, and *that* . . . well, that would *never* do. And so he reached forward, lifted the silky mass of it in his fingers . . . and slowly, slowly he knelt before her and pressed his lips against the satin mound of her belly, and then dragged them lower, lower, lower, until his tongue nestled against—

Gideon abruptly threw the rest of his port into the fire, where it hissed and smoked like a demon vanquished.

Chapter Nine

The barnacle scraping and hull polishing continued: deportment and conversation in the morning, reels before dinner to build the appetite, cards with Lord Lindsey midday to break up the lessons. And, though the process certainly wasn't entirely painless, Lily began to take on the sheen of gentility; it had been there, all along, of course, beneath the barnacles. She could now conduct skillfully vacuous conversations, *eat* rather than devour, and respond to questions about her life in Sussex with some knowledge and a good deal of imaginative embellishment. The quiet of Aster Park seemed less oppressive and alien now; her head didn't swim in astonishment when her meals were placed in front of her three times a day.

Her curtsies were things of beauty; her walking left Gideon Cole in despair.

And nothing Gideon said, no threats or cajoling or irony, could seem to alter it. Perhaps her walk and the angle of her chin were built into her, she thought, the way her own spine was built into her. She'd presented that theory to him; he'd merely regarded her with a look of mystification and amusement.

During the four nights following their picnic, Lily stared at her ceiling while Alice snored next to her, wondering whether Gideon was stretched out in a chair in front of the fire in the library. So far her courage had failed her, or her judgment had come to her rescue—or perhaps they were working in tandem to preserve her virtue, though this seemed unlikely—but she had not returned to the library.

Yet.

But by her fifth day, when she was five pounds away from freedom, she began losing at cards. In earnest.

"What happened, Miss Masters?" Lord Lindsey asked as she prettily shrugged away another loss. "Have you lost your knack, or have I improved?"

"Surely it's the latter, Lord Lindsey."

And Lily would apologize for being such a poor opponent and arrive for her afternoon quadrille lessons with empty hands.

The first two times it happened, Gideon teased her. The third time, he glanced down at her hands . . . and then into her face . . .

And then he smiled, that slow, devastating, heart-stopping smile.

He *knew*, the beast.

Madame Marceau swept in with the crispness of a March wind. Servants trailed her carrying trunks and parcels of all shapes and sizes.

"Lily, Lily, Lily! Come! I aver, you will be a swan, and I simply cannot wait to see you in my creations. Off with that old bag of a gown, now! Excuse us, *please*."

She looked down her long nose and delivered this last

order to the servants. They deposited their parcels and scurried from the room while Madame Marceau unwrapped each gown reverently, as though she were excavating jewels. She located the gloves and slippers and hats to match, and arranged the ensembles over the chairs and across the settee. And then she stood back, gesturing to it all with a flourish.

Lily gaped: shimmering silks and satins, fine wools and muslins and lawns, evening gowns and walking dresses, kid slippers and gloves and stockings. Much of it in the blues and greens and golds Gideon Cole had suggested, the colors of sea and sky and sun.

Her hands began to tremble at the bounty before her; she hardly dared touch one thread of it. How could she put anything so fine on her *body*? Shouldn't it be framed and hung on the wall instead? Locked in a closet and counted each night, the way Mrs. Plunkett inventoried the silver plate?

Madame Marceau's smile grew soft with understanding. "You will more than do them justice, I promise you. This one first, my dear. This style is all the rage in Paris." She scooped up a gown in an unusual shade of blue satin; it drooped across her arms like a fainting maiden.

"For your first ball. For you will only ever have *one* first ball. Step out of those drawers, now."

Again, Madame Marceau was so businesslike Lily didn't think twice about complying with her request. She obediently dropped her drawers and lifted her arms, and Madame Marceau poured the blue gown over her head. It shivered down over her skin, as light and cool as water. The modiste circled her, deftly doing up the laces that closed the back of the dress, and then she plucked up a pair of soft white gloves and pushed them over Lily's hands one at a time. Finally, startling her, Madame Marceau seized Lily's heavy hair and skillfully twisted it into a knot, securing it with pins extracted from her pocket. She turned Lily to face the mirror.

"Tell me I'm wrong, Miss Lily Masters," Madame Marceau demanded. "Tell me you are not a diamond of the first water."

Lily's mouth parted, but she could find no words. The creature that gazed back at her from the mirror could not possibly have anything to do with *her*. She saw vivid eyes made brilliant by the exquisite shade of the gown, luminous skin made more luminous still by the gleam of satin. Her delicate features and slim contours were revealed by the lift of her hair, the cut of the dress. Forgetting for a moment she had an audience in Madame Marceau, she reached out a gloved hand and touched a tentative finger to the mirror.

Madame Marceau laughed, pleased with herself. "Perfectly splendid. Fits like a dream. Now off with that dress and on with . . . What are your plans for this afternoon?"

"Dancing," Lily said faintly. "I've a dancing lesson."

"This one, then." The modiste scooped up a white muslin gown that was so fine it looked nearly transparent. The neckline was deep, and tiny buttons closed its back. Satin ribbon in the same pale shade as the dress edged the hem and the waist.

"Mr. Cole will not be able to take his eyes from you."

Lily flushed. She knew it was futile, knew it was foolish . . . knew he intended to marry the daughter of a marquis. And yet . . . *he rarely takes his eyes from me, anyhow. He is always watching, watching.*

1:00 to 3:00 The Waltz

Lily arrived precisely on the hour; the clock was just striking one. She hovered a moment at the entrance of the doorway, shy in her delicate new dress and soft slippers; the air touched the back of her neck and made her feel exposed and strangely vulnerable. In fact, bereft of the embrace of Mrs. Plunkett's big borrowed dress, she felt altogether bare.

The mirror in the red room had told her she was beautiful. *Beautiful.* Not just St. Giles pretty. And Madame Marceau had told her she was beautiful.

She would believe she was beautiful when she saw it reflected in Gideon Cole's eyes.

They were chatting in low voices near the pianoforte, bent over the sheet music; Gideon said something and Kilmartin laughed, and Gideon turned slightly toward the doorway.

And saw her.

Slowly, slowly, he straightened to his full height, and went very still.

Her heart stopped her throat. *He will not be able to take his eyes from you.*

Gideon held her there, suspended in the beam of his eyes, and it seemed to Lily that his entire self was distilled in the fixed heat of his gaze. She could not seem to move or look away from him.

And so I am beautiful.

Lily at last remembered to curtsy. To her undying regret, it seemed to be the thing that enabled Gideon to tear his eyes from her.

Kilmartin was gawking at her, too. "You are . . . you are looking quite well, Miss Masters. The new gown . . ." He abandoned gentility for enthusiasm. "Good God, but that new gown suits you, Lily. You're really very stunning."

Lily took a deep breath and smiled at him. "Thank you . . . *Laurie.*" She curtsied to him, too, a beautiful low dipping, a veritable masterpiece of a curtsy.

"All right, Kilmartin, that's quite enough gaping,"

Gideon said mildly. He had turned and was steadfastly looking away from Lily, fussing with the sheet music perched on the pianoforte. "This afternoon, Miss Masters, you will learn the most important, though simplest, of dances." He took a deep breath and turned back to her. "The waltz."

Lily, inevitably, had a question: "Why is it the most important?"

"Perhaps because it is the most . . . daring, Miss Masters. It was, in fact, once considered quite scandalous. For a waltz requires only two people: a man and a woman who . . . touch each other throughout the dance, in something like . . ." He paused awkwardly and cleared his throat. ". . . Like an embrace."

Lily regarded him, scarlet. Gideon gazed back at her, eyebrows lifted in challenge.

"I prefer reels," she announced airily. As though she'd been performing them all of her life.

"Ah. Well, I fear the waltz *does* require a certain amount of grace." Gideon's tone was sympathetic. "Rather more than a reel requires. Perhaps if you don't feel *equal* to it . . ."

Lily sighed. He knew very well that she understood his stratagem, and yet she still could not resist it. "Very well, Mr. Cole. How does one waltz?"

"First, you must place your hand in mine." He waved the fingers on his outstretched arm coaxingly.

Lily's gloved hand rose tentatively to meet his, and he gently folded his fingers around hers.

Gideon looked down. Lily's head was averted.

"You must step closer to me, Miss Masters." He said it softly.

"I must?" Two faint words.

"Again, I am afraid so."

Lily inched forward.

"Closer, Lily," he murmured.

Lily flushed a deep tortured rose, but obediently inched toward him until they were very nearly touching. The scent of her rose up to him, something subtle and complex, musky and sweet, released by the warmth of her body. He was close enough to hear her quick shallow breaths.

His heart was thudding strangely in his chest, making his own breath come swiftly.

"And now I must place my hand . . . like so . . . against your waist." His voice had gone strangely husky.

Torturously slowly, he moved his hand until it just hovered over the small of her back, just above where her waist flared into her slim hips. Tension vibrated through Lily; he could feel it in the stiffness of her small hand.

At last, he pressed his palm softly against her.

She was so slim; his hand nearly spanned her back. Through the fine fabric of her new dress, even through his glove, he could feel the pearls of her spine and the rise and fall of her rapid breathing, see the gentle curve of her breasts, and for a moment he went still with wonder.

He slowly lowered his head to look at her. Lily's lashes cast trembling shadows on the curves of her cheeks; the muted light of the ballroom glinted off the down at the tender nape of her neck, off the tiny buttons that closed the back of her dress.

Buttons that could be opened with one skillful flick of a finger.

Desire spiked so suddenly and violently through him he nearly swayed from it.

Gideon stood very still, his breathing quiet and swift, as though the moment itself was a skittish creature that could be frightened away with a sudden move.

He had not been prepared for what it would be like to

touch her. To stand this close to her. To take in her scent with every breath.

It was nearly a minute before he could speak.

"Lily." His voice was hoarse. He cleared his throat. "Look at me."

She glanced up, and her face was still scarlet, her eyes ever so slightly wary.

Gideon managed to smile slightly. "One does not regard their dancing partner with wariness, Miss Masters."

"Oh?" The word was a little weak. "How *does* one regard one's partner?"

Her husky voice was like a soft finger dragged against the short hairs on Gideon's neck. It inspired a number of dangerous little answers: *With desire* was one of them. *With warmth* was another.

Think of Constance, he ordered himself. Golden, confident Constance, who had skin as firm and warm as a peach and who took the dance floor with the majesty of one of Nelson's tall ships and was the daughter of a marquis. How did Constance look at him when they danced the waltz? And how did he look at Constance?

"Regard your partner with . . . polite interest," he told Lily. This was true, he admitted to himself with some surprise; this *was* the expression with which Constance regarded him, and with which he typically regarded Constance. "Smile, but not too frequently. Never frown, unless you're gravely insulted, which, I might add, is not likely to happen in a London ballroom. And always," he said, smiling down at her softly, "look up at your partner, and not down at your feet, the way you are now."

"Good God, Cole, are you ever going to dance?" Kilmartin called over to them grumpily. "My fingers have frozen in the shape of this waltz."

"Sorry, Laurie. Follow me, Lily. Yes, I know you prefer not to follow anyone," he added wryly, "but I must lead you. It is simply how things are done. Do you think you can do it?"

Lily's chin went up.

"Begin the waltz, Laurie," Gideon called over to Kilmartin.

Kilmartin's fingers fell against the keys, and a slow French waltz, sweeping and stately, took shape. Gideon took a tentative step into the music; Lily moved with him stiffly. It was a bit like trying to drag something up from the bottom of the Thames.

"Step and *glide*, Lily."

She followed; still, it was more of a haul than a glide. For such a slight girl, she had remarkable powers of resistance.

He couldn't continue towing her about the floor. How to explain the movement of the waltz to her . . . ? "Miss Masters, pretend you are . . . a bird. And the music is a current of air. And I am the wings you use to just . . . sail over it."

It sounded absurd even to him, but Lily looked up at him, surprised, a small pleased smile curving her lips. She closed her eyes briefly.

When she opened them again, she was like air in his arms.

Step . . . and glide. Step . . . and glide. One, two, three . . . One, two, three . . . One, two, three . . .

Effortlessly, united in breathless surprise, they eased into the slow circles required of the waltz. And in moments, Gideon felt exempt from gravity.

"Oh." Lily laughed up at him, her face radiant, embarrassment forgotten. "This is lovely! It *is* like flying."

Gideon laughed, too, giddy; dancing with Lily was like . . . dancing with music itself.

Eyes locked, they spun about the room in mutual, precarious wonder, as if they had each been given a new set of wings to play with and feared they would soon be taken away. *This,* Gideon thought, astounded, looking down into Lily's glowing face. *This is what a waltz is supposed to feel like. I understand it now.*

And then a realization tore the breath violently from him: *This is what* everything *should feel like.*

He stopped abruptly, stunned, and shook free of her hand. Lily stumbled in surprise.

"I've an appointment, Laurie." Gideon raised his voice so Kilmartin could hear. "Sorry, old man, must have forgotten. Tomorrow, then?"

The waltz jangled to a messy halt mid-measure. Kilmartin swiveled, startled, to stare at Gideon.

Gideon strode to the doorway. He paused when he reached it and pulled his grandfather's watch from his pocket; he hefted it thoughtfully in his hand. And he waited for Lily's eyes to go to it, waited, deliberately, for the sparkle in them to fade to bleakness.

"Just wanted to be certain it was still there, Miss Masters."

He strode out of the ballroom.

Chapter Ten

Blindly, Gideon strode down the hall; he could hear his boot heels striking hard on the marble floors, but he had no sense of his surroundings; clocks and portraits and vases and sconces passed in a blur. He wasn't fleeing, he told himself. But he could not seem to stop moving. This hot jagged thing he took in with every breath . . . it wasn't rage, exactly. Or rather it *was*, but it was mostly about . . . betrayal.

Of whom?

Of myself.

Oh, he had asked for it, hadn't he? He had no one to blame but himself, and this infuriated him.

He had lived his life according to a Master Plan, and he had always assumed this plan would make him happy. He had excelled as a student, as a soldier, as a barrister, and he had thought this was happiness. He had danced with Constance Clary, the daughter of a marquis, and he had thought this was happiness. He would inherit his uncle's beautiful property, and he had thought this was happiness.

But he now knew the truth: the only pure happiness he had ever known had been crystallized in a single moment in his uncle's ballroom, in the arms of Lily Masters. And it could—*she* could—never have anything to do with his future.

He had brought this unspeakable cruelty upon himself.

He seemed to be heading in the direction of the main entrance. He thought he passed a servant; he had a general impression of a woman, mouth agape and eyes wide with alarm. *Good God, what must my expression be?* Murderous was his guess.

And then he collided with Gregson, who was holding a wrapped parcel in his hand.

"What the bloody hell is *that*?" Gideon snapped.

If Gregson thought this degree of passion about a mere package was excessive, it didn't show on his face.

"A package arrived for Lord Lindsey, sir."

Gideon snatched it from Gregson. " 'McBride's Apothecary,' " he read aloud from the package. *McBride?* Who was he to Lily?

It didn't matter. More to the point, it *couldn't* matter. Gideon closed his eyes briefly against a wash of desolation.

He opened them to see Gregson watching him, his brow furrowed in deep concern.

"Sir?"

"I'm all right, Gregson." His voice betrayed otherwise. "I'll take the package to my uncle. Thank you. And I apologize for snapping at you."

"*Did* you snap, sir?"

Gideon almost smiled.

Lily and Kilmartin remained frozen in stunned silence for a moment or so, staring at the doorway through which Gideon had practically stormed.

"He's a . . . passionate sort," Kilmartin finally ventured,

an attempt to explain his friend's appalling behavior. "Driven. Subject to the occasional mood." He frowned a little. "More subject than usual, it seems."

Lily's face still felt hot from Gideon's pointed cruelty and abrupt abandonment. He had touched her, she had circled the room in his arms, and her very *blood* had rejoiced: *at last, at last, at last*. And now it still heated her veins, flushed her skin, as if enraged his hands were no longer upon her.

"How do you *stand* him?" she blurted.

"Gideon?" Kilmartin sounded surprised, and then sat back, reflecting, and shook his head. "Oh, I suppose it's because he's never boring. He's a . . . brilliant chap. A thinker. Exceedingly loyal. Kind to a fault. Well, usually," he added, somewhat sheepishly. "But where you are concerned, Miss Masters . . ." He paused, looking puzzled for a moment, and then shrugged and pushed himself away from the pianoforte and stood. "I suppose I can stand Gideon mainly because . . . well, Gideon Cole is perhaps the most innately decent man I've ever met. It often causes problems for him, but there you have it."

Lily knew it to be true; she *felt* it to be true. But as Kilmartin said: where *she* was concerned . . .

Kilmartin was watching her; bless him, he looked concerned for her. Lily smiled weakly. "I'm sure he thinks the same of you."

Kilmartin gazed reflectively toward the doorway through which Gideon had disappeared. "I would like very much for Gideon to be happy. I just wish . . . I wish I knew for certain what it was that would make him . . ."

He trailed off and shook his head, and then turned to Lily again and smiled reassuringly. Kilmartin's was not an extraordinary face—but it was growing strangely dear. "You're not a bad sort, either, Miss Masters," he said. "Now,

I best go see if I can find him. I imagine you can call this time your own, if you like."

He bowed to her, she curtsied in return, and Kilmartin left her alone in the ballroom.

Fresh air should cool her flaming cheeks and clear her mind of Gideon Cole, Lily decided. If fresh air couldn't, then nothing could.

Well, she suspected *nothing* could, but cool air would feel lovely, anyhow.

She wasn't due to play cards with Lord Lindsey for another few hours or so. Today Alice had been excited about visiting the pigs: Lily thought she might like to see them, too, not to mention her sister. *However,* Lily thought, looking down at her lovely new dress and her gloved hands, *I probably shouldn't wear a white ball gown to visit pigs.* She'd best choose something else from the bizarre wealth of dresses that hung in her wardrobe.

She peeked into it, feeling a little like a servant intruding upon grand visitors. Walking dresses. Ball dresses. Dining dresses. Morning dresses. And things to cover them up—pelisses, shawls, aprons.

Perhaps, Lily thought, there should be dresses simply for sitting. Or for thinking. Perhaps there should be a *reading* dress. She almost laughed at the thought. Perhaps she should start a fashion, like that paragon Lady Constance Clary. *She starts fashions and ends them,* Gideon had said of Constance. As though this were an accomplishment akin to building Brighton Pavilion.

She managed to undo the tiny buttons on the back of her dress without any assistance—their tricky location posed no challenge whatsoever for the deft fingers of a pickpocket. She selected a dress—*Which one is the pig dress?* she wondered half whimsically. The one she chose was a soft shade of brown, trimmed with a minimum of fripperies, and it demurely covered up every bit of her.

There. And now, if she could find her way about London and about this great house, she could certainly find her way to Aster Park's outbuildings and to the pigs.

She found her sister perched on the edge of a pen, gazing down at an enormous sow and a collection of piglets jostling for teats. Alice's own dress appeared to be trimmed in about two inches of muck, and she looked every bit as happy as the pigs.

A grime-coated man stood nearby, watching and listening to Alice, who never seemed to need people to talk much. Fortunately, people often seemed content just to listen to Alice.

"Hello, goose! I thought I'd join you here this morning. How do you like the pigs?"

"Lily! Aren't they *lovely*? I've named all of them: that's Daisy, Phillip, Margaret, Fanny—she's the loud one—and Lily. I named Lily after you."

Lily looked down at her namesake; the pink of the piglet's skin showed through her coarse white piggy hair, and she had black spots on her rump and bristly pale eyelashes. She was very handsome, as piglets go, and she was winning the battle for a teat, Lily noted with satisfaction. "I'm flattered, Alice. They *are* lovely."

"And soon they will all be dinner," Alice said stoically.

Lily blinked. She glanced up at the grubby man standing nearby; his eyes were glinting with amusement. "Yes . . . well . . ."

"But then again, I *like* dinner. And that's just what life is like here on the farm." Alice sounded sage. "Every animal has a role to play."

Lily fought a laugh. "You've learned a good deal about farming, then, have you?"

"Oh, yes. Boone and Dawson—Lily, this is Dawson—" —the grubby man nodded to Lily; Lily nodded back— "think I might make a very good farmer one day. I'm a quick learner, they say," she added proudly.

"You always have been." She tugged Alice's braid.

But her smile faded as a realization intruded. This new ambition of Alice's was a far cry from girlish dreaming of grand houses and shoes. Alice had begun thinking of an actual, practical future. She would return to St. Giles with visions of pigs in her head.

And there were no pigs or peacocks in St. Giles. No acres upon acres of green lawns and tall spreading trees, no lakes or fountains. *No matter what I've told her, she will blame me when we leave.*

Standing over the pigs, the realization she'd been holding at bay charged her: damn him, but Gideon Cole was right; he'd always been right. He'd only been trying to make her see.

That she could not stay in St. Giles forever. Not for her sake or Alice's.

She held still, gathered her courage, and let her largest fear crash over her: *What will become of us?*

What was she suited *for*, anyway? A lodging house owner, a prostitute? An apothecary, a fence? She'd arrived at Aster Park a patchwork creature, half lady, half urchin . . . all pride. But what had the previous week made of her?

Lily had begun to suspect she'd be a creature divided her whole life: divided between gentility and the streets, between desperation to flee so she could call her days, her life, her own again . . .

And between wanting to stay, no matter what he did or said, to see how this particular story ended.

Gideon found Uncle Edward in bed, but the curtains were pulled open and a bar of sunlight fell across his legs, and there was evidence that he'd been up and about. An easel was set up in the corner; a palette stiff with dried paint lay next to it. A half-finished view of Aster Park as viewed through his window sprawled on the canvas. Uncle Edward had at one time dabbled in watercolors; today, it seemed, he was taking advantage of the sunlight to explore it again.

Lord Lindsey looked up from the book he was reading. It was Lily's *Encyclopedia of Natural History*, Gideon noted, fanned open to a page about antelopes.

"Oh, it's you, Gideon. Do come in." His voice was distracted; Lord Lindsey barely lifted his head from the book. Apparently he found antelopes captivating.

"You needn't sound so *enthusiastic*, Uncle Edward."

Lord Lindsey seemed oblivious to his sarcasm. "Did you bring that little minx with you? I must say, that Miss Masters is a breath of fresh air."

"But you don't *like* fresh air, Uncle Edward." Gideon now sounded as surly as a dockworker.

Startled, Lord Lindsey gave Gideon his full attention then, and something he saw made him frown. "Gideon, your face is— Come over here, lad."

Gideon hesitated.

"*Now*," Lord Lindsey commanded.

Gideon moved closer, and his uncle's eyes widened in concern.

"Good God, what is it, boy? What has happened? Is it an

investment? A case? It can't possibly be a—tell me it isn't a *woman*, Gideon. Is it that Constance chit? Sit down and tell me."

"I've brought a parcel addressed to you, Uncle Edward."

"Never mind that. Something is eating at you, and I doubt it has anything to do with that package."

Gideon lowered himself into the chair next to his uncle's bed. He slumped there for a moment, wishing he hadn't come up to his uncle at all, wishing he had gone through the main door and kept walking, maybe to . . . Dover, or something. But he decided he'd better speak.

"I can't tell you about it, sir. But thank you."

"Oh, nonsense, son. Look up at me. Are you in any trouble? I'll fix it straight away."

This made Gideon smile weakly. "No. It's nothing like that, I promise you. I apologize for the dramatics. It's a mood; it will pass."

"Do you have a mistress, Gideon?"

"*Uncle Edward!*"

"Honestly, you are far too serious; you work far too hard. If you don't intend to take a wife soon, you best take a mistress. Mistresses can do wonders for . . . 'moods.' "

Gideon studied his uncle for a moment. "Did *you* have a mistress, Uncle Edward?"

"Of course." Lord Lindsey smiled rakishly.

Gideon regarded him in intensely curious silence.

"Go ahead: ask me, lad."

"*While* you were married to Aunt Beatrice?"

"Well. I loved your aunt, Gideon."

"That's not an answer, Uncle Edward."

"Let me finish: I loved Beatrice. We had a wonderful life together, and there were the boys . . . But Therese, well . . ."

He paused, and something passed over his face; a

remembered pain, perhaps, or a remembered pleasure. "Therese *was* life."

Gideon sensed it would be unkind, selfish, to press him for more. But suddenly it seemed critical to know. "Did you love Aunt Beatrice when you married her?"

His uncle regarded him again for a moment thoughtfully, perhaps mulling over how to answer the question, or whether to answer it at all. Gideon held his breath.

"Beatrice and I were fond of each other when we married, Gideon." Lord Lindsey's voice faltered a bit, as though these were thoughts he had never before shared. "Life, and time, and shared joys and sorrows—that's how it became love. It is like that with most marriages. But I saw Therese as often as I could."

"Did you love Therese? Or was it just . . ."

Lord Lindsey inhaled deeply; he exhaled gustily. "In for a penny, in for a pound. I suppose I may as well tell you. Gideon, I loved Beatrice. But if we are being truthful, I was *in* love with Therese. It was often inconvenient, but it was never . . . it was never 'just.' "

Gideon absorbed this; it was less of a shock than he would have expected. "What became of her?" he asked softly.

"She decided to marry, for reasons of her own. A farmer. She moved to Devonshire many years ago and refused to see me after that. It very nearly killed me."

The deeply felt words hung in the room. Gideon and his uncle sat together for a time without speaking, immersed in separate thoughts.

"There was no one else after her," Lord Lindsey added distantly.

"Uncle Edward . . ." Gideon took a deep breath. "Did you ever regret your choice?"

"Choice, Gideon?" The baron looked surprised. "There was no choice. A well-bred young man does not marry his mistress. I loved and was loved by two good women. And I knew profound passion with one of them."

Gideon wished again he could leave the room so he could be alone with his thoughts, sift through his own feelings. He jounced his knee restlessly.

"I'm not sure you came in here to interrogate me about my romantic past, Gideon, but perhaps you did, and I hope I've said something of use to you. You're a good lad. You've indulged me above and beyond the call of duty, and I know it's not just because you hunger for a title. I loved my boys, as well you know. But I am proud of you, Gideon, and I think of you . . . well, I think of you as a son."

Good God. The old buzzard might just make me cry. Gideon reached out his hand; Lord Lindsey gripped it and gave it a startlingly firm squeeze for one supposedly enfeebled. And then he gave it a brisk pat and released it.

"Enough sentimental claptrap, eh, m'boy? What's in the package?"

"It's addressed to you, Uncle Edward."

Lord Lindsey tore through the paper like a child on Christmas morning. Two wide-mouthed brown bottles emerged, along with a sheet of foolscap.

Lord Lindsey read the note aloud. "'Compoments of McBride.'"

"'Compoments'?" Gideon frowned. "What the devil is a 'compoment'?"

"Oh!" Lord Lindsey was excited. "I think it's meant to say 'Compliments.' 'Compliments of McBride.' Lily's apothecary friend?" The baron handed one of the bottles to Gideon.

Gideon uncorked it and sniffed, then reared back,

blinking. "Good God. I think this is pure gin." He peered into the bottle. "Correction . . . it's gin with bits of something floating in it."

He passed the bottle back to his uncle, who took a deep appreciative sniff. "Ah, now *that's* what I call an elixir. Shall we?"

"Do you really think you should, Uncle Edward?"

"It will either kill me or cure me, Gideon, and I'm quite all right with either possibility. Ring for some glasses."

Suddenly, getting drunk on McBride's elixir in the middle of the day sounded like a capital idea. Gideon rang for the glasses.

Lily was just about to cross the threshold to Lord Lindsey's chambers for her game of cards when she heard a great, rending . . . snort. Followed by a series of soft, snuffling noises.

Rather like the nest of piglets competing for teats.

She thought it best, at that point, to approach the room cautiously. She peeked in.

Gideon and Kilmartin, bootless and in shirtsleeves, were layered across Lord Lindsey's bed, and across Lord Lindsey himself, like puppies. The room reeked of gin. And feet. And man.

All three men were snoring, at astonishingly different rhythms and pitches. It was a veritable respiratory symphony.

She tiptoed farther into the room and spotted two familiar large brown bottles tipped on the table. So McBride had received her note! And someone, clearly, had read it for him, because he'd delivered the requested elixir. She plucked up the sheet of foolscap near the bottle. " 'Compoments of McBride,' " she read aloud, softly. It was a reminder of home, of someone who cared for her for simple reasons, and a simpler if significantly more risky way of life, as the snorts rose and ebbed around her.

And then it occurred to her that a true luxury was at hand, one she thought she'd never be offered: the freedom to gaze unobserved at Gideon Cole.

She almost crept over to the bed; she jumped when Kilmartin twitched and murmured and flung an arm out. Her heart battering sickeningly at the walls of her chest, she looked down.

Gideon's lashes, nearly as thick as a girl's, shivered against the curve of his cheekbones; it seemed his dreams were as restless as his days. His eyebrows, by contrast, were ferociously masculine and wildly mussed, as though he had spent a good portion of the afternoon facedown and had finally rolled over. His firm, beautiful mouth was parted slightly; a beard was starting, darkening the hollows of his cheeks. His hair was pushed back, exposing the vulnerable blue-white of one temple.

She must really be gone on him if she found the man captivating even when he was stone drunk.

A short time ago this man had been deliberately cruel: *You're a thief, Lily, nothing more*. That had been the intent of his words, anyhow. And yet . . . his words and actions had carried the bite of hurt and fear. As though he had been defending himself against her.

But what can I possibly do to him?

And oh, this tempting suspicion: *Perhaps the very same thing he does to me.*

"You're good for him."

Lily jumped. Mrs. Plunkett was standing in the doorway, observing the mildly debauched scene with the dispassionate air of one who has seen everything, twice. She swiftly ducked out of the room again; Lily could hear her footsteps moving down the hall, the heavy tread that Lord Lindsey had once described to her.

Lily darted to the doorway. "Mrs. Plunkett!" she called. "Good for who?"

"Whom," the housekeeper corrected, without turning or pausing, and continued down the hall.

Dinner was served in their rooms that evening, which didn't surprise Lily in the least. She doubted the gentlemen of the house would be fit for any activity, with the exception, possibly, of retching. So Lily and Alice took their meal together, and Alice chattered on about the gardens. And the pigs. And the servants, who, it seemed, lived astonishingly vivid lives.

Lily brushed her sister's hair out in long strokes as they prepared for sleep. "In a day or so, Alice, I will be going on a trip with Mr. Cole and Lord Kilmartin. We shall be away for"—Lily wasn't certain how long their stay in London would last—"for a time. But not a very long time."

Alice absorbed this information. "May I come along?"

"Well, it really is a trip for . . . older people, dearest. You will find it quite dull. We thought you'd like to stay here with Mrs. Plunkett and Boone to help take care of Aster Park while we are gone. Dawson may need some help with the pigs."

Lily had never been apart from her sister since she was born. She had a very strong suspicion that the separation would trouble her a good deal more than it would trouble Alice.

"Lily?"

"Yes?"

"Are you going to marry Mr. Cole?"

Lily froze mid-brush. "No, Alice." She drew the brush

through her sister's tangles again. And for some reason, uttering those two words was like swallowing glass.

"But you should. Perhaps I shall ask him to marry you. Ow! Lily, that pulls!"

"Alice?"

"Yes, Lily?"

"Please make me a solemn promise that you will ask him nothing of the sort."

Alice frowned. "But I am certain he wouldn't mind marrying you. Then we could all live together forever. And have picnics and such."

It was moments like these that Lily almost hated Gideon Cole. When the game was over, when Gideon was finally engaged to Lady Constance Clary, it would be Lily who was left to explain to Alice why they would never see him again.

But then again, it was more or less Lily's fault that she and Alice were here at all.

"We shall have other adventures, dearest," she told her sister finally, her voice thick.

And Alice still looked puzzled, but she refrained from fussing. Bless her, but Alice never fussed.

Chapter Eleven

The tap came at the accustomed time, and Lily, awake hours earlier in anticipation, bounded to the door. She took her tray from Mrs. Plunkett. Eggs and bread and coffee and—

Where was her note?

A strange little clutch of fear tightened her belly; she looked up at Mrs. Plunkett and prayed her eyes showed nothing of what she felt.

"You're to go down to the ballroom when you've finished your breakfast, Miss Masters. And then you're free to do as you like with your day. The gentlemen have . . . other plans."

Casting their accounts all day, no doubt.

"Lord Lindsey, as well?"

Mrs. Plunkett hesitated, and . . . was that the faintest hint of a smile on her lips? "Lord Lindsey will be sleeping for the greater part of the afternoon. He sends his regrets. Dinner will be brought to your room tonight."

"Thank you." Lily's voice was threadbare from nerves.

Alice skipped away with Mrs. Plunkett; Lily could hear her chattering away to the taciturn housekeeper, as though she were ever likely to reply.

* * *

There was a man in the ballroom, but it wasn't Gideon Cole or Lord Kilmartin. A bespectacled chap, slight, with curly hair trimmed close to his scalp, stood diffidently near the pianoforte. His coat was of a dark blue cloth with brass buttons, not nearly as fine as anything she'd seen Kilmartin or Gideon wearing; perhaps he wasn't a slave to the fashion requirements of the *ton*.

"Miss Masters?" He bowed.

Lily curtsied; odd how natural the motion had become. "Yes, Mr.—"

"Paul." He had a soft kind voice.

"Forgive me, sir, but I must know your surname."

"Forgive *me*, Miss Masters," the man stammered. "I was not merely being presumptuous. My surname *is* Paul."

Lily was confused. "You are Mr. Paul Paul?"

"I am Mr. *Geoffrey* Paul, Miss Masters. I am a pianoforte teacher."

"Oh." Lily frowned puzzled. And then, as understanding seeped in: "*Oh.*" She breathed the word reverently. "Were you sent here . . ."

"To give you a lesson? Yes."

He knew, she told herself, almost afraid to believe it. She'd longed to touch that pianoforte since she'd arrived.

Gideon Cole sees everything.

The maddening man. Her heart felt like a bud bursting into sudden bloom.

"Have you ever before played the pianoforte, Miss Masters?" Mr. Paul said when it appeared Miss Lily Masters did not intend to speak again.

"No. Well . . . yes, but I was very small. I knew only simple tunes, and I doubt I still know them."

"All tunes are simple once you know them, Miss

Masters." He smiled at her. "And you may be surprised by what your fingers still know."

Sheet music rustled in Mr. Paul's hands; he settled it on the pianoforte. "Can you read music at all, Miss Masters?"

"No, sir." She lowered herself slowly to the pianoforte bench and stared down. All those keys, all those songs waiting to spring from them. How could she touch only a few? How did any composer ever decide which ones to include in a song?

Lily tentatively positioned her fingers over middle C, closed her eyes, struck two notes. She opened her eyes and looked down at her hands, but her fingers seemed to grow shy and lose their way, so she looked up again and let them do what they wanted to do. Little by little, a halting tune comprised half of wrong notes emerged.

She stopped and stared wonderingly up at Mr. Paul, awed by her own music.

Mr. Paul, that kind man, smiled at her. "I recognize the song, believe it or not, Miss Masters. It's 'The Dew on the White Rose.' It's a lullaby, of sorts. Shall we practice it?"

"Oh, yes, please."

"All right. Why don't we begin again?"

"Why don't we?" Lily agreed happily.

He hovered at the edge of the doorway for a long while, watching her. He watched her through her first attempt at the song, and the second, and the third. He watched her laugh delightedly at her mistakes, and turn her shining face up at Mr. Paul, asking for guidance.

And really, Gideon decided as he watched her, he could watch Lily do anything at all, for hours on end. Picking her teeth, perhaps. Reading a book. Eating. With both hands, even.

Familiar acts are made beautiful through love.

He reared back from the thought as though it were a rat

that had suddenly scurried across his feet. Who had said that? Some bloody poet, probably. He really needed to stop reading poetry; it would rot his mind, and a barrister needed a sharp mind.

Thanks to McBride's elixir, pain still played tympani on his temples, and truth be told, the pianoforte music was killing him. His uncle, damn the man, seemed almost entirely unaffected, apart from an expressed desire to sleep away the day. If anything, he seemed even more cheerful than usual. Poor Kilmartin, on the other hand, was still casting his accounts in a chamber pot upstairs. Both he and Kilmartin would be useless to anyone today. Gideon wanted strong tea and a dark room.

But this morning, he'd been alert enough to dash a note off to Mr. Paul, a respected local music teacher. The inspiration had been there for some time now; McBride's elixir had presented the opportunity.

And after a little more thought, he'd decided to engage Mr. Paul's services to play waltzes. Kilmartin, Gideon decided, could dance with Lily, and Gideon would . . . well, he'd do something else during that time.

For he didn't dare touch her again.

When the endlessly patient Mr. Paul took his leave of her, Lily was faced with another luxurious stretch of time to herself, so she decided to visit the library once again. She approached it cautiously, lest she find Gideon Cole in there.

He wasn't. But she felt his presence as strongly as if he actually were. Her eyes landed on the chair nearest the fire; her memories filled it with him reciting Shakespeare by firelight, his eyes tracing the length of her and going unreadable again.

She tried to cram the disparate things she felt for Gideon

into the scratchy hair shirt of cynicism: *It's simple, Lily. He simply wants to get his hands on you, have his way with you, and his precious pride can't bear the very idea of wanting a* pickpocket *from St. Giles. That's all.*

But they were too large and shining and nebulous, all the things she felt. They slid right out of that hair shirt, because it was like trying to dress a ray of light.

He'd sent her a book and stockings and a pianoforte teacher.

I'm not sure why I care, Miss Masters. But I do.

Lily shook her head, sending these thoughts scattering, and settled into the chair; she could smell him faintly on it, and she closed her eyes, imagining, for a moment, it was indeed Gideon: his arms would close around her, she would arc her head back so his lips could reach her throat, so his hands could reach down to her—

Really. She often regretted ever reading that little French book, for the stories returned to her constantly now, feeding her already roaring imagination like shreds of hay.

She opened her eyes again and noticed the thick book resting on the little table next to the chair: *Elements of English Law*. It gapped a little in the middle; Gideon had tucked something there to hold his place, no doubt. Perhaps he'd been reading up on pickpockets. She almost smiled, and then she began to worry a little that it might be true, so she pulled the book open to the marked page.

But it wasn't the page he'd marked that was interesting. It was the marker he'd used: a little red book. It was the book he had turned over in his lap the night she'd surprised him in the library, she was certain of it.

The Collected Poems of John Keats.

Imagine *that*. Gideon Cole read poetry and hid it within the pages of the book he probably thought he *ought* to be reading.

Lily tucked her feet up underneath her, opening the little book tenderly, as though she were cracking open his heart. All the pages looked well thumbed; one of them sported a faded reddish stain; port, perhaps. She decided to begin reading there.

Thou still unravish'd bride of quietness,
Thou foster-child of silence and slow time,

She read the words aloud, astonished by the feel of them on her tongue, by the music they made. She read on, slowly and solemnly, as though she were reciting a spell that would open up a seam in time through which she could actually see Keats's Grecian urn.

This is Gideon, she thought. *Pure beauty hidden among a great heavy book of codes and rules.*

She read the last lines of the poem aloud, softly.

Beauty is truth, truth beauty,—that is all
Ye know on earth, and all ye need to know.

Lily lowered the book slowly into her lap. *All ye need to know.*

He was a capricious, impatient, maddening man who insisted on stifling the best part of himself. Who lived his every moment in preparation for some future day. But as far as she was concerned, Gideon Cole was beauty. And truth. And, at the moment, all she ever wanted or needed to know.

She closed her eyes to shut out everything in the library, to be alone with this awareness. It was like being suspended in a warm, brilliant light, in that place between flight

. . . and falling.

Chapter Twelve

LM—Here is your schedule for today:

10:30	*Dancing*
12:00	*Luncheon and cards with Lord Lindsey*
1:30	*Deportment*
6:00	*Dining and packing for London*

The morning will be devoted to the waltz, as previous appointments have interfered with your lessons. The evening will be devoted to packing for our trip to London. Dinner will be taken in our respective quarters.

Lily read the note again. And then realization set in; her hand rose to touch her face in a tiny gesture of joy, of trepidation, of anticipation. They were to waltz all morning.

Gideon's hand on her waist, his hand covering hers, his eyes warm upon her, his scent surrounding her . . .

They were to waltz all morning.

* * *

Gideon and Kilmartin were waiting for her in the ballroom, both still a trifle pale and bleary-eyed in the aftermath of the elixir episode.

"Good morning, Miss Masters."

The voice came from near the pianoforte; Lily turned in surprise to find Mr. Paul.

"Oh! Good morning, Mr. Paul." She gave him a curtsy.

There was a strangely awkward silence, and then Gideon cleared his throat. "Mr. Paul has been invited to play a variety of waltzes for you this morning. Kilmartin will dance with you today, Miss Masters, as we believe it is beneficial for you to experience a . . . variety of dancing partners."

The words knocked the wind from her. "I see," she said softly, finally.

Gideon took an audible breath, and his words were rushed and nearly toneless, as though he'd rehearsed them. "I have business elsewhere on my uncle's estate. I shall see you and Lord Kilmartin this afternoon for our . . ." He glanced at Mr. Paul.

He could hardly call it a "deportment lesson," Lily thought, in front of someone not privy to their little charade. "I shall see you this afternoon," he said finally.

Lily found she had nothing to say to that.

Gideon bowed to all of them. He would not meet her eyes as he left the ballroom.

Reeling with hurt, she turned her head away from his retreating back to find Kilmartin's kind eyes upon her.

"Let's take a spin, then, shall we, Miss Masters?" he said gently. "But not so fast as usual, perhaps, Mr. Paul. A slow waltz."

Mr. Paul smiled. "Certainly, Lord Kilmartin."

"Miss Masters?" Kilmartin extended his arms, inviting her to step near.

She stepped into them, numbly. After all, they were to waltz all morning.

The view of Aster Park from Lord Lindsey's window now filled the entire canvas. Lily admired it over his shoulder as the baron pondered his next play.

"You're a bit subdued, child. Dreaming of London, are you?" Lord Lindsey had won the first hand; they were now in the middle of the second. "You are leaving soon, are you not?"

"Tomorrow, Lord Lindsey."

"Ah. And no doubt you will find more worthy card partners in the *ton*."

"Nonsense. None so worthy as you, Lord Lindsey."

The baron smiled. "Well, of course not. I was testing you, Lily. You see, I've won every hand today." He sipped at his tea and replaced it in his saucer; porcelain rang against porcelain. It had become a comforting sound now. *Every time I hear it, from now on, I'll think of Lord Lindsey.*

"I am glad you insisted on our daily games, sir, for you have much sharpened my skills."

"Oh, I never insisted, Lily, though I *would* have if my nephew hadn't. He sent you up to me the day after we met. And the next day, and so on."

"I'm glad he insisted, too, Lord Lindsey." Her voice had gone thick.

"You'll get yourself engaged in London, no doubt, child. Will you come again to see me after that?"

She almost didn't trust herself to speak. "Yes, sir, of course," she lied softly, finally.

For what was one more lie in the midst of all of the others?

* * *

Lily appeared in the ballroom for her deportment lesson looking subdued, Kilmartin at her side.

How many ways are there for a man to despise himself? Gideon thought dryly. Infinite, surely. He'd been behaving like a lunatic, warm and playful one moment, all childish fits the next. No wonder she looked subdued.

"Gideon, do you need me for this portion of the lesson? I should like a dark room and a cool rag across my forehead."

Gideon turned to Kilmartin. Laurie *did* look a trifle green; perhaps spinning about in the waltz had not been the wisest thing for him to do in the wake of the elixir episode. And so Gideon felt guilty about that, as well.

"Well, we can probably do without you, Laurie. I believe we shall simply spend our remaining time on walking, since Miss Masters still holds her head up like a pugilist and tends to flee rather than walk."

He watched Lily's chin go up stubbornly at his assessment. *Good.* Stubborn was better than subdued.

"Thank you, Gideon. Don't forget we are to see Cunnington's mare this afternoon. I will very likely see you . . . tomorrow morning, Miss Masters, if not at dinner? For we leave first thing."

"Very good, then, Lord Kilmartin." Lily curtsied for Laurie.

And so Gideon was left alone with Lily. They regarded each other for a moment, awkwardly; her chin was still up high. Lord, but her neck was lovely and long, he thought absently, a delicate thing rising up out of her pale gown. Like a swan.

Like a swan!

"Follow me, Miss Masters." He spun about and all but dashed out the ballroom; he heard Lily's slippers clacking frantically on the marble behind him. Gideon led her down the stairs and out of the house and into the back garden; he stopped when they reached the fountain and swept an arm toward the three great white swans sailing haughtily in the waters of it.

"Now, see how the swans *glide*, Miss Masters, their necks high and proud, but not *too* high and proud? You can do that. Your chin is always up there, anyhow, high and proud." He imitated her, stuck his chin skyward. She smiled a little. "Just lower it a notch. The tiniest notch. Give it a try."

She poked her chin up defiantly, and swept through the grass, the hem of her dress darkening as it touched the dew. "How is this?"

"Hmmm . . . your shoulders are good, but lower your head just a little bit more and . . . glide. No, do not scurry. Remember, you've nowhere in particular to go, nothing to run from or to, you are . . . well, pretend you are a queen. There is no need for defiance, for you rule all, you *own* all. And all eyes are upon you."

Lily gave herself a little shake, as though unraveling a poorly knitted stitch, and recomposed herself. And then . . . shoulders back, chin ever so slightly up, her hands loose . . .

She glided. Beautifully. At last.

"That's it, Lily! Splendid! Like a . . . queen."

His voice trailed off. For she did look exactly the way a queen should look, delicate and fiery and proud, the sun turning her dark gold hair into a gleaming coronet.

She stopped gliding. "Was that it?" Hope widened her eyes.

"Yes." He smiled down at her. "You did it beautifully." A single hair lay against her neck, a glinting thread; Gideon reached out a hand and idly lifted it up, as if to show it to her. And as he did, his fingers gently brushed against the skin of her throat.

Lily went very still.

Gideon frowned faintly. For a long moment he was dimly aware of other things: the fluttering of the lace at her neckline. A swan fanning its wings in the fountain. The scent of old roses.

And then Lily's eyes, the curve of her lips, became the universe.

Gideon cupped his hand around Lily's neck and continued gazing down at her; his thumb began to stroke, slowly stroke, the silky skin beneath her jaw. Her eyes trembled closed.

"Forgive me, Lily." The words were almost a sigh.

He lowered his head.

It was a breath of a kiss, a testing kiss. But it could not remain that way; the desire had been too long denied. Her lips beneath his were a miracle, all softness and give; and Gideon's lips became gently insistent, moving over hers until they parted to allow his tongue to stroke tentatively between them. When Lily made a soft sound in the back of her throat, a soft sound of wanting, Gideon slid his hands down over her shoulders and wrapped his arms around her slim waist, and Lily's hands glided up his chest to clasp behind his head, settling into his embrace.

And then she tilted her head back, opening fully to him.

There was nothing of artifice or expertise in her kiss, just want and instinct. Dizzy with wonder and greed, Gideon's mouth took hers; her lips met, moved with his in equal hunger. Their tongues twined, withdrew, twined again, as Lily's fingers dragged softly over the nape of his neck.

The pleasure was sweeter, more piercing than anything he had ever known.

Gideon drew a path with lips from her mouth to her throat, and then delicately tasted the fragile skin there, felt her heart beat there; Lily sighed, murmured something softly. He pulled her closer still, tightly up against him so she could feel the hard swell of his arousal, so she could know what the feel of her, the taste of her, did to him; she buried her face in his throat, her breath, her lips, hot against his skin, and pushed herself closer, closer, moving her hips against him, seeking her own pleasure and driving him closer to the edge of frenzy. *She wants me, too.*

And the realization spurred his hands; he grew bolder, more insistent, more rash and eager. His lips took her mouth again, more deliberately, and he began to gather her dress up in his fingers, in a fever to touch the skin between her thighs, to cup the heat between her legs, to delve his fingers into the moisture he knew was gathering there, to make her shake in his arms, cry out for him. *I can take her now. I will take her here in the garden—*

And then a swan made an irritated sound, and sense seeped back into Gideon's consciousness.

He lifted his lips from hers at once and held her loosely away from him in a sort of shock; Lily leaned her forehead against his chest. They stood that way for what felt like minutes, breathing roughly, the summer sunshine beating down.

At last Gideon pulled away from Lily's embrace and looked down at her. Her cheeks were flushed, her lips stung pink, her eyes dazed and heated still.

Gideon sank onto the little wrought iron bench and slumped there, his hands flat against his thighs. He looked hunted.

"Lily, I've no right . . . I should not have . . ."

She slowly lowered herself onto the bench, a careful distance away from him. In the silence that followed, she could hear the fountain pouring itself endlessly into the swan pool.

Her senses reeled, drunk with Gideon Cole. Ghosts of sensation lingered on her fingertips, her lips and throat, as though they'd been held up to a fire. Her hands in his silky hair, on his warm skin, his sweet hard mouth joined with hers . . . and the taste of him, the salt and musk . . . it was far more potent than anything, *anything* she could have lived in her imagination, or read in a book.

"She is all that is worthy," Gideon said finally, half to himself. He turned to look at Lily, then turned quickly away, as though the sight of her was too painful. "Constance, that is. She has . . . wealth and position. She is the daughter of a marquis." It sounded as though he was trying to explain something, both to himself and to her. Lily waited.

"You see . . ." Gideon took a deep breath. "My sister, Helen . . . well, her husband is not a . . . good man." He paused. "He . . . he drinks."

"Oh." There was something more; Lily sensed it. "Papa drank."

Gideon's head turned toward her swiftly. "Did he ever hurt you?"

"No. He merely drank up everything we had." She smiled sadly. But then all at once she understood. "Mr. Cole—your sister's husband—does he—?"

Gideon closed his beautiful dark eyes wearily. When he opened them again, they were old and tormented. His hand fluttered up to his cheekbone, a sort of hopeless gesture. "Here. She's had bruises here, Lily. The sort that . . . that a fist would leave. More than once I've seen them. Helen has not stated so outright, but . . . I'm certain of it. He drinks," Gideon concluded grimly, "and then he hits her."

"Oh, Gideon." Lily's voice had gone faint.

"And you see, Lily . . . Helen and I, after we lost our parents, there was very little money, and much debt. Crushing debt. And well, I was a boy, Lily. I confess I was . . . a little afraid. I sold our home to pay the debts, and Helen and I had very little money left. We discussed it, and Helen decided to marry a man who offered for her, so I could continue on at Oxford with what money we had. She was seventeen at the time, but she claimed to *like* the idea of being wed. But now I think . . . well, if I'd gone into soldiering rather than staying at Oxford . . . perhaps my tuition could have become her dowry . . . perhaps I could have secured a better marriage for her. But I," he added bitterly, "*wanted* to stay on at Oxford. I wanted to somehow restore all my father had managed to lose. To build and keep a fortune, restore our family's honor, such as it was. And Helen knew I wanted it. I think that may be part of the reason she agreed to this marriage. I don't think her husband was always quite like this. But over the years his drinking has worsened. As has his . . . conduct."

Lily closed her own eyes against the ache that swelled in her. Gideon Cole, protector of the weak and defenseless, tormentor of pickpockets, occupied a hell on earth. Because he had not been able to protect his own sister.

"Your uncle . . . perhaps she could come here . . ."

"Well, Helen's ashamed, you see; my uncle was dead against the marriage from the start. They argued bitterly about it and haven't spoken since, and she won't come to Aster Park. It was like Uncle Edward *knew*. . . . Anyhow, when I marry Lady Constance Clary . . . among other things, I believe I can persuade Helen to come to live with me. At the very least, I will be able to set her up in her own household."

And now Lily understood what Gideon was really telling

her. He was a good man, a kind man, a beautiful man. A *human* man. And an honorable man, in his way. But nothing had changed. His Master Plan remained. And Lady Constance Clary was the key to his future.

"I will not keep you if you wish to leave Aster Park, Lily." He looked away from her to say these words; his voice was frayed, soft with emotion.

I love him. The realization struck Lily as cleanly as a rock to the head, though it had been dawning for days now. She loved him. It was a strange, delicious anguish, a birth and a death. She traced Gideon's profile with her eyes, numb with a sense of unreality that something that seemed so clearly meant for her could never, ever be.

She listened to the fountain pouring endlessly into itself and thought: *So this is love. It fills you up, so you must give it away or it will flood you.*

"I will go with you to London, Gideon. I will help you to win Constance." Her heart was in the words; she hoped Gideon knew it. "I will make very certain that you do."

He smiled, that slow gift of a smile that—oh God—carved her heart right out of her chest.

"Thank you, Lily."

He did not look like a grateful man. He looked like a man in agony.

"But once you are engaged to Lady Clary . . . I will go," she added gently.

Gideon slowly skimmed her features with his eyes, as if memorizing her face. "If that is what you desire." His voice had gone husky.

But they both knew that Lily, proud Lily, would have it no other way. *Never allow yourself to be at the mercy of any man, Lily.*

"It is what I desire." Gently said, but firmly, too.

He nodded once. "What will you do then?"

"What I have always done. Survive." She tried for flippancy, but her voice broke a little, spoiling it.

Another silence passed between them; to Lily, it felt like a widening of the inevitable gulf.

"Ho, Gideon, are we going to see Mr. Cunnington's mare this afternoon?" Kilmartin's hearty voice rang across the garden.

"I'll be there in a moment, Laurie."

Gideon stood up, and Lily followed. "Until dinner, then, Miss Masters?"

"Very well, Mr. Cole." She curtsied, beautifully, and a hint of a smile touched his lips.

"I would have no worries about the *ton*, Lily. You are perhaps the truest lady I've ever had the pleasure of knowing."

He bowed low to her, and she watched him walk, his hair glowing like lit coal in the sun, away from her and toward Kilmartin's impatient voice.

Chapter Thirteen

"Another demned relative, eh?" was how Aunt Hester greeted the three of them when they arrived at her London town house.

Aunt Hester studied Lily through a quizzing glass, which made her watery blue eyes look enormous, and magnified the millions of fine lines that hatched her face.

"You don't look like any of the other Mowbrys, but I aver, Lawrence's branch of the family mated like rabbits," she pronounced flatly, finally, her scrutiny completed. "Can't keep track anymore. No matter: pleased to meet you dear, welcome, and if you're a relative, well, you can call me Aunt Hester. I've been called into service as chaperone here, and I hope you appreciate it. Bloody dull, if you ask me."

And with that, Aunt Hester turned abruptly and wobbled out of the room, her cane thumping the floor.

The three of them stared after her open-mouthed.

"Well, *she's* certainly charming, Laurie," Gideon managed at last.

"She's *old*, Gideon. She probably wouldn't care if we entertained a cast of Drury Lane actresses in the downstairs sitting room. Nor would she hear it, come to that. But she's all the respectability we need. And look out for her cane. I felt it more than once across my legs as a lad—she has a wicked swing."

"She said 'demned' and 'bloody.'" Lily was awed. "And she never curtsied once."

"She gave all that up long ago," Kilmartin explained. "The privileges of being old and rich, I suppose. And if she attempted a curtsy, she'd probably never be able to straighten herself to a standing position again."

"I like her," Lily declared.

"Don't let it give you any ideas, Miss Masters." Gideon smiled a little. "*You* will be curtsying and saying 'goodness.' Now, let's get settled into our rooms. Where are the footmen with our trunks?"

On cue, a series of footmen—surprisingly young and handsome and virile-looking footmen—paraded in with the trunks containing Lily's London finery and proceeded up the stairs.

Gideon pointed to a tray overflowing with little white cards. "I sent word to various acquaintances that we'd be returning to the *ton*, as did Laurie, and he mentioned you'd be along, too. That blizzard of cards and invitations is the result. Everyone is curious to see *you*, Miss Masters, for you are a new face, and any new face on the scene excites curiosity. Tonight, we will begin in earnest—we will be attending a ball. Lady Braxton's seasonal do. Do you think you can manage it?"

As he'd expected, Lily's chin went up. Gideon smiled a little. Lily did defiance the way other people breathed.

"Watch that chin," he told her softly. "Think 'swan.'"

And then he was sorry he'd said it. Because "swan" reminded both of them of the garden, and the sun beating down, and an extraordinary kiss. He watched a flush slowly tint Lily's cheeks; he felt an uncomfortable warmth in his own. He decided to make a great show of following the footmen up the stairs, issuing orders as he went.

He tried and failed to pretend he couldn't feel a pair of aquamarine eyes on his back.

The smell of something cooking rose up to Gideon in his room. Aunt Hester certainly had a decent household staff; they would not waste away while they stayed with her. She probably paid her servants well. Or perhaps they were simply afraid of her cane.

He sat down on his bed and opened the little box; it hadn't been touched in years, and the lid creaked, protesting. But the necklace, a single tiny, round diamond on a gold chain, had lost none of its gleam. He lifted it out and looped it over one finger; it swung gently, the tiny diamond frisking with the light.

The necklace had been his mother's, one of the few things his father hadn't gambled away or pawned. She had cherished it, his mother, and Gideon and Helen had known that when it appeared around her neck, the occasion was special indeed.

Lily would need a necklace to wear with her finery. At one time he'd thought he'd give the necklace to Constance once they were wed, but he'd since thought better of it: doubtless the tiny diamond would confuse and embarrass her. He could give it to Helen . . . but it was entirely possible her husband would take it from her and pawn it.

But why give it to Lily? She was only an ephemeral part of his life; she would leave him when their charade had ended. And if he could stop thinking of the kiss in the garden, of course, that memory would fade eventually, too.

But he couldn't stop thinking of the kiss in the garden.

A hot weakness swept through him again, a desire unlike anything he'd ever experienced. Last night, lying awake, he had thought he would die if he couldn't someday—*soon*—take Lily Masters.

But he would not use undue persuasion. He wanted her to choose him for his own sake, rather than for . . . for the sake of having a protector. If she did not come to him willingly . . . well, then, it could never, ever be.

He gave himself a shake. *Good God, get a hold of yourself, Cole.* All of this internal Byronic drama had been exacerbated, he was sure, by the fact that he had been virtually cloistered with her and Kilmartin in the country. That he had not tasted or touched a woman intimately for far too long.

He simply could not imagine losing control and inching Constance's dress up in the garden. He half smiled; making love to Constance would require a certain amount of ceremony. *The minute I see Constance again I will come to my senses.* Constance was glorious, a true aristocrat; she was the future he'd devoted years to securing.

He decided, then, he would go out to White's instead of dining with Lily and Kilmartin; their carriage could stop by to fetch him before the ball. But he would leave the necklace with Kilmartin with instructions to give it to Lily. For Lily's glowing eyes when he gave her the necklace were not images he could risk adding to his gallery of memories.

The fewer memories he had of Lily Masters, the less likely they were to haunt him when she was gone.

"We've lost Gideon for the time being, Miss Masters," Kilmartin announced cheerfully, "but then again, that means more dinner for the two of us. We'll fetch him at White's before the ball. My *God*, you look a peach."

Such unwelcome news delivered in such a cheerful voice was jarring. And when it was followed by a *compliment* . . . For one moment, Lily was utterly rattled.

"Er . . . thank you, Lord Kilmartin," she finally managed. She usually enjoyed Kilmartin's honest appraisals. She knew his heart was firmly in the hands of Lady Anne Clapham, and he had no use for flattery; therefore, his compliments were all sincerity.

But where *was* Gideon, then? Her disappointment was acute. She was wearing the blue satin, the one that Madame Marceau had assured her made her look a veritable diamond of the first water, and Lily wanted to see this confirmed in Gideon's eyes. It would have given her courage.

"Oh! He left something for you." Kilmartin produced a little box. "Necklace. We should have thought of it before, for of course any young lady would need a necklace to go with all her finery. So here it is." He thrust the box at Lily.

"Oh." She stared at the box dumbly for a moment, and then, her hands trembling a little, she pried up the lid. Her heart skipped. Was it actually a . . . *diamond*? On a *gold* chain? Had Gideon given her a *diamond*?

"It's a diamond," Kilmartin said. "Albeit just a speck of one. I think it belonged to Gideon's mother. He wanted you to have it."

"Oh," Lily said faintly, again.

"Umm . . . do you need help with the clasp?" Kilmartin looked uncomfortable. Clearly he did not want to fumble about at Lily's neck.

"Oh, no, I can manage it all on my own, thank you."

And Lily held the box as though she were holding Gideon's beating heart.

* * *

The ride in the carriage to the Braxton ball was a silent affair, for the most part; the three of them, Kilmartin, Gideon, and Lily, were as tense as three highwaymen about to accost a mail coach.

Lily sat across from Gideon, bathed in shadows. A silk shawl covered her; he wondered which of Madame Marceau's creations she had chosen to wear for this momentous evening, and if perhaps he should have helped her choose.

Aunt Hester sat next to Lily, snoring softly. She had agreed to accompany them, for propriety's sake, but only long enough to be noted as a chaperone, and then make an exit, as surreptitious an exit as a formidable countess forever draped in black bombazine could make.

"You look an absolute peach, Miss Masters," Kilmartin said again, reassuringly. He'd said it at least three or four times; it had become something of a nervous stutter. It was grating on Gideon's nerves.

They'd discussed it: Lily would enter with Kilmartin; Hester would enter behind them. And Gideon would wait, and enter last of all, mingling with the crowd, watching Lily and Kilmartin's progress through it, to meet up with them again to conspicuously greet Miss Masters.

"Parry everything," Gideon reminded her softly.

"Stories," Kilmartin added nervously. "Don't forget the stories."

Lily smiled, and her smile was like a little wedge of light in the darkness of the coach. It was almost as though she were reassuring Kilmartin and Gideon, when in fact, Gideon thought, it should really be the other way around.

* * *

It began subtly enough. Kilmartin and Lily entered the party, through the lit arch of the doorway, past the phalanx of footmen; Gideon lingered behind them, and watched.

He saw a head—it belonged to Lord Stanley—turn idly; perhaps he was looking for a friend in the crowd.

But then Lord Stanley's casually searching gaze lit upon Lily.

His head went rigid.

He stared.

A moment later Lord Stanley tore his gaze away from her and whispered to his companion, Lord Something-or-Other; Gideon could not recall the man's name.

Lord Something-or-Other joined Lord Stanley in staring.

As Lily and Kilmartin made their leisurely way through the crowd, another head turned. And another. And then another and another . . .

It was like watching the path of a lit fuse.

Lily, gliding like a swan, made her shimmering way through the crowd escorted by Kilmartin, who was flushed with all the unaccustomed attention and with the pleasure of appearing with one of the loveliest girls in London on his arm. The candlelight set Lily aglow, from the dark gold of her hair down the length of her gown—a silver-blue satin with an overlay of fine patent net; like mist floating over a dawn sky. Madame Marceau was a genius, Gideon thought. Lily was a shining thing. Almost otherworldly.

And he alone of the people in this ballroom knew how fully *of* this world she was. For he alone of anyone here had felt the frantic beat of her heart beneath his lips.

He took a deep breath. He was supposed to be keeping an eye out for Constance.

And as Constance was always difficult to miss, he soon found her: looking like Spring itself in gold-trimmed willow green silk, surrounded by a group of lesser mortals, her handmaidens among them. She did rather stop the breath, Constance did. Like one's first sight of the Parthenon.

And Constance, too, was watching Lily's progress through the crowd, wearing an expression Gideon had never before seen on her face—speculative and narrow-eyed.

The crowd swallowed Kilmartin and Lily up and Gideon lost sight of them.

Constance became aware of Gideon's eyes upon her. Her face transformed immediately; she smiled, a cool, dazzling smile of welcome, and gave a subtle nod. Gideon responded with a slow sultry smile that made feminine hearts, and maybe a male heart or two, palpitate all over the ballroom, and bowed in return to her.

And then he ignored her and all the hands and voices that reached out for him in delighted greeting and pursued Kilmartin and Lily through the crowd.

It's like one of my stories. I've walked into one of my stories.

Lily decided to treat the event as a dream; for in dreams, one merely followed where the dream led, and marveled at the things that unfolded, and—most importantly—woke unscathed. Her heart, which had been throwing itself violently against her rib cage, slowed to a more civilized pace.

She'd never seen so many clean, beautiful people massed in her life. They glinted, these people, as though the chandelier light had been specifically designed to point out jewels to her: rings and necklaces, bracelets and tiaras. Just *one* piece would support her and Alice for life.

But she was here for Gideon and his bloody Master Plan, not to shop for her future.

They came at her for introductions, handsome, scrupulously groomed young men, their eagerness straining at the confines of their fine manners. Lord Jarvis, a smiling affable blond gentleman, claimed a waltz. She bestowed reels on a few others, offering up her dance card while Kilmartin looked on protectively and a little nervously.

Gideon arrived just as Lily was extracting her hand from the paw of the handsome young George Willett.

"Very nice to meet you, Mr. Willett," she said. "I look forward to our dance."

Overcome with admiration, Mr. Willett's mouth opened and closed a few times, and then he abandoned the notion of speaking and simply bowed and backed away.

"Oh, hello, Mr. Cole. I believe you know my cousin, Miss Masters?" Kilmartin measured the words out as though reciting them from a script.

"*Do* try to be a little more subtle, Laurie," Gideon murmured. "A pleasure to see you again, Miss Masters," he said, raising his voice a bit for the benefit of anyone who might be attempting to eavesdrop. He bowed lingeringly over Lily's extended hand, and then straightened and met her eyes.

Lily realized she and Gideon had been gazing silently at each other for an inordinately long time only when she noticed the disconcerted expression on Kilmartin's face. She withdrew her hand from Gideon's and it went up to touch her diamond, almost unconsciously; Gideon's eyes followed it there, and he looked, for a moment, shaken.

"Before you came up to us, Gideon, Lily made the acquaintance of Lord Jarvis," Kilmartin told him, his voice low but thrumming with excitement. "And Lord Jarvis claimed a *waltz*."

"*Very* good news indeed, Laurie. One less waltz he can

share with Constance. Will you do *me* the honor of a waltz or two, Miss Masters?" His eyes on her were gently amused.

Lily could only nod. Her chin was up and proud, she realized; she adjusted it to a less combative angle, and Gideon gave her a crooked smile.

A swoop of vivid color caught her eye then; Lily looked up to find an alarmingly beautiful woman, a vision in green and gold, gliding over to them, her bearing as innately, indolently, graceful as a leaf drifting from a tree. Lily spent a moment gaping in simple awe: it was like watching the coming of *Spring*, for God's sake; the woman's arrival felt that momentous. An accompanying celestial chorus would not have seemed inappropriate.

And then Lily knew with sickening certainty: this was Lady Constance Clary.

So much for pretending it was all a dream.

Everything Gideon had said about the bloody woman was obviously true, only more so. And all at once, Lily *deeply* regretted her promise to help him win Lady Constance Clary. How on earth could she rival a goddess? From her book of Greek myths, Lily knew what became of mortals who tangled with the denizens of Olympus: they became bulls and trees and whatnot. Clearly that kiss in the garden had wreaked havoc on her judgment. *No one* should be held to any promise made in the wake of such a kiss, Lily thought desperately. Her heart was flinging itself at her ribs again. *Let's leave right away, shall we?* it coaxed her.

"Good evening, Lady Clary," Gideon said to the woman, as though she were a mere mortal. "Allow me to introduce Miss Lily Masters, Lord Kilmartin's cousin from Sussex."

Constance turned cool gray eyes on Lily; lovely things they were, large and pale-lashed and so clear Lily could swear she could see her own reflection in them. Lady Clary curtsied, and the curtsy was, of course, flawless, all fluid grace.

"How do you do, Miss Masters?" she said.

And if Constance's tone had been warm and kind, Lily might have been completely undone; she might have bolted screaming into the night, tearing Madame Marceau's creations from her, leaving a trail of shredded satin in her wake: *She's too perfect! I can't do this!* But there had been a metallic sheen to that drawled "How do you do," rather like a sword drawn from its sheath, and Lily was intrigued; her innate fighting spirit reared up.

So she dipped into one of her own signature lovely curtsies and arranged her features into an expression meant to convey both warmth and indifference.

"How do you do, Lady Clary? 'Tis a pleasure to meet you."

Constance's eyebrows went up as she registered the sultry instrument of Lily's voice. "Likewise, Miss Masters. And may I say, your gown is very . . . striking." She purred the last word ironically.

Gideon's and Kilmartin's heads turned in tandem toward Lily.

"Oh! Thank you! And yours is"—Lily's eyes skimmed over Constance, and then she went studiously expressionless, as though graciously overlooking a social faux pas—"singular, as well."

Gideon's and Kilmartin's heads swung back toward Constance.

The tiniest, tiniest of furrows appeared between Constance's eyes. No doubt she'd expected stammering confusion or a mortified blush by way of reply, and wasn't quite accustomed to encountering confidence. "May I ask who made your gown, Miss Masters?"

"Certainly, Lady Clary. Madame Marceau of London is my modiste of preference." "*Of preference*," Lily congratulated herself. *Clever of you, Masters.*

Constance's smile held a hint of condescension. "Oh. I see. I've not heard of Madame Marceau."

"Oh, *haven't* you?" Lily was all sympathy. "But then, she *is* rather exclusive. *She* selects her clients, rather than the other way around. And 'tis considered quite an honor, really, to be selected by her. I now have quite a collection of her exquisite work. Her Reading dresses are the finest I've ever seen."

Constance's eyes flared for an almost undetectable second. " 'Reading dresses'?"

Lily saw Gideon and Kilmartin swing their heads back toward her.

"Yes." And then understanding, followed by sympathy, dawned on Lily's face. "Oh, have Reading dresses not yet reached London? They are all the rage in Paris."

Constance's fine features briefly went utterly immobile. "Of course," she said finally. "I just *adore* Reading dresses. My own modiste excels at them. Is . . . is your Madame Marceau very dear?"

Lily was nearly beside herself with glee that Constance "adored" Reading dresses.

"Dear?" Lily repeated, her brow wrinkling a little. "I suppose that depends on what you mean by . . . dear." And then she cast a speaking look up at a startled Gideon, making her innuendo as clear as a summer sky.

Constance's fine eyes darted from Lily to Gideon and back to Lily again. "I suppose my question concerned whether Madame Marceau is *costly*." Her tone had acquired a bit of an edge.

"Hmmm. I suppose she *might* be . . . for someone concerned with cost, that is." Lily smiled beatifically at Constance.

Constance was forced to smile in return.

Gideon spoke up then, cheerily. "The country air seems to have suited you, Constance. You're looking healthy."

Lily almost laughed. She sincerely doubted it was the sort of compliment Lady Constance Clary would have liked to receive in the presence of the mysterious Miss Lily Masters from Sussex.

"Thank you, Gideon," Constance said regally, her eyes flicking toward Lily as she said it. *See? I am allowed to call him by his first name* was the unspoken message.

Lily remained blandly unaffected. Or at least her expression did.

"Miss Masters has honored me with a few of her waltzes, but perhaps you'll honor me with one as well, Constance," Gideon ventured.

"Oh, Gideon, what a shame." Constance's tone was about an octave too sweet. "I've promised all my waltzes to Lord Jarvis."

Lily's brows dove into a gently puzzled frown. "Oh dear, *have* you promised all your waltzes to him? For I have promised Lord Jarvis a waltz as well, and— Oh! See, here he is to collect."

And as Constance went scarlet, Lily smiled radiantly upon Lord Jarvis, who didn't look the least bit guilty as he bowed to Constance and Gideon and Kilmartin. He led Lily proudly out to the dance floor, and she went without a backward glance.

Gideon stifled an errant impulse to pull her back by the elbow.

"As for *my* waltzes, they are all promised to Lady Anne Clapham," Kilmartin said contentedly. He bowed and went in search of his partner, leaving Gideon alone with Constance, who was glowing a singular shade of pink and wearing an expression of patent disbelief.

Gideon would not have thought Jarvis so susceptible to novelty, but he'd seemed eager enough to run off to dance with Lily. Would Lily be all right? Would Jarvis be a gentleman, would Lily be afraid, would Lily be—

He stopped his thoughts, smiled softly. Lily had been . . . simply amazing. She was *always* simply amazing. And she could take care of herself, because she always had.

He turned to the beautiful bright pink woman standing next to him and felt a twinge of conscience; interesting how quickly Constance had resorted to lying—and clumsily at that—to salvage her wounded pride. Then again, Gideon couldn't recall Constance needing to salvage *anything* before; perhaps she was new to it. He seized the opportunity to play the hero.

"I would be delighted if you would honor me with this waltz, Constance, as Lord Jarvis seems to have forgotten one of his commitments this evening."

The feverish color faded from Constance's cheeks; after a moment's hesitation, she took his proffered arm with a gracious smile. And he smiled back at her. She truly *was* a spectacular creature. He *did* honor her. She would make a splendid wife.

He led Constance out onto the floor, and promptly craned his head to look for Lily.

Who knew that hell came equipped with an orchestra playing waltzes? It was not at *all* how Lily would have pictured it.

She'd made Lady Constance Clary's perfect eyebrows rise, she reflected, as Jarvis manfully steered her about the dance floor; there was some satisfaction in that. She thought she might even have rattled the woman's composure a little. But Lady Clary's composure, Lily was certain, was built on bedrock: difficult to move off its foundations indeed.

Gideon was touching Constance now, Lily was sure of it, and the thought made her heart clench. His hand would be on the small of Constance's back, as the music swept them along; perhaps he would laugh with her, wrap her in that slow inclusive smile. The two of them looked glorious together; they *both* could easily have been refugees from Olympus. Lady Constance Clary, Gideon's future wife. If all went according to plan.

Lily *hated* Constance Clary.

Oh wait—Jarvis was talking. She'd better charm him, for that was her purpose here.

"And from where do you hail, Miss Masters?"

"I'm from Sussex, Lord Jarvis. Near Wilmington."

"Charming place, Sussex. Have you been to Brighton?"

"My father takes us once a year. We enjoy the sea ever so much."

"Wonderful! Do you generally enjoy the outdoors, then?"

"Oh yes! In fact, riding is one of my favorite pastimes. I've a lovely horse named McBride. I named him for my father's old groom, for he has a long somber face, just like McBride did." And despite herself, Lily felt the momentum of her story begin to buoy her; there really was nothing like a good story for distracting one from one's troubles.

"'Did' ? What became of McBride the groom?" Jarvis looked intrigued.

"He married the local barmaid and sired nine children. Died of happiness a few years ago, or so Papa says."

Lord Jarvis laughed, and Lily smiled up at him, pleased. "Miss Masters, where *have* you been hiding?"

"Oh, this is my first season, Lord Jarvis. Papa thought it was time we go to London instead of Brighton. 'About time you let the lads get a look at you, m'dear,' he said."

Lord Jarvis laughed again; he seemed delighted with her.

It was working! She was charming him!

And yet her heart still felt so much like an anvil it was a wonder Lord Jarvis was able to spin her about at all.

"It is wonderful to see you again, Constance. And may I say, the green of your dress does magical things for your eyes?"

"Doesn't it?" Constance agreed. "My modiste . . ." she trailed off. Clearly, she had slightly less confidence in her modiste than she'd had a moment before—she had Lily to thank for that. "My modiste assures me that she kept the fabric aside especially for me, as no other woman of the *ton* had the strength of presence to carry it off," she finished bravely.

"And I know how that sort of things pleases you," Gideon murmured.

"Perhaps I should investigate another modiste." *Ah, now she is fishing.*

"Perhaps, Constance. Although I would hate for you to change even a hair. Your own modiste so clearly suits . . . *you.*"

Constance seemed uncertain whether to be pleased with this assessment; it wasn't altogether an unqualified compliment. She changed the subject. "Have you known Miss Masters long, Gideon?" She gave the words a casual lilt.

"Oh, two weeks or so." His answer was just as airy. "We were much thrown together in the country."

"Were you?" Constance paused. "Perhaps I shall invite her to one of my dinners. I should like to know her better. She seems very . . ." She faltered a bit. "Agreeable. Yes, very agreeable."

"Oh, she *is*. She is *very* . . ." Gideon paused, as though searching for just the right word. ". . . Yes, she is . . . agreeable." He allowed his voice and his gaze to drift dreamily out over Constance's head, implying that no words were truly adequate to describe Miss Masters, so "agreeable" would have to do.

"Well, one *so* wants people to be agreeable, of course," Constance continued smoothly. "Especially when they are the relatives of our special friends. What is her family like?"

"Oh, her father is rich."

"Rich?" The word was a feeble squeak.

"Very, *very* rich," Gideon confirmed. "Very, *very* rich," he embellished, for his own amusement. "He owns virtually everything near Wilmington. Houses, land, horses. Quite fortunate in his investments, you know."

"But he hasn't a title," Constance guessed, a hint of triumph in her voice.

"Well . . . no." Gideon frowned a little, as though puzzled why such a thing would matter in the least.

Constance abruptly changed tack. "Papa asked after you today, Gideon. He's very fond of you."

"Oh, please do send your father my regards. I am fond of him as well."

"He said he'd be willing to introduce you to a few *very* important people at a dinner when he returns from the country. I do believe they're now ready fill the new position in the Treasury."

And at her words, the little band of tension that always tightened his chest whenever he danced with Constance loosened just a little, and Gideon allowed himself to savor this very small victory. He smiled upon her warmly. "Please tell your father, Constance, that I would not object in the least to meeting . . . a few *very* important people. Or discussing a position in the Treasury."

Lily had just jounced about in a reel partnered by George Willett, and she was reasonably satisfied that she'd performed it with a convincing enthusiasm and conviction. George Willett seemed to think so, anyhow; he claimed to want to speak with her again sometime later in the evening, if that was quite all right with her. Poor sod had stammered out the words.

"I'd be delighted, Mr. Willett," she'd told him gently, to ease his torment.

She was just fanning herself when she looked up to find Gideon standing before her, his dance card in hand.

"Miss Masters? I believe this is our waltz."

She stared up at him. How well he looked in evening clothes, in stark black and starched white, a sober-colored waistcoat; the colors suited his fair skin and those dark, dark eyes. Still, she preferred him in an open-necked white shirt, sleeves rolled up, his head tilted back to catch the sun on his face. Butterflies rather than silk fans fluttering nearby. She knew, in his heart, he preferred it, too, and she felt a surge of irritation with him.

"That's quite a breeze you're creating with that fan, Lily. Best be careful, or all these muslin gowns will fly up."

"And then perhaps this event will be *truly* enjoyable." She said it more tartly than she'd intended.

Gideon laughed and extended his arm. Heads turned when he laughed, and eyes went to Lily curiously, and then the heads moved closer together to discuss her. It was the way Gideon wanted it to be, she knew; he wanted people to notice her. And so she swallowed her pride and impatience and rested her gloved hand on his arm, gliding out to the dance floor with him. Like a swan.

They eased into the slow circles of the waltz, and Lily's perception narrowed to his hand on her back, to his hand closed over hers, to his eyes searching her eyes. A telling heat rose in her cheeks. She was grateful that it could be mistaken for the flush of exercise, and not, God forbid . . . *desire*.

"Thank you for the necklace," Lily said softly at last, because it seemed he would never speak. He was only *looking* at her.

"I beg your pardon?" Her words seemed to startle him.

She raised her voice. "I said, thank you for the necklace." Lily could feel her face growing warmer. Bloody fair skin of hers. *Don't make me bellow it, Mr. Cole.*

"Oh," Gideon said uncomfortably. A warm pink had settled into his cheeks as well. Was Gideon *blushing*? "Yes."

An awkward silence settled over them.

"Well," Lily asked brightly, finally, since the necklace was clearly an uncomfortable topic, "has Lady Clary succumbed to your charms? Are you engaged?"

Gideon lifted a brow. "That eager to marry me off, are you?" When she didn't reply, he added, "I do believe she's rather . . . taken note of you."

"She really is spectacular," Lily admitted. "Constance, that is."

"You thought perhaps I'd been exaggerating?" He smiled down at her.

Don't smile at me, you maddening man, Lily thought. *It hurts when you smile at me.*

"I can't say that I like her, however." Lily was surprised when she realized she'd said it aloud.

"It isn't necessary that you do," Gideon said quietly.

Lily looked away from him; she saw Kilmartin sail by in the grip of a pleasant-looking brunette. Ah, Lady Anne Clapham, of course. If even half the world was anywhere near as content as Kilmartin looked at the moment, it would be an entirely different place.

"But the two of you look very well together. You and Constance." Lily's voice was a little weak.

"Thank you, Lily."

"Well, you do. Look well together, that is."

"No, I meant . . . thank you. Thank you for . . ." Gideon faltered; he cleared his throat. "Just thank you." His gaze dropped to her mouth. He seemed momentarily transfixed.

He was remembering. She had to make it stop.

"Pleased I can help," she said crisply.

Gideon started; she had successfully jarred him from a deeper foray into sentiment. He smiled a little again. "I overheard Jarvis extolling your charms. He repeated a story about a groom named McBride who'd sired nine children and died of happiness."

Lily smiled despite herself. "I *am* clever that way."

Gideon turned somber again. "I think our plan just may work."

Our plan? It certainly wasn't any plan of *hers*. "You invested thirty pounds in me, Mr. Cole," she told him softly. "It's the least I could do."

He laughed again, and heads turned again to see Gideon Cole enjoying himself so thoroughly with someone who wasn't Lady Constance Clary.

Chapter Fourteen

"Do you know what they are calling her, Gideon?" Kilmartin was beside himself with excitement. "*La Belle Lily*! She's already been given a *nickname*! We have succeeded beyond our wildest dreams."

"Quite." It was the evening after Lily's debut in the *ton*, and they were all attending yet another ball, this one presented by Lady Delloway, who had thoughtfully arranged all of her velvet-covered furniture into groups suited for intimate conversations. Lily was perched on the edge of a settee flirting with the Willett lad. Once dismissed as shy, George Willett seemed to bloom in Lily's presence.

Gideon was suddenly very irritated with Lady Delloway's clever seating arrangements.

"And—it gets even better, Gideon—there are bets in the books at White's that wager you will transfer your affections from Constance to La Belle Lily and announce your engagement before the end of the season! And a few related bets wagering that any number of other females will cast themselves off bridges and out of windows at the announcement."

"Oh?" Gideon replied distantly. Lily was laughing now;

he watched her toss her head and tap young Willett on the arm with her fan. The lad was red-faced with pleasure.

"And Constance will give birth to His Majesty's bastard child come autumn."

"Very good, Laurie, very good," Gideon said absently.

"Gideon," Kilmartin said sharply.

Gideon turned on him and frowned. "Need you take that tone, Laurie? What the devil is the matter?"

"You've not heard a word I said."

"I've heard a few. Lily is popular, blah blah blah."

"It's time to further refine our strategy, Gideon, if you'd like to secure your engagement to Constance before the end of the season, and perhaps even win a pound or two from the betting books at White's while you're at it. I *know* you could use a pound or two."

Constance? Where *was* Constance? Gideon looked about for her.

Her found her across the room . . . watching him . . . watching Lily.

Gideon smiled at her encouragingly; Constance promptly outdid him with a smile as hard and bright as a string of diamonds. It irritated him a little, a new sensation where Constance was concerned: must she always best everyone at *everything*? But she was her usual breathtaking self tonight: draped in gold-trimmed white, her hair intricately curled and piled high to show her long smooth neck to its best advantage. He glanced almost imperceptibly lower and—

Good heavens. Intriguing long shadows moved beneath her very sheer dress, and—well, if he was not mistaken, Constance had completely forsaken a petticoat.

The evening instantly took on a decidedly more interesting cast. Perhaps Constance harbored hidden . . . *depths*. For she'd been known to be daring, but never . . . provocative.

"But Gideon, this is perhaps the best bit of news of all," Kilmartin continued breathlessly. "A group at White's ranked the young ladies of the *ton* this season . . . and our Lily is first! Constance is second. Word got out, of course, as word will. I must admit that I helped a little to make sure that word got out."

Ah. Gideon sighed inwardly. Forsaking a petticoat was merely Constance's way of escalating her game. And yet—and this cheered him—the very absence of a petticoat meant Constance believed there *was* a game. "Next to Newgate, I would imagine 'second' would be Constance's least favorite place to be," he said wryly.

"I think Jarvis is making a serious run for Lily, Gideon. He's certainly been attentive."

"*What?*" Gideon rounded on Kilmartin, who took a step back. "Has sense completely deserted the *ton*? She cannot have fooled *everyone* so easily."

"Calm yourself, old man. You're missing the point. Lily *is* quite a marvel—she's doing a smashing job, you can't deny it. And with Jarvis out of the way, and Constance wearing nearly transparent clothes to impress you, I imagine you'll be ensconced in the Treasury and calling the Marquis Shawcross 'Papa' in two shakes of a lamb's tail. Go on. Take a twirl about the dance floor with Constance. I imagine that gossamer gown will improve your mood."

Several admirers now ringed Lily; poor Willett was forced to compete for her attention. Gideon eyed them discreetly, to see if any of her conversational companions would begin to pat their pockets in bemusement, having just noticed they were missing a watch. But no, all of Lily's conversation partners displayed a uniformity of expression: captivated.

As if to compare, Gideon glanced again at Constance. She was watching Lily, too, and he was startled to find her wearing a tremendously unappealing expression—one that bordered on the sour. It was gone in an instant, as if it had merely been the product of shifting shadows.

Lord Stanley, darkly handsome, was leaning over Lily now. Gideon watched, tensing, as the man moved slowly closer to her, and closer still, until his lips were hovering near her ear. And then Stanley curled his white-gloved hand over Lily's wrist, and his lips moved, murmuring something.

Lily's head jerked upward, her complexion crimson, her spine rigid. She gave her wrist a little tug. Stanley held her fast.

Later Gideon couldn't recall the steps he took toward them; one moment he was observing from a small distance, the next he was standing over them. Their heads, Stanley's and Lily's, turned up to him; Stanley's sullen and intent, Lily's uncertain and fiercely angry.

"Unhand her, Stanley. Now." Gideon's voice, low and lethal, silenced every man in the perimeter of the settee as effectively as a fired musket.

Stanley's eyes flew wide; an unpleasant smile cut across his face. His hand remained on Lily's wrist.

"Gideon." He thought he heard a man's voice, a quiet warning. But Gideon was focused on the hand gripping Lily. He forced his own hands to remain uncurled; he was afraid his fist would launch of its own accord.

"I'm a dead shot, Stanley," Gideon said mildly instead. "Care to test me?"

"*Gideon.*"

The voice finally penetrated the static of rage in Gideon's mind. He turned; a pale Kilmartin stood next to him.

"You don't *do* that anymore, Gideon," Kilmartin said quietly.

Stanley's hand flew from Lily's wrist; he stood abruptly.

He was pale now, too. As was every man in the perimeter of the settee.

"My apologies for any offense I may have caused, Miss Masters, Mr. Cole," Stanley said coldly. He bowed, a shallow insolent bend, and strode quickly away. Lily absently rubbed at her wrist and stared up into Gideon's face, her eyes wide and hot with lingering outrage.

A waltz struck up; swarms of dancers moved in pairs toward the floor, oblivious to the little drama that had just taken place over the settee.

Gideon took a deep breath. "You're all right, Miss Masters?"

"Yes. Thank you, Mr. Cole." Her eyes locked with his.

Gideon turned away from her swiftly. Had he really nearly called a man out for touching a pickpocket's wrist? Had he really nearly lost all control?

"Pity Constance didn't witness that, Gideon. You'd have increased your appeal a thousandfold," Kilmartin murmured to him. It sounded like a jest, but Kilmartin's voice wasn't entirely steady. "Perhaps the blokes at White's will help to spread the word."

"All part of the charade, Laurie." He gave Kilmartin a smile that was meant to be reassuring, but in truth, Gideon was a bit shaken, too.

He looked at Lily as though she was a stranger. And she gazed back at him until an uneasy Willett gently reminded her she'd promised him this waltz.

Gideon bowed and went to Constance; with some relief, he led her in all her golden magnificence to the dance floor. There was little danger of calling anyone out over Constance. No one would have dared touch Constance.

* * *

"So, Constance, how has life treated you since last we met?" Remnants of rage clung to him; the waltz with Constance would shake them off, he decided.

"Since yesterday evening, you mean?" She smiled, acknowledging his mild teasing. "Splendidly, as usual. For one, my new horse arrived in London—Papa bought it especially for me from a breeder in the country. And I've decided to hold a dinner party—my aunt will be there, of course, since Mama and Papa are in the country. I thought I'd invite—"

"Constance, your new horse—what is its name?"

Constance blinked. "My horse, Gideon? It's a bay mare. It cost a fortune, too, Papa said. Its sire was a—"

"But what do you *call* her? What is her *name*?" The question, for some reason, struck Gideon as urgent.

Constance had begun to look uncomfortable. "It's a *horse*, Gideon, not a person. It doesn't require a name. I call it . . . *my horse*." Constance had clearly begun to find the conversation a little troubling.

"For example, *my* horse, Constance," Gideon continued doggedly—he'd begun to use his barrister voice—"is named Horatio. I named him after Nelson, you know. Because he's a valiant sort of horse. A big brown fellow. Suppose horses, like people, required baptizing and registering in the public record. *What then would you name your horse*?" His voice had definitely gone up in volume.

Constance's mouth dropped open; she stared at him as if he'd sprouted another eye. He couldn't blame her, really. But it just, somehow, seemed imperative to know. Who *was* Constance? What did she think about? What *would* she name a horse?

She closed her mouth, finally, and pressed her lips together tightly, thinking. *Thinking of what?* Gideon wondered desperately. *What does she really think about anything?*

"Oh, let's talk of other things, shall we?" Constance cajoled. She gave a nervous little laugh.

She'd decided to placate him. He stifled a sigh.

"Well, then. How about a favorite color? Do you have a favorite color, Constance?"

"My goodness, Gideon, I think you've been spending too much time in the courtroom. You've begun to speak only in questions. No matter: I can answer that one for you. It's blue."

Gideon pounced on this information eagerly. "Why blue?"

"Because it looks very well on me!" She sounded triumphant.

Well, of course.

He could have asked: Which blue? The blue of a summer sky? The blue-green of the ocean? The blue of the sky at midnight? The blue of bluebells? But suddenly it had stopped mattering. He felt defeated.

What was the *matter* with him?

"You're right, Constance. Blue does look very well on you." Gideon gave her a smile, the kind she had come to expect from him, and Constance looked relieved. "As does the dress you're wearing," he added. "It's quite spectacular." She smiled, as content again as a baby freshly fed on mama's milk.

"Now, about my dinner party, Gideon . . . I shall invite Lord Kilmartin, of course, and Lady Anne Clapham, because we must have both—"

"And Kilmartin's cousin," Gideon suggested nonchalantly. "Miss Lily Masters."

There was an almost undetectable pause. "Naturally," Constance said evenly. "I'll have Miss Masters. And we'll have cards; perhaps some dancing . . ."

And so Gideon learned all about Constance's dinner party as they finished their waltz. But he couldn't help but notice that it never once occurred to her to ask him if *he* had a favorite color.

Lily was more at home in crowds than in the rambling fields of Aster Park; still, she was small and she was surrounded by an awful lot of people, most of whom had been strenuously dancing and sweating. And the *jewels* . . . it was difficult not to view accessorized people the way she had viewed them for years . . . like trees ripe for the plucking. She needed a little air.

A Lord Something-or-Other escorted her from the dance floor back to where Kilmartin and Lady Clapham stood, but she was able to duck away from them before they saw or acknowledged her return. Fortunately, there was an empty space on her dance card; she had lied, sweetly of course, and told a number of admirers she had promised that particular waltz to someone. To *herself*, was the truth.

She wove her way through the crowd toward the double doors that opened onto Lady Delloway's balcony, aware of eyes on her the entire time. Admiring eyes, for the most part, and speculative, too; she resisted the urge to shrug them off and scurry out of view as quickly as possible. She'd never before *wanted* to be seen; being seen was a definite liability for a pickpocket. But now . . . in order for Gideon Cole's plan to work, everyone needed to know who Lily Masters was. So she glided like a swan, and took the stares. For Gideon.

For Gideon, who had nearly called a man out . . . simply because another man had touched her. More specifically, touched her and then murmured an astonishing suggestion in her ear. It hadn't been anything Lily hadn't heard before in

St. Giles; in other circumstances, she would have dispatched Stanley with a knee or elbow. But in a London ballroom . . . well, she supposed that's why young ladies needed men about—to shoot men who made untoward suggestions, Lily thought wryly. Seemed excessive, but then everything about the *ton* was excessive.

That murderous look in Gideon's eye had seemed authentic enough, however. She should know: she'd seen it before, when he'd closed his own wrist over her hand the day she'd tried to steal his watch. And truth be told, it had been a trifle thrilling: before Gideon Cole, no one had ever come to her rescue. For any reason.

But Gideon had his hand on Constance's back right now, the music sweeping them along in circles. Constance would be close enough to *smell* him, to see the one or two gray hairs sneaking into his red-kissed dark hair. Lily had seen them when she had combed her fingers up through his hair . . . in the garden . . . right before his mouth had covered hers . . .

Oh, for God's sake, she told herself sternly. There really was no point in tormenting herself over a moment that could simply never recur.

She reached the double doors at last and inhaled; the smell of horse dung and dirt and coal fires and swarming humans rose up to her from the street. *Ah, London.* She took great breaths of it.

A giddy female voice wafted out to where she stood.

"Meggie, Meggie! I danced a reel with him! With Mr. Cole!"

"Oh, then he must have actually *touched* you! And yet you haven't yet swooned," her friend teased.

Lily peeked into the room; a group of girls, all in light-colored muslin, had clustered near the door. She'd met most of them, she was certain, briefly; the names all seemed to end with an "ee" sound. Mary? Meggy? Polly?

"Yes! As a matter of fact, he touched me right *here*," the girl called Meggie said proudly. She stretched out her hand, and her friends gathered around her, giggling and pretending to make a great fuss over the hand in question.

"He's so *heavenly*," one of them sighed.

"Oh, yes, *heavenly*," several of them echoed.

Good God. Well, Gideon *was* heavenly, but how could any man bear up under this kind of adulation without becoming insufferable? Not that Gideon Cole *couldn't* be insufferable . . .

Lily imagined joining their giddy, girlish conversation: "Well, if you think he *looks* heavenly, you should *taste* him! And oh my *goodness*, he has the most enormous . . . well, *you know*. Why, I felt it pressing against me just the other day. In the garden. While we passionately kissed." What would they say to *that*?

"Well, I swear to you he looked at *me*," another of the girls chimed in. "Right at me. *Appreciatively*. While he was dancing with Lady Clary."

"Oh, bosh. He was looking *over* you to look at *her*. You know—Lord Kilmartin's cousin."

Lily's heart bumped. Was he? Had Gideon been looking at her? And then she recalled: *Of course he was looking at me. It's all part of our charade.*

"Lord Kilmartin's cousin? Miss Lily Masters? I hear she has piles and piles of money."

"My father says he knows her father. Made a fortune in shipping, or what have you."

This was interesting, Lily thought, given that *she* had never met her fictional father. Perhaps she should just close her mouth from now on and let the story do what it would, as it seemed to be taking on a fascinating life of its own.

"She *is* very pretty," one of the allowed. "And agreeable."

"Oh yes, very agreeable, so agreeable," they all chorused.

Lily bit her lip to stifle a laugh.

"But she makes all of us that much more invisible."

Imagine that! Lily Masters, who had made an art form of being invisible, was making *others* feel invisible.

"Mr. Cole wouldn't look at us anyway. He only has eyes for the Lady Clarys and the Lily Masters of the world."

If they only knew.

"Do you think Mr. Cole will marry Miss Masters instead of Lady Clary?"

"Not if Lady Clary has anything to say about it." They giggled, but one of the girls made a nervous shushing noise, as if Constance was omnipotent and bound to overhear.

Lily supposed it *was* funny. But still it hurt, and brought with it another rush of impatience for Gideon, who was intent on marrying the daughter of a marquis so he could live his father's life over again, only without the disaster this time.

Lily knew him in a way none of these innocents, these girls no older than herself, did or ever would. She wondered if Constance knew Gideon the way she knew him, or if she only knew the public Gideon: the one who smiled often but not *too* often; who charmed but was not effusive or passionate or moody; who was witty but not silly. The Gideon who was always all that was appropriate, everything that the odious little brown book said he should be. Did he care for Constance? He'd never once said that he did.

Perhaps Gideon has revealed himself to me because he knows I am of no social consequence. Deep down, she knew this wasn't true. McBride had once told her that herbs were most potent when harvested beneath a full moon, because the moon drew their strongest qualities to the surface, much the way it pulled tides to the shore. And Lily knew somehow she had drawn Gideon's true self to the surface—probably because, under the skin, they were the same. And this, Lily thought, with a wretched smile, probably bothered Gideon more than a thousand stolen watches.

The strains of the next waltz drifted out to her. Ah. It was her turn once again to dance with the "heavenly" Gideon Cole. She slipped back into the drawing room like a shadow, thinking that in this instance Gideon couldn't possibly object.

"Well, I'm for bed." Kilmartin yawned. "More parties tomorrow. And the next day and the next," he added cheerfully. "Well done, Lily. You'll win a bride for Gideon yet!"

Lily had never appreciated a compliment less. "Good night, Lord Kilmartin."

"Laurie?" Gideon said suddenly, just as Kilmartin was about to mount the stairs.

"Yes, Gideon?"

"When do you intend to propose to Lady Anne Clapham?"

Kilmartin froze in his tracks. He twisted his head back toward Gideon, his eyes huge with alarm.

Gideon smiled mischievously. He was almost too enchanting when he was being a rascal, Lily thought. "Ah, forget I said anything, old man. Go to bed. I shall see you in the morning." He was grinning broadly now.

Kilmartin gave him a quick dark frown and huffed up the stairs. "*I'm* not the one with a Master Plan, Cole. *I've* all the time in the world."

"But what if someone else snaps her up while you're 'taking your time'?" Gideon teased.

Kilmartin paused on the landing, and his expression was one of gentle, almost pitying amusement. "Oh, no one else will snap her up. We are meant for each other."

And with that supremely, peacefully confident statement, he bowed to them and disappeared from view.

Gideon was quiet after that, pensive. His long fingers tapped an absent tattoo on the arm of his chair; he caught himself and stopped.

Lily stood, prepared to follow Kilmartin up the stairs to her own room. "Well, Mr. Cole, good—"

"Do you miss Alice?" Gideon said suddenly.

Lily turned to him, surprised; she slowly lowered herself back into her chair.

"Well . . . yes I do, very much," she admitted. "We've never been apart since she was born."

"We'll return to Aster Park soon."

Lily nodded. She supposed he'd meant it to be reassuring, but when they returned for Alice, it would very likely mean that Gideon's engagement to Constance Clary had been achieved, and that she and Alice would be leaving Aster Park for good.

Leaving Gideon for good.

"Well, no doubt Alice is too diverted by Aster Park's many pleasures to miss *me* much." She smiled wryly.

He was silent for a moment. "It is . . . it is difficult to imagine that anyone . . . would not miss you." His voice had a catch in it.

And suddenly Lily knew he was saying two things at once. Her heart jolted.

His eyes were on her, softly, softly burning. With longing.

I should leave the room. Now.

She wanted to lean forward and cup his beautiful face in her hands, stroke the strong lines of his cheekbones, touch her lips to his and drink the longing out of him. The ferocity of her sudden wanting turned her breathing shallow; Gideon's own breath was coming more swiftly, too. His eyes heated to black; they never left her. They willed her closer; she could feel it from where she sat, the strength of his desire. Her skin prickled, remembering the feel of his hands on it. *God, just to touch him . . .*

Lily stood up quickly. "I should retire for the evening."

Gideon went very still, surprised. And then he nodded once; he looked down into his lap a moment, as if ashamed. And then he slowly rose to his feet, as ever conscious of manners.

She turned and moved toward the stairs.

"Lily?"

She paused, turned back toward him.

"You are . . . you are remarkable." The words were softly said, but urgency thrummed through them; a yearning that thrilled her and terrified her.

Her lips curved into a hint of a smile. "I know."

Gideon gave a short pained laugh, and turned his head away from her.

And with extraordinary difficulty, Lily turned her back to him and mounted the stairs.

How foolish she was. Here she'd thought Gideon Cole had already broken her heart. She recalled her book of Greek myths, and she now understood that she was like poor Prometheus chained to the rock: as long as she remained near him, Gideon Cole would have the power to break her heart over and over again, and the pain of it would be fresh every single time.

Chapter Fifteen

Lily wanted to be alone with Constance Clary about as badly as she wanted to be transported to Australia. And so far she'd been fortunate: at social affairs, she was usually buffered by a collection of new admirers, or by Gideon and Kilmartin. The woman's Olympian impact had always therefore been somewhat diluted.

But tonight, just two nights after Lady Delloway's ball, Lily was in Constance's territory—the town house Constance's father owned and that she shared with her aunt—for a dinner party, and Constance had just issued an invitation directly to her:

"Miss Masters, would you like to accompany me to the withdrawing room? I do believe my hair is coming loose of its pins, and I could use some assistance."

Gideon was absorbed in a conversation with some elderly gentleman Lily didn't recognize. Kilmartin was dancing attendance upon Lady Anne Clapham.

And Constance clearly wanted to be alone with Miss Lily Masters.

Lily thought of her *Encyclopedia of Natural History.* It

described how a lion would separate a zebra from its herd in order to make a meal of it. Lily suddenly knew just how the zebra felt.

"Oh, certainly, Lady Clary," she said. For what other response could she offer? A truthful one?: "Not on your life, Lady Clary"?

Resignedly, struggling valiantly to float like a swan and not shuffle like a prisoner being led off to the racks, Lily followed Constance. She caught a glimpse of the two of them in a long mirror as they passed: two lovely blonde women, one tall and buxom and glowing with health and self-satisfaction, the other petite, slim, looking a little apprehensive. She was reminded of a gnat buzzing after a great horse.

The gilding in the little withdrawing room fairly blinded Lily: the mirror, the legs on the chairs, the trim on the bureau—all were polished to a supernatural brilliance, no doubt so Constance could see herself reflected in as many surfaces as possible. Everything else—the settee, the stools and chairs, the curtains—was fashioned of silver-blue satin, heavy and lustrous, corded in gold. Practically mirrorlike in sheen, as well.

Constance settled onto a plump stool in front of the vanity and eyed herself in the mirror, turning her fine head this way and that to examine her hair. A tendril had escaped. She frowned a little at her hair's blatant insubordination.

"I'm *so* pleased you could attend my party, Miss Masters."

"I wouldn't miss it for the *world*, Lady Clary. I'm honored to be included." *A bigger pair of hypocrites,* Lily thought, *cannot be found in all of London.*

"And are you enjoying London, Miss Masters?"

"More than I can say, Lady Clary."

"And do you perhaps enjoy some amusements . . . more than others?"

Lily almost sighed. Constance really wasn't nearly as clever as she believed she was. "I'm sorry, I do not take your meaning, Lady Clary." Lily's gaze met Constance's in the mirror innocently.

Constance's eyes narrowed slightly. "Is there perhaps one . . . *activity* . . . you prefer more than all others?"

"By activity, do you mean parties and balls, things of that sort?"

"Yes. Or perhaps dancing with a particular . . . *person.* That sort of thing."

"Oh, no. I rather enjoy *all* that London has to offer," Lily replied cheerfully.

She watched Constance's face go closed and expressionless, like a pot lid clamped over the bubbling stew of her thoughts.

Lily decided to change the subject. Her eyes went to the impressive object circling Constance's throat; a series of small blue stones and small white ones. "Your necklace is stunning, Lady Clary."

"Thank you, Miss Masters. It's new." Constance fingered it possessively. "Papa gave it to me for my birthday. And it's not paste, you know. It's three sapphires and two diamonds."

Sapphires and diamonds! McBride would have fainted on the spot. Lily's fingers itched to at least *touch* it. "My papa would never buy me anything quite so grand. He says it's a job for my future husband."

Constance pounced on this like a fox on a hare. "Oh? Are you *engaged*, then, Miss Masters?"

Lily donned her enigmatic expression. "I suppose one could say that."

She watched Constance draw in a breath and hold it in an

agony of anticipation. And Lily waited, and waited, until she decided she'd better speak before Constance actually turned blue and toppled from her perch.

"That is, engaged in *becoming* engaged. But then, aren't we all, this season?"

She met Constance's eyes in the mirror once again. Constance released her breath and pressed her lips tightly together. Her gray eyes were now downright wintry.

And in that moment, Lily knew: *I have officially made an enemy.* Which suited her perfectly.

Lady Clary studied her coolly in the mirror, no doubt wondering why it was so difficult to cow Lily Masters the way she'd cowed all the other girls in the *ton*. Lily would have loved to tell her exactly why: None of the other young ladies had actually been *schooled* in Lady Constance Clary.

Do you even care for Gideon, you . . . you . . . creature*?* It took all of Lily's self-control to keep the thought nothing more than a thought. *If it doesn't matter to Gideon, why should it matter to me?*

She tamped down her impatience and anger and gathered her manners about her. "Lady Clary, perhaps we can tuck up your loose hair now. Your guests will be missing you, no doubt."

Constance, obviously accustomed to being administered to, waited while Lily gently pushed the wayward tendril of hair back into place and pinned it. Her face was contemplative, but not in a soothing way, as she watched Lily in the mirror.

Lily's fingers brushed the clasp of the necklace; she imagined she could feel the dazzle of it shoot right through her fingertips.

* * *

Slowly, Lily reminded herself. *Not as though I'm digging to China.* She lifted the heavy silver fork to her mouth and tasted the pickled vegetables; she fought the urge to pucker. *Perhaps a slice of beef would help wash down the taste . . .* She peered at the platter and noted that the beef was swimming in sauce. *Everything* seemed to be swimming in sauce. She didn't mind, really; a layer of sauce added a layer of mystery to the food. Lily liked being surprised by tastes each time she lifted her fork to her mouth.

There was an intriguing pyramid of little round balls at the end of the table, stacked atop a sort of elegant silver platform; they had the look of sweets. She was dying to have a crack at those. Perhaps she should ask one of the army of footmen—nearly one to a diner, she guessed—to fetch some for her. They were liveried in blue and gold, the footmen, like the furniture; in the candlelight, from a distance, it was sometimes difficult to discern them from the chairs.

Lily was unsurprised to find she'd been relegated to the table's equivalent of St. Giles; to her left sat a surly elderly man who had belched audibly several times now. Lily was sympathetic. She was certain the pickled vegetables were at fault. Kilmartin and Lady Anne Clapham were in neutral territory, a few more seats toward the middle.

Gideon, on the other hand, was at the far end of the table, seated, of course, next to Constance. Lord Jarvis sat directly across from Constance. Constance had ensured that she was, in fact, the filling in a sandwich of admiration and competition.

"*Oh!*"

The amiable conversation and clinking of silver and porcelain came to an abrupt halt. All eyes turned toward the piercing little cry of distress.

Which had issued from Constance, if her wide eyes and

the hand splayed across her chest were any indication. "I know I would have seen it fall." She directed her breathless words to no one in particular. "I would have *felt* it fall. . . ."

Everyone stared at her blankly.

"My necklace! It's gone!" she clarified indignantly. "My new necklace is gone!"

An alarmed collective murmur started up; as if on command, everyone sitting at the table dove beneath it to take a look. Much rustling about ensued, mingled with a few undignified giggles. One by one, heads popped back up and seats were retaken.

But no one had retrieved a necklace.

"We shall find it, Constance," Gideon soothed. "No doubt it slipped from your neck and is somewhere nearby. We'll all help to search for it, is that not so?" Gideon's tone, gentle though it was, brooked no argument. Again, as if on command, all the heads at the table nodded vigorously.

Constance lowered her voice. "Perhaps one of the servants . . ."

"If one of the servants found it, they would never dare keep it from you, Constance." He matched her low tone. "But we shall investigate that possibility, as well. Meanwhile, we'll all do a proper search. When did you see it last?"

"Well . . . I believe it was when Miss Masters and I repaired to the withdrawing room. Miss Masters admired my necklace excessively," she added. "She said that her papa would never buy her anything so fine—that it was a job for her future husband."

Gideon almost smiled; *how* did Lily come up with these little embellishments?

"Well then, we shall look in the withdrawing room, of course," he told Constance. "But can you describe to me anything you may have done there—without divulging all of your feminine secrets, of course—that may have jarred your necklace from you?"

Constance cocked her head. "Well . . . my hair seemed to be coming loose of its pins, so Miss Masters offered to help me to put it up again. And that's when she admired my necklace, and said all those kind things about it. And then we put my hair up, and we returned to my guests. The clasp was a bit loose, but I was certain it would hold."

Gideon pictured it: the two lovely women facing the mirror, Lily's slim fingers lifting Constance's hair—

Suspicion struck the air from his lungs.

I am an excellent thief, Mr. Cole.

It made a terrible sort of sense: Their plan—*his* plan—had succeeded so brilliantly it would never occur to anyone that the lovely, genteel Miss Lily Masters of Sussex—La Belle Lily, whose father was very, very rich—would steal a necklace. He'd provided Lily with the disguise; Constance had presented the opportunity. Lily's light fingers had sustained her and Alice for years, but the income from the sale of Constance's necklace would mean Lily would never have to steal again.

His suspicion sickened him. Perhaps Lily had never dreamed Constance would announce the loss in such a public fashion, but he knew that if even a whiff of suspicion wafted her way, Lily, who so excelled at telling stories, was capable of gazing into anyone's eyes and . . . lying.

Perhaps even to him.

No, not to him: for he wouldn't give her the opportunity.

What will you do? he'd asked Lily that day in the garden. As though her life could not possibly go on without him after their kiss. He now felt like a callow fool.

What I have always done, she'd replied. *Survive.*

* * *

After dinner, Constance's guests repaired to the drawing room for cards and chatting. A search party was dispatched to the withdrawing room, and those whose eyes were deemed the sharpest fanned out to search the rest of the premises. But the necklace remained stubbornly missing.

Constance recovered from the trauma rapidly enough, however. A necklace could be replaced, and the prospect of new things always pleased her beyond measure.

In the drawing room, two simultaneous card games were assembled; a few other guests were distributed about the chairs and settees, idly chatting. Once Constance was seated and holding a hand of cards, Gideon appeared at Lily's elbow.

"A word, Miss Masters."

He gestured subtly with his chin to the next room and walked in that direction; she followed. He paused by a short pillar supporting a sprawling fern.

"Where did you put it, Lily?"

No preamble; just a swift decisive blow. Lily was thunderstruck.

And then her chin snapped up. "That's it? Not even '*Did* you take it, Lily?' "

Gideon remained silent; his face was ashen. His eyes burned down at her, scouring her soul for the truth.

"Or how about, 'Would you like to split the take, Lily?' " she hissed. How could she possibly defend herself? She could only use words, and he would believe what he believed. And apparently Gideon believed she was a thief.

Because she *was* a thief.

"You admired the necklace, Lily, and then it disappeared."

"Oh yes, and that's just the sort of thief I am. I announce what I'm about to take, and then I take it."

He took a deep breath. "I know you dislike her, and I can understand the temptation—"

"*Stop.*" Her voice was low and furious. "Just stop. Don't try to explain away my 'actions,' Gideon. Don't try to be a *barrister* with me. I didn't take the necklace."

He didn't reply. He simply watched her. He was always watching, watching; as though if he watched long enough she would reveal some essential truth about herself to him.

She wanted to lash out, to free herself from his gaze.

"I didn't take it, Gideon. But could you blame me if I *had*? For what will become of me when your *game* is over? How do you suppose I will continue looking after myself and Alice? Perhaps I should begin receiving 'gentlemen' callers."

He flinched. *Good.* She was glad she had the power to hurt him. Or at least shock him.

She watched him, waiting for a sign, willing him to believe her, to smile at her, to—

"You can give the necklace to me, Lily." His voice was low and tense. "I'll simply tell Constance I found it. We'll speak no more of it, I swear it."

Lily closed her eyes briefly; she refused to allow him to see on her face what those words had done to her.

Her voice was a dead thing when she spoke. "I'll see your game through, Gideon. That is, if you trust me to remain under Aunt Hester's roof. You never know. I might steal the silver plate and copulate with the footmen."

Gideon's mouth parted a little as though someone had just kicked him squarely in the ribs. And then—and this frightened her more than anything had in a very long time—the searching light went out of his eyes.

What replaced it was indifference.

"You can remain with Aunt Hester, Miss Masters. What you choose to do there is none of my concern, for I shall repair to my own lodgings for the duration of our stay in the *ton*. And of course you will see our *game* through, Miss Masters, if you wish to remain out of Newgate. For it would be a simple thing for me to put you there."

He bowed to her, and sauntered back into the room full of card players, right into the rays of Constance's welcoming smile.

Chapter Sixteen

All right, old man, the note read, *if this is a strategy, it's working: Constance has asked after you several times, in her own subtle fashion, and she seems increasingly nervous. I have told her you were called away on business. Meanwhile, Jarvis seems more and more enamored of Lily, though he has still enjoyed a few waltzes with Constance. Still, it would have been helpful to be privy to this part of the plan, if it is indeed part of the plan. Yrs—Kilmartin*

After Constance's dinner, Gideon disappeared into his own lodgings for three days, wallowing in his dim rooms until he could scarcely tell day from night, drinking all manner of things, ignoring the concerned and then irritated and then *deeply* concerned messages sent to him by Kilmartin. He didn't know precisely why he was so darkly, furiously miserable; every time a reason began to swim into coherence—betrayal? desire? ambition?—he drowned it ruthlessly with whiskey. *Take that,* he told it grimly. He didn't want to know.

In short, he'd behaved abysmally. Like a child. *Completely* out of character.

But Kilmartin's last message had struck a new note; Gideon could practically hear the taxed patience and hurt feelings in it. It cut through his self-absorption, and he managed to sober up enough to feel ashamed.

And so he pulled himself together: washing, shaving, dressing. And showed his face again at last at Aunt Hester's town house.

"Why, Gideon," Kilmartin drawled when he saw him standing in the parlor.

Gideon shook his head once, abruptly, a warning.

And Kilmartin, good friend as always, heeded it, shaking his own head.

"I apologize, Laurie," Gideon added, a little defensively.

"Perhaps you should apologize to Miss Masters, too," Kilmartin suggested gently.

Gideon's jaw tightened; he said nothing.

Kilmartin didn't press him; he sighed. "The plan is still on?"

"It is still on."

"I heard word that Constance intended to ride in the row today. Perhaps you'd better take out my high flyer. And Lily."

So Gideon took the high flyer. And Lily.

Lily sat next to him now in stubborn silence, looking delicately smart in a blue riding habit.

Gideon didn't know what to say to her. Part of him clung to the perverse hope that she *had* stolen the necklace. Because it would be much, much simpler to say good-bye to a thief who had betrayed his trust than to the remarkable girl with whom he had shared an unforgettable kiss.

The deepest, truest part of him was certain she had not taken it.

Almost certain.

Odd that Kilmartin had never voiced any sort of suspicion; instead, his face had reflected only reproach when he'd reappeared. As though *Gideon* was the only one who had committed any sort of transgression. *She's gotten to all of us,* Gideon thought.

Well, it wasn't as though a rash of jewel thefts had been reported about the *ton*, was it?

The problem was this: Ever since Lily Masters had appeared in his life, Gideon had grown increasingly unsure about who he was. Or perhaps the problem was in fact the opposite: It was increasingly clear *who* he truly was.

But it had very little to do with who he intended to be.

Rotten Row was teeming with people and horses and stylish equipages, but Constance was easy to find. Constance's posture—regal perfection—was unmistakable, as was the air of complacent serenity that surrounded her like a nimbus. She was perched on what must be her nameless bay mare.

And then he noticed her companion: Lord Jarvis. "Bloody hell."

Lily jerked in the seat next to him, as though he'd shaken her awake, and followed Gideon's gaze; her features settled into comprehension, and then became opaque. "Don't worry," she said quietly, her first words to him in nearly an hour. For some reason they seemed almost excruciatingly intimate for that very reason. "I will honor my *promise*, Mr. Cole."

The word "promise" fairly sparkled with malice, but when he slid a glance sideways, Lily's expression was rosebud-sweet. Gideon pulled the high flyer up near Constance.

"Why, Cole! How goes it?" Jarvis beamed at him from

atop his handsome mount and tipped his hat. Jarvis continually bemused Gideon; he didn't seem to realize he was Gideon's rival. Or perhaps he merely considered the search for a bride a benign, manly sort of competition, like grouse hunting—no hard feelings when all was said and done, and may the best man bag the best grouse.

"Hullo, Jarvis. Good afternoon, Lady Clary." Gideon tipped his hat while Lily sweetly echoed his greeting.

Constance nodded; the plume on her hat nodded along with her. "Mr. Cole. Miss Masters." Her voice was cool. "Lord Jarvis and I were just discussing Lady Pemberton's ball of last night. The orchestra she engaged was most accomplished."

"Oh, was it grand? I was terribly sorry to miss it—and the opportunity to dance with you." Gideon was all sincerity. "Unfortunately, I had some pressing . . . business to conduct." And then he smiled at Constance, the sort of smile that could coax a return smile from a corpse. Constance, not being a corpse, smiled back at him, officially thawed.

"Yes, *business* to conduct," Lily echoed, with an enigmatic smile, as though Gideon's business had everything to do with her.

Constance's smile vanished abruptly. "*You* were at the ball, Miss Masters." She sounded terse.

And Gideon had never before heard Constance sound anything other than *mellifluous*. At last: an obvious ripple in her aristocratic serenity. No doubt because Lily Masters had been steadily skipping little stones across it for days now. Gideon began to feel more cheerful.

"Yes, and it was truly a pleasure to see you there, Lady Clary," Lily allowed. "But oddly, I did not enjoy it as much as the others this season. It was just that something seemed to be . . . *missing*." And then she poured a gaze so melting over Gideon that he felt like a fly trapped in amber.

Constance's cool gray eyes moved from one to the other of them. Two thin white lines of agitation appeared on either side of her patrician nostrils.

More and more interesting, Gideon thought.

"Splendid animal, Constance," he commented mildly. "Your mare."

"Yes. It's the new horse I told you about." She glanced at Lily. *See? I still hold private conversations with him.*

"What is her name?" Lily asked brightly.

"It hasn't a name." Constance sounded amazed to be answering horse questions again.

"She looks like a Mavis," Lily mused.

"It looks like a *horse*," Constance corrected grimly.

"Constance is a marvelous horsewoman," Lord Jarvis volunteered.

"Thank you, Malcolm." Constance pointedly and warmly delivered his first name. "Do *you* ride, Miss Masters?"

There was a pause. "Oh, yes, Lady Clary." Lily's voice was a slow velvet caress. "I do so like to go for the occasional . . . *ride*." And her gaze slid sideways ever so briefly toward Gideon.

It seemed to Gideon he had never heard a more prurient sentence in his life.

He felt his face growing warm; he risked a glance at Jarvis. Jarvis was rosy, too, and his mouth had dropped open just slightly in amazement. *Probably wondering,* Gideon thought with some dark amusement, *if he'd heard her correctly.*

Constance, disappointingly, seemed to have missed the innuendo entirely. But then she had never lived downstairs from a prostitute.

A barouche full of young ladies rolled by. Fragments of giggled conversation drifted in their wake; Gideon caught the words "heavenly" and "divine" and "Mr. Cole" and "Miss Masters."

The white lines on Constance's face deepened.

Lord Jarvis spoke up at last. "Perhaps Miss Masters would like a ride—that is, perhaps we can all ride together someday," he corrected hurriedly, flushing again.

"Perhaps," Gideon allowed, smiling in a way that meant he did not intend to make any plan of the sort at the moment.

"Mr. Cole! Mr. Cole!" They all turned with a start; none of them had noticed the man huffing up to them on foot, hat in hand, until he was nigh upon them. "Oh, I knew it was *you*, Mr. Cole! Ye're a big 'un, and I says to meself, Wesley, I says, that's Mr. Gideon Cole."

The man, tall and broad-backed, cheeks and nose and hands ruddy from a life spent mostly outdoors, grinned up at Gideon and thrust one of those ruddy hands up; Gideon seized it in his own and shook it.

"Hullo, Mr. Wesley." For this was the son of the man who had died and left him his infamous thirty pounds. Mr. Wesley, a farmer, was no doubt on a rare visit to London.

Constance's eyes went to where Gideon's hand, covered in its fine glove, joined to Mr. Wesley's weathered paw. And then she looked into Gideon's face. Her expression was much the same as the one she'd worn when he'd insisted she give her horse a name: confused and anxious.

"I'm in London just the day, ye see, Mr. Cole, and when I saw ye I wanted to thank ye once again on behalf of me da. We miss 'im, rest 'is soul, but we're prosperin', and 'tis all yer doin'. If ye didna time and again take on the likes of us fer no—"

"You're quite welcome, Mr. Wesley," Gideon said

swiftly, and then said no more. He was certain Mr. Wesley was about to say "no pay," and those two little words might inspire Constance to ask dangerous questions. Such as, "Where do you get your money if you take on clients for no pay, Gideon?" And the truthful answer to that question would be: "What money, Constance?"

Mr. Wesley, puzzled by the abrupt response, moved his eyes between Constance and Jarvis. He took in their mildly repulsed expressions, and his smile vanished, replaced with a sort of stoic understanding.

A swift surge of anger took Gideon by surprise, an alien thing when it came to Constance. He wrestled it back. He supposed he couldn't fault her for it, really; no doubt she had never been exposed to someone like Mr. Wesley—a man of rough dress and speech and questionable cleanliness.

A man whose labor put food on the tables of the *ton*'s aristocrats.

But then, marriage to Constance would mean he could take on *every* client for no pay, if he so chose. A veritable battalion of Mr. Wesleys.

"You received our bequest, Mr. Cole?" Mr. Wesley asked. "Dodge passed it on t' ye?"

"I did," Gideon said gently. "And I thank you." *And look what I bought with it!* He was perversely tempted to add, with a gesture at Lily.

But he said nothing more.

"Well, I'll be off, then, Mr. Cole," Mr. Wesley said with great dignity. "My thanks again, sir, and bless you." He bowed and strode away, pulling his battered hat back down upon his head as he went.

Wait! Gideon was tempted to call after him. But he didn't. He simply stared. And felt ashamed.

"Good *heavens*," Constance said with a breathy little

laugh. As though Mr. Wesley had committed a social faux pas simply by virtue of being.

Again, that surge of anger. Gideon tamped it back. He glanced at Lily; she was watching Mr. Wesley become a speck in the distance, her expression softer than he'd seen it all day.

"Handsome dress, Miss Masters," Constance said finally, with the air of one who thought she was rescuing the conversation.

Dresses. With Constance, it was always, always *dresses*.

"Thank you, Lady Clary." Lily sounded genuinely touched by the compliment. "By the way, I have alerted my modiste to your interest in her services. She has agreed to observe you from a distance to see whether you would make a suitable client."

"A . . . a suitable *client*?" Constance's horse danced a little beneath her, as though she had squeezed her thighs in outrage.

Well, Gideon thought. If talk of dresses could lead to an obvious loss of composure in Constance Clary, perhaps it was worth it, after all.

"That is," Lily explained hurriedly, "she wishes to ascertain whether her skills can do your figure justice, of *course*."

Constance managed to get her dancing horse under control. "I see. Well, I should still like to see how she does Reading dresses. I have yet to see any of *yours*, Miss Masters." Constance looked out at Lily through hooded eyes.

Lily's brows dipped a little in puzzlement. "Well . . . I suppose that would be because you wouldn't wear a Reading dress for a ride in a high flyer, now, would you, Lady Clary? Or to a ball or dinner?"

Constance regarded Lily for a silent moment. "Of course not," she agreed weakly.

It was like watching two people duel with flower-tipped rapiers, Gideon exulted. Something had definitely shifted. Lily Masters had ceased to become a curiosity; she was officially a rival. And Constance had never *had* one of those before.

We've done it, Gideon quietly marveled.

"Well, we must move along." Gideon tossed the words breezily into the silence. "Will the two of you attend the Ryce-Martin party?"

"Certainly." Jarvis beamed at them.

Constance, for her part, merely nodded curtly. "And Gideon," she said coolly, "my father would still like to speak with you about the position in the Treasury. They hope to fill it by the end of the month."

It was too soon for celebration. But nevertheless, he felt a firefly-sized flare of elation.

"I would be delighted to meet with your father at his convenience, Constance. And I shall look forward *greatly* to the Ryce-Martin party." He fixed her with a long, meaningful gaze meant to soothe away her agitation. And after a moment Constance's jaw seemed to loosen and she was able to show all of her teeth in her signature smile.

Gideon slapped the ribbons over the backs of Kilmartin's brown geldings and the high flyer lurched forward.

"Pleasant chap," he heard Jarvis commenting as they rolled away.

He wondered what Constance would reply to *that*.

Lily was silent again, her face shuttered—as though a curtain had come down over the performance. And what a performance it had been. *Reading* dresses? *Mavis?* Against all odds, it was *working*. Constance had been officially thrown off her game; it was breathtaking to witness. It remained, of course, a delicate situation, and would need to be managed carefully. But at this rate, he wouldn't be surprised if Constance proposed to him solely to spite Lily Masters.

He almost turned to Lily to share the joke, the small triumph. But layers of confusion and hurt and distrust prevented him from turning his head; he kept his eyes on the backs of the geldings. Better that he nurture this wall between them, he thought. *Better, in the long term, for both of us.*

Lily stood on the walk and watched Kilmartin's geldings, two horses as beautifully and ideally matched as Gideon Cole and Constance Clary, pull the high flyer and Gideon swiftly away.

Gideon had deposited her back at Aunt Hester's as if she were a . . . hod of coal. With *exactly* that much ceremony and care. He had swung her down from the high flyer, and then his hands had practically flown from her, unwilling to remain on her a second longer than necessary. And then he'd touched the brim of his hat. She was sure he resented the compulsion to do so.

Fine, she thought furiously. If Gideon became engaged to the odious woman, at least Lily would get some satisfaction from knowing that she had bested her, even if Lady Constance Clary would never know it.

By some satisfaction, she actually meant a very, very minute *particle* of satisfaction.

For three strained nights, Kilmartin and Aunt Hester had escorted her to parties and balls; for three strained nights, Kilmartin had made clumsy apologies for Gideon, assuring Lily that *disappearing* was merely all part of Gideon's plan. And Kilmartin's solicitousness on those three nights had been excruciating, for it meant he suspected she was hurting. And here she thought she'd been doing a *splendid* job of keeping that a secret. Her pride had fairly throbbed every time Kilmartin said something to her in a gentle voice.

And then this morning, her heart nearly stopped when Gideon appeared at Aunt Hester's town house. His face had been pale and there were dark rings beneath his eyes; his expression had been unreadable, of course, his hands fidgeting with his hat. The sight of him shaved the sharpest edge from her anger: for it was clear that Gideon was hurting, too.

Good.

She'd encased herself in icy silence. And it had nearly worked; she had almost felt nothing as she sat next to him in the high flyer; she had almost been able to derive nothing but pure enjoyment from tormenting Lady Constance Clary. Until Mr. Wesley appeared, and Gideon was confronted with his two selves.

And one of those selves was the man she loved.

She'd seen it in Gideon's face today; his coolness to Mr. Wesley had not come naturally. But he could expect that sort of discomfort if he continually stifled the best part of himself.

The fool.

He *deserved* to get what he wanted so desperately. She was certain it would make him bloody miserable. With some difficulty, she restrained herself from throwing her bonnet on the floor and stomping on it in frustration.

One of Aunt Hester's impossibly handsome footmen appeared before her then, startling her. They were always doing that: Thanks to the thick carpets everywhere, they were as silent as cats.

"There's a visitor for you in the parlor, Miss Masters. A Madame Marceau. I took the liberty of bringing in some tea."

"Oh!" This was good news. Madame Marceau's frank

company would go a long way toward cleansing her mind of the horribly oblique Lady Constance Clary. "Thank you! Splendid. Have you any cakes, too?"

"I brought in cakes." The footman smiled; the entire household had become familiar with Miss Masters's fondness for food of any kind.

Madame Marceau rose to greet Lily. She was, as usual, stunningly turned out in one of her own creations, a dress of a deep claret hue, severely and exquisitely cut to show off her elegantly tall form.

"Miss Masters! How lovely to see you! And I don't mind saying that your dress is smashing."

Lily smiled at Madame Marceau and curtsied. "I know a wonderful modiste, if you'd like her name."

Madame Marceau laughed. "She *is* wonderful, isn't she? And she has a delicious dilemma, entirely caused by you, she suspects."

"Oh, dear! What could that be?"

"I received an urgent message a very short time ago—from a Bow Street Runner, if you can imagine it—inquiring if I were the modiste who dressed Miss Lily Masters, and, if so, would I please consider making, and I quote, a 'Reading dress' for a certain Lady Constance Clary. *The* Lady Constance Clary! Daughter of Marquis Shawcross! And they had bribes in hand if I would do it straight away! I was simply flabbergasted, as you can imagine."

Lily clapped her hand over her mouth in glee. "Oh," she said faintly, struggling with laughter. "I had no idea . . . it worked so amazingly well . . ."

"Miss Masters? Would you care to share with me what is going on?"

"It's just this, Madame Marceau: I told Lady Constance Clary, who is simply insufferable, that you are my modiste of choice, and that *you* choose your clients, rather than the other way around. Today I even told her you might be watching her from a distance to determine whether she would make a suitable client."

Madame Marceau's mouth dropped open in astonishment, and then she threw back her head and laughed raucously. "*Ohhhh*, Miss Masters, that is the most *marvelous* tale." She wiped her eyes. "And what on earth is a *Reading* dress?"

"Well . . . I suppose that's up to you. Although I do know that they're very, very, *very* expensive."

"Expensive, are they?" Madame Marceau's eyes gleamed like guineas.

"Very, *very*," Lily confirmed with a wicked smile. "I think you should make quite a few of them for Constance."

"Perhaps something with a long sleeve . . ." Madame Marceau mused.

"And perhaps with a book dangling from it somewhere."

They laughed together again until they nearly choked.

Chapter Seventeen

Lily wore sea green silk that night, and Lord Jarvis and numerous other men assured her it suited her magnificently. Splendidly. Beautifully. Superlatives were flung at her all evening; her favorite thus far compared her hair to the color of Roman coins. Imagine—not just coins: *Roman* coins. *That* one was courtesy of Lord Ryce-Martin, their host for the ball this evening. It was difficult not to enjoy being so excessively admired; if not for Gideon and Lady Constance Clary she might even enjoy herself.

While Lily sat on the settee and listened to Lord Jarvis talk about himself, Gideon stood across the room, talking with Constance, his face gently amused and attentive. And then his eyes flicked up, caught hers, held briefly, flicked away again.

Why am I doing this? Lily asked herself again. *Participating in this charade? Because I made a promise.*

Because I love him.

But did she really? She loved the man he was beneath his masks. The kind man, the gentle man, the whimsical man, the passionate and impatient man, the man who noticed everything. Who cared deeply. Who admired leaves.

The man he was determined to smother so he could marry the daughter of a marquis.

Five nights now he'd repaired to his own lodgings. For five nearly sleepless nights, she'd listened to Aunt Hester snore—it penetrated all of the walls in the town house—and despite herself, Lily's entire world seemed diminished.

When did he intend to propose to Constance? She supposed the moment would knell in her heart; perhaps that was all the warning he intended give her. Lily wondered what it might be like to marry Jarvis or one of these other oh-so-attentive men, none of whom she'd given any specific sort of encouragement. She imagined she might even enjoy the engagement until the time came for her to introduce them to her fictional father.

"Miss Lily Masters? A message for you."

She looked up. One of Lady Ryce-Martin's footmen stood before her, extending a folded sheet of foolscap.

"Oh! Thank you."

Miss Masters,

Miss Alice is very ill. The doctor has suggested that you come home at once. A hired carriage waits outside.

Yrs.,

Ada Plunkett

Lily stared down at the horrible words, and her limbs slowly turned to ice.

"Miss Masters, is everything quite all right?"

She'd forgotten about Lord Jarvis. Lily attempted a polite smile; but her lips seemed made of ice, too. Somehow she made them move, form words. "Thank you for asking. It seems . . . my sister is unwell, and I have been called home. If you will excuse me?"

She rose and curtsied—odd how strangely comforting this gesture had become—and moved through the room like the Lily of old, swift and wraithlike, to the carriage waiting outside.

"Gideon, you really should hold another house party at Aster Park. All that lovely land—splendid for riding and picnics and archery. And all those lovely rooms perfect for . . ." Constance trailed off.

Gideon was immediately alert. Could it be that Constance had just issued her very first *innuendo*? "Perfect for *what*, Constance?" he coaxed silkily. *For private meetings* would have been a splendid response, preferably delivered in sultry tones. But he would have been satisfied with a coquettish sideways glance between her pale lashes. Something. *Anything*.

Constance frowned a little. "Oh, my apologies. I was momentarily distracted by Lydia Burnham's new gown. That color doesn't suit her, does it? What I meant to say is that the rooms are perfect for dinner parties and cards and dancing, of course."

Gideon sighed inwardly. Constance was a genteel lady, after all, and virtually an innocent in many ways, gossamer gowns notwithstanding. She would no doubt require a considerable amount of . . . sensual education. Then again, perhaps her competitive streak would work in his favor in the bedroom. He imagined how he'd go about it: "Well, Lord Rawlston told me *his* wife is quite skilled at—"

Constance was still speaking, so he returned his attention to her. "You could ask Kilmartin, too, and . . . Lord Jarvis. And perhaps I could ask a few other friends."

She'd cushioned Jarvis's name with a strategic little pause, Gideon noted, half amused. *Perhaps she means to force my hand.* And the more Gideon thought about it, the more practical, the more desirable a house party seemed—for many an engagement had been sealed at a house party. And it suited him to have his hand forced: he was weary, *weary* of his charade.

He barely spoke to Lily beyond pleasantries now; for five nights now, including his embarrassing little . . . *retreat*, he'd slept in his own lodgings. And already his thoughts were calmer, more rational, more clear of purpose—rather, in fact, the way they were before Lily entered his life. Perhaps this was evidence that Lily *was* merely a passing fever.

But Lily hadn't once faltered in keeping her promise. As though she, too, hoped to force matters to a conclusion.

Lord Kilmartin strolled up to Gideon and Constance, his face a little ruddy from his vigorous turn about the dance floor.

"Constance was just suggesting I host a house party at Aster Park this weekend, Laurie. What do you think of the idea?"

"Oh, splendid! You will invite Lady Anne Clapham of course. And my dear cousin Lily."

Constance's vivacity dropped a notch. "Oh, of course. We must have Miss Masters as well. Dear, *dear* Miss Masters. When, by the way, does your *dear* cousin Lily return to Sussex?"

"Well . . ." Kilmartin looked up at Gideon meaningfully. "Possibly . . . never."

Constance fixed Gideon with a gaze so penetrating he was amazed a smoking hole didn't appear between his eyes.

"Yes," Gideon said equably, "I shall of course invite Lady Clapham and Miss Masters to Aster Park, too. Rest assured, Constance, you shall have no competition"—he waited for Constance to begin to smile—"when it comes to archery."

Constance's smile congealed mid-curve. Kilmartin coughed, skillfully disguising a laugh.

Gideon felt a twinge of conscience: He wasn't entirely proud of the means by which he was corralling an aristocratic wife, but it *did* seem to be working. He even half suspected Constance would approve of his methods, because her own attempts to get the things she wanted were not precisely irreproachable. But it was exhausting. It seemed such a long time since he'd been able to just . . . *be*.

"It's decided, then, is it?" Kilmartin said brightly, just as Lord Jarvis approached their group and bowed. "We shall all repair to Aster Park the day after tomorrow."

"Jarvis!" Gideon greeted enthusiastically, just to confuse Constance further. "I'd like to invite you to a house party to commence the day after tomorrow at my uncle's home, Aster Park. Kilmartin and Lady Clary and Miss Lily Masters will be joining us there, as well as a few other . . ." Gideon thought of the people Constance was likely to invite, and because he wasn't sure what to call them, he decided upon ". . . friends."

Unbidden, Lily's words came to him: *Everyone is your friend, and yet everyone is a stranger*. Almost unconsciously, he flicked his eyes toward the settee; she was no longer there.

"Oh, thank you, Cole. That sounds wonderful!" Jarvis beamed at the three of them. "Perhaps Miss Masters's sister will be recovered by then."

What an odd thing to say. Gideon frowned a little. "I beg your pardon?"

"While I was conversing with Miss Masters a few minutes ago, she received a note summoning her home. Something about her sister. She—Miss Masters, that is—seemed quite distressed, in fact. I thought you might have known, Kilmartin, as she's your cousin. I shall miss—that is, she will be greatly missed," Jarvis stammered.

"Home, did you say?" Constance's face was positively radiant. "Miss Masters has been called *home*? To Sussex? That *is* a shame. And listen, Gideon, the orchestra has just struck up our waltz."

"Gideon?" she repeated, when he did not reply.

"Constance." Gideon could hardly hear his own voice over the roaring that had started up in his ears. Some great weight was limiting his breathing, too. "I think . . . I think your idea of a house party is so splendid that I should repair at once to Aster Park to begin preparations. I would very much like you to see it at its best. You *do* understand? You *will* forgive me if I miss just this waltz? I am certain there will be many others for us." He offered a smile; it felt like his face was cracking in half, and he distantly hoped it didn't look as hideous as it felt.

Kilmartin was staring at him as if he'd gone mad.

"Well . . . it does seem a trifle unusual . . ." Constance was frowning slightly. "But I do understand, Gideon. If Aster Park were *my* home, I should like it to look its best as well." The words throbbed with significance.

But Gideon took no notice. "Wonderful," he said. He bowed, then turned and wove his way toward the exit of Lord and Lady Ryce-Martin's town house.

As quick as a thief.

Chapter Eighteen

Gideon threw a handful of pound notes at the groggy hack driver and ran for Aster Park's main house, crashing through the huge double doors. Every lamp in the house was snuffed, all the fires in the main rooms doused. He bolted up the darkened stairs.

"*Lily!*" He ran down the hallways toward their chamber. The door was ajar, the room was cold; Lily and Alice weren't there.

He scrambled up another flight of stairs, which led to the nursery. A spread of soft light from the open door told him a fire was blazing—he had found them.

Lily was staring into the fire, the dim light illuminating the network of fine wrinkles the hours-long coach ride had irrevocably crushed into her gown.

A small form was humped under a number of quilts on the bed: Alice. His heart gave a thud; he looked closely, and saw the rise and fall of Alice's breathing. He closed his eyes briefly against a wave of relief. At least she lived.

Lily turned slowly to face him. She seemed a bit dazed,

but unsurprised; no doubt she had heard his footsteps in the hall.

Gideon hesitated on the threshold of the room. "How is she?"

"The doctor said . . . well, it was very serious. But she is . . ." Lily's voice shook; she took a breath to steady it. "She is a sturdy little girl. Her fever broke earlier, and already she improves. She's sleeping more restfully now. The doctor was here, but he has gone home now."

Gideon's throat tightened with all he could not put into words. They regarded each other across a thick silence, the air shimmering with unspoken things.

"She is . . . she is all I have." A tremulous, almost apologetic smile touched Lily's lips.

Gideon was beside her in a few steps.

He pulled her into his arms and folded himself around her, holding her tightly. The feel of her, the relief of having her in his arms again, was almost too much to bear. Lily clung to him, trembling.

"That's not true, Lily, my Lily," he murmured. "It will be all right. I am here."

His hands moved over her back in long soothing strokes; he brushed his lips tenderly across her brow, across her temple, across her cheekbone and eyelids, nuzzling her, murmuring her name, murmuring incoherent syllables of comfort. She did not cry, but she shook with the fear of loss, and he held her, willing his warmth into her.

He could not have said how long they stood there. But slowly, little by little, her shivering body softened beneath his hands. And Lily, her eyes half closed, began to tilt her face so his lips would fall against the tender place beneath her jaw . . .

The corner of her mouth . . .

Her lips.

His lips hovered over hers, a breath away from touching. His hands stilled on her. He cautiously lifted his head; he felt her hands fumbling against him.

Gideon looked down and watched, as if in a dream, her slim fingers slowly work open a button on his shirt.

"*Lily*. Lily, you should not . . ."

"Hush." She paused and covered his lips with two fingers. "You are forever telling me what to do."

He smiled against her fingers. And slowly, while Gideon barely drew breath, she worked open another button, and another, and then the next. And he let her. Until his shirt hung open in two panels and the cool air of the room struck his bare flesh.

Lily gently parted his shirt and the flat of her cool hands landed on his skin; she slid them up, with excruciating leisure, over his muscled ribs. Tributaries of desire ignited everywhere in him, like the myriad fires set by a single strike of lightning.

Her hands paused; she placed a single soft kiss over his heart.

"Please," she whispered.

And it was as though he'd been waiting to hear this word, in her voice, all his life.

It was no tentative exploration this time. He sank slowly, irrevocably into the hot bliss of her mouth; he cupped her face and tilted her head back so his tongue could plunge deeply, so he could find all the texture and sweetness of her. Lily reached up to wrap her arms loosely around his head, and their tongues tangled, graceless and impatient; his hands shaking, he dragged his fingers over the curves of her cheeks, down the column of her throat, down to trace, lightly, the fine bones at the base of her neck. And oh, her skin was soft, indescribably soft.

Gideon pulled away from her abruptly and took her by the hand, leading her to the little maid's room that adjoined the main chamber.

The room was cool; the warmth of the main room's fire had not reached it. And here he kissed her, solemnly, almost chastely; a tender press of the lips, a signal of intent. *He would make love to her in this room.*

"Turn around, Lily," he ordered softly.

Slowly, she did as ordered. Gideon tugged with trembling hands at the fine laces that closed her gown, loosening them until the shoulders of it drooped; as he did, he dragged his lips along the silky length of her neck, stopping to nip a tender kiss at the place where it joined her shoulders, and saw the gooseflesh rising along her arms. Lily's head went back; he wrapped his arms around her slim waist and trailed his tongue along the arc of her neck, stopping to savor the pulse beating in her throat with his lips; he could feel her breathing quickening beneath his hands.

And then, with a touch as delicate as moth wings, he pushed the sleeves of her gown down, down, down, until the bodice drooped to her waist with a soft rustle.

"Oh, Lily. My Lily. How I have wanted you," he sighed into her ear. Her breathing was rapid now, and it excited him unbearably. He ran a single finger reverently down the beads of her spine to the cleft of her buttocks, feeling the gooseflesh rise in its wake; he fanned his hands to slowly savor the way her hips curved gently into her waist, stopping tantalizingly just shy of her breasts. When Lily arced back against him reflexively, whispering his name, urging his hands to go farther, he felt a surge of triumph, but he did not oblige her.

Instead, he unfastened his trousers with hands gone suddenly clumsy, and shook his shirt away from his shoulders until it dropped to the floor.

"Turn around, Lily," he ordered softly, again.

Lily turned again, slowly, her arms coming up to cover her breasts, the gown still clinging to her hips. Her eyes were pale and bright in the dark; she took in his nudeness and his arousal with unabashed, avid wonder.

Fairly shaking with the effort to hold his desire in check, Gideon leaned down to kiss her parted lips again, softly nuzzling, tasting her breath, while he searched her hair for pins. One by one he found them and pulled them; they fell to the floor with little pings. He loosened the dark gold glory of her hair, and combed it away from her face.

And then he pushed his fingers up through it and pulled her head back, taking a kiss almost marauding in its force.

Lily's arms came away from her breasts and folded around his neck, and she pushed herself up against him, meeting his released hunger with her own. Tongues and lips and teeth clashed in this deep, endless kiss; her breasts chafed against his chest; her soft belly dragged against his shaft. *Dear God.*

Patience slipped his grasp; he pushed at Lily's gown until it at last slid down over her hips and sagged into a soft heap at her ankles, and his hands cupped her small round buttocks, lifting her up against his hardness. "Feel me, Lily," he whispered against her lips. "Do you want me?"

"I want you." Her low velvet voice was ragged with the truth of it.

He held her back away from him to look, to briefly savor. Lily now stood bare except for her stockings and garters, her skin glowing like the surface of the moon in the dark of the room. As he looked, her shoulders were back, her chin up. She was so beautiful, so perfectly her.

"*Oh God.*" Did he say it? Did she? It was impossible to know; it was all the same now. His hands twining in her hair, her hands roaming over his chest, he kissed her, backing her slowly up to the bed, until her knees bent and she sat down upon it. And then he pushed her gently until she lay back, her hair spread out behind her, her eyes half closed with desire. He stretched out on the bed alongside her.

His palm skimmed over one of Lily's small, upthrust breasts, and she breathed in sharply; he lowered his head and closed his mouth over it, taking the silk crepe of her nipple first with his tongue, then his teeth; her fingers combed through his hair, holding him to her, and she arced with a soft keening whimper.

He was of a mind to satisfy his need quickly.

Gideon pulled her into his arms, covering her briefly, and dragged his tongue down the seam that divided her slim ribs, to her nest of damp curls, where he savored the fresh singular taste of her with his tongue; she rippled beneath his hands and mouth like quicksilver, encouraging him, whispering his name. With his hands, he gently parted her slim legs covered in their fine stockings, and savored her again; he cupped her buttocks, lifting her up to meet his mouth, and her hips began to move in time with his relentless tongue, until her breathing was hoarse and swift, until she begged him with incoherent syllables and gripped the coverlet.

And then he moved up the length of her body again, taking her mouth in a deep kiss, because he wanted to feel her entire body against his when she found her release. He slipped one finger slowly, deeply into the damp heat of her and crooked it ever so slightly.

She came apart with a long, nearly silent cry, bowing up beneath him, pulsing wondrously.

It has to be now, he thought. *Or I will die.*

Gideon moved her knees apart with his hands and fitted himself to her, and, rising up over her, he entered her quickly; Lily gave a shocked little intake of breath, but she lifted her hips to meet him, to ease his passage. They breathed roughly together; he groaned until he was seated deeply in her.

And then he knew, without a doubt, that he was her first.

"Lily . . . I'm sorry," he whispered, foolishly.

"Don't be ridiculous," she whispered.

And though he tried, God knows, he could not be slow about it; the need was too great and too long contained. He moved in her, and his release was swift and explosive; it seared his every nerve with astounding pleasure, sending him out of his body. He heard his own hoarse cry as if it had come from someone else entirely.

Stunned and spent, he rolled away from Lily and threw one arm over his face, breathing heavily. He lay alongside her for a long moment without touching her, the cool air of the room chilling the perspiration on his body.

"Did I hurt you?" he asked, finally.

A pause.

"No." A single soft word.

"Liar."

She laughed softly. He pulled her into his arms and held her tightly against him, stroking her sweat-dampened hair away from her face. He touched her lips, her brows, the curve of her chin, wonderingly, as though she were a magical being, something he'd only just discovered, and she smiled up at him.

"It can be so wonderful, Lily, I promise you."

"It *was* wonderful."

"Was it?" *God, I sound like a boy,* he thought. He felt shy and proud.

"Mmmm," she confirmed languorously.

"I should have been more gentle . . ."

"Hush. Gideon, it was . . . extraordinary. I wasn't sure . . . that is . . ."

He smiled in the dark. *She* was extraordinary. "But you suspected."

She laughed softly. "I had a book."

"I *knew* you could understand more French than you let on."

She laughed again and shifted a little in his arms, and his hands slid down over her belly. With just that little movement, he was hardening again. He moved his hands up over her breasts, languidly exploring the satin shape of them, until her breath came in little gasps.

"*Gideon.*"

This was it: This was what he had feared. For he could sink into the sea that was Lily and happily never come up again; he feared he would never, ever be sated.

It seemed they still could not go slowly, though he had intended to try. He sat up, pulling her into his lap; he gently nipped the silky back of her neck, and covered her breasts with his hands; he eased into her as she straddled his thighs. His hands moved down to the cleft in her legs; he urged her up and down his shaft until he groaned his own release, shuddering from it. He held her as Lily again pulsed around him, gasping his name like a cry for help.

She collapsed against him, and he rolled her over into his arms and buried his face in her hair, murmuring her name. He felt the rise and fall of her ribs beneath his hands. Nothing had ever felt more miraculous.

What am I going to do?

Don't think, he told himself. *There's only today.*

They were silent together, languid for a time. No sound but breathing filled the room.

"I didn't take the necklace," Lily said suddenly.

Gideon tensed. "It doesn't matter."

She pulled away from him a little and leaned on one elbow, her hair falling over her face. "Gideon, I swear to you—"

"What I'm saying, Lily, is that I know you didn't take it. I think I've always known. But . . . it wouldn't matter if you had. I still would have come to you."

Neither of them said anything more after that. Lily settled back into his arms, and he held her like a gift.

After too short a time, Lily pulled gently out of his arms again; he released her reluctantly. She sat up on the bed, and he admired the pale curve of her waist and hips as she twisted her hair into a loose knot. She lifted her dress up from the floor and stood to pull it over her head.

She turned to him. "Alice," she said simply.

She returned to sit briefly on the edge of the bed. Gideon reached out his hand; she took it in hers and their fingers twined. She kissed his knuckles, and then she leaned down to kiss his lips softly.

"I will stay with her," he told her. "You can sleep."

"Thank you. But if she wakes, she'll want me, Gideon."

He knew this was true. "I want you, too," he said softly. "I always have."

She said nothing; she merely gazed down at him for a moment, a small smile hovering on her lips. And then she bent down to kiss him on the mouth, and slowly withdrew her fingers from his.

* * *

Gideon remained stretched out on the narrow little servant's bed for a long time, thinking. He finally roused himself to dress, and then walked through the sickroom to find Lily kneeling on the floor next to Alice's bed, her head resting on the bed, cradled on her arms. Both girls were fast asleep.

Gideon settled his coat over Lily's shoulders, and then rested the back of his hand briefly, lightly on Alice's forehead. She was cool; her breathing seemed even.

He was not in the habit of thanking God, but he uttered a silent prayer of thanks anyway. Today, his gratitude for everything was so large a whole planet could not contain it. He thought he had best thank God, if only to relieve himself of a little of it.

He used the poker to coax the dying fire higher. And then, quietly, he left them.

Chapter Nineteen

Lily awoke to a bright room and the feel of someone's little fingers drumming her head.

"Thank goodness, Lily. I thought you had died."

Lily smiled, weak with relief. "*Somebody* is feeling better."

Alice still looked a little peaked, but her eyes were bright—not with fever, thankfully, but with curiosity. She frowned at Lily. "*You* look terrible, Lily. It's purple underneath your eyes. And why are you wearing a man's coat?"

Startled, Lily reached her hand up to her shoulder. She hadn't noticed the weight of the coat, but the rush of Gideon's scent nearly felled her.

"Well, thank you very much, Alice, but you aren't exactly looking radiant this morning, either. You've been very ill, goose, and I've been very worried. How do you feel?"

Alice gave it some thought. "Hungry."

"Perhaps the doctor should have a look at you. How is your breathing? Do you hurt? Take a deep breath and see."

Alice inhaled deeply. "No. It doesn't hurt anymore. But I like the doctor. Let's have him come anyway."

Lily smiled. "Perhaps Mrs. Plunkett will bring you some broth."

"And some cakes."

"All right. Perhaps some cakes, too."

Lily stood and stretched. Her body was stiff, and there was a soreness between her legs which surprised her until she remembered: *Of course. Last night.*

And then suddenly the memory of last night flooded her heart and mind. Gideon lifting her up against him, her first feel of his naked flesh against hers. *Do you want me, Lily?* The breathtakingly tender, and then rough, demand of his very accomplished lips. His fingers gliding over her skin, the feel of him moving inside her, the smooth skin of his hard back, the curling hair of his chest.

I love him.

Lily's restlessness drove her to the threshold of the little maid's room near the nursery. The most astonishing things had taken place upon that narrow, austere little bed, all because, like a wanton, she'd asked for something for the first time in her life: *Please*, she'd said to him. She'd sought comfort, and relief from weeks of pent longing. He'd given it to her.

Lily smiled a little, even as her throat tightened with tears. The *power* of it was indescribable, terrible in its beauty. The moment Gideon had touched her, there had been no thought or choice. If she'd known how terrifyingly, exhilaratingly *final* it would be to make love to him . . .

I want you, she'd told him last night. *I want him*, she'd told herself for weeks. If she'd known what it really meant, she might have fled long ago.

Never willingly put yourself at the mercy of a man, Lily. Her mother had known the bittersweet danger of it.

"Mr. Cole was here this morning," Alice called from the bed.

Lily's heart gave a jump. "Was he?" she asked casually.

"He didn't know I saw. He looked in at us for a long time, and then he left."

"He cares for you, Alice."

"And for you, Lily." Her words were innocent.

But even if they were true, it would not change a thing. Nothing could come of it. *We cannot stay here any longer.*

Gideon had been unable to sleep for more than a few fitful hours. Finally, at dawn, he'd visited the nursery to look in on Lily and Alice. Reassured that they were both still breathing, he stopped himself from touching Lily.

He simply could not face her yet, so he left them and trudged through the chilled, sweet, predawn air out to the stables. He needed space in which to unravel his tangled heart and mind, to examine his thoughts one by one, so he could arrive at some sort of conclusion. He sent the sleepy stable boy back to the loft and saddled Horatio himself. He trotted out of the stableyard, and then kneed him into a run.

He galloped over the soft spreading green of the park deep into his uncle's land. The dawn air was heavy with moist earth and green things, and he took great draughts of it, hoping it would clear his mind.

But Gideon's thoughts kept pace with him, so he finally dismounted and led Horatio along the lake, surrendering to the need to think . . . and decide.

For the first time in his life, he had truly made love to a woman. *Made love*. Not just for the physical release, or the savage pleasure of it, or just because he could. But because he wanted to become a part of *her*, to give pleasure and comfort solely to *her*.

And this thing he felt . . . whatever it was . . . it threatened to override his good sense, his plans, his control. Like a weed—

He half smiled to himself; good God, even the prose in his *thoughts* was going purple. *Bloody poetry*. No, not a weed. For Lily *was* life, not a thing that strangled life.

And then he realized his uncle had described Therese in just the same way.

Oh God.

It very nearly killed me. Those had been his uncle's words, too. Gideon had known grief in his life; he'd known enough of life's valleys to be suspicious of the peaks. Nothing so immense had ever before touched him. He should send Lily away before the rest of his life became a pale coda to these past few weeks with her.

For he, in his way, with his whim and his weakness and thirty pounds, had brought this down on all of them. Although he supposed he could allot a little of the blame to Lily. She *had* tried to steal his watch. He smiled a little.

Meanwhile, for his sake and for hers, he would keep his distance. He'd spent the last decade or so of his life keeping his distance from risk, from want—how difficult, really, could another week or so be?

Lily stayed with Alice in the nursery all day, reading stories to her, napping when she napped, eating when she ate. The servants, one by one, stopped by to say hello and to see how Miss Alice fared. Even Boone the gardener and Dawson the pig keeper made an appearance, each of them as grubby as two potatoes freshly pulled from the ground. Mrs. Plunkett looked distinctly nervous to have the two of them in the house.

Alice, it seemed, had made friends everywhere at Aster

Park. *But Alice,* Lily told herself stubbornly, *will make friends everywhere she goes. She has that kind of spirit. She will be fine when we leave. We will* both *be fine when we leave.*

Coach fare to London was probably about four shillings. Perhaps over the next few days she could win as much at cards from Lord Lindsey; instead of handing it over to Gideon toward her debt, she would keep it, find some way to send word to the coaching inn . . .

Twilight's mauve shadows now filled the nursery room, and Alice was snoring softly. The remnants of their dinner—soup, cold meat, bread—littered a tray on the floor. Mrs. Plunkett would no doubt be by to fetch it a little later. The housekeeper had promised to stay with Alice tonight.

"Sleep in your own room, Miss Masters. You need a good night's sleep, or you'll have the fever, too."

It was so lovely to be cared for that Lily didn't put up an argument.

Gideon had not appeared all day.

So Lily kissed her sleeping sister softly on the forehead, and took her candle down the hall to her room. She slid the bolt on the door and wrapped the blankets tightly around her as though they could keep everything out. The world. Pain.

Love.

Brandy hadn't helped. He thought perhaps he'd move on to whiskey, and then considered how the combination of brandy and whiskey would make him feel in the morning, and rejected *that* idea. Not to mention the effect too much drinking would have on his nearly empty stomach. For he had not eaten a thing tonight. He had taken his meal in his chambers, and the cold meat had gone down like ashes. He hadn't even attempted the peas.

And so Gideon had gone to the library and pulled books from the shelves and taken them back to his chambers with him, a desperate attempt to lull himself to sleep. But the poetry he usually found as lulling as a soft symphony had only made it all worse.

And so, punitively, he had tried Plutarch. But his mind seemed unable to get any purchase on the words; it slid over them and right back off again. He tossed Plutarch aside. He considered going for a moonlit swim in the lake, but rejected that notion as too absurdly dramatic.

His blankets itched; he threw them off irritably.

And then he spent the next half hour staring up at the shifting shadows on his ceiling, cast by the flickering light of his taper.

It was no use.

Gideon stood and slowly pulled his trousers on and stuffed his shirt into his trousers, with hands that trembled a little. He lifted the candle and cupped his hand around it, and went out the door of his bedchamber.

The tap came close to midnight; she knew because she had heard the hour struck by one of Aster Park's many clocks. Lily's heart leaped up like a fish breaking the surface of the sea.

Don't open the door. You shouldn't open the door.

Another tap. So softly she could almost have imagined it. Three times.

It's foolish. It's dangerous. Nothing good can ever come of this.

A pause. Her heart nearly stopped.

And then another soft tap.

She leaped from her bed and dashed to the door before he

could change his mind, her hand fumbling impatiently at the lock to slide it open.

Gideon was dressed only in trousers and a shirt open at the neck, a lit candle illuminating his face. She stepped aside, and he entered the room, setting the candle with great care on her dressing table. She closed the door and slid the bolt, turned to face him.

Her arms went around his neck just as he was reaching for her, and then his lips were on hers, excruciatingly tender.

She stepped back from him and raised her arms, and Gideon lifted her dressing gown over her head; it drifted, ghostlike, to the floor. She stood nude before him; impatient, he pulled her into his arms and sought her mouth again. They joined in a long, drugging kiss as his hands roamed feverishly everywhere, sliding down over her breasts, cupping her buttocks and lifting her up against him, stroking the tender flesh inside her thighs, until she was nothing but sensation. His lips were on her throat and shoulders, her mouth again; he traced the whorls of her ear with his tongue. She took her mouth from his and buried her face against him, sighing with pleasure; she rippled beneath his hands, submitting to, encouraging his exploration.

Neither of them had yet said a word.

Gideon turned her to face the mirror over her dressing table and stood behind her. By candlelight, she saw her own face, flushed and heavy-lidded, her hair a riotous tangle. Gideon traced lacy figures over her nipples with fingers at first delicate, and then rough, and she arched her head back, trembling with the pleasure of it; he bent his head to nuzzle her throat. In the mirror she watched his hair fall over his brow.

"See how beautiful you are, Lily." Lily watched in the mirror, mesmerized, as Gideon's palms covered her breasts and circled over them, then slid in tandem down over the curve of her belly to the silky triangle between her legs. Her breathing grew rough with anticipation; but he was only teasing her; his fingers merely trailed across her damp curls before gliding back again to her breasts; she sighed a protest. His hands left her body altogether for a moment to unfasten his trousers, and then she felt his erection pressing against her. His breath came in harsh gasps in her ear.

"I need you *now*, Lily."

"Yes." Her own voice was a taut whisper.

He gently urged her to bend forward, and nudged her legs farther apart with his knee; she braced her hands on her dressing table. She could feel his shaft tease the cleft in her legs, and then he was sliding into her, slowly, filling her gloriously full. His hand came around to touch where she ached to be touched, and his hips pulled back, and then slowly thrust forward again. She watched their faces in the mirror, Gideon's above his white shirt flushed, his eyes distant, intent, her own face avid and possessed.

He stroked into her again, and she moaned from it. He did it again, exquisitely, agonizingly slowly, his hand stroking in rhythm. She watched, held in thrall by her own reflection, by the beautiful man joined to her, watched his dark eyes meet her own in the mirror in a conspiracy of desire. He filled his hands with her breasts, and moved in her again.

"*Gideon. Please.*"

The sound of her voice spurred him on; the relentless, building rhythm of Gideon's hips banked the want in her higher, and higher, and higher still, until she was begging, until her breath burst from her lungs in short harsh puffs, until at last, *oh God*, at last, she shattered into glittering shards of pleasure, her own sharp exultant cry ringing in her ears, mingling with Gideon's.

Gideon swept her up in his arms before her legs could buckle and carried her to the bed. He stripped off his trousers and shirt and joined her there, pulling her into an embrace. Their sweat-sheened limbs twined around each other. He kissed her, softly.

"Shall we go slow this time, Lily? Do you think we can?" he whispered, teasing.

She pulled out of his arms. "Hold still," she told him. "Don't move at all."

Gideon was still breathing hard; he didn't look as though he could move even if he wanted to. He smiled faintly, his chest still rising and falling from exertion.

Lily wound her fingers in the curling hair on his chest and kissed the indentation between the bones at the base of his neck; she tested the soft leather of his nipples with her tongue. His hand rose reflexively to touch her hair.

"I thought I told you not to move," she whispered sternly.

She felt his chest quiver with a laugh; his hand dropped obediently.

He was so *big*; so long in length and broad at the shoulder. Lily dragged her hands down over Gideon's hard chest to his belly; it wasn't perfectly flat, but it was more endearing for its slight softness. She liked him this way; she liked this evidence of the vulnerability he kept so well hidden. She dipped her tongue into his navel, tasting the salt and musk of him; rubbed her cheek against his belly, feeling it lift and fall beneath her lips as his breathing quickened. She found a scar across his hip, a long thin one, the skin stretched white; she traced it with her nail, as if she could undo whatever hurt had caused it.

And then she raised her head from him and dragged her

fingers down over his furred, hard thighs, finding and stroking a silky bare place between them where riding horseback had rubbed the hair away. Gideon hissed air in between his teeth.

"Good?" she whispered.

Gideon gave a short strangled laugh. So she kissed him there, on the silky bare place, she touched her tongue to it. He moaned her name softly and shifted restlessly, opening his thighs; his shaft stirred and swelled before her eyes. She kissed it, dragged her tongue down it.

"*Holy God almighty . . .*" he groaned.

She laughed softly. And did it again. And then again. He began to move his hips, encouraging her.

"No moving." It was an order, a whisper.

"Sadist." A choked laugh.

She exulted in giving pleasure to him; she wanted to give and give to him, to this vulnerable, strong, beautiful man. *I love you* was in her every touch; she wished she could transfer her love to him through his skin, so he would feel how it felt to her. *I love you.*

Gideon suddenly rolled over on his side and seized her in his arms, pulling her up over him, and she shrieked softly in surprise.

"You are," he said, enunciating each word wonderingly, "so *unbelievably* beautiful."

She smiled down into his soft dark eyes. Her hair fell over his face; he blew his breath out and it lifted away.

She could feel him hard and insistent and very, very ready against her. She moved her hips, a primal instinct, seeking her own pleasure.

"Are you tender?" he whispered. "Can you take me?"

Yes, I am tender. Yes, I will take you. "Take me."

She thought people only said things like that in erotic French stories. She understood now why they would.

Gideon gently rolled her over, gazed down into her eyes, and she wrapped her legs and arms around him, opening for him. He stroked into her, and her head went back on a gasp; she could feel him everywhere in her body, in her throat and fingertips, the soles of her feet. He pulled back from her, and she heard a long groan escape from him; he moved again.

Slowly this time, and it was exquisite torture, it built and built in her until she thought she would die from it, and still it built. And then they moved together blindly, together and alone in their race for release, and for her it came on a burst of white light behind her eyes.

She thought she may have bitten him, on the shoulder, perhaps.

"I think you bit me," he murmured lazily after a moment.

She smiled; too limp to do anything but feel.

". . . Thirteen, fourteen, *fifteen*! Fifteen," Gideon announced. He felt utterly replete. Almost stupid with happiness.

"Fifteen?" Lily's delicious velvet voice was languid.

"Freckles. You've fifteen freckles. Seven on one side, eight on the other. The very first day I saw you, I wanted to count them. And now"—Gideon touched a finger gently to each one, one at a time—"I have. Fifteen little golden freckles, like . . . angel tears."

Lily laughed, and Gideon feigned feeling wounded.

"What? What's so amusing about angel tears?"

"You've been at the poetry again, Gideon."

He went still. "What do you mean?"

"I saw the book you tried to hide from me in the library

that night. John Keats. And I read a little. It was wonderful. About an urn, and truth and beauty."

Gideon smiled a little sheepishly. "I like Keats."

"When I saw the book, I understood how you . . . well, '*You are a bird,*' you said, '*and the music is a current of air. And I am the wings you use to sail over it.*' It was beautiful, Gideon. And it worked, you know. You taught me to waltz with those words."

Gideon felt shy. "You remember that?"

"I shall never forget it. And then there was, '*Pretend you are a willow, bending in the breeze . . .*' You've a poet in you, Gideon."

Gideon threw an arm over his eyes and smiled a little pleased, embarrassed smile. "It's you, Lily. You bring it out in me."

"Perhaps. But I think it was always in there to be *brought* out. Like my stories."

"Like your stories," he repeated softly. He was quiet for a moment. "I love Byron, too. And Wordsworth, though I prefer Byron's wit."

"I've not read Byron."

"Oh, you'd like him very much," Gideon enthused. "Beautiful and passionate and witty. Much like you."

Lily giggled. He thought perhaps it was his favorite sound in the world.

"I'll find the book for you in the library," he added. "We shall read it together. The next time we make love."

Lily said nothing. He was distantly aware that he had said something that implied a future, but rigorous lovemaking had pummeled from him all ability to control his words.

He could not let her go; the very idea of it now seemed delusional. But would she consent to be his mistress, knowing what her role in his life would be? Furtive visits, stolen time? That he would have children with another woman, with Constance?

And what if Lily became pregnant? An enormous happiness bloomed at the thought. A boy, a girl . . . it wouldn't matter. As long as either one of them resembled her.

And yet . . . what sort of life would that be for a child? And what of Alice? And what sort of man would he be if he supported his mistress and her sister with his wife's money?

A man like just about any other, he thought wryly. *An ordinary man.*

Perhaps he *could* be like his uncle. Perhaps he could know passion with one woman, and social acceptance and status and wealth with another. Perhaps he could have a wife *and* a mistress, both of them beautiful and adoring. He would be vastly more fortunate than most men could ever dream of being.

If only he could make Lily understand, and see the wisdom of it. For it was the only way they could be together. And it was unthinkable to him that they should ever be apart. The very idea made his lungs seize with panic.

"You should let me take care of you, Lily." He held his breath. "There is no shame in allowing someone to take care of you."

There was a beat of silence.

"You're one to talk," she murmured.

He gave a short laugh, and yet the moment for him was deadly serious. He was asking her to give up her independence for him.

"Say it, Lily. Say you will allow me to take care of you. Say you will not leave me." His fingers stroked the inside of her thigh, tracing the tender flesh there; he felt her stir against his hand, her legs falling slightly open, inviting his hand to wander higher, and, against all reason, he felt himself growing hard again. "Say it." His fingers trailed up her thigh to cup the furred warmth of her; his fingers played lazily in her curls. "Say it." He was being unfair, he didn't care.

"All right. Yes." Her voice was weak, but the words were vow enough to satisfy him.

This hunger for each other . . . it fed upon itself. It astounded him.

And it exhausted him, frankly. His eyes were growing heavier and heavier, even as his hand wandered over Lily's soft body.

"You should return to your room," Lily whispered. Her hand was circling aimlessly over his chest.

"Yes, I should," he agreed sleepily.

It was the last thing he remembered saying.

Chapter Twenty

D*rip, drip, drip.*

With the logic of the dream-fogged, Lily decided the sound was water dripping from the eaves of Mrs. Smythe's lodging house. Had it rained during the night?

Drip, drip, drip.

The sound was *maddening*. She was just reaching for a pillow to cover her head when a whisper rudely shattered what was left of her sleep.

"Lily—the door. Someone is tapping."

Lily attempted to sit upright, but her limbs were entangled with Gideon's.

Gideon. It was his voice waking her, still raspy from sleep.

When she turned anxious eyes toward him, his face softened; he kissed her lips gently, pushing her sleep- and passion-tangled hair away from her face with one hand.

"You'd best answer the door, love," he whispered.

Her heart leaped. *Love*. It was a casual endearment. The sort of thing all those men in the French book said to the naked women in their beds. And yet . . .

Tap, tap, tap.

Lily slid out of bed, Gideon's hand trailing the length of her spine as she did. She scrambled into her night robe and caught a glimpse of herself in the mirror: hair like an owl's nest, cheeks and lips flushed from sleep and kissing. She looked a complete wanton. Unless the person outside the other door were a child, they would be left with no doubts as to what sort of activities she'd been engaged in the night before.

Behind her, Gideon ducked under her blankets.

Lily cautiously pulled the door open a few inches and peeked out. Mrs. Plunkett was standing there, as impassive as ever. She was holding a breakfast tray, which, oddly, held two plates of eggs and bread and two cups for tea.

And Mrs. Plunkett knew full well that Alice was sleeping in the nursery.

Lily felt her face burst into flaming embarrassment.

"Good morning, Miss Masters," Mrs. Plunkett said smoothly, as if she hadn't been knocking unattended for several minutes at least. And then she raised her voice slightly, as though she wanted to reach the back rows in a great hall. "I thought you might like to know, Miss Masters, that the guests for Mr. Cole's house party have begun to arrive. A certain *Lady Constance Clary* is instructing our footmen how to unload her trunks. And there are other young ladies, too. I've set the maids to preparing the rooms."

"*Holy*—" the single muffled word came from the direction of Lily's bed. Mrs. Plunkett's face revealed nothing, but Lily was certain she was not the least bit fooled.

Gideon had been right about one thing: one could always default to manners in untenable situations. "Thank you, Mrs. Plunkett," Lily managed to stammer at last, relieving the housekeeper of her tray. "That is . . . helpful information indeed." Mrs. Plunkett nodded and dipped a quick little curtsy and plodded off down the hallway.

Lily's hands were shaking. She backed into her room slowly and closed the door with her hip, and then settled the tray with a rattle on her dressing table. *I can't look at him. I can't bear to look at him.* The shame, the sense of betrayal, was so corrosive it nearly made her retch. She stood very still and crossed her arms over her body, an attempt to soothe the pain of it.

And the worst of it was, she had no right to feel this way.

Oh, she was a fool. Two nights before, she had virtually thrown herself upon Gideon, and he had enjoyed her thoroughly, as any sensible man would do. And he had *enjoyed* her knowing Lady Constance Clary, the woman he hoped to make his wife, would be at Aster Park in a few days for a house party.

Would a gentleman have led a lady by the hand into a servant's room to make passionate love to her? Certainly, if the lady in question was not really a . . . *lady.* If she were, for instance, a pickpocket from St. Giles instead.

Say it, Lily. Say you'll stay.

What had she thought? That this was one of her stories? That it would end in the prince marrying the pickpocket? The man wanted a mistress.

"Lily?" Gideon's voice was low and taut with unease. She heard him slide out of bed, heard the soft rustle of blankets as they crumpled to the floor, heard him pad over to her. His arms went around her gently from behind. She squeezed her eyes closed, a defense against the enveloping musk and warmth of him. Her body, the weak traitor it was, wanted him still.

"Lily, believe me, I completely forgot about the house party. I would give anything for all of them to go home."

"*All* of them?" Her voice sounded faint and brittle to her own ears.

He said nothing. And his silence went through her like a blade.

"Don't worry," she said, as lightly as she could. She felt numb; it amazed her that her heart continued to beat, that she was still able to breathe. She took a step out of his arms, and they fell away from her, stiff as two boards. "I will continue to help you, Gideon. I promised I would, and I meant it."

She turned to face him then; he too looked as though he had stopped breathing. Like two animals poised to attack, they studied each other wordlessly for a long, awful moment.

And then Gideon bent to collect his trousers. He hurriedly slid into them, jerked his shirt on, plucked up his boots in one hand, and strode toward the door, his movements frenetic.

He paused when he reached it and turned.

"Lily . . ." It sounded like a plea.

She shook her head gently, refusing to meet his eyes.

A moment later she heard the door shut behind him.

"I would most definitely have this marble removed, and perhaps put in a mosaic instead. This marble is so . . . *very* dated." Constance's voice was lowered, but the acoustics of the great old house were such that it carried up to where Gideon stood on the landing. He paused, wanting to hear more decorating advice from Constance. "As for that clock . . . it's simply hideous. And all that dusty velvet-covered furniture. A clean sweep—that's what this place needs. Bring it up to the first stare of fashion."

He heard a murmured chorus of female agreement. The

handmaidens, no doubt, and possibly Constance's aunt as well.

It occurred to Gideon suddenly that it was Constance who had always assessed Aster Park with a thief's eye: for value.

Lily had always eyed it like the treasure it was.

Gideon rubbed his jaw; he'd shaved so quickly it was a wonder he hadn't severed his head in the process. Although he wasn't convinced a severed head wouldn't be preferable to spending several days in a house full of people.

Up the stairs, down two hallways and two doors to the right was a warm bed musky from lovemaking, and with his entire being he longed to return to it. Lily was in that room, dressing; no doubt she would emerge looking as innocent as a flower.

God, but the look on her face this morning . . . Later . . . later he would soothe her wounded pride with kisses. Night could never come soon enough.

He ran his hand over his jaw, testing; it was smooth enough, he supposed. He patted his shirt, making sure it was safely tucked into his trousers, straightened his cravat, and then marched with heavy footfall down the stairs so Constance would hear him approach.

She turned a beaming face up to him.

"Gideon! Thank you *so* much for inviting us."

"Us"? I only invited a few of you. The two other young ladies, each attractive but not *too* attractive, because Constance would never allow it, were wearing concertedly bright expressions. Constance's aunt, Lady . . . Musgrove? Mangrove? . . . hovered behind them, more servant than chaperone.

Lady Anne Clapham, no doubt, would arrive separately.

Lady Clapham had never seemed tempted to orbit Constance.

"Welcome, ladies. Your rooms are being prepared. Perhaps you'd like to take breakfast in the—"

Kilmartin burst into the house just then. "Make way, Gideon, I've brought Aunt Hester."

Sure enough, a steady *thwack thwack thwack*ing could be heard through the open door: Aunt Hester's cane striking the marble steps as she ascended them.

Kilmartin vanished out the door again to escort his aunt. "Step away, youngster, I'm not a cripple!" everyone heard.

Finally Aunt Hester herself appeared in the doorway, looming in black bombazine.

Kilmartin made the introduction. "My aunt, Countess Avery."

The ladies dipped pretty curtsies, and Aunt Hester studied Constance and her friends for a long silent moment through her quizzing glass.

Then slowly, slowly, in silence still, she lifted her cane. It rose, and rose, trembling in her grip; the eyes of the girls followed it as though they were all little cobras in the throes of mesmerism. And still it rose, until it pointed to about their midsections.

"If any of you so much as *thinks* an improper thought at this house party," Aunt Hester snarled, "mark my words, you'll taste this cane!"

The cane wavered in the air for another beat or two. And then Aunt Hester lowered it with a *thunk* and burst into uproarious laughter. "Oh, you should *see* your faces."

She thumped farther into the house, still laughing delightedly. "Enjoy yourselves, young people. I need a brandy. Where's that baron? Kilmartin promised me cards and a brandy."

Gregson magically materialized and escorted Aunt Hester away. The *thunk* of her cane gradually faded off into the bowels of the house.

Kilmartin looked at Gideon and shrugged. "Constance has brought *her* aunt," Gideon said, meaning, We already have a chaperone.

"And I have brought mine." Kilmartin grinned at him.

Gideon smiled, shaking his head. He agreed with Lily: she was a little terrifying, but he rather liked Aunt Hester. Ironically, neither of the aunts made appropriate chaperones. Constance's aunt was too timid; Kilmartin's too old and frightening and sleepy. It was a veritable recipe for hijinks, if any of the young ladies were so inclined to indulge.

"And how is Miss Masters?" Constance asked Kilmartin carefully.

Damn.

Kilmartin looked at Gideon. Gideon looked at Kilmartin. They spoke at once.

"She is—"

"She arrived—"

Kilmartin and Gideon looked at each other again. Gideon lifted a brow. Kilmartin, bless him, understood it meant, "*I'll* do the talking."

"That is to say, ladies," Gideon said smoothly, "Miss Masters's sister is doing quite well, and no longer has need of her. Miss Masters is just now shaking off the dust of her journey. She will join you momentarily in the solarium."

"Well," Constance said predictably, "I'd rather like to shake off the dust, too. Wouldn't you, ladies, as well?"

Three heads nodded and affirmed in a chorus of girlish voices.

"The rooms are prepared, Mr. Cole." This came from

Mrs. Plunkett, who had, bless her, appeared just in time. "I'll take the ladies to them."

"Thank you, Mrs. Plunkett. I shall see all of you in the solarium in a half hour's time?"

A prettier collection of curtsies could not be seen in all of England as the girls took their leave of Gideon and Kilmartin. He watched them sail up the stairs, trailed by Constance's aunt, who really seemed more of a servant to her formidable niece.

"How does Lily's sister fare?" Kilmartin asked in a lowered voice.

"She is doing well, thankfully."

"You're fond of her." Kilmartin was watching Gideon closely.

"Yes," Gideon answered, after a pause. He didn't know whether Kilmartin was referring to Lily or Alice, but it was most certainly true in both cases.

Kilmartin opened his mouth to say something more, but Gideon spoke first. "And when can we expect Lady Anne Clapham?"

Kilmartin's eyes went dewy. "Soon, but not soon enough."

In the past, Gideon would have rolled his eyes, or teased his friend. But what he felt today was envy so profound it was like an ache, and an understanding that made his past teasing seem reprehensible. "Good," he replied softly.

Kilmartin looked up, surprised again. He frowned a little, and opened his mouth as if to say something, but Gideon interrupted.

"I'll meet you in the solarium at half past the hour, Laurie."

Gideon went up the stairs, two flights up, to visit someone he cared for.

* * *

Lily considered whether she should go downstairs. Perhaps she should plead a headache, or an even more explicit feminine complaint, and refuse to join the . . . *festivities*. Take her meals in her room, wait stoically for the entire party to leave, the way one waited out any ailment. But then she considered how happy that would make Constance, and decided it was not an option at all. She had a *duty*, she decided, to make Lady Constance Clary as uncomfortable as possible. And today, of all days, she would *relish* it.

She sighed and pulled one of her lovely muslin morning gowns over her head, twisting about to do up the tiny buttons. She took her hair in her fist and prepared to pin it up, but a scent arrested her; she lifted her hair to her nose and smelled *him*: a musky male scent, unmistakably Gideon. A rush of memory and primal longing that overrode every practicality, every resentment, came at her; she remembered trailing kisses over Gideon's sweat-sheened body last night, her hair dragging the length of him. She breathed her hair in deeply and closed her eyes.

Would anyone else notice? And even if they did, would they recognize the scent she wore? *Eau de Gideon Cole*?

She didn't care. She would sit in that room with Lady Constance Clary, as prim as any of those young ladies, with the scent of lovemaking in her hair.

She twisted her hair and pinned it up in just the way Madame Marceau had showed her, and examined the result in the mirror.

She had expected to see a wan face reflected there, a face that reflected how she felt about everything at the moment, but her cheeks were still rosy from the heat of the bed and her lips were still stung full from a night of passionate kissing. She looked splendid.

Bracing herself, she made her way down the hallway and followed the sound of feminine chatter, a high-pitched incessant chirping that sounded like nothing so much as trees full of birds. The solarium, then, was where they were.

Using all of her will not to drag her feet, Lily took herself toward the room. And when she reached it, she paused in the doorway in astonishment.

Constance and her handmaidens were draped artfully over the furniture. But this wasn't the astonishing thing.

The astonishing thing was this: they were all wearing long-sleeved, high-necked, richly ruffled gowns, and from the wrists of their gowns dangled . . .

Tiny books.

At last, Lily beheld her own invention: Reading dresses.

"Well, Miss Alice, it is very good to see you feeling better. What is this you have here?"

Alice was sitting up in bed holding a very large book. "It's a book about pigs," she told Gideon happily. "And only pigs. Mrs. Plunkett found it in the library. I cannot read all of the words, but there are a great many pictures."

"Libraries are wonderful things," Gideon said solemnly.

"Pigs, too," Alice said. "You just missed Lily. She is going to a party downstairs. I am sound enough to go, too, but she will not allow me to leave the bed."

"Lily is very wise, in that regard, I am afraid. I must go to the party, too, Miss Alice."

"Will you come see me again later?"

"Yes, I will come up to see you again later." He smiled at her. "Perhaps I'll read you a story."

"Something with a battle?"

"I'll see what I can do," he promised her solemnly.

*　*　*

Constance, perhaps predictably, had insisted on archery after their morning repast. And so the entire party was now gathered in front of targets in the park—Jarvis had arrived shortly after Constance and the handmaidens, so their group was now complete—and had made ready to begin the competition, when their attention was suddenly riveted by the approach of two more people.

"She wanted to come out," Kilmartin whispered to Gideon. "I could not dissuade her."

They stood together and watched, in a sort of silent fascination, as Aunt Hester, a great bombazine dome in the distance, hobbled toward them, her cane no doubt taking divots out of the lawn on the way. And this was remarkable enough, but the greater miracle was Lord Lindsey strolling solicitously next to her, his pace matching hers. As though he'd taken strolls in the park every day for the past five years instead of lying in a darkened room. A veritable English Lazarus.

Behind them a brace of footmen followed very, very slowly, carrying two chairs, as though ready to catch either one of them if they should begin to topple over.

"Hester and I thought we'd get in a game of lawn tennis," Lord Lindsey called to Gideon.

The last time his uncle had set foot on his own grounds his two cousins had been alive. And it was Lily, Gideon realized. Lily had somehow rolled back the stone that no one else had been able to budge.

Aunt Hester's voice floated over to them. "I don't like that Constance. She's too big. I rather prefer the little one. Makes a good houseguest, that one."

"She's not *big*, Hester. She's tall. And she's the daughter of a marquis." This came from the baron, patiently. Gideon almost smiled at his uncle's loyalty to him, given that his uncle had described Constance in precisely the same words a few short weeks ago.

"Big," Aunt Hester corrected adamantly. "She's too big, too everything."

"Hear, hear," Kilmartin whispered.

"Hush, Laurie," Gideon hissed.

The young ladies were all riveted by Aunt Hester's approach; fortunately, they'd missed the hissed words. Gideon turned to Lily; she was staring in the direction of Aunt Hester, too, wearing an expression of faintly amused gratitude. Gideon knew her pride must be stinging; he couldn't blame her for refusing to meet his eyes. And yet, for selfish reasons, he wished she would.

"Hester," Lord Lindsey was explaining patiently, in as low a voice as he probably thought Hester could still hear, "I know you think you are speaking quietly, but I am afraid that you are *not*."

Hester turned a truly surprised look on him. "I wasn't trying to speak quietly."

Gideon turned to Constance, who was holding a bow and arrow almost speculatively now, as though contemplating Hester as a target.

"Constance, you remind me of nothing so much as Diana, Goddess of the Hunt," Gideon said, his voice raised as though none of them could hear Aunt Hester at all. "You look as though you were born with a bow and arrow in your hands."

Lily rolled her eyes. Jarvis looked crestfallen that he had not thought to say something as clever, and turned his head hopefully toward Lily. And the two hot pink spots that had risen in Constance's cheeks at Hester's remarks faded. Gideon had restored order to her world with a single compliment.

"Thank you, Gideon," she said regally. "And what shall be the prize in our little tournament?" She tilted her head coyly.

"I would ask you to name it, Constance, but you are certain to win, and that would hardly be fair to the rest of us, now, would it?" He smiled, to make it clear that he was teasing.

Constance dimpled. "Oh, now, I *shall* be fair. I would suggest that the winner"—she drummed her fingers thoughtfully against her chin for a moment—"shall win a stroll alone with the person of his or her choice." She touched glances on everyone in the circle, but Gideon and Jarvis were favored with lingering ones.

Jarvis, Gideon decided, needed to work on his game face. He looked as hopeful as a hound seated next to a dinner table.

"That sounds fair, Constance," Gideon said evenly. "Does anyone object?"

Resounding silence met this question. He glanced at Lily; her expression was inscrutable.

"I do think," Constance said, as she lifted the bow to her shoulder, "that archery is a fine activity for young ladies. Don't you agree?"

"Quite!" "A fine activity!" "Certainly fine!" Constance's handmaidens echoed.

"'A fine activity'?" Aunt Hester pondered. "Certainly—if one requires one's mate to pull down venison for the evening meal."

Lily coughed to disguise a laugh, and Gideon watched Constance's face go stony.

With dramatic precision, Constance slowly drew the bowstring taut and squinted one eye at the target. She *did* look handsome; her form was flawless, and typically her aim was, too; he'd seen her arrow cleanly pierce the red center of a target any number of times in the past.

Constance allowed a moment to beat by so the suspense could build and so that everyone present could thoroughly admire her form.

And just as she was about to release her arrow, Aunt Hester cleared her throat loudly and messily.

Constance's arrow flew wildly wide of the mark, in the general direction of the footmen. The two footmen threw themselves to the ground, flattening. Everyone else flung their arms frantically over their heads.

"Good God, now she's trying to impale the footmen," Aunt Hester complained.

"Missed," Constance muttered, her cheeks flushed. Gideon wasn't sure whether she meant the target or Aunt Hester.

After a moment, one of the footmen peered up and, determining no other arrows were heading his way, scurried forth to retrieve the wayward one.

Constance suddenly whirled on Lily, who really *had* done an admirable job of not laughing aloud. "Won't you demonstrate *your* prowess for us, Miss Masters? It would make the contest ever so much more interesting."

"How could it possibly get any more interesting?" Kilmartin whispered to Gideon.

Lily's face was instantly serious again, but Gideon noticed the wicked glint in her eye. He knew a moment of worry.

"Oh, I'm afraid . . . well, I used to be quite an archer, too, Lady Clary. And then . . . well, I had to stop."

"An injury?" The word was sympathetic, but Constance's eyes gleamed hope; Gideon imagined she would have loved for Miss Masters to be horribly disfigured beneath her lovely muslin gown.

"Oh, no," Lily assured her. "It's just that . . ." She dropped her voice. "Well, haven't you heard about what happened to those girls in France?"

Like a crooked finger, Lily's lowered voice brought Constance and the handmaidens nearer; Constance lowered her own voice to match. "Girls in France?" she urged.

"They were all quite adept at archery. They won prizes; they practiced as often as they could; it was the delight of their lives. And then . . . one day . . ." Lily paused and bit her lip, as if she could hardly bear to go on.

The girls leaned forward. And so did Kilmartin and Gideon, dying to hear what had happened to the fictitious French girls.

"Well, it seems they developed . . ." Lily cast her eyes downward and whispered the word, as though it were the vilest profanity. "*Humps*."

"*Humps*?" It was a soprano chorus of horror. Three feminine arms flew backwards simultaneously to frantically pat at three backs, feeling for bulges.

Lily squeezed her eyes shut and nodded sadly, as if the plight of the French girls moved her profoundly. "Yes. *Large* humps. They woke up one morning . . . and . . . well, there they were. *Overnight*. The French doctors determined it was because the . . . well, the physiques of women are not built for archery, you see, and all that pulling on the bow caused their *own* backs to bow . . . And now the poor young ladies cannot lie flat in their beds, and it is difficult to sew dresses to fit them, so they now only have one or two dresses to choose from. It's very, very sad."

Constance's grip on the bow grew slack; it fell from her hand to the grass.

Gideon wanted to drop to the ground and roll like a colt. She was extraordinary, really. Even poor Lady Anne Clapham was surreptitiously feeling her back for the start of a hump. Gideon glanced at Kilmartin; he was gazing at Lily in bald admiration.

Lily's jaw was set with something like grim satisfaction.

"*What*?" Aunt Hester bellowed. "I didn't hear a word of that."

It was a pity she hadn't heard; no doubt she would have enjoyed the tale immensely.

"Is there to be no archery, then?" Lord Lindsey asked mildly. His expression was strangely thoughtful.

"Archery is dull, Edward. Try *napping*," Aunt Hester declared. She closed her eyes and proceeded to try it herself.

Constance recovered rapidly, as usual. "Since I am the only one to release an arrow, I think I shall declare myself the winner of the tournament," she announced. "Unless someone else would like to fire an arrow?"

Resounding silence. Hump horror apparently had overcome them all. Gideon was fairly certain an objection would have shocked Constance to her bones anyway.

"Good," Constance continued. "Now, *whom* shall I choose to accompany me on my stroll? Perhaps . . . perhaps I shall have all of you guess the number I am thinking, and the winner shall accompany me. Yes? Well . . . I am thinking of a number between one and ten."

"Five!" shouted one of her handmaidens eagerly, clearly oblivious to Constance's intent.

"Oh, I'm so sorry . . ." Constance feigned disappointment. "Care to try . . . Malcolm?" She turned to Jarvis.

"Three?" Jarvis hazarded.

"Oh, I'm afraid not," she sympathized. "Gideon?" Her gray eyes pinned him.

His heartbeat began to accelerate oddly. Because Gideon knew it wouldn't matter what he said: he'd been chosen. He was perversely tempted to shout "six and three quarters!"

"One," he said, instead.

"Gideon! How lovely! You are absolutely correct. It shall be you, then." Constance turned to Lily. "Miss Masters, I'm so sorry you did not get an opportunity to . . . choose."

"Oh, please do not trouble yourself over it, Lady Clary. It was so very interesting watching you . . . *choose*." Her tone was venom-laced honey.

Constance opened her mouth for a moment as if to reply, but then closed it again—tightly—and turned away. "Gideon?"

Gideon found he couldn't look at Lily as he walked away at Constance's triumphant side, his own heart thumping in anticipation of what was to come. He rehearsed the words in his head: *Constance, will you do me the honor of . . .*

"See? This is precisely what I mean, Gideon. These unruly American trees." Constance gestured to a big oak, clustered with a number of other old spreading oaks. "Trees should be planted in lines, don't you think? Neatly? To emphasize the borders of a property."

Trees should be planted in *lines*? Gideon had never heard anything so ridiculous in his life. "I rather think they're fine just the way they are, Constance," he told her mildly.

He turned back and noticed Lily speaking to Kilmartin alone, somewhat apart from the group; Laurie's head was down, his posture one of intent listening.

"Gideon?"

He was still looking toward Kilmartin and Lily. They seemed to be having rather a *long* conversation. Gideon began to feel absurdly jealous. Where was Lady Anne

Clapham? Ah, he saw her now: she was being a good girl; she had engaged the baron in some sort of discussion, as Aunt Hester had her head thrown back, napping.

"Gideon?" Constance repeated.

"Yes, Constance?"

"Don't you think it's time we announced our engagement?"

It took a moment for Gideon to absorb what Constance had said. And then her words detonated, one by one, in his mind.

Gideon's head swiveled toward her so quickly he nearly dislocated his neck. "It's time we announced our *engagement*?"

"Oh, good. I'm *so* glad you agree." Her smile was a brilliant thing; she was as pleased as if she had just watched her arrow cleanly pierce the red heart of a target.

He stared at her, momentarily dumbstruck. Imagine: Constance, with a little of her characteristic maneuvering, had done the work for him. He knew a moment of breathless admiration for the *strategy* of it all.

"And as we are engaged, Gideon, you may kiss me now."

Gideon started at that, and stared at her as if he were seeing her for the first time. Constance's pale brows curved as neatly as commas over her handsome gray eyes; her lips, a perfectly matched set that fit neatly one atop the other, were handsome, too. It was a face a portrait painter would love for its purity of line, a face that would look right at home in his uncle's sculpture garden.

Perhaps this was why he felt that kissing her made about as much sense to him as kissing a statue.

She was going to be his wife. It was everything he'd always desired. Of *course* he wanted to kiss her.

Should he touch her? Put his arms around her? With Lily, he was guided by impulse; his hands knew precisely what they wanted to touch and when. But no such instinct emerged to guide him at the moment. He turned toward Kilmartin and Lily swiftly, to see whether either of them was watching. They were still absorbed in their conversation.

He turned back to Constance.

She was waiting expectantly. And if he left her waiting any longer, the moment would become irretrievable.

His hands discreetly at his sides, Gideon slowly moved his face down toward her. Her pores, the fine hairs in her nose, a hint of down on her upper lip came into view . . . these features would become as familiar to him as his own as the years went by. His *wife*. She would be his *wife*.

He applied enough pressure to ensure the contact could be considered a kiss and then straightened, and Constance looked briskly satisfied, as though she had accomplished something important, like ordering a new pelisse.

"Well, *fiancé*," she said brightly. "I shall begin planning our wedding immediately! Papa will be so pleased. It will be the largest event London has ever seen—short of a coronation."

"But shouldn't I speak to your father about this first? Ask his permission?" Gideon wondered why he was looking for reasons to delay his engagement.

"Oh, I suppose you may do it as a formality, if you wish. But Papa has already told me he wouldn't mind a bit if you were to offer for me. He *is* fond of you."

"So you've said," Gideon said weakly.

"And I imagine the position in the Treasury is as good as yours now."

"I count myself a fortunate man, Constance." His head was spinning oddly.

"Shall we tell the others?" She looped her arm through

his possessively. He heard the unspoken words: *particularly Miss Masters.*

"Perhaps not quite yet. Let's allow it to be a secret between the two of us for now." He smiled at her, with some difficulty. He really wanted to be alone with his thoughts at the moment, and that seemed all wrong. He'd just become *engaged,* for God's sake. He should very much want to be alone with Constance.

Having a secret from all the others, thankfully, seemed to appeal to Constance. "All right," she agreed.

"Perhaps, then, we shouldn't walk arm in arm just yet."

Constance withdrew her arm from his with apparent reluctance. Side by side they walked back to the others, and Constance talked and talked about the wedding she'd planned. Gideon suspected she'd had the details arranged in her mind for years, and had only needed to decide which man to insert into the picture next to her. And as Constance talked, Gideon waited for his sense of triumph to emerge.

Perhaps it would when this numb surprise was through with him.

As Constance and Gideon approached the group, everybody looked up to greet them. And at last, Lily looked at him, too, and now Gideon knew why she would not meet his eyes earlier.

Because everything was in her eyes: pain and pride and sheer joy in the fact that he simply . . . *was.* Herself laid bare. He knew it was foolish to stare, but he couldn't seem to free his eyes from hers. Nor did he want to.

A well-bred young man does not marry his mistress.

The urge to bolt was suddenly overwhelming. He wanted time and space to think.

Too late, he noticed Constance watching him. And watching Lily.

And wearing an odd, tiny smile.

"Everybody, we have the most wonderful news," she sang out. "Gideon and I are engaged."

Gideon's vision blurred.

"He's *marrying* the big blonde girl?" Aunt Hester sounded positively astounded.

"It appears so," Lord Lindsey soothed. "And she's lovely and tall, yes."

Gideon looked at Constance, stunned. She was smiling at him triumphantly and a trifle indulgently, as if she had just done something for his own good.

Perhaps she had.

They came at him: Kilmartin, the handmaidens, his uncle, even Aunt Hester. With patting hands and cheerful voices, saying the rote things one says when a suitable engagement is announced. But he only heard one of the voices. The low velvet one. He heard it like a voice in his own head.

"Congratulations, Gideon." And he could have sworn she meant it.

It was decided—by Constance, of course—that a celebratory luncheon was in order. The crowd was moved indoors, the cook was alerted to the need to add a few festive elements to their midday repast—perhaps some special cakes or sauces—and the ladies went upstairs to change their clothing. Again.

Lily was grateful for her ironclad pride. Because she would never, *never* allow Lady Constance Clary to see that she viewed the news of her engagement to Gideon Cole as anything other than delightful. And as a matter of supreme indifference to her.

Ah, she thought bitterly, *I am learning so much about love*. Specifically, she had just learned it was entirely possible to love a complete idiot. For only a complete idiot would consign himself to a lifetime with Lady Constance Clary, regardless of her money and beauty and position and—

Lily stopped her thoughts. Enumerating Constance's assets was not a soothing pastime.

Jarvis had transferred his attentions wholeheartedly to Lily. She was tempted to swat his solicitous face away like a fly.

She was feeling a good deal of contempt for men as a species at the moment.

With the exception, perhaps, of Lord Kilmartin. For the second time in her life, she had asked for something—for coach fare and enough for ship's passage to *anywhere*, if he could spare it—and wonder of wonders, Kilmartin had given it to her, with no questions, just kindness, his face sad but eloquent with understanding. And she'd asked him because she'd watched Gideon and Constance stroll away together and she'd known . . . she'd known.

I'm not running *away,* she told herself. *I'm* leaving. *There's a difference.*

Kilmartin had agreed to make the arrangements for her; he'd promptly sent word to the nearest coaching inn through a servant. Three hours from now, a coach would roll up behind the main house and a footman would carry a packed trunk down through the kitchen as a favor to Kilmartin. The girls would then board the coach and be whisked away.

All that was left was for Lily to plead a headache and return to her room to pack for herself and Alice.

She itched to move now, before all her feelings caught up to her in earnest. But she decided to linger and make pleasantries, if it killed her. For if she disappeared immediately, it would please Constance to no end. And if Constance were any more puffed and pleased with herself, Lily thought, she would explode and splatter the fine furniture in Aster Park's drawing room.

Besides, there was something Lily needed to know before she left.

"Lady Clary." She could hear the sweet, convincing concern in her own voice; she was glad. "Did you ever find your necklace?"

Constance turned her gray eyes toward Lily. Glittering things, cold as diamonds. "Oh, yes, Miss Masters. Thank you for asking. In an *urn*, if you can imagine. It must have slipped from *me* into *it*." She gave a tinkly little laugh. The handmaidens giggled, too.

Lily could feel Gideon's eyes upon her; she couldn't look at him. She could pretend very well that she was unaffected by his engagement, but it was too much to ask of her to look into his eyes and pretend.

A benign somnolence had descended upon the party after the luncheon, brought on by the abundance of sauces, no doubt. Lily pleaded a headache and disappeared upstairs; everyone else had gathered in the parlor to play cards, or read, as the sun lowered in the sky. His favorite time of day. *It gilds everything,* Lily had said. *Everything is allowed to be beautiful then.*

Suddenly, Gideon's cravat felt too tight. Or perhaps it was just that his trousers were chafing him. No . . . that wasn't the problem, precisely, either. But he *did* feel as though he were suffocating. The cards were boring him, the conversation was boring him.

A stroll outside, maybe? With Constance?

No . . . somehow that didn't sound like a good idea, either.

I'm engaged to be married. Shouldn't he be rejoicing? Shouldn't he be savoring the moment, Constance's every word, storing the images for review on some night twenty years hence, when he and Constance were old and gray? After all, he now stood at the very pinnacle of his Master Plan.

Love will come, he told himself. As it had come for Uncle Edward. Shared joys and sorrows . . .

Meanwhile, he would share every moment possible with Lily. And there should be many of them, since his business was in London, and he'd decided he would find lodgings for her there. Would Lily take him in her arms tonight if he came to her? Perhaps he could ease her wounded feelings with kisses, soothe her aching head with a stroking hand, talk to her of where she might like to live in London, as his mistress. Plan the time they would spend together after he was wed to Constance. Laugh with her, talk of poetry . . . kiss her soft mouth . . . touch his tongue to her little, up-tilted breasts . . .

Was it wrong to be growing hard over thoughts of his mistress while his fiancée sat across from him, pretending to be interested in the book she was reading but really wondering who might be watching and admiring her?

He obliged Constance by glancing across the table at her. Ten years? Twenty years? Thirty years? When would it become love? In the lamplight she looked, as usual, pristine, magnificent, every inch the aristocrat she was. And odd, but he still wasn't even tempted to touch her. He was no longer even curious. She had ceased being a challenge.

She was like . . . a court case he had won.

The aptness of the analogy panicked him. And all at once,

his idle musings and his pervasive sense of unease gelled into a single coherent thought:

I may have made a horrible mistake.

He shifted uneasily in his chair. Maybe he just needed to eat an opponent alive in the courtroom; it would be lovely to return to work. It would be a great pleasure to win Madame Marceau's case for her. Or perhaps he needed a hard run across parklands.

But then Gideon had an inspiration: *I'll go see how Alice fares, just for a moment. And maybe . . . and maybe Lily. And then I'll return.* Gideon immediately felt more cheerful.

He stood up abruptly. "Excuse me for just a moment, will you . . ." He almost said "dear," thinking he may as well try it out, but the word stubbornly refused to spill from his tongue. ". . . Constance? I'll return in just a few moments."

She smiled graciously, granting him the moment away from her.

He tried not to leave with unseemly haste.

Gideon stopped in the kitchen for some lemon cakes before heading to the nursery. No doubt Alice had been plied with them more than once today, but the girl could use a little more fattening up. He stopped in the library, too, for he was certain he would be able to find a book on reptiles. Now, *reptiles* . . . they were sure to delight the gory tastes of a ten-year-old.

He trudged up the several flights of stairs to the nursery, his arms full of offerings.

"Little Miss Masters," he called cheerfully as he entered the room, "I've a book full of monsters that you may wish to see."

He'd expected an exuberant "hurrah!" or at the very least a "hullo, Mr. Cole!"

He was greeted with silence.

"Alice?" Gideon stepped all the way into the chamber; the bed was empty. He frowned. Was Alice sound enough, then, to move out of the nursery and back into the room she shared with Lily?

Gideon peered into the little maid's room. He touched the narrow, austere bed; memories flooded him. Lily murmuring a single word against his heart: *Please.* The luminous beauty of her slim bare body. The exquisite friction of her breasts against his skin.

Her laughter. Her low velvet voice in his ear.

He simply could not imagine a moment when he would not want her. He wanted her now.

Gideon backed out of the room, driven by an odd sense of urgency. He would go to her now, inquire after her headache, and perhaps find Alice, too. He would spend a few moments with them. *Only a few,* he told himself sternly. And then he would return to his fiancée and all of his other . . . friends.

He may as well get accustomed to it, for this was to be his life: a few stolen moments with Lily, the rest with the woman who sat decoratively in the drawing room downstairs, a woman who would confer wealth and power and status and security upon him with a single vow.

And share his bed, his life, his home, for the rest of his life.

"Stop feeling my forehead," Alice groused, pulling away from Lily's hand. "I am quite well. Why can't we return to Aster Park? I want Mr. Cole."

The coach had eaten the road with astonishing speed. They were already on the outskirts of London; she knew because the smell of London, specifically the docks, had infiltrated the coach.

"Do you remember, Alice, when I told you I'd be in Mr. Cole's employ for a short time? Well . . . that time has passed. It's time for a new adventure. I've heard there are grand palaces in Italy, and roads made all of water . . ."

Alice began to cry softly, and mumbled something under her breath. It sounded like, *"Mrs. Smythe, shall I sweep the floor today?"*

Lily wanted to cry, too. But she was not one for crying. All she knew was that moving, and moving swiftly, had always helped before. When one lived from day to day, from hand to mouth, and kept moving, the future remained a pleasant stranger, and there was no time to think or suffer.

Lily's chamber door was ever so slightly ajar, and the short hairs at the back of Gideon's neck began to prickle in warning. He half suspected what he would find within the room; his heart thudding, he gave the door a gentle push wider to confirm it.

At first glance, nothing seemed amiss, and he allowed himself hope.

But then he glanced at her dressing table. Her books were gone. All except *Sense and Sensibility*. In their place, the necklace he had given her, his mother's necklace, was arranged neatly.

The sight of it could not have cut more deeply if she had dragged the diamond across his skin.

He crossed the room in three steps and flung open the wardrobe. Only the ball gowns remained, listless and gleaming dully, like wallflowers at a dance.

His hand fumbled out to touch the sea green satin dress she'd been wearing the first night they'd made love; it hung limply, crumpled beyond redemption. He took a bit of it between his fingers, as though if he longed for her just hard enough Lily would materialize inside it. He lifted it to his face; it held the ghost of her scent.

Gideon finally lowered himself to the bed and sat there, staring blindly. He felt hollow; his skin seemed to have acquired a fine coating of ice. He was distantly aware of a point of agony that seemed located at the very center of him; he didn't know what to call it. Rage, grief, disbelief: it was all of a piece.

But she had *promised—*

No, that wasn't true. He had coerced her into promising. Used her own desire against her.

Why shouldn't she go? She had a pride as unbending as his own. And still she'd stood there like a bloody *hero* while Constance announced their engagement. There was only one reason *he*, with his own formidable pride, would have ever done such a thing.

He would have done it for someone he loved.

And if Lily loved him . . . witnessing that moment was more, he realized, than she ever should have had to bear.

He sat there on the edge of her bed feeling cold and hollow and faintly ridiculous. The things he had wanted all of his life, the things he had had been convinced would give his world meaning, security, certainty . . . he felt like a child now, who had craved after tin toys. None of it meant a thing when cast in the shadow of love.

Gideon rose to his feet.

To hell with all of it. He needed Lily.

Chapter Twenty-One

Compared to Mrs. Smythe's boarding house, the Tiger's Nest may as well have been Aster Park. Still, it was on the wrong side of savory, that was certain.

Alice had stopped crying and was intrigued, as usual, by anything new or different. Ships creaked and bobbed in the oily dark of the water, and Lily began to feel a little surge of something that felt almost like hope: each of those ships was bound for someplace new. Infested with rats as they no doubt were, staffed by ruffians and stocked with bad food . . . Lily could handle all of it. Could embrace it, even. As long as they kept moving.

What she couldn't handle, apparently, was love.

"Thank you, sir," she said primly to the driver, who touched his fingers to his hat, a gesture she had come to expect and which would have been foreign to her only a few weeks ago. She deposited a gratuity into his palm, which prodded him into a burst of generosity: He carried their trunk into the Tiger's Nest for them and deposited it on the floor there.

"Hold my hand, Alice, and don't let go," she murmured to her sister.

Once upon a time she would have been inconspicuous here in the Tiger's Nest, an urchin in tattered clothing adept at disappearing into crowds. Now she looked like a lady traveling alone with a little girl, which meant she was a target for any number of things: advances, theft.

She'd need a story.

Well, *that* shouldn't be difficult.

The murmuring and clanking of glasses and laughter didn't exactly stop as she entered the room, but she felt avid eyes upon her, sensed the halt of a few conversations. It would have been much easier to be unobtrusive, Lily thought, if she wasn't wearing a fine blue wool pelisse created by Madame Marceau, designer of the Reading dress.

She paused in the doorway, her hand still tightly gripping Alice's. And then she turned and called over her shoulder out the door.

"I told you, *dear*, no one will even notice if you bring that gun in here." She turned to the two men sitting nearest her, who were gazing up at her warily, and raised her voice a little to include anybody else who might be eavesdropping. "Husbands," she confided with airy exasperation. "He has a very large gun, you see, as he is an exceptionally large man, and he is shy of bringing it places. 'It's embarrassing, Lil,' he says—he calls me Lil—'I wish I could carry an ordinary gun just like everyone else's.' I tell him he's fine the way he is, you see, that it doesn't matter to *me* what size his gun is, but he just won't believe me. I do wish, however, he'd repair the locks on it. The thing tends to go off with no warning."

She turned to the innkeeper, who was now eyeing the front door of his establishment uneasily, anticipating the entrance of an armed behemoth.

"I'll have a room, upstairs, if you would. My husband will be joining me in a moment."

"Er . . . yes, ma'am."

"Oh, and if you would . . . our trunk?" Lily said sweetly.

"Of course." The innkeeper swept it up in his thick arms and practically scurried up the stairs, Lily and Alice following.

"That was a bit much," Alice whispered.

Lily squeezed her hand to shush her.

"Laurie, may I have a word with you?"

Kilmartin looked up from his hand of cards. "Of course, old man." He waited expectantly for Gideon to speak, while Lady Anne smiled at him over the top of her cards.

Gideon glared significance at him, and comprehension finally lit Kilmartin's face. He pushed his chair back and followed Gideon's long stormy strides into the adjacent drawing room.

And once there, Gideon began pacing madly, his hand raking up through his hair. "She's gone, Laurie. Gone. Lily and Alice are gone."

"Yes. I know."

"I went up to see Alice and—"

Kilmartin's words finally registered. Gideon went rigid, like a man who has been shot before he drops to the ground. And then he pivoted very, very slowly to face his friend.

"You know," he repeated flatly.

Kilmartin nodded sadly.

Gideon squeezed his eyes closed, opened them again. "Laurie . . . how . . . why . . . ?"

"Gideon . . . she was deeply unhappy. She came to me today to ask for help. And . . . well, I helped."

Gideon's mouth worked, but no sound came out.

"I care for Lily, too, Gideon. Not, of course, in the way that I care for Lady Anne Clapham," Kilmartin added quickly. "But I'm not blind, you know, my friend. I saw how things were with . . . with the two of you. I was growing more and more concerned for you both. So when she asked, I gave her money and sent a note to the coaching inn. They sent a driver for her an hour ago."

"An *hour*—" Gideon gave a choked laugh and abruptly sank down onto the settee.

They didn't speak for a time. Someone in the other room laughed a tinkling laugh.

"It's just . . . I care for her, Laurie." The words so insufficiently described what Gideon felt that they might as well have been a bald lie.

Kilmartin lowered himself into the seat across from Gideon and leaned forward. "You know I care for you, Gideon. God knows why," he added wryly. "But Lily wanted very much to leave as soon as possible, to spare you, and Alice, too, a good-bye. She felt she'd accomplished her mission and paid off her debt. I'm terribly sorry—if I'd known . . ."

"You could not have known, Laurie. *I* didn't quite know."

"If you had seen her face, Gideon . . ." Kilmartin continued despairingly. "I promise you, you could not have said no to her, either. And then when you announced your engagement . . . well, I thought it might be for the best."

"Laurie." Gideon's voice sounded faint; he felt ill. "She could even now be carrying my child."

Kilmartin's face went gray, as though someone had punched the air from him. "God, Gideon." His voice was faint, too. "I didn't know it had come to that."

"Oh," Gideon said bitterly. "It came to that."

Kilmartin sat very still, wordlessly absorbing this.

"Are you ashamed of me?" Gideon asked desperately.

After a moment, Kilmartin shook his head. "Imagine that. Gideon Cole is human. You've behaved like a real member of the nobility, you know." He tried a smile.

"I've made rather a mess of things, haven't I?"

Kilmartin paused. "It rather looks that way, yes."

Gideon looked up sharply, but Kilmartin, bless him, was smiling ruefully.

"You're a good friend, Laurie. I cannot thank you enough for all you have done. And yet . . ." Gideon paused.

"And yet . . . ?" Kilmartin prompted softly.

Gideon was in hell. "I love her, Laurie. I *need* her."

Kilmartin's eyes went wide; he sat straight up and took a deep breath, and then released it. They were silent together for a moment; more laughter floated in from the next room.

"Well, Gideon," Kilmartin asked gently, "does this change your Master Plan?"

Gideon closed his eyes again. He'd worked his entire life . . . only to discover that Lily Masters *was* his Master Plan. "Yes. Yes, God help me, but it does." He thought of Helen; he would find a way . . . there had to be a way. But that way *had* to include Lily.

Kilmartin inhaled sharply and stood, and did a little pacing of his own. And then he turned to face Gideon again. "You *do* understand what this could mean for you? What it could do to your career as a barrister, any future political career, your position in the *ton*?"

"Laurie. No one is more aware of those things than I, and you know it. They . . ." He could hardly believe he was about to utter the words, but they were true. "They no longer matter. I will survive. I shall manage. But survival will be worth nothing . . . without Lily."

How would his life look? Simpler, certainly. He could do

without the fine lodgings, the fine clothes, the parties and balls. He considered all of them, and realized he wouldn't miss them in the least. A barrister not subject to the fashion and social requirements of the *ton* could live well enough. He could move in next door to Dodge. He almost smiled at the thought.

But he didn't need to plan his life now; all he needed was Lily, and his life would find him.

Kilmartin paced a little more, shaking his head thoughtfully now and again. Gideon was distantly amused; he could not recall ever seeing his friend quite so agitated.

And then Kilmartin finally paused, his expression resigned. "She did ask me not to tell you, Gideon . . . But she thought she'd take a ship out to Italy in the morning."

"*Italy?*"

"You didn't really expect her to go back to St. Giles, did you?"

"Yes . . . no . . . but *Italy*?"

"The weather is very fine there," Kilmartin said defensively. "It was my idea. Anyhow, there's an inn by the docks, the Tiger's Nest. She knew of it."

Gideon leaped from the settee and seized a shocked Kilmartin in an embrace, lifting him off the ground. And then he dropped him again and bolted for the door.

But Constance was blocking the doorway, one hand perched on her hip.

"We *wondered* where the two of you had got to! We thought we'd try a moonlight walk in my—our—that is, your uncle's sculpture garden."

The handmaidens and Lord Jarvis clustered behind her and the whole lot of them crowded into the room. Lady Anne Clapham hovered politely in the rear.

From Gideon's heart to his mouth, with no pause for filtering, came these words:

"Constance, it's no good. I'm sorry. I cannot marry you."

Constance went as stiff as one of those sculptures, and all of the mouths of all of the people standing dropped open into perfect little ovals of astonishment.

Truthfully, Gideon was just as shocked with himself as they were. Really, he could have done it more graciously. Or at the very least, more privately. But the bindings were off of his heart now, and his heart had control of his faculties.

Constance's confidence, however, was a breathtakingly impenetrable thing. "Don't be silly, Gideon," she replied evenly, composure regained. "Of *course* you can marry me. I don't mind a bit that you don't have a title, so you needn't worry on *that* account. You will have a perfectly splendid career in politics, Papa said, and I've money enough for anything we could possibly desire, and we'll have Aster Park. Now let's go for a walk in the moonlight, all of us, shall we?"

Gideon smiled at her, a smile so brilliant with his sense of liberation. "No, Constance. You don't understand. I'm not in love with you."

Constance's smile slowly distorted into a grimace of irritation. "Oh, Gideon. That hardly matters, does it? Please abandon this nonsense."

That hardly matters? Her words sounded like so much blasphemy. And just a few short weeks ago he probably would have agreed with her.

"Constance." The bloody woman was forcing him to use his barrister voice. "Constance, it's all been a game, don't you see? You've been playing at it, and I've been playing at it . . . and you don't really want *me*. You want to *win*. Perhaps I've been despicable, but if you think about it, you'll see that I'm right and—well, as I said, it's no good."

"But Gideon . . . it's how it's *done*." Constance was genuinely bewildered. "I don't understand. We're going to have a lovely large wedding. *Everyone* will be there."

Gideon felt something akin to pity. He wasn't exactly proud of himself at the moment, but he'd just learned that pride was a frivolous thing when love was at stake.

"I'm terribly sorry, Constance. But you're not in love with me, and as for me—I'm in love with someone else entirely. And I've no idea whether she loves me, too, but I'm about to find out. If she does, I fully intend to marry *her*. Again, I'm terribly sorry."

"Miss Masters?" Constance sounded incredulous. "She *cannot* have won."

"Oh, Miss Masters did not win."

Constance's face began to ease back into some semblance of self-satisfaction.

"She did not win," Gideon clarified, "because in truth, there never really was a contest. It was *always* Lily."

Constance seemed to *inflate* then; she drew herself up to her entire regal height and glared at Gideon, in the way, he was sure, that kings and queens throughout the ages had done just before they ordered the execution of a rebellious peasant.

"Gideon, if you do not cease this nonsense at once, I shall never, *ever* forgive you. And Papa shall most *definitely* hear about it. You will be ruined."

"I would not expect you to forgive me, Constance," he said gently. "But I find, strangely, that I do not care whether you do or not. And please do give your papa my regards."

Constance stared at him, and truthfully—and this did wound his pride, if only just a little—she looked more *thwarted* than heartbroken. She was clearly having difficulty absorbing the fact that, for the first time in her life, she would not be getting exactly what she wanted.

"If you will excuse me?" Gideon moved forward, toward all those horrified faces perched atop bodies stiff with outrage; they parted to let him pass.

And then he broke into a run and ran like a wild thing, with abandon, through the hallways out the door of the house, snatching his coat from a beaming Gregson on his way.

To Lily.

Chapter Twenty-Two

Once the innkeeper had deposited her trunk in the room, Lily barred the door and pushed the trunk in front of it. Just in case one or two of the customers downstairs were unafraid of a large husband with an unreliable gun.

Alice tested the bed first thing. "It's not at all comfortable, Lily."

Wonderful. Her sister had become a connoisseur of beds.

"In our lifetimes, Alice, we will likely know a great many kinds of rooms and beds." She kept her tone bright for Alice's sake. But now that she'd stopped moving, doubt caught up to her and washed over her in great cold paralyzing waves.

Had leaving Aster Park truly been the right thing to do for Alice? For *herself*?

"Will Mr. Cole be coming along for it?" Alice looked hopeful. "For our adventure?"

Alice might as well have taken a knife to her heart. "No, I am afraid not, dearest."

Lily looked into Alice's face, and guilt and misery twisted in her. It was she who had put that stoic and closed expression on her sister's face; Alice was trying to pretend this newest loss didn't matter at all, when in fact it bewildered her and cut deeply.

Lily pulled her sister into a swift hard hug then; anything more lingering and tender would have had both of them sobbing like ninnies. And of the many things Lily and Alice could be considered, "ninnies" was not one of them.

"Alice, I want you to know that, no matter what, *I* will *never* leave you." Tears clogged Lily's throat. She absolutely refused to indulge them even a little. She threw her shoulders back. *She* was the mistress of her destiny.

She reached down to feel Alice's forehead again, and Alice dodged away. "I *told* you . . ."

Lily sighed. "You've still a bit of a cough, Alice. I'll fetch something hot from the kitchen downstairs in a few minutes."

"Cakes?" But it was a halfhearted suggestion. As though Alice had already accepted there would be no more cakes.

"Tea. Why don't you climb into bed and I'll tell you a story, and then I'll fetch some tea? And perhaps some soup, or stew. They are cooking something lovely in the kitchen, I can smell it." Actually, "lovely" was an overstatement, but such was the power of Lily's persuasion that Alice looked mollified.

Lily tried to think of a story. But they'd already lived their favorite story: the one with the great house, the peacocks, the food.

And the prince.

How could she ever invent a new story to rival it? Exhaustion finally robbed her of speech. *Why on earth am I running?*

Because she *was* running. Running *away*. And the truth was: because she was afraid.

Well, it was fear *and* pride, really. And now that the feverish impulse to flee had ebbed, she felt deeply foolish. For who was she, to hold fate to her own exacting standards? She'd been given an opportunity to love a beautiful, astonishing man, to make him smile, to hear his thoughts, to revel in his body. To experience astounding pleasure beneath his hands. Gideon Cole made her feel exquisite and protected and loved for the first time in her life. It was more than *anyone* deserved, she thought, let alone a pickpocket from St. Giles. And she knew, no matter what happened, no matter what turn his life took, Gideon would make certain that both she and Alice were safe and comfortable.

And yet she'd run from him. Just because circumstances weren't precisely as she wanted them. Because she hadn't the courage, truthfully, to trust him. To surrender her independence to him, and trust she would not feel trapped . . . only loved.

She would have to share him with another woman.

Her hands went up to her face in agitation. It was torture to imagine him with Constance. In bed with Constance, touching her . . .

Oh, God.

Could she do this?

She knew one thing to be true: *The greater part of him will always be mine.* And no one would take that from her. Or from Gideon.

She froze mid-pace, spellbound by her own decision.

"Lily?" Alice's concerned voice came to her.

Lily turned. "Alice . . ."

"Yes, Lily?"

Lily inhaled deeply. Once she'd said the words to Alice, she could not take them back. She couldn't do that to Alice yet again.

So she said them. "We're going back to Aster Park."

"Hurrah!" Alice bounced on the hard little bed. "For good?"

Inwardly, Lily crossed her fingers. "Perhaps."

An hour or so later, when Lily went downstairs again for tea, she was greeted by an astonishing sight.

Gideon was standing in the center of the room looking baffled, his head swiveling from side to side.

All of the men in the inn seemed to have disappeared.

And then Lily found them: they were crouching under the tables.

Lily saw the top of the innkeeper's shiny head poking up from behind the bar, like the moon sinking over the horizon. Slowly, slowly, it rose, and then his eyes appeared, and then his nose. But that seemed to be as far as he intended to rise.

"Ma'am," his voice quavered politely, "would this be your husband?"

"Oh, yes," she agreed at once. "This is my husband. The one with the big . . . gun."

Gideon turned to her. "Gun?" he queried softly. His eyes upon her were burning significance, but the corners of his mouth were turned up a little in amusement.

It was wonderful to hear his voice in this place.

They gazed and gazed at each other across the inn, while dozens of men cowered under tables, their tankards of ale left unattended.

"Yes. You know . . . *dear* . . . your gun," she said softly, when she could speak again. "Your very big gun with the lock that doesn't work properly."

Gideon was fighting a number of emotions, it seemed. Amusement was clearly one of them.

"Of course . . . *dear*. I'll see to it one of these days."

Big, beautiful man. How she loved him.

"I would like to speak to you privately, Lily," he said at last. He now sounded very stiff and formal.

"Alice is upstairs."

"I would like to speak to you . . . alone. If you please. It won't take but a minute."

"I do not want to leave her for long."

"Outside for just a moment, then?" He'd begun to sound a little desperate.

She nodded once, acquiescing, her heart pounding so hard she could hear the blood whooshing in her ears. *Why is he here?*

Gideon pushed open the door, motioning for Lily to precede him through it.

Heaving a collective sigh of relief, all the men crouching under the tables crawled out from under them and took up their drinks again.

Gideon stared into the water; a fat full moon had turned it black and glossy. He was certain the dank fishy smell of the harbor would permeate his clothing. It was the most romantic smell he could imagine.

Anywhere Lily was would always be romantic.

"There may be cutthroats about," Lily warned.

"I shall shoot all of them with my big broken gun."

This made her smile; thank God he could still make her smile.

He felt very awkward suddenly. He longed to touch her; would she shy away from him? No: together they were incendiary; they would forget everything else instantly if they touched each other. He wouldn't touch her until he learned what he'd come here to learn.

He cleared his throat. "I suppose you're wondering why I'm here."

She regarded him thoughtfully for a moment. "Are you wondering why *I'm* here?" she countered softly.

"No," he answered just as softly. "I know why you're here."

The water slapped, slapped, slapped, rhythmically against the pilings. Lily turned away from him; she seemed hypnotized by it momentarily.

"Lily . . . it's . . . well, it's as I told Constance—in front of everybody, it just slipped out, you know, and a very unpleasant business it was—it's no good, Lily."

"No good?" she repeated, frowning a little.

"Yes. I've been horrible."

She looked up at him, confused now. "Gideon, you've never been hor—"

"Lily—listen to me please: I've been . . . *such* a fool. I've come to tell you . . ." God, but this was difficult. If his courtroom opponents could see him now . . . He took a deep breath. "It's just that . . . I love you, Lily."

Lily went very still, her eyes as round as the bright moon.

"I love you." Once he'd said it, he quite liked the sound of it. He wanted to say it again and again. "I love you, and I've told Constance as much. I've quite sealed my fate with her, and no doubt with the *ton* at large. Dear God, you should have seen her face, Lily—I know you would have liked to have seen her face—the bloody woman looked *thwarted*, not heartbroken—"

Lily laughed breathlessly, caught up in the giddy rush of his words.

"I never proposed to her, by the way, but I will tell you about that later. And I've made it very clear to her that I don't want to marry her. I very much want to spend my life with *you.* I don't know how you will ever forgive me for what a fool I've been, how obliviously cruel; God knows, I should find it difficult. But I want to marry you, Lily, and keep you by my side forever, and spar with you and make love to you and have children with you. Nothing else matters. I bless the day you tried to pick my pocket, I bless that thirty pounds, I bless—"

"Gideon?"

"Yes?"

She waited; the timbers of a ship groaned as it shifted in the water. "I was coming back. To Aster Park."

He frowned a little, puzzled. And then a wondering smile slowly curved his lips as understanding dawned. "You were . . . you were coming back?"

Lily nodded somberly.

"You would . . . you would have done that for me? Even if . . . even in spite of Constance?"

Lily nodded again, a soft smile lighting her face. Tears had begun to gather in her eyes; they glittered in the moonlight.

"Then . . ." He sounded gently mystified. "Perhaps you love me, too."

"Rather." Her voice had gone husky.

"Say it aloud then," he ordered her gently.

"I love you?"

"Yes. But make a statement of it, not a question."

Lily laughed softly. "I love you, Gideon."

"You do?" He was all shy delight.

"So much. I love you . . . I . . . well, I love you. Will that do?"

Gideon smiled, that slow sultry smile that filled his eyes and lit his face and was now all for Lily, forever. He reached for her, and Lily's hands went around his neck.

"Yes. That will do," Gideon murmured. "But just to be perfectly clear: Does that mean you will marry me?"

"Mmmm . . . persuade me."

His mouth came down softly over hers in a kiss so tender and claiming she felt it fanning out to the reaches of her soul, winding around her heart, sealing her to him forever.

Suffice it to say, she was persuaded.

"Shall we go tell Alice now?" Lily said when she could breathe again.

"When I've finished kissing you."

He finished a long moment later.

And when Gideon pushed open the door of the Tiger's Nest, every man in it dove under the tables again.

Chapter Twenty-Three

With some difficulty, Gideon had persuaded a London hack to take them back to Aster Park. They arrived just past dawn, and much to Gideon's surprise, a yawning Kilmartin was in the drawing room when Gideon and the two sleepy girls entered the house.

"Congratulate us, Kilmartin," Gideon said quietly. "I believe you know my fiancée, Miss Lily Masters?"

"Congratulations, Lily." Kilmartin smiled upon both of them. "And to you, too, Miss Alice. You're getting a new brother."

Alice merely yawned and rocked one fist in her eye.

Lily, however, was flushing pink with happiness. "Thank you, Lord Kilmartin." She curtsied.

"Oh, now . . ." Kilmartin said. He seized her quickly by the shoulders and kissed her on one cheek and then the other. "It's 'Laurie' from now on."

Gideon turned to his fiancée. "Lily . . . may I have a moment alone with Kilmartin? Perhaps you can get some sleep in your room."

Lily smiled and mounted the stairs hand in hand with

Alice. As she did, she sent a look back over her shoulder that heated his blood to a distracting degree.

He turned back to Kilmartin, flustered. Kilmartin looked greatly amused.

"They cleared out right after you left. Constance and her handmaidens. And Jarvis, too. Pleasant chap. Bit of a cipher, though."

"Lady Anne?"

"Still here. As is Aunt Hester. I told her about your little . . . scene. She was gravely disappointed to have missed it."

Gideon smiled a little. "Do you think I'm sunk, Laurie?"

"Well . . ." Kilmartin drew out the word. "I, for one, shall never cut you. It remains to be seen what the rest of the *ton* thinks, once word gets out. And then there's your uncle."

"Ah, yes. My uncle. Does he know yet?"

"He knows."

Gideon felt as nervous as a ten-year-old boy who had just been caught applying gravy to the banister, or swimming naked. His uncle had thrashed him for both transgressions more than a decade ago.

"He's waiting for you, in fact, in his room. Which is why I stayed down here. I felt I should warn you, should you return this morning."

"You're a good friend, Laurie."

Kilmartin smiled. "And you're happy, Gideon?"

The word "yes" did not begin to answer the question, but Kilmartin saw the answer in Gideon's face.

"Good," Kilmartin told him softly.

Gideon awkwardly patted him, and Kilmartin patted him back, and then they gave up on the patting and hugged each other.

Once they'd gotten *that* over with, they stood back from

each other again, all business. "Good luck with Lord Lindsey," Kilmartin said.

Gideon was freshly nervous. "You *would* have to say that."

He went up the stairs to the sound of Kilmartin's soft laughter.

"Ah, Gideon." His uncle was sitting up in his armchair, looking freshly shaved and just as alert as if it were noon instead of just past dawn.

"Good morning, Uncle Edward," Gideon said cautiously.

"You look as though you haven't slept all night, lad."

"Haven't, Uncle Edward."

Edward said nothing for an unconscionably long time.

Gideon stared at his uncle, attempting to read his thoughts.

Lord Lindsey continued to stare back silently at Gideon, thoughtfully.

"*Boo!*" he shouted finally.

Gideon jumped, and then put one hand on Edward's table for balance and the other one over his heart. "*Christ*, Uncle Edward."

Edward laughed. "Good God, boy. I can't take a strap to you anymore, so you may as well relax. Oh, good, here's Ada Plunkett with the tea. Thank you, Mrs. Plunkett." Mrs. Plunkett settled the gleaming silver service on the table and left the room as quietly as she'd entered it.

"You'd best have some tea, Gideon, for we'll be having a talk. Take a seat."

Gideon settled himself carefully at Uncle Edward's table and slowly lifted the teapot to pour. Thankfully, his hands didn't shake.

Very much.

"So . . . you had *one* fiancée last night. And do you have an entirely different one this morning?"

"Yes, sir," Gideon admitted.

"Miss Lily Masters?"

"Yes, sir."

Edward nodded. "She's not the daughter of a marquis," he mused.

"No, sir."

"And you somewhat publicly jilted the daughter of a marquis last night."

"Yes, sir."

Lord Lindsey was quiet for a moment. "Did you ever actually propose to the Shawcross chit, Gideon?"

Gideon stared at his uncle, startled. How had he *known*? But honor prevented Gideon from betraying Constance's little maneuver. And as he could not tell the truth, he said nothing.

Lord Lindsey nodded in satisfied confirmation. "Something about your face when Lady Clary made her announcement yesterday . . ."

Gideon remained steadfastly silent.

"Is Miss Lily Masters really Kilmartin's cousin?"

Gideon paused. "No, sir."

Uncle Edward nodded, pleased with himself. "I thought not. Too much spunk in that girl. Who is she really? Do you know her family?"

"No, sir."

"Does *anyone* know her family?"

"No, sir. Her sister, Alice, is what remains of it, sir."

"Then who is she?"

"She . . . is simply Miss Lily Masters, sir. Orphaned. Hails from . . . London."

Uncle Edward didn't press him. "It wouldn't matter who her family was, would it, Gideon?" he asked softly.

Gideon paused. "No, sir." He smiled; he couldn't help himself.

Uncle Edward lifted a brow. "You've made rather a mess of things, haven't you, boy?"

Gideon considered this. "Yes, sir."

Lord Lindsey grinned. "*Good.* It's about time."

"I beg your pardon?" Gideon was startled.

"Some of the finest decisions are made when you don't think and *plan* so bloody much, Gideon. See what you've done? You've gone and made yourself happy at last, quite by accident. Which makes me, and everyone who cares for you, happy too. Your father didn't have it completely wrong, Gideon—every now and then a risk is exactly what's called for."

Gideon was speechless.

Uncle Edward was not. "You'll need a wedding gift. I have one for you."

"Uncle Edward, that's very kind of you, but that won't be necessary, I assure you. We will be just—"

"It's Aster Park."

Gideon slowly, slowly lowered his hot tea to the table. "Ast—Aster Park? Uncle Edward . . . but . . . you cannot . . ."

"I can and I will. It's yours. And, yes, I *know* you were bound to inherit, but allow me to make a grand gesture, will you? The whole place, the land, the cattle, the sheep, the servants, it's all yours to do with as you like, for I've a mind to get in a good bit of traveling before I go to my reward. Egypt. Devonshire. Places of that sort. It's all for you and *Mrs.* Cole. You can divide your time between here and London. See if you can't make the park earn a fair bit more than it earns now. Wasn't there something about sheep?"

"The Leicester Long Wool," Gideon said faintly.

"Right. Buy some sheep. You aren't going to *cry*, are you, Gideon?" Uncle Edward looked worried.

"Um . . . no, Uncle Edward."

"Do you think our soon-to-be Mrs. Gideon Cole can manage a great house?"

Mrs. Gideon Cole. Gideon smiled faintly. If there was one thing Lily could do . . . it was manage. She would learn. "Yes. She can manage the household at Aster Park."

"She cured me," Lord Lindsey mused. "I'm quite fond of her."

She cured me, too. "*You* cured you, Uncle Edward."

"Yes, but she was the tonic, you see."

"Yes." Gideon smiled. "I do see."

"Best get married straight away, lad. Do the right thing by that girl." Gideon started guiltily; did Uncle Edward suspect—

"No, don't say anything more, son, and for God's sake, don't take it in your head to thank me endlessly. Boring, is what *that* would be. I already know how you feel."

So Gideon simply reached for his uncle's hand. His uncle clasped it tightly for a moment in that startlingly strong grip of his. And it was Uncle Edward who had suspiciously moist eyes when he finally gave Gideon's hand a manly pat and released it.

And that, Gideon decided, was quite enough of male affection for one morning. He was more in the mood for *female* affection. Would it be rude to wake her up?

Oh, he'd apologize later.

The wedding itself may not have been remarkable, but the guests certainly were. A prostitute, an apothecary, a solicitor, a modiste, a baron, a housekeeper and a butler, and a doctor and all his rosy daughters filled the little church near Aster Park and watched Gideon Cole and Lily Masters pledge to love and honor each other as long as they both lived.

Lily's wedding gift to Gideon was his own gold watch. They'd decided to make it a tradition, of sorts; she'd give it to him for his birthday and all major holidays.

Kilmartin stood up with Gideon. Alice strew flowers in their path with an excess of enthusiasm. And a beautiful, dark-haired young woman, veiled so as to be unobtrusive, sat quietly in the back of the church.

Helen Turner. Gideon's sister.

He'd persuaded her to come to stay at Aster Park, now that he was more or less master of it. All was not perfect; Helen had agreed to a life in limbo, of sorts, for even if her husband consented to a divorce, her status in society would always be tenuous.

But she loved Lily and Alice. She'd reunited with her uncle; she'd forgiven him and had been forgiven in turn. And she was safe at last.

Now the three women Gideon loved, Lily and Alice and Helen, lived under his own roof, where he could cherish and protect them.

And that, and that only, was his new Master Plan.

About the Author

Julie Anne Long originally set out to be a rock star when she grew up, and she has the guitars and the questionable wardrobe stuffed in the back of her closet to prove it. But writing was her first love. When playing to indifferent crowds at midnight in dank sticky clubs finally lost its, ahem, *charm*, Julie realized she could incorporate all the best things about being in a band—namely drama, passion, and men with unruly hair—into novels, while also indulging her love of history and research. She made the move from guitar to keyboard (the computer variety) and embarked on a considerably more civilized, if not much more peaceful, career as a novelist.

Julie lives in the San Francisco Bay Area with a fat orange cat (little known fact: they issue you a cat the moment you become a romance novelist). Visit her Web site at www.julieannelong.com, or write to her at Julie@julieannelong.com.

THE EDITOR'S DIARY

Dear Reader,

Food is the spice of life. Whether it's chili that's so hot you're breathing fire or chocolate whose decadence indulges your senses, take a bite out of life—and love—in our two Warner Forever titles this April. After all, what fun is one without the other?

Jambalaya isn't the only thing that's spicy in the bayou. Check out Rene LeDeux in **Sandra Hill's** latest, **THE RED-HOT CAJUN**. Fed up with DC politics, Rene moved back to Louisiana with only one goal: to build his cabin in peace. But he'll never find peace there. His wacky, matchmaking great-aunt is determined to get Rene married and his activist friends devise a kidnapping scheme to bring media attention to their cause. Rene just never expected his friends to kidnap his high school nemesis Valerie "Ice" Breux, now a TV personality, and stow her at Rene's beloved cabin. And he certainly never expected the heat wave that began when she walked through his door. She swears she'll tolerate him when alligators fly, but he's always liked a challenge...and soon the weather won't have anything to do with the heat. Pick it up and see why *Publishers Weekly* raves "some like it hot and hilarious, and Hill delivers both."

Romantic Times Bookclub called her last book "dazzling" and "impossible to put down," so grab **Julie Anne Long's TO LOVE A THIEF**. The story of Pygmalion never seemed so romantic—or so sensual. Lily Masters has a silver tongue and the fastest fingers in all of

London. Skilled at picking pockets, Lily has provided for herself and her sister in the city's slums without being detected. But records are meant to be broken. When Lily is caught and threatened with prison, Gideon Cole comes to her rescue. A broad-shouldered barrister with a heart so charitable it leads him into trouble, Gideon can't resist buying the aquamarine-eyed beauty's freedom. In exchange, Lily must invade polite society and pose as the object of Gideon's desire to snare him a wealthy bride. Before the scheme can begin, Gideon must first teach her proper speech, dancing, pianoforte, etiquette—everything a lady knows. But does Gideon's pupil, with her stubborn and sensual nature, have something to teach him?

To find out more about Warner Forever, these titles and the authors, visit us at www.warnerforever.com.

With warmest wishes,

Karen Kosztolnyik

Karen Kosztolnyik, Senior Editor

P.S. Fate has a funny way of breaking the best laid plans in these two irresistible novels: Amanda Scott weaves the sensual and unforgettable tale of a Scottish lord whose scheme leads him to marry the wrong sister but fall in love with her for all of the right reasons in LORD OF THE ISLES; and Lori Wilde debuts her latest hilarious and sexy story of an impulsive PR specialist who teams with a brainy archeologist to reunite two Egyptian star-crossed lovers with a magic amulet in MISSION: IRRESISTIBLE.